Bedford Pim

The Gate of the Pacific

SALZWASSER
VERLAG

Bedford Pim

The Gate of the Pacific

Reprint of the original, first published in 1863.

1st Edition 2022 | ISBN: 978-3-37500-375-3

Verlag (Publisher): Salzwasser Verlag GmbH, Zeilweg 44, 60439 Frankfurt, Deutschland
Vertretungsberechtigt (Authorized to represent): E. Roepke, Zeilweg 44, 60439 Frankfurt, Deutschland
Druck (Print): Books on Demand GmbH, In de Tarpen 42, 22848 Norderstedt, Deutschland

THE
GATE OF THE PACIFIC.

THE

GATE OF THE PACIFIC.

BY

COMMANDER BEDFORD PIM, R.N

LONDON:

1863.

PREFACE.

Deeply impressed with the political and commercial necessity of opening a great Highway to the Pacific, free to all nations, and independent of the American monopoly at Panama, I found myself in the unenviable dilemma of either quietly looking on and seeing the dearest interests of my country permanently sacrificed, or making a bold effort to secure for them the consideration which their importance imperatively demanded. In adopting the latter alternative I have not shut my eyes to the difficulties of the task. In order to do any good, I had to call a spade a spade, nail my colours to the mast, and denounce a timid and un-English policy. Moreover, Central American affairs, and their bearings upon those of Great Britain, are so little understood by the general public, that all I might write would appear mere verbiage, unless my readers could be placed in possession of all the facts of the case, hitherto dispersed in a variety of official documents and trustworthy publications. How to do this, and at the same time produce a readable book, was a difficulty at which experienced writers may smile, but which looked rather formidable to a man like myself, who has spent fewer years at school than he has amongst the icebergs of the Arctic regions, or under the scorching rays of tropical suns.

My best thanks are due to those kind friends who have furnished me with information, and enabled me to embellish my work with illustrations. I am especially indebted to Sir William Gore Ouseley and Mr. Sewell for their spirited sketches of Nicaraguan scenery, and to Captain Anderson, of the King's Own Staffordshire Militia, for putting all the illustrations into shape for the lithographer.

BEDFORD PIM.

Belsize Park, Hampstead, N.W.
February, 1863.

CONTENTS.

CHAPTER I.

CHAPTER II.

CHAPTER III.

CHAPTER IV.

CHAPTER V.

CHAPTER VI.

CHAPTER VII.

CHAPTER VIII.

CHAPTER IX.

CHAPTER X.

CHAPTER XI.

CHAPTER XII.

CHAPTER XIII.

CHAPTER XIV.

CHAPTER XV.

CHAPTER XVI.

CHAPTER XVII.

CHAPTER XVIII.

APPENDIX.

Maps and Illustrations.

MAPS.

ILLUSTRATIONS.

THE

GATE OF THE PACIFIC.

CHAPTER I.

ENGLISH GOOD SETTLERS.—BEST MEANS OF SECURING THE ATTACHMENT OF COLONIES.—GENERAL OPPOSITION TO QUICK LOCOMOTION.—MONROE DOCTRINE.—PANAMA ROUTE NO HIGHWAY OF NATIONS.—POLITICAL AND COMMERCIAL NECESSITY OF A NEW TRANSIT LINE THROUGH CENTRAL AMERICA.—COLONEL WALKER.—MY SURVEYS AND EXPLORATIONS.—GREYTOWN HARBOUR SILTING UP.—SURRENDER OF IMPORTANT RIGHTS.—ENDEAVOURS TO ESTABLISH AN INDEPENDENT LINE.

THE English seem to excel all other modern people in fitness for colonization; and to their pioneering energy may be attributed the enormous increase of commerce, the rapid advance of civilization, and the spread of Christianity; but it cannot be denied that in spite of this natural advantage the nation has been singularly unhappy in the management of its colonies, and profited little by former trials or dearly-bought experience.

When sanctioning the formation of a colony, the mother-country should regard it as a primary object to ensure the permanent attachment of her offspring, by facilitating a certain, speedy, and safe exchange of ideas and commodities between herself and the interesting young stranger. Those ties which affection, a community of interest, or a love of gain, weave between a kindred people, are not the less strong because they are unseen; and once established, furnish the best guarantee for permanent peace and lasting goodwill.

A rapid, certain, and safe means of communication between the different nations of the earth has now become the great aim of all well-wishers of mankind, and our colonies should be the first to experience the benefit of this state of things; unfortunately, the opening of new roads, and the improvement of the means of locomotion, has hitherto been viewed in this country in a narrow spirit. The introduction of stage-coaches, it was asserted, would be the sure forerunner of national degeneracy; people would no longer choose to ride on horseback, but prefer to "loll at ease" in those effeminate contrivances, which were pronounced "one of the greatest evils that had happened to the kingdom."

The introduction of railways met with equally ridiculous objections; and one is almost at a loss to comprehend how sane men could utter such absolute nonsense against that great blessing of the human race which the genius of a Stephenson was about to confer upon the nation. It may be argued that a great many who spoke against the introduction of railways could have had no clear conception of what they were talking about; but no excuse of this sort can be advanced with regard to the late Thames embankment question. Everybody could understand that; everybody had more or less suffered from delays, and been annoyed by the crowded state of our London streets, and the unhealthy condition of our great river, yet it was gravely questioned whether the embankment would be an improvement or not; and future generations will behold with astonishment the ridiculous aspect of this controversy.

If such or similar shortsightedness prevails with regard to the means of locomotion at our very doors, no surprise can be felt at the utter blindness displayed regarding localities so distant that public opinion cannot be brought to bear upon them in any great force. A recent instance was afforded by the late transportation of troops to Canada. Owing to the absence of a direct road, which ought to have been constructed years ago, we were compelled to send our soldiers by a roundabout way, and at an outlay which almost equalled the cost the construction of a good railway would have involved.

The overland route to India was entirely established by an individual, and in the teeth of direct opposition; the Government of the day openly discountenancing the scheme, and the India Board distinctly stating that they required "no steam to India" at all; indeed, that struggle for a transit is a stranger tale than fiction. Fortunately for us, Lieutenant Waghorn, R.N., persevered in his great undertaking. His route was successfully opened, its value distinctly proved,—in no case more than in the great Indian mutiny,—and a new source of wealth and happiness opened to our nation. But what was the reward of him who sacrificed all he possessed, who spent his entire property, devoted his health, ay, life itself, in order to ensure the success of so noble a cause? He did not receive anything, either for himself or his family!

The vast benefits which resulted from opening a short route to the British possessions in the East, by way of Suez, naturally drew attention to the great Isthmus of the New World, Panama (the high-road to a great portion of our wealth), in the hope of obtaining similar benefits for English colonies and interests in that direction. But it was not the good fortune of Great Britain to possess another Waghorn in this Western field, and all the efforts made to obtain a footing in Central America signally failed. The truth is, that each and every attempt was frustrated by the United States, ever anxious to prevent any nation but itself from enjoying the commerce of the New World, to which, according to the Monroe doctrine, it has the sole and exclusive right. In this instance the Americans spared no pains to secure for themselves the monopoly of the transit over the Isthmus of their continent, and they have succeeded perfectly.

With the whole field to themselves, our transatlantic cousins lost no time in opening their route; a railroad was built which will ever be a monument of skill and enterprise, and the value of which has far surpassed every calculation. Its political importance to the United States is immense; by means of it the real control of the Pacific commerce falls into the hands of our rivals; and our policy must of necessity be cramped when we reflect that our unscrupulous offspring have the power, in the event of war, to inflict disaster upon our squadron, menace our possessions, cut up our trade, or destroy our cruisers in detail, before we could even inform our countrymen that hostilities had broken out.

An opportunity occurred about the time the transit *viâ* Panama was secured in favour of the United States, to open a new route, partly through Mosquito and partly through Nicaragua, starting from Greytown: but again, although the Atlantic port was under our protectorate, and everything in our favour, we were beaten out of the field by our ubiquitous rivals, who opened a steamboat communication by the river San Juan and across Lake Nicaragua, while we were squabbling about the Mosquito question. Once more an opening presented itself during Walker's sojourn in the country; but the same shortsighted policy, the same weak submission to transatlantic intimidation, prevailed; and not content with overlooking the chance thus offered, we actually went out of our way to destroy it.

If the Panama route were a great highway of nations open to the whole world, there would be no cause for disquiet or distrust on the part of England; but it cannot be repeated too often that it is the *only* transit, and belongs *exclusively* to the United States. It is true that the soil is the property of New Granada, and that the Americans simply hold a lease of it; but that wonderful people make no secret of their intention to convert their leasehold into a freehold, *malgré* the rightful owners. That this is not mere wordy declamation has been evidenced on more than one occasion; and, doubtless, long ago the matter would have been settled in this wise, had not all parties in the United States been fully occupied with the internal troubles of their own country. An unmistakable exposition of the popular determination in this matter has very lately been given by the seizure of Confederates upon neutral ground, and their forcible conveyance as prisoners across the Panama Railway, in direct violation of the neutrality of New Granada; remonstrance and protest only eliciting the startling reply, that the line was held to be the property of the United States.

The time has arrived when the eyes of the public ought to be opened to the true aspect of affairs in Central America. Sooner or later, nothing but disaster will be the result of tamely submitting to this close monopoly of the transit. We are permitted to traverse the line only on sufferance; and by-and-by, when accustomed to its use, and unable to carry on our Pacific trade without such a speedy means of communication, then, without notice, we shall find the gate closed against us, and incalculable injury inflicted upon our commerce and prestige. This was more than shadowed forth in the speech of our Colonial Secretary (the Duke of Newcastle) from his place in the House of Lords last session (1862), when he said, "A short time back, when there was an apprehension of hostilities with the United States, (the 'Trent' affair,) he was unable to communicate with the Governor of British Columbia for the space of six weeks, there being the possible chance of any dispatches sent *viâ* Panama falling into hostile hands." Time was when a British Minister would not have dared to make such an admission of governmental weakness and pusillanimity; but in the present day, after the meekness with which repeated insults have been borne when coming from the other side of the Atlantic, one is not surprised at anything; and no doubt even the 'Trent' outrage would have been quietly put up with if it had not come within the scope of public observation. The energetic measures taken on that occasion no more emanated from the Government of the day than did the raising of the Volunteer Rifle force, or any other really useful project.

The United States, by the untiring energy, skill, perseverance, and patriotism of its citizens, and the fostering care and foresight of its government, had passed the mother-country in the commercial race, when the present deplorable struggle commenced; that event has, of course, put a decisive stop to all progress; nevertheless, when peace is restored, our rivals will possess an immense vantage-ground in the Panama Railway; and while it continues the only gate to the Pacific, of which they hold the keys, they must be the winners. The English will be blind indeed if they throw away the chance now offered. There are other parts of Central America which present even greater facilities for a transit than Panama; and it is in the power of England to open more than one new route for herself exclusively if she chooses; but, if she is wise, she will make a highway free to all nations.

Some explanation of my connection with the subject of transit routes may be due to my readers. Long practical acquaintance with the efforts to discover the North-West Passage first drew my attention to the matter, and impressed me with the importance of shortening the road between the scenes of my countrymen's commercial enterprise and the mother-country. Strongly imbued with this feeling, an invitation to accompany the late Mr. Robert Stephenson, M.P., to the Isthmus of Suez, was eagerly accepted, and the opportunity of studying the question of transit with one of the ablest engineers of the day thus afforded. Afterwards I found myself, in the course of service, stationed as senior naval officer on the Atlantic side of the great American Isthmus, the entire Pacific side of which (with Panama as head-quarters) I had formerly been made familiar with by constant employment in surveying duties. At Greytown I found the question of transit of absorbing interest to the inhabitants; without commerce their town sinks to the level of a wretched swampy village, but with it becomes the *entrepôt* of a very extensive trade. It is this fact which has caused it to be coveted by Nicaragua, and made the United States strain every nerve to deprive us of footing at a place so important, not only in a commercial but in a strategical point of view. Neither the Americans nor the Nicaraguans ever cared one straw whether or not England exercised a protectorate over Mosquito; but the possession of the port of Greytown has ever been the real bone of contention in the Mosquito question; and that unseemly squabble would never have taken place had not this harbour, so valuable for transit purposes, been included in the Mosquito territory.

Thrown in the very midst of this most important and congenial discussion, it is but natural that I should have manifested the warmest interest in the subject, and very soon discovered that the question affected British interests much more nearly than is suspected by the public at home. England has never had her attention properly aroused to the importance of possessing a ready means of access to her possessions and commerce in the Pacific. The Government has tabooed the subject by every means in its power, frightened, no doubt, by the Yankee scarecrow which is for ever dangling before its eyes, and which, to its vision, is always on the point of assuming vitality.

Whilst simply crossing the ocean was the only means of transit, we were able to hold our own against all comers; but now that the genius of a Stephenson and a Waghorn has curtailed both time and distance, it is a widely different affair: those men have effected a revolution, and we must abide by the work of their hands. A giant innovation has taken place, and we must stand to it for better or for worse; for better if we keep pace with it, for worse if we lag behind. Already the glaring error of allowing the United States to monopolize and control the only avenue of approach to the Pacific is apparent; and it is to be hoped, now that the governmental apprehensions have been quieted by American *dis*union, that a vigorous effort will be made to open a new and independent route.

The territory of New Granada being closed against any rival to the Panama Railway by the terms of its contract,* which grants to the citizens of the United States the *exclusive* privilege of transit, it follows that we must look elsewhere for the means of crossing expe-

* See chapter on Panama.

ditiously from ocean to ocean. Nicaragua offers the best field for such an undertaking; but here again we have been out-generaled, and the route through that republic would also have been completely in the hands of Americans, had not, fortunately for us, causes of both a political and physical nature combined against them. Their transit was eminently successful, in spite of its various transshipments, until Colonel W. Walker was driven to interfere with it, with destructive effect both to himself and the undertaking. During the conflict which ensued, the river was so seriously impeded by artificial obstacles, as also the port of Greytown, that the navigation soon became barred against even the smallest vessels.

In the first place, I turned my attention to the river, with a view to ascertain if it could again be used for traffic, but my surveys and explorations failed to give any hope of such a consummation. The favourite project on the spot was to dam the Colorado, and by thus forcing all the stream into the San Juan branch, to cause the descent of so strong a current and large a volume of water as to scour out and deepen the channel and harbour. This, no doubt, might be done; but it will be as well to say nothing of the time and cost. In short, there is but little question that the days of Greytown are drawing to a close; its once fine port, in which a number of heavy ships could have been anchored with ease and convenience, will now admit only the smallest vessels, as is proved by the last survey (April, 1860), when only eleven feet could be found on the bar; and the sand-spit which forms the seaward face of the port had extended itself, and therefore narrowed the entrance, during the preceding fifteen months, no less than two hundred yards. Greytown, like its neighbours, Blewfields, Pearl Cay, and Cape Gracias, must fulfil its destiny. Each of those places once boasted a splendid harbour, but what are they now? Lagoons—mere shallow sheets of water: and to this Greytown must shortly come, and therefore its commercial and strategical importance will soon belong to the past.

The certainty that Greytown was doomed, and with it any hope of transit in that quarter, prompted me to examine the nature of the coast more minutely than had hitherto been attempted, and thus the deep bay formed by the projection of Monkey Point became known. This bay, which I have designated Gorgon Bay, after H.M.S. Gorgon, then under my command, is about thirty miles to the northward of Greytown; it proved to be capacious, free from shoals, easily entered by day or night, well sheltered from the Northers, and in every respect admirably adapted for the Atlantic terminus of a transit route. The distance to the Lake Nicaragua did not much exceed sixty miles, with indication of an easy gradient the whole way; while from the Lake terminus to the Pacific the road and the steamers left by the "Accessory Transit Company" could be at once made available.

The absolute necessity for an alternative route in the interests of British commerce had so impressed itself upon my mind, that I felt nothing could have been more opportune than the bringing to light of such a port as that just described; and now came the question—how to secure it? In this, not so many obstacles were experienced as I had been led to suppose. I found the King of Mosquito quite alive to the many advantages that would accrue to his people from opening a transit through his territories, and consequently he was quite prepared to grant a liberal concession for a railway, and to allow me whatever land I required. No time, therefore, was lost in effecting the purchase of the entire bay, from Monkey Point to Little Monkey Point, including the adjacent islands, and in obtaining his signature to a concession of land for transit purposes.

Having taken the above step, the next thing to be done was to advise our minister, Mr. Wyke, of the altered aspect of affairs on the coast of Mosquito, and of the rapid deterioration of Greytown Harbour; and this seemed to me the more important, as rumours had reached me that, as usual, Greytown was the stumbling-block in the way of his negotiating a treaty with Nicaragua. For various reasons, it was improbable that a dispatch would ever reach its destination; besides, time was very precious; and therefore, taking all things into consideration, I deemed it best to pay a visit to Mr. Wyke myself. I cannot say that I met with the least encouragement from that gentleman, and afterwards found, by a comparison of dates, that just before my arrival he had concluded a treaty, giving up everything—protectorate of Mosquito, boundary, etc.; in short, each and every point which we had maintained and held long before the United States became a nation. There was probably not much difficulty in effecting such a treaty. I cannot, however, help saying that Mr. Wyke struck me as being ashamed of the work upon which he was employed; and a perusal of the treaties made by him will, in my opinion, show that at least there would have been some reason in being so. I do not, however, saddle Mr. Wyke* with the entire blame, as it is not improbable that he acted under direct orders from a *Liberal* Government, urged by that dread of the Yankees which has been the stumbling-block of their party for the last twenty years.

A lengthy official correspondence ensued touching the action I had taken, the upshot of which was that my Lords of the Admiralty, instructed by Earl Russell, visited me with a reprimand for having purchased the land; but, as I continued in my command for a considerable period afterwards,—although, to be consistent with the terms of the reprimand, this ought not to have been the case,—I contented myself with settling, at least to my own satisfaction, that the American scarecrow was probably again dangling in the eyes of the authorities, and that they had prepared themselves with a written disclaimer in case their old enemy should really assume vitality, and demand to know what right England had to look after her own interests, or to presume to originate a transit intended to be independent of their monopoly at Panama.

Before proceeding further, I would entreat all whom it may concern, namely, every intelligent Englishman, to interest himself that this important subject shall

* Since knighted for his services—Sir Charles Lennox Wyke, C.B.

not be burked, and England once more be deprived of a means of independent transit, by which alone her young colonies of Vancouver Island and British Columbia can be properly governed, and her commercial interests in the broad Pacific be fostered and developed.

CHAPTER II.

BOUNDARIES OF CENTRAL AMERICA.—POLITICAL DIVISIONS.—EXTENT AND AREA.—COMPARISON OF THE TWO GREAT ISTHMUSES OF THE WORLD.—ISTHMUS OF PANAMA (PANAMA AND VERAGUAS).—PROVINCES OF MEXICO (YUCATAN AND CHIAPAS).—BELIZE.—COSTARICA.—SAN SALVADOR.—TRADITION.—HONDURAS AND BAY ISLANDS.—ABANDONMENT OF FELLOW-COUNTRYMEN.—GUATEMALA.

In defining the boundaries of Central America, I shall not restrict myself to the narrowest part, commonly called the Isthmus of Panama, but include the entire country, from the first narrowing of the land of North America at the Isthmus of Tehuantepec, between the 16th and 18th parallel of north latitude, and 94th meridian of west longitude, to its expansion into South America at Darien in the 7th parallel of north latitude and 77th west meridian. In this definition I have been guided, not by political divisions, but by what appear to be the strict geographical limits of the centre of the New World. Central America, then, lies between the 7th and 18th parallels of north latitude, and the 77th and 94th of west longitude; its least breadth from sea to sea is 27 miles, at lat. 9° N., long. 79° W. The extent of its coast-line, counting all the sinuosities, is about 3000 miles, its length from end to end about 1350 miles, its direction north-west and south-east, and its area about

300,000 square miles, or about the size of Great Britain and France put together.

It is hardly possible to conceive anything more widely different than the nature of the connecting links joining together the continents of the Old and New Worlds. In the former we have a broad, flat, low expanse of parched and arid country, rather more than seventy miles across, a complete desert; in the latter, a mountainous surface and very irregular coast-line extending over many hundreds of miles, teeming with animal and vegetable life, and only, at its narrowest part, about half the width of the Old World isthmus. There is another striking dissimilarity,—the one possessing the earliest records of the human race in readable hieroglyphics, and crowded with historical associations of the deepest interest to mankind, whilst the other is a comparatively modern addition to the history of the world, with writings still an enigma to science.

There are so many well-written accounts of Central America, from its conquest and partial occupation (the first European settlement was formed by Columbus, in 1502) until the final expulsion of the Spaniards, between the years 1820 and 1823, that it seems superfluous to enter upon its earlier history; and I shall therefore simply confine myself to a brief notice of the various states and dependencies, and only enlarge on Nicaragua and the Mosquito territory, so long a cause of contention between this country and the United States, because on that portion of the Isthmus is centred the chief interest; but should any one wish to go more deeply into the subject, a complete list of books has been appended, from which may be obtained a detailed account of all that is known of this interesting part of the world.

Within the limits I have defined as the natural boundaries of the centre of the New World are included two provinces of New Granada (Panama and Veraguas, commonly called the Isthmus of Panama), two of Mexico (Yucatan and Chiapas), an English colony (Belize, or British Honduras), five republics (Costarica, San Salvador, Honduras and the Bay Islands, Guatemala, and Nicaragua), and the Indian kingdom of Mosquito. The five republics number altogether forty-five districts, each with a capital, and 253 towns and villages, exclusive of capitals. Costarica has eight districts, San Salvador four, Honduras twelve, Guatemala thirteen, and Nicaragua eight, making in all forty-five.

PROVINCES OF NEW GRANADA,

COMMONLY CALLED THE ISTHMUS OF PANAMA.

The Isthmus of Panama lies between the 4th and 10th parallels of north latitude, and the 77th and 83rd of west longitude; it belongs politically to the Republic of New Granada, and comprises the provinces of Panama and Veraguas, and the territories of Darien and Bocas del Toro. Its least breadth, from sea to sea, is twenty-seven miles, and its configuration is that of a bow, the coast of the Caribbean Sea forming the convex line, that of the South Sea the concave. Bounded on the north and north-east by the Atlantic, on the south and south-west by the Pacific Ocean, on the east by the rivers Atrato and San Juan, and on the west by the republic of Costarica, the population amounts to 129,000; and it presents, including the adjacent islands, a surface of 34,000 square miles, an extent of territory nearly equal to that of Portugal.

In the province of Panama is situated the celebrated Atlantic port of Portobello, lat. 9° 34′ N., long. 79° 44′ W. The harbour of the same name was discovered on the 2nd November, 1502, by Columbus, but the town was not commenced until the reign of Philip II. Soon after its foundation it became of importance, by being made the port through which all the trade between Spain and Western America was carried on, and by the great annual fair held there. On account of these advantages, Portobello was looked upon with envy by other nations, and suffered frequent attacks; the first time by Francis Drake, in 1595, during the wars between Philip II. of Spain and Elizabeth of England. It was sacked twice by the buccaneers, in 1624 and 1673; and again, when in the reign of George II. war broke out between Great Britain and Spain, Portobello was taken, and nearly reduced to ashes, by Admiral Vernon, on the 22nd of November, 1739. Nine years later, the Spanish galleon and the great fair were abolished, when Portobello, which had always been dreaded on account of its climate, was almost deserted; it fell, never to rise again, for after the war of independence the traffic was conducted by way of Chagres, which, though not a regular harbour, has several advantages over Portobello. The town of Chagres is, like Portobello, one of the most miserable and unhealthy in the country; it lies at the mouth of the river of the same name, in lat. 9° 18′ 6″ N., long. 79° 59′ 2″ W., and is guarded by the castle of San Lorenzo, a dark-looking fortification. This castle is situated on a high rock at the entrance of the river, and was destroyed in 1671 by command of Henry Morgan, but a few years after was rebuilt by the Spaniards. Chagres contains about one thousand inhabitants, nearly all of whom are negroes or people of a mixed origin. Aspinwall, the great *entrepôt* of the Isthmus, will be mentioned below.

PROVINCES OF MEXICO.

Yucatan and Chiapas.—In 1506 Juan Dias de Solis and Vincent Janez Pinzon discovered Yucatan, but it was not explored until 1517. Like the rest of the continent, the country was overrun by the Spaniards, but not without harder fighting than they met anywhere else. It was a separate Captain-Generalcy until the revolution, when it joined the Mexican Confederation; since then, in common with other Spanish-American States, it has been filled with anarchy and confusion, and at present the country is almost in the hands of the Indians. The capital is Merida, the population of which is about 20,000. This province was in a forward state of civilization when discovered, as is attested by the magnificent ruins so ably described by Mr. John L. Stephens. The area of Yucatan is about 53,000 square miles, and the population, by rough calculation, amounts to 600,000. Our knowledge of this part of America is still imperfect. Yucatan is a peninsula, 120 miles from Cuba; it lies between lat. 18° and 21° N. and long. 87° and 91° W., having north and west the Gulf of Mexico, east the Caribbean Sea, and landward Belize, Guatemala, and Chiapas. The chief port is Campeachy, but it does not deserve the name of harbour. Chiapas does not approach Yucatan in size and population, does not exceed 39,000 square miles, and 200,000 souls is probably the extent of the population.

BELIZE.

Belize, or British Honduras, owes its settlement to the buccaneers, who maintained a footing in spite of all the efforts of the Spaniards to dislodge them. The district has been in the possession of England for more than 200 years, and comprises a territory of about 160 miles in length by about 60 at its broadest part, equal to an area of 9600 square miles. The population is estimated to exceed 25,000, of whom the greater portion are coloured. The town of Belize forms a remarkable contrast to those of the neighbouring states: while the latter seem to be gradually decaying, the former strides forward every year, and bids fair to become shortly a most thriving settlement. Mahogany is the chief article of export: about 20,000 tons per annum are shipped, requiring 16,000 trees: a single tree has been sold for £1800. Plantations of considerable extent are now being cleared, and probably cotton and sugar will before long be largely exported. Belize is governed by a Superintendent appointed by the Home Government; it is under the diocese of Jamaica. There are several good schools, besides a number chiefly conducted on Sundays.

TABLE SHOWING TEMPERATURE AND FALL OF RAIN AT BELIZE.

Months.	Maximum Temperature.	Minimum Temperature.	Fall of Rain.
January	82° Fahr.	66° Fahr.	2·7 inches.
February	85	73	4·2 „
March	83	75	none.
April	89	74	none.
May	89	75	2·5 „
June	90	77	4·3 „
July	90	78	3·3 „
August	90	78	0·6 „
September	91	76	8·2 „
October	87	75	4·8 „
November	85	68	9·9 „
December	86	75	6·7 „
Average mean temperature for the year, 79° Fahr.			46·9 inches.

COSTARICA.

Of all the states of Central America, Costarica is the most prosperous: its exports at present reach a large amount, viz. 1,000,000 dollars; other exports, 350,000 dollars; total, 1,350,000 dollars. The late ruling President has done much to develope its resources, but perhaps the greatest benefit he conferred was by keeping, for many years, a firm hold on the presidential chair, thus avoiding the calamities usually attendant upon elections in these countries. He was in reality dictator, and this is probably the secret of the national prosperity. It is really astonishing what progress these countries make, if only allowed a few years' peace and quiet. Under firm and determined rule their growth is quite tropical; but directly political freedom is allowed, revolution follows revolution, and the most frightful excesses lay waste the country.

The Roman Catholic religion is declared by law to be the religion of the country; the constitution guarantees it the protection of the Government, while it tolerates every other persuasion. By a concordat with Rome, dated October 1852, tithes were abolished, and 10,000 dollars per annum settled on the diocese. Costarica was ecclesiastically subordinate to the bishopric of Nicaragua until 1850, when it was erected into a separate diocese. There are forty-five churches and sixty-one priests.

San José is the capital, and 4500 feet above the level of the sea; the houses are whitewashed, with red-tiled roofs, only one story high, and built of adobes, or sun-dried bricks. The city has a clean and cheerful look; it was commenced about 1775, and is therefore comparatively modern.

"The natives of Costarica are extremely jealous of foreign influence, and though willing to be benefited by foreign capital, they are desirous of reaping this benefit in a most selfish manner, by absorbing all the wealth which such capital will create. This feeling induced them, when they formed a company for the building of a road from the capital to the Serapiqui river, to exclude all foreigners from participation therein, by enacting that none but a native could be a stockholder. In this shortsighted policy they have persisted ever since, and will persevere, until they have learnt, to their irretrievable cost, that without foreign aid they are unable to do anything. The Costaricans appear fated to do the reverse of what civilized nations have done: they exclude foreigners from their public works, such as roads, etc., while they allow them to hold real estate. I am convinced that this contradiction in their acts proceeds, in a great measure, from the exclusiveness of their egotism, rather than from any want of knowledge of their true interests."*

Their jealousy of foreigners was exemplified by their declaration of war against the filibusters in Nicaragua, and the decree that all taken with arms in their hands should be shot. The result of their jealousy and meddling was the loss of more than 2000 of their best men, a large increase of debt and misery, with nothing to show for it but a glass case, erected at San José, containing the national colours and the following inscriptions:—

"On the 15th July, 1857, the national flag which floated above the walls of Fort Castillo during the siege, together with the names of the superior officers who defended it so brilliantly, were deposited in this urn, by order of his Excellency the President of the Republic, Don José Rafael Mora. Eternal honour to the heroes who defended the Castle of San Juan."

"On the 15th February, 1857, 400 filibusters, under the command of the so-called Colonel Titus, attacked the Castle of San Carlos, which was in a dilapidated state, and garrisoned only by thirty-seven men. But animated by the brave Colonel, Don George F. Cauty, and the worthy comandante of the fort, Lieutenant-Colonel Faustine Montes de Orca, the little garrison heroically resisted the enemy, until the 19th of the same month, on which day seventy-seven riflemen, under the command of Captain Jesus Alvarado and Don Joaquin Ortiz, who had been sent to the relief of the fort by the General-in-Chief, Don José Joaquin Mora, fell upon the filibusters with so much bravery, that they dispersed them in an instant, compelling them to throw away their clothes so that they might fly with greater ease. This brilliant feat of arms, planned so admirably by our General, decided the happy issue of the holy war which was sustained by the republics of Central America against their invaders."

* Letters from the British Consul.

The boundary-line between Costarica and Nicaragua is still in dispute. The old boundary, by charter of 1574, commenced at the mouth of the river San Juan, and extended up that stream within fifteen leagues of the lake, whence a line was drawn due west to the head waters of the Rio Salto, and down that stream to the Pacific. To the north and west of that boundary lies the district of Guanacaste, which was annexed to Costarica after the independence, by the freewill of the inhabitants in 1824, and their action was approved by the Federal Congress of Central America in 1825. Guanacaste has since then been in actual possession of Costarica, and its northern boundaries would therefore be those of Costarica, viz. the remaining fifteen leagues of the Rio San Juan, and now the entire length of that stream, thence along the borders of the lake to the Rio Sapoa, and from the source of that stream to the beautiful harbour of Salinas Bay, on the Pacific. The whole republic lies between 8° 30′ and 10° 40′ N., and 82° and 85° W., and comprises about 25,000 square miles, with a population of about 135,000 inhabitants. There are two or three harbours, but Punta Arenas, on the Pacific, is the chief port of entry.

SAN SALVADOR.

San Salvador is the smallest of the five states, being 165 miles in length, by 69 in average breadth, and containing about 11,385 square miles of territory; it enjoys a beautiful climate and fertile soil, and only requires a fostering care to become the garden of the Pacific. Its population is relatively the largest in Central America, and numbers 290,000. It has only one seaport worthy the name, and that is La Union, in the Gulf of Fonseca. It is well watered, having no less than twenty-two rivers, varying from 260 to 30 miles in length, and seventeen lakes. The country is eminently plutonic, an entire chain of volcanos extending along the Pacific coast-line; many of the lakes are merely extinct craters filled with water, which overflowing have made beds for themselves and become rivers: an example is afforded by the stream from the Lake Guija, which for more than two leagues has worn for itself a channel in the lava, and so rapidly has this process been going on that in some places the banks have attained an elevation of from fifty to sixty feet. In the same manner the Lake of Ilopango has forced for itself a channel through exceedingly high precipitous land, to unite with the deep-flowing river of Giboa.

It is impossible to say when these operations of nature took place, certainly a long period before the conquest of America, nor is it probable the natives ever knew anything certain about it; if they had any tradition in relation thereto, it has been lost amid the bustle of subsequent immigration and political events.

The current tradition of to-day is, that on the site of the Lake of Guija there existed a populous city, which was destroyed similarly to Sodom and Gomorrah of the Old World. There is nothing impossible in the story, seeing that we still find many flourishing cities at the base of volcanos; but that the silver vases, candlesticks, etc. etc., said to have been found in the lake, have come from the lost city, is more than doubtful. It is more probable that, in the political tempests which have passed over these countries, some of the inhabitants may have committed their treasures for greater security to the waters of the lake, and may afterwards have perished without divulging the secret, or have been unable to find the deposit, until, long after, accident or avarice may have brought to light the hidden treasures.

San Salvador lies between the parallels 13° and 14° 10′ north, and the meridians 87° and 90° west. It is bounded on the south and west by the Gulf of Fonseca and the Pacific, and on the north and east by Guatemala and Honduras, a formidable range of mountains constituting the inland barrier. The topography of the country is remarkable: there are two steppes,—that on the coast, about fifteen miles in breadth; and then again, at an elevation of about 2000 feet, the second steppe, more than twice as broad, well watered, and fertile beyond description; the far interior consists of high broken land. The capital of the Republic is named after the state, or rather the state after the capital; it was founded in 1528 by George Alvarado, brother of the great conqueror. Its elevation is upwards of 2000 feet above the sea. In April, 1854, it was destroyed by a violent earthquake, after having survived several shocks,—twice in the sixteenth century, the same in the next, again in 1728, and lastly in 1839. There appears to be more political contentment and stability in San Salvador than in any other part of Central America, without exception; unfortunately its geographical position and want of ports is the great drawback to its progress.

HONDURAS AND BAY ISLANDS.

Columbus made his first landing on the continent of America in Honduras. In 1502 he discovered Guanaja, named by him the "Isle of Pines;" thence sailed towards the mainland, and on the 14th of August stepped ashore on the point now called Cabo de Honduras, close to the present town of Truxillo, which was founded by Fernando Cortez a few years after the death of the great navigator. Honduras comprises an area of nearly 40,000 square miles; it has a coast-line of about 400 miles on the Caribbean Sea and about 60 miles on the Pacific; all of the latter is included in the Gulf of Fonseca. There are several islands, both on the Atlantic and Pacific, which pertain to this state; it also possesses more than one good harbour, and it is second to none in its natural wealth. The topography is similar to that of the other states. The population amounts to 350,000, containing a larger proportion of whites than any of the other states; the black element also is large, owing to the establishment in the country of the Caribs. These people constitute all that remains of the original inhabitants of St. Vincent. They gave their English masters so much trouble, that in 1796 they were deported, to the number of nearly 6000, to Roatan, in the Bay of Honduras; since that period they have steadily increased, and now form by far the most hardworking and industrious part of the population of Honduras. They are mostly mahogany cutters, and the amount of work they perform is marvellous; they are tall, fine-looking men, powerful, and by their provident habits are generally well off; most of them speak both Spanish and English. They are said to be the best woodmen in the world.

The Bay Islands, situated on the Atlantic, within sight of the Republic of Honduras, lately ceded to that state, are Bonacca, Roatan, Utilla, and a number of smaller islands and coral Cays. The group was almost depopulated by the early conquerors, who carried the aborigines as slaves to Cuba. At the commencement of the seventeenth century the buccaneers made such constant forays upon the remaining inhabitants, and the harbours afforded such excellent shelter for their ships, that the Spaniards determined to abandon the settlements; and accordingly all the people were transported in 1642 to Truxillo. The buccaneers lost no time in taking possession, and speedily fortified themselves; but in 1650, after some hard fighting, they were expelled. The Spaniards not occupying the islands, they continued a desert waste until 1742, when the English took possession. During the next hundred years the group appears to have witnessed several changes, but finally by occupation came under English rule. The extreme fertility of the soil and its commanding geographical position attracted many settlers, who, numbering some thousands, declared their wish to be under English government. In 1852 they were formally annexed to Belize, and called the Colony of the Bay Islands, and from this period appear to have increased considerably in population and prosperity; but unfortunately for the settlers, the Government of the United States chose to object to the establishment of any colony on or near the American continent, save and except such as emanated from themselves. Accordingly the English government, after a weak and puerile defence of their policy, relinquished the point, and by treaty, dated November, 1859, totally abandoned the Bay Island colony to Honduras, thereby causing the ruin of many British subjects, and, what was of scarcely less importance, lowering the prestige of our nation in the eyes of the whole world, by taking up the matter with one hand and laying it down with the other. No one can say to what lengths the bullying propensities of the Yankees would have been carried, and how long our Liberal Government would have borne the constant humiliations to which they were subjected, had not an end been put to the system by the division in the United States, which, for the present at all events, gives the people of that country quite enough to do to mind their own affairs. In the Appendix will be found the treaty with Honduras, by which this weak and disgraceful abandonment of fellow-countrymen in a distant part of the world was consummated.

GUATEMALA.

Guatemala is the largest state, and is famous for the beauty of its scenery. Its great drawback is want of seaports and the absence of roads; it will therefore probably remain undisturbed for many years, and even then civilization will most likely find its way into the country from the northern side, *viâ* Mexico, as that is by far the most accessible. The area of Guatemala is about 60,000 square miles, and the population numbers about 800,000, very few of whom are whites; two-thirds at least are

Indians. There is a great paucity of negroes throughout this state.

Guatemala, at the time of the Spanish conquest, was further advanced in civilization than any other part of Central America; it is said that in those days the natives possessed a written language, which is more than was the case either with the Aztecs or the Incas.

It is difficult to find a name for the form of government; it is totally unlike that of the other states; the present ruler is called Captain-General and President for Life, and has even the power of naming his successor. He is a pure Indian, and has so much influence with the Indian tribes and lower orders that every attempt to unseat or destroy him has proved a failure; under his *régime* bigotry and intolerance in religious matters have been rampant. The Jesuits, expelled from the liberal states, here flourish in rank luxuriance, and have set their seal on the people, so that it is not difficult to foresee the abject condition to which all classes will be reduced if this state of affairs continues. Under such a government commerce and industry languish, and accordingly, by the last accounts, the imports and exports had dwindled down to a very low figure. Guatemala is bounded on the north by the Mexican states of Chiapas and Yucatan, but the boundary-line has ever been in dispute, and there is no prospect of its settlement. On the south and west the Pacific washes its shores, and the Republic of San Salvador adjoins on the south-east; on the east and north-east, Honduras, the Atlantic, and Belize form the boundary line. The ports on the Atlantic are Izabal, on the Gulf of Dulce, lat.

15° 24′ N., long. 89° 9′ W., which gulf is in fact a large body of fresh water,—a lake to which access is obtained by ascending its outlet, the Rio Dulce, having only six feet on the bar,—and San Tomas, lat. 15° 45′ N., long. 88° 40′ W., at the head of the Bay of Amatique, its length is about four miles, breadth two miles, easy of access at all times; the greatest depth is five fathoms, gradually shoaling towards the shore; the entrance is open to the north. On the Pacific Guatemala does not possess any ports, the two shipping-places, Istapa and San José, being simply bad and exposed roadsteads; the former was used by Alvarado to build the vessels employed in the conquest of Peru.

New Guatemala* is the present capital of the state; it is the third of the name, and was founded in 1776. The first was founded by Alvarado; its ruins are known as *Ciudad Vieja*; it was destroyed in 1541. The second was destroyed, or nearly so, in 1773; it is called *Antigua Guatemala*, and lies about thirty miles to the westward of the present capital, which is situated on the northern border of a vast plain, 4500 feet above the sea, in lat. 14° 35′ N., and long. 90° 45′ W. The locality is most healthy, and the scenery lovely in the extreme; the mean average temperature for the year is 65°.

* Guatemala is said to have received its name from the word *quauhtemali*, which, in the Aztec language, means a decayed log of wood, because the Mexican Indians who accompanied Alvarado found near the palace of the kings of Kachiquel an old worm-eaten tree. Some writers, however, state that the name is derived from *uhatezmalha*, which signifies "a mountain that throws out water," in allusion to the volcano contiguous to the city. I am inclined to think the latter derivation the most probable.

CHAPTER III.

BOUNDARIES OF NICARAGUA.—CLIMATE.—TEMPERATURE.—EARLY ACCOUNTS.—ABORIGINES.—COSTUME.—LITTLE CHANGE SINCE THE CONQUEST.—CHARACTER OF INDIANS.—THE SPANISH RULE.—HISTORICAL NOTICES.—COLONEL WILLIAM WALKER.—FILIBUSTERISM.—DESTRUCTION OF THE TRANSIT.—WALKER'S BATTLES.—DEFENCE OF THE GUADALUPE CHURCH.—EXPULSION OF WALKER.—HIS REAL OBJECT AND POLICY.—SELFISHNESS OF THE OTHER STATES.—WALKER'S EXECUTION.—ADMINISTRATION OF PRESIDENT MARTINEZ.

NICARAGUA is unquestionably the most important of all the states of Central America, if only from its geographical position, affording as it does a ready means of access from sea to sea. Its boundaries are the same which pertained to it as a province, namely, the Mosquito territory on the east, the Pacific Ocean on the west, Honduras on the north,—following the river Wanks from Cape Gracias-á-Dios to its source, and thence down the Rio Negro to the sea in the Gulf of Fonseca,—Costarica on the south, the actual boundary-line being still in dispute between the two Republics. Nicaragua is very irregular in its outline, and therefore it is difficult to define its geographical position; but it may be said to be between the 14th and 11th parallel of north latitude and 84° 15′ and 86° 30′ of west longitude. It contains an area of rather more than 30,000 square miles,—about the size of Portugal.*

* "Nisaragua, one of the five sovereign states of Central America, is about

The climate of Nicaragua is varied; in the plains it is tropical, but any degree of temperature may be obtained by resorting to the hill-country at the northern extreme of the lake, where the Andes appear to be effectually broken by the great transverse valley from sea to sea. The absence of mountains towards the Atlantic permits the trade winds to sweep across the country, and ventilate it to such a degree as to make the temperature very agreeable to health and feeling, even in the plains. There are two seasons, wet and dry, or summer and winter; the wet lasts from May to November, but often considerable periods elapse without a drop of rain or a cloud obscuring the deep blue of the sky. The maximum range of the thermometer is from 80° to 90°. In the dry season the temperature is much cooler and often quite chilly, clear sky, passing showers, and fine bracing atmosphere. Few observations have been taken, but the following will afford a fair average:—Total annual

half the area of Great Britain, but contains a population of only a quarter of a million, of whom nearly half reside in towns. The country is mostly a dead level, covered with perennial forest, growing on a soil of apparently extreme fertility. Its climate has two marked seasons, the wet and the dry, of which the former is called the winter, on account of its chillness, though the sun is at that time vertical. The whole territory is eminently volcanic, such hills as there are being either active or extinct volcanos. The chief exports of Nicaragua are hides (about 50,000 annually) and various woods. One-half of its population are pure Indians, and the rest, excepting very few pure Spaniards, are of intermixed races. Nearly the whole are Roman Catholics, and speak Spanish. They are exceedingly illiterate; even a high official doubted whether or no London was a town in England. Nicaragua has been chiefly famous for its civil wars. Its Government—as those in the four neighbouring Central American republics—consists of a President, elected for four years, and a Senate, and a House of Representatives."—'A Sketch of Nicaragua.' By Gerard Raoul Perry, Esq., H.B.M. Vice-Consul for that State. Proceedings of R. G. Society, vol. vi. no. 111, p. 74.

rain, 97·7 inches; rain fell 139 days, rest dry; mean highest temperature 86·45°, mean lowest 71·15°, mean average of the year 77·42°.

The early accounts of the habits and customs of the natives are vague and unsatisfactory. Perhaps the most reliable chronicle is that of Gonzales Hernandez de Oviedo y Valdez, historiographer of the Indies to the King of Spain, who was in Nicaragua when the country was attacked and conquered, about 1522, by Gil Gonzales de Avila.

In Nicaragua "Nature has lavished her richest gifts and assumed her most magnificent forms; high volcanos, gentle slopes, level plains, and broad and beautiful lakes and rivers, are here combined with a fertility of soil and a salubriousness of climate, probably unsurpassed by any equal extent of country under the tropics. These were conditions eminently favourable for bringing together primitive communities of men, and for nurturing and sustaining a vast population. That it did so, we have the testimony of all the early chroniclers; and he who has passed over its broad plains and luxuriant slopes, and observed its attractions and resources, will be prepared to credit the assertion of the pious Las Casas, that it was 'one of the best-peopled countries in all America.'

"The Indians of Nicaragua enjoy equal privileges with the whites, and may aspire to any position, however high, both in the Church and State. The system of *peonage* (slavery under a less repugnant name) is here unknown; yet the Indian retains his traditionary deference for the white man, and tacitly admits his superiority. Their dress is exceedingly simple. On ordinary occasions the women wear only a white or flowered skirt, fastened around the waist, leaving the upper part of the person entirely exposed, or but partially covered by a handkerchief fastened around the neck. In Masaya and some other places, a square piece of cloth, of native manufacture, and of precisely the same style and pattern with that used for the same purpose before the Discovery, supplies the place of the skirt. It is fastened in some incomprehensible way, without the aid of strings or pins, and falls from the hips a little below the knees. The guipil and nagua are however adopted in nearly all the large towns, and are everywhere worn on festival days and Sundays. The men wear a kind of cotton drawers, fastened above the hips, but frequently reaching no lower than the knees. Sandals supply the place of shoes, but for the most part both sexes go with their feet bare. The taste for ornament is universal. They are also fond of flowers, and the girls are seldom without some of them, entwined amongst the luxuriant locks of their long black hair, or braided in a chaplet, and encircling their foreheads.

"The aborigines of Nicaragua, as also of the other states of Central America, still constitute numerically the predominating portion of the population; and if we include the people of other races amalgamated with them, they undoubtedly comprehend three-fourths of the entire inhabitants. Most of these are what may be called civilized; but there are many tribes occupying large tracts of unexplored country, generally denominated 'Indios Bravos,' who are more or less savage, and whose numbers we have no means of estimating. They undoubtedly retain their primitive habits, very little modified from what they were before the period of the Discovery. But amongst the civilized Indians of Nicaragua, although mingling freely with the inhabitants of European descent, there has not been that change from their original habits which might at first be supposed. Indeed it is, in many respects, hard to say whether the conquerors have assimilated most to the Indians, or the Indians most to the Spaniards.

"The Indians of to-day occupy the towns that their ancestors occupied; and the departmental and other subdivisions of the country coincide very nearly with the ancient principalities or chieftaincies. The prefects, or heads of these departments, have only supplanted the caciques; and the existing municipalities only supply the place of the *Guegues*, or councils of old men. Many of the social as well as civil institutions of the country have been recognized and perpetuated by the Spaniards; and some of the ceremonies of the aboriginal ritual have also been incorporated amongst the rites of the Catholic Church.

"Thus much may be said of the Indians of Central America generally, but the following observations must be understood to refer specifically to those of Nicaragua, although perhaps quite true of those of the other states. In character they are singularly docile and industrious, and constitute what would in some countries be called an excellent 'rural population.' They are a smaller race of men than the Indians of the United States, but have fine muscular developments, and a singularly mild and soft expression of countenance. In colour also they are lighter, and their features less strongly marked. Some of the women are exceedingly pretty, and, when young, have figures beautifully and classically moulded. They are entirely unobtrusive in their manners, seldom speaking unless first addressed, and are always kind and hospitable to the stranger. They are not warlike, but brave; and when reduced to the necessity, fight with desperate obstinacy. The agriculture of the state is almost entirely carried on by them."*

The population of Nicaragua does not exceed 300,000, and of this number scarcely one-tenth are whites; the remainder consist of Indians, Mestizos, and Negroes. The consequence is, that the authorities are for the most part chosen from the two latter classes, universal suffrage being the law of the land. This is the more to be regretted, inasmuch as the coloured races of Nicaragua, as everywhere else, cannot by any stretch of imagination be considered sufficiently intellectual to govern; while, on the contrary, the white natives are intelligent, courteous, and hospitable.

After continuing under Spanish rule for three centuries, the conquerors were expelled the country they had so shamefully misused. During their lengthy sojourn in the land, the Iberian immigrants seldom or never identified themselves with the new country: all their settlements are in ruins or falling to decay; they came not to develope the soil, not to render the mineral wealth accessible, not to clear and settle the land, but to get together by any means, however wicked, sufficient wealth

* Transactions of the American Ethnological Society.

to ensure them a life of luxury and indolence. With such pioneers of civilization, it is no wonder that the Spanish raid has not left an impress for good on any part of the New World. Contrast North America, from which the Spaniards turned aside with disdain because there was no speedy means of obtaining riches. What astounding results have not been produced there during the three hundred years worse than wasted in the southern part of the continent!

In 1815 Nicaragua attempted to throw off the yoke of Spain. In 1821 the Central American states, namely Guatemala, Honduras, San Salvador, Nicaragua, and Costarica, declared their independence; and in 1822 they were incorporated with Mexico under the Emperor Iturbide. This arrangement lasted but a short time, and was followed by the creation of the five states into a federation similar to that of the United States. The Republic of Central America only lasted two years; the National Assembly met in Guatemala, but its measures are not worth recording, save and except the abolition of slavery throughout the states. In 1825 the Federation dissolved. In 1829 it was reconstituted under General Morazan, but again destroyed by Carrera. During the next twenty years a series of revolutions and intestine quarrels followed, the tendency of which has been to reduce the country to a condition less civilized than when first discovered. In 1851, Honduras, San Salvador, and Nicaragua formed a union; in 1852 it was broken up; and since that period the five states have maintained a separate government, although subsequent events in Nicaragua have proved that a strong fellow-feeling exists between them. In 1853 a sharp contest for the Presidency took place in Nicaragua between Señors Castellon and Chamorro; the latter obtained the victory, and banished his opponent, who however while in Honduras succeeded in organizing an expedition against Chamorro. At Leon, the real capital of the state, he was well received; and adding largely to his forces, met his adversary in a pitched battle, and completely routed him. Chamorro then took refuge in Granada, the rival capital of Nicaragua, and Castellon at once laid siege to that place. The city withstood every effort to overcome it. At this stage of the proceedings Castellon fell back upon that most ancient of expedients, and decided to call in foreign aid. His choice fell upon Colonel Walker, who at that time had attained considerable notoriety, from an effort to establish an independent republic in Sonora, a province of Northern Mexico, where he had displayed great military skill and daring. Walker agreed to act with Castellon on certain conditions, and appears to have made the arrangement more to gratify ambition and love of daring adventure than from any sordid motive; and no doubt the majority of his followers were enlisted with the same views. In June, 1855, General Walker and fifty-six men joined themselves to the army of Castellon. Any number of Californians might have been engaged to follow the fortunes of Walker, especially as these men, in their passage through Nicaragua, had seen with longing eyes the beauty, fertility, and richness of the country; but a small number was deemed sufficient, particularly as they were picked men. General Walker's first fight was at Rivas; his force consisted of 55 Americans and 100 natives, against the troops under General Boscha, numbering upwards of a thousand. The hundred natives fled at the very commencement of the action, nevertheless the Americans stood their ground; but after losing twelve of their number they were compelled to retreat. This fight, however, had a most salutary effect on the enemy, as they had a practical opportunity of proving the material their new adversaries were made of. General Boscha owned a loss of 180 in killed and wounded. In the next fight, at Virgen Bay, Walker was victorious. His reputation was now established; and the capture of Granada, the deaths of the chiefs of the respective parties, Chamorro and Castellon,* as well as other favourable circumstances, acting in his favour, he became virtually the head of the state. The account of proceedings in Nicaragua at this period have an interest for Englishmen, as it is a sort of reflex of their own history some centuries ago. The struggle for power was between two great sections of the state, Leon and Granada: the former styled their chief Director, and wore a badge of *red* ribbon in their hats; the latter named their leader Presi-

* Castellon was a man of large and enlightened views. He keenly felt the fallen state of his country, and did his utmost to restore her. It was he who corresponded with the present Emperor of the French when a prisoner at Ham, with a view to induce his Majesty to adopt Nicaragua.

General Walker thus describes his first interview with him:—"Castellon received the new-comers with frank cordiality, and expressed the lively pleasure he felt at their arrival. It did not require many minutes to see that he was not the man to control a revolutionary movement, or to conduct it to a successful issue. There was a certain indecision, not merely in his words and features, but even in his walk and the general motions of his body; and this trait of character seemed to be aggravated by the circumstances about him."

dent, and mounted the *white* ribbon; and, curiously enough, many of the phases of this struggle closely resemble the Wars of the Roses in other respects besides the distinctive badges of the two parties.

At this time the office of President was tendered to the American General, but he declined, and instead nominated Don Patricio Rivas as provisional President for fourteen months, with a Cabinet composed of the following members, four of them Nicaraguans, and two Americans. At the same time the standing army was fixed at 150 Americans and 150 natives.

CABINET.

Don Patricio Rivas	*President.*
General William Walker	*Commander-in-Chief.*
General Maximo Xeres	*Minister of State.*
General Ponciano Corral	*Minister of War.*
Colonel Parker H. French	*Minister of the Hacienda.*
Don Fermin Ferrer	*Minister of Public Credit.*

This arrangement was made in October, 1855, but was not destined to continue long in its integrity; a fortnight had hardly elapsed before a correspondence of General Corral was intercepted, and he himself proved a traitor on the clearest evidence. Walker, being convinced of his colleague's guilt, ordered him to be shot, which sentence was at once carried into effect.

General Walker was born in 1824; his father was a banker in Scotland, but emigrated to the United States in 1820. He graduated successively in law and physic, but settled down as an editor of a paper in New Orleans; thence he went to California in a similar capacity, and left that employment to become a leader of filibusters* against Sonora, one of the northern divisions of Mexico; his object was to erect that magnificent district into an independent republic; but the time was not well chosen for the attempt, and he failed. General Walker was a small wiry man, height five feet four inches, very light hair and thick moustache, no beard or whiskers, eyes prominent and large, of a singularly light grey colour; his manner was grave and taciturn, habits most temperate; highly ambitious, but careless of acquiring wealth; brave without being reckless, resolute and determined, he proved himself a model leader for the desperate and lawless men with whom he had afterwards to deal.

General Walker, directly he was able, devoted himself to the development of his adopted country; he caused explorations of the land to be made, and did his utmost to encourage enterprise and industry. Immigration met with his especial favour, as the true means of enriching the State; while in council he introduced an enlightened policy which would no doubt ultimately have proved most beneficial, had not the opposition he met with from his own country completely neutralized all his efforts. The United States, after vacillating for some time, refused to acknowledge the new government of Nicaragua, and this decided the

* The word 'filibuster' is a French and Spanish corruption of the English word 'freebooter,' an appellation which, in former days, from its being frequently assumed by a certain class of men, who disliked the harsher name of 'pirate,' became familiar to the inhabitants of the West India Islands and Central America; but as filibusterism is now used, it expresses the action of the American people, or a portion of the people, in the acquisition of territory which does not belong to them, unrestrained by the responsibilities of the American Government.

hesitating states of Central America, who viewed with jealousy and aversion Walker's progressive tendencies; they speedily assumed a hostile attitude, soon followed by an open rupture. In March, 1856, the Costarican army met a force of 207 men, under Colonel Schlesinger, and utterly routed them, the Colonel being the first man to run, for which Walker sentenced him to be shot, but he escaped. The Costaricans then murdered a number of shopkeepers and innocent persons at Virgen Bay, after which they marched upon the town of Rivas, and succeeded in occupying it with 2500 men. General Walker now took the field in person, and at the head of 500 men attacked Rivas. The battle continued the whole day; all the staff were killed or wounded, and a loss of 130 men compelled Walker to retire. The Costaricans admitted a loss of more than 500 men, and although they remained masters of the town, yet after a few days they considered it prudent to retire with all haste into Costarica. Another attempt to induce the United States to acknowledge the Government of Nicaragua was successful, although the political conditions were the same as when the previous application had been made two months before. The recognition, however, came too late to be of any use: the hostility of the surrounding states had been stirred up, and to the extraordinary diplomacy of the United States, added to the enmity of a powerful countryman, whom Walker unavoidably provoked, may be traced his downfall.

The great mistake of Walker at this period of his career was the acceptance on his part of the presidential chair; and this mistake was the less excusable in a man of his intelligence, because he could not have been at a loss to find a native to fill that place who would have been entirely subservient to him.

To maintain himself in power, it was absolutely necessary that the approaches to the Lake of Nicaragua should be kept open, so as to allow of the free arrival of a constant succession of recruits to feed his Nicaraguan army; but the infusion of Anglo-Saxon intelligence and energy into the council and tactics of the Costaricans turned the balance. A series of masterly movements, made in December, 1856, by their troops, under command of Captain Spencer and General Mora, placed all the approaches in their power; and rapidly following up this success by the defeat and destruction of a body of filibusters at the mouth of the Serepiqui; by the seizure of all the transit steamers; and, by the capture of the forts Castillo Viejo and San Carlos, on the river San Juan, they virtually sealed Walker's doom by cutting off his communication with the Southern States of America, and thus stopping his supplies of men and munitions of war. About 300 recruits for Walker's army arrived at Greytown from New Orleans on the very day Captain Spencer seized the river steamboats, and these men were just in time to see their only means of transport to the interior disappear up the shallow waters of the San Juan, where it was impossible to reach them.

In the meantime Walker fought the battles of Masaya and Granada, and stood his ground manfully against fearful odds. The obstinate valour of the filibusters, as displayed by holding the walls of the great church of

Sir Wm G Ouseley del — Brooks, at

Granada against eight times their number, reads more like romance than reality. When I visited the spot in 1860, I was much struck by the appearance of the ruins, which were absolutely covered with rifle bullets and shot-holes; the place seemed to be quite shelterless; nevertheless General Henningsen, with 400 men, defended the bare walls for nineteen days against upwards of 3000 Central Americans; the besieged lived on their horses while they lasted, and then sustained life by eating the dead bodies of their comrades; their sufferings were awful, yet not one thought of surrender. On the nineteenth day only 150 were left out of the 400, and General Henningsen determined, as a last resort, to cut his way through the enemy; but that night General Walker, with 175 men, landed from the lake in the rear of the besieging army, forced his way over three successive breastworks, and after a most gallant and daring attack, though with the loss of nearly half his number, effected a junction with Henningsen. The allied Central Americans retreated in despair, and began to quarrel amongst themselves. This would have been the time for Walker to strike a decisive blow, but the paucity of his numbers paralysed his movements, and the news of the success of their friends on the San Juan once more gave the Central Americans encouragement and cohesiveness.

It was now simply a question of how long Walker could withstand the pressure against him. He disputed every inch of ground, but was slowly forced to retreat towards San Juan del Sur; his last halt was at Rivas, where a desperate stand was made. But all his efforts were of no avail against the overwhelming forces opposed to him; each encounter, although actually a victory, was in reality a defeat, from the number of his men disabled, whom it was impossible to replace. Thus, early in 1857, Walker, with a mere handful of men, after performing prodigies of valour, found himself most reluctantly compelled to seek shelter on board a man-of-war of the United States navy, by which vessel himself and the remnant of his followers were conveyed away from Nicaragua.

After an occupation of the country for nearly two years, the filibusters were finally expelled, having lost, in killed and wounded, nine-tenths of their numbers. The daring valour of these men made them respected throughout the land, and there can be no question, that had Walker maintained a footing in the State, he would have completely regenerated it; he would then have been worshipped as a great man, but failing, he has been hunted to death. The upper class, the real descendants of the Spaniards, were favourable to the infusion of a foreign element; they were quite tired with the constant anarchy, ruin, and misery, characteristic of Central America, and any foreign influence capable of guaranteeing peace to their country would have been welcome; but their voice in the State was too weak, chiefly because their number was small, and even amongst themselves they were not united; consequently their opportunity was lost.

The object of General Walker has been thoroughly misunderstood in this country, and wilfully misstated in the United States, where his plan was well known; but the formation of a powerful independent Central

American Federation was not palatable to the Cabinet at Washington, for the principal reason, that the monopoly of transit across the Isthmus would no longer be in the hands of Americans, but be open to the world. Our Ministers, therefore, were quietly allowed to entertain the erroneous opinion that annexation was Walker's purpose, and then, by a mixture of cajolery and bullying (in which the Yankees have long held a monopoly as regards England), were made to assist, or rather made to do the dirty work, in the downfall and murder of a man who would have proved a true friend, if only left alone. General Walker never had the slightest intention of adding another State to the American Union: at the invitation of Castellon he threw himself boldly into Nicaragua, with the ambition to restore that magnificent country to its proper position among nations. He saw at a glance that the germ of commercial success was there, if only from geographical position; and this view was more than confirmed by a subsequent inspection of the overflowing richness of the mineral, vegetable, and animal kingdom.

To elevate a nation into fit companionship with other peoples was surely a worthy aim, and this appears to have been Walker's sincere purpose. Not a single case of cruelty or maladministration is recorded against him; on the contrary, he seems to have governed with wisdom, courage, and firmness, and to have been decidedly popular with the people, who unanimously voted him President; but the combination against him was too strong. Honduras, Guatemala, San Salvador, and Costarica joined against him, not because they cared to save Nicaragua, but to save themselves from merging into a Federation, the government of which would doubtless have fallen for the most part into the hands of the superior state of Nicaragua as soon as that country devoted itself to developing its grand geographical position.

The troops of the native states would have been powerless to stay Walker's progress, had it not been for the enmity of individual Americans, who infused an energy and ability into the operations of the native forces which they never could have attained by themselves; and, the efforts of the allied naval forces of Great Britain and the United States to effect his destruction, by keenly watching his every movement, and by the latter power in effecting his capture and basely consigning him to death. Intervention as regards small and weak powers is usually the policy of England, and certainly was that adopted in this case; and if the authorities did experience any qualm of conscience, it was silenced by the call from the United States, who have only to speak to our rulers in a sufficiently peremptory manner to command immediate attention. Considering "the intimate relations that have generally subsisted between our policy and our interest," it is marvellous the amount of blindness and flunkeyism we displayed in the case of Walker. Our policy is *non*-intervention in the disunion of a *great* power, our Ministers probably thinking in this instance that if the contending parties are left alone we may escape in future the quantity of "dirt" which the States, when united, from time to time compelled the mother-country to swallow.

The subsequent career of Walker is soon told. He was landed at New Orleans, and devoted himself to the organization of a new expedition, but from various causes so many followers do not appear to have rallied around his standard as he expected; in the meantime every avenue of approach to Nicaragua was so strictly guarded, chiefly by British cruisers, that Walker did not effect his purpose of re-entering Nicaragua at all. He however succeeded in the States in organizing a very formidable band, with which he sailed for Greytown, and even landed his men at Punta Arenas; but here his further progress was put a stop to by an armed party from the U.S.S. Wabash, under her first lieutenant, who seized Walker and his men, and conveyed them as prisoners on board the frigate, ultimately landing them at New Orleans. In August, 1860, the last and fatal attempt was made. Walker landed near Truxillo, and stormed the fort with a mere handful of men; he proclaimed that he came not to war on the people but on the government;* but misfortune dogged his footsteps, and he was very shortly under the necessity of giving himself up to an English man-of-war, whence he was transferred to the authorities of Honduras, by whose order he was shot at Truxillo on the 25th of September, 1860. It is stated that ten shots were fired at him amid the cheers of the natives, and he was afterwards buried by foreigners. He met his death as became a soldier, without flinching, and with the utmost calmness. General Walker, shortly before his

* In which he imitated English policy in China in 1857:—"We do not war upon the people, but only on the mandarins."

execution, penned the following protest for publication :—

"I hereby protest before the civilized world that when I surrendered to the captain of her Majesty's steamer Icarus, that officer expressly received my sword and pistols, as well as the arms of Colonel Rundler, and the surrender was expressly, and in so many words, to him, as the representative of her Britannic Majesty.

(Signature) "WILLIAM WALKER.

"On board the steamer Icarus, September 5, 1860."

General Walker was the only victim; Colonel Rundler was imprisoned, and the remaining filibusters were landed at New Orleans by H.M.S. Gladiator.

After the expulsion of Walker in 1857, the choice of President fell upon a wealthy merchant, Thomas Martinez by name, who has administered the affairs of the State with judgment and prudence, and may lay claim to having advanced the interests of his country more than any of his predecessors. He established the seat of government at Managua, a town about midway between Granada and Leon, the rival capitals, and by this act did much to quiet the two great factions; although as regards the Granada of to-day, it can hardly be called a town, as the greater part of the city has been destroyed; and I could not learn that there was much prospect of its ever being restored, the more ecpecially as it is not well situated, either in a commercial or a sanitary point of view. The Republic is once again slowly rising from its ashes, and will, no doubt, ere long fulfil its destiny, by becoming a great highway of nations, and at the same time the garden of America; its geographical position fits it exactly for the former, its fine climate and wonderful fertility will enable it to become the latter, by the infusion of a little energy and enterprise. In reference to the climate, the following are the impressions of Walker on the soothing nature of the balmy, "soft, mild air, which seemed a fluid altogether different from the atmosphere of the northern climates. You felt as if a thin and vapoury exhalation of opium, soothing and exhilarating by turns, was being mixed at intervals with the common elements of the atmosphere."

The northern part of the Republic is mountainous, but the southern consists entirely of the great transverse valley of the lakes, completely interrupting the Cordillera, which do not again attain any elevation until far within the territory of Costarica. This great valley is about two hundred miles long, by about one hundred broad, and consists for the most part of magnificent savanas. The country teems with precious metals, while animal and vegetable life are most abundant and prolific. The lakes shoal gradually towards the shore, and can be navigated with ease and safety in all directions; there is only one outlet, and that is by the river San Juan, at the southern extremity. The land on the western side is thickly wooded, while that on the eastern is mostly undulating and grassy, upon which large herds of cattle are raised, the hides of which constitute a large item among the exports of the country.

The natural products of Nicaragua are multifarious; cotton, sugar, indigo, tobacco, rice, cacao, coffee, etc., may be produced in overflowing abundance; the cotton is of a superior quality. The cacao of Nicaragua has long been celebrated for its quality and value. The sugar-cane is slenderer than the variety cultivated in the West India Islands, but contains more saccharine matter. Two crops, and when the fields are irrigated, three crops, are taken from the same ground annually. The crystals are remarkably large and fine, and the sugar itself, when carefully manufactured, nearly equal in beauty to the refined sugar of commerce. The indigo is produced from an indigenous plant called juiquilite (*Indigofera disperma*, Linn.), and has a high reputation in commerce. Coffee flourishes well on the higher grounds. The same may be said of tobacco, which is a government monopoly, and its production is not allowed except in certain quantities. Maize grows in great perfection, and, made into *tortillas*, constitutes a principal article of food. Dye-woods, chiefly the *braziletto*, are extensively exported. All the edible roots and fruits of the tropics thrive well—plantains, bananas, beans, tomatoes, yams, arrowroot, citrons, melons of all kinds, limes, lemons, oranges, pine-apples or ananas, guavas, cocoa-nuts, and many other kinds of fruits and vegetables. Among the vegetable productions which enter into commerce may be mentioned sarsaparilla, annatto, vanilla, ginger, gum-copal, gum-arabic, copaiva, caoutchouc, dragon's-blood, etc.

The mineral resources of Nicaragua are also abundant; gold, silver, copper, lead, and iron, are found in considerable quantities in various parts, but chiefly in the districts of Segovia and Chontales. The production of these metals has greatly fallen off since the independence from Spain; still the produce is considerable, and with capital and good roads the overflowing treasures of the country might be worked with profit. Sulphur may be had in inexhaustible quantities, crude and nearly pure from the volcanos; nitre is also abundant, as also sulphate of iron. Notwithstanding the variety of its products, and the ease with which they may be prepared for the market, the commerce of Nicaragua is very limited.

The political organization of the Republic provides that the executive power shall be vested in a President elected by popular vote for four years, and that he may be re-elected for another term; he must be a native of Central America, resident five years in the state, and thirty years of age. There is a Senate and Congress. The Senate consists of twelve members, two from each of the six districts; they must have all the qualifications of the President, besides property to the extent of one thousand dollars. The office is held for four years, three of the number retiring each year, but they may be re-elected. No ecclesiastic can be elected to this body. Members of Congress are chosen in the proportion of one for every 20,000 inhabitants, they must be twenty-five years of age, have resided one year in the state, and may be either secular or ecclesiastic. All males are electors, but some become so at eighteen—married men for instance.

The rights of the citizen are defined to be, "Liberty, equality, security of life and property; all of which are inseparable and inalienable, and inherent in the nature of man." Again, "Every man is free, and can neither sell himself nor be sold by others." The Catholic religion is recognized by the State, but all other religions are tolerated. A concordat has just been received from the Pope (August, 1862), by which tithes are abolished, and a fixed sum paid to the clergy out of the revenue. Liberty of speech and freedom of the press are guaranteed, and the inviolability of the domicile recognized.

The Judiciary consists of a supreme court, the members being named by Congress and approved by the Senate; there are three judges in each department, one of whom is nominated the presiding judge over each of the six districts; these six judges meeting annually in the capital constitute a court of appeal. They hold office for four years, but are eligible for re-election.

From the above, and the general description of the country which is here given, it will be seen that Nicaragua possesses great fertility and vast resources, and that nothing is wanting but a firm government, and moderate energy and industry, to raise it, in a short space, from the slough of despond into which it, in common with most Spanish American states, has for so long been plunged.

CHAPTER IV.

SKETCH OF THE MOSQUITO SHORE.—PAPAL BULL OF ALEXANDER VI.—NELSON AND MOSQUITO.—DISGRACEFUL TREATY.—DEFEAT OF THE SPANIARDS AT BLACK RIVER.—EXPULSION OF THE NICARAGUANS.—GREYTOWN.—ITS DESTRUCTION.—SILTING UP OF GREYTOWN HARBOUR.—REMARKS ON THE CLIMATE.—MOSQUITO INDIANS.—MORAVIAN MISSIONARIES.—BLEWFIELDS.—CORN ISLANDS.—POPULATION AND AREA OF CENTRAL AMERICA.

In order to complete this general view of the present position of the Central American nationalities, it is necessary to sketch the history of the Mosquito shore, and narrate the state and condition of that most important portion of Central America. The boundaries of the Mosquito territory have, from time immemorial, been in dispute, and to enter fully upon the subject would fill volumes. I shall in this place define the country, as included between the river San Juan on the south, and Cape Cameron on the north, as the points within which the Spaniards and their descendants have never succeeded in establishing themselves. The whole country, it is true, belonged to Spain under the Papal bull issued in 1524 by Alexander VI., the father of the Borgias, Lucretia and Cæsar, with this additional privilege, "that should the natives refuse to embrace the Romish faith and acknowledge her sway, they might be extirpated." The Spaniards, however, do not appear to have availed themselves of this generous permission to seize upon the Mosquito Indian's body and soul; and in no instance did they effect even a temporary footing within the limits I have designated, while to this day the natives retain their freedom and language; and so far from owning the allegiance of either Spain or her revolted dependencies, they entertain the most bitter animosity to the whole Spanish race. Early in the seventeenth century the Mosquito Indians allied themselves with the buccaneers, and from that period their friendship for the English may be dated. This predilection of the natives has on several occasions been most useful, especially against the Spaniards in 1780, when they proved themselves very worthy allies; indeed, but for their bravery and fidelity, the expedition up the river San Juan, and on to the Lake Nicaragua, under Nelson, would have perished to a man, as is testified in the account of the attack given in the 'Life of Nelson,' whose name, by the bye, is as much venerated in Mosquito as in England.

In 1786 a treaty, quite as unnecessary as that signed in 1860, was made with the King of Spain; no reason has ever been given for this foolish act, which of course entailed ruin on hundreds of British subjects, who upon the faith of a British protectorate had established themselves in Mosquito. By the terms of this treaty it was agreed that "the Mosquito country should be evacuated by the subjects of his Britannic Majesty, and that he should disown in the most solemn manner any obstruction to such evacuation." His Catholic Majesty, on his part, "prompted solely by motives of humanity, promises to the King of England that he will not exercise any severity against the Mosquito Indians inhabiting in part the countries that are to be evacuated in virtue of the present convention, on account of any connection which may have subsisted between the said Indians and the English."* His Catholic Majesty kept his word by making forays along the coast, but in spite of every effort no head could be made against this indomitable aboriginal race; and in 1796, the Spaniards having suffered a signal defeat at Black River by a Mosquito force, gave up their attempts in despair, and the natives were not again molested by Spain.

From this it is clear that, during the suspension of friendly relations on the part of England in 1786, the Mosquito Indians were able to maintain their freedom and independent existence, and therefore by no perversion of words can they be said to be or to have been ever under Spanish rule.

During the wars of Napoleon, little was heard of Mosquito; a limited commerce was carried on, and a new king was crowned by the English at Jamaica, after the manner of his forefathers, a custom which origi-

* 1670. The Mosquito Indians placed themselves under the protectorate of Great Britain, and their king was acknowledged during James II.'s reign, under the Great Seal of Jamaica, by the Duke of Albemarle.

1730. English settlements were formed at Black River, Cape Gracias-á-Dios, and Blowfields.

1741. Civil government was established, forts built and garrisoned by British troops.

1763. At the peace, civil and military authorities were withdrawn by treaty.

1776. The establishments were placed on their former footing, but again withdrawn in 1788.

nated in 1687, and is still in force, the present king having been crowned at Belize a few years back. But the great events which had convulsed Europe found an echo in the remotest corners of the earth. The period had now arrived when the narrow policy of Spain recoiled upon herself, and lost her the proudest jewel in the king's crown. The struggle for independence in Spanish America of course attracted the attention of Europe towards that part of the world; and the immense importance, both in a commercial and strategical point of view, of the narrow strip of land which connects the continent was then made manifest.

From that period Europe paid considerable attention to the movements of the new nationalities, especially in the vicinity of the "Isthmus of the Americas," as affording a vast opening for commerce; at the same time England renewed her alliance with the Mosquito Indians, who gladly welcomed their old friend back again. Meanwhile, the new republics were busily engaged cutting each other to pieces, and preparing for themselves years of poverty and misrule; no effort on the part of the nations of Europe could persuade them to settle their differences, and turn their attention to the arts of peace; in short, nearly twenty years elapsed before quiet was in any degree restored to this distracted land. Indeed, even now there is poor promise for the future; and probably nothing will regenerate the country but the introduction of a purer and more energetic race.

The repeated attempts, and the anxiety displayed, by various people to increase the commerce of their respective countries by the discovery of a practicable route for the construction of a canal from sea to sea, of course attracted the attention of the natives of the soil, and especially the people of Nicaragua, who could not fail to observe that the only means by which they could reach the Atlantic was by way of the river San Juan, an outlet of their magnificent lake, but forming a harbour at its mouth, within the territory of Mosquito. The value of the entire stream was thus made apparent to them; and trusting to the forbearance of England, they made an attempt to take possession by force. In 1836 a body of Nicaraguans descended the river, and seized upon the settlement at its mouth. The population, composed of British settlers and Mosquito men, was too small to offer any resistance, and accordingly the Nicaraguans held the place *vi et armis*. As soon as the King of Mosquito heard of this outrage he communicated with Colonel Macdonald, superintendent of Belize, and that officer lost no time in entering an appearance in the harbour; he displayed equal celerity in ejecting the intruders. Colonel Quijano, the commandant, at first declined to depart, but he was not requested to do so a second time, and speedily found himself at another part of the coast, and his followers dispersed. Hardly, however, had Colonel Macdonald returned to Belize before the Nicaraguans again occupied the port; this time they were not disturbed, but allowed to remain until the question had been considered in England; where the deliberations led to the *request* that Nicaragua would state upon what grounds she founded her claims. After waiting a long time for a reply, the King of Mosquito himself gave notice that unless the port was restored to him within a given period he would take forcible possession; this he did, aided by a small number of British seamen and marines, at the expiration of the time allowed; but no sooner had the allies departed than the Nicaraguans sent troops to pull down the Mosquito flag, and capture the Mosquito authorities. It now became necessary to act with decision in the matter; and a force under Captain Lock, R.N., proceeded there, dislodged the Nicaraguans, and drove them up the river. Captain Lock followed, and captured Fort San Carlos, situated at the junction of the lake; he was accompanied by a number of Mosquito Indians, who proved themselves as brave, faithful, and useful as when with Nelson in the same locality seventy years previously; and no doubt he might have landed his force at Granada, and have captured that city, had the necessity existed; but the President and Congress signed a treaty on the 7th March, 1848, by which, reserving the right to prove their claim, they undertook not to molest Mosquito in her occupation of the point in question.

This treaty has been a fruitful source of annoyance ever since. It was a great mistake to treat at all; but it was an act of folly to invite litigation on the subject. The claim of Mosquito was just and valid, and the Nicaraguans ought simply to have been punished for their presumption, and warned to be more careful in future. They were, of course, anxious to possess the harbour of San Juan, or, as it is more commonly called, Greytown, because the immense importance of the position was apparent to the meanest capacity; but they had, in reality, no more claim to the country than Spain has to Portugal.

The gallant old conquerors failed in all their attempts on the Mosquito shore; and even, it is said, made the obstructions in the river San Juan, by which the navigation of that stream is impeded, for no other purpose than to keep out intruders, of whom the Mosquito Indians were perhaps the most dreaded. How then can their descendants presume to lay claim to the land? Even supposing the ancient rights of the King of Mosquito to be pronounced null and void, there is the fact in his favour, that, on the evacuation of the continent by Spain, he was the first to establish a settlement at the harbour of San Juan, and therefore by the act of occupation he has a right to the soil: besides, at the time when the Nicaraguans sent to take the place, there was not even one representative of their country living in the vicinity, neither was there even one habitation owned by a Nicaraguan citizen; the town consisted entirely of British settlers and Mosquito Indians. The first house was built in 1824 by Messrs. Bowden, Shepherd, and three others. Captain Shepherd had, before this date, possessed a store on the opposite side of the harbour, and carried on a trade between Jamaica and Granada. San Juan was named Greytown after Sir Charles Grey, Governor of Jamaica, by direction of the King in council, December 8th, 1847.

Greytown was not permitted to pass even its seven years' apprenticeship in peace, but was wantonly destroyed by Commander Hollis, of the U. S. corvette

Cyane, on the 13th of July, 1854. Not satisfied with bombarding an unresisting town, the commander landed his men, and burnt the place to the ground, under circumstances of peculiar insult to the English and their flag; in fact, during the last ten years every sort of indignity has been heaped upon the *protectors* of Mosquito by the Americans, who have never made any secret of their intention to monopolize the whole of the continent for themselves, and to drive out interlopers by foul means if unable to do so by fair. Our Government has, indeed, been kicked and cuffed, and made to eat any quantity of dirt; and there is no knowing how much further a weak Administration might have helplessly drifted, with every probability of shipwreck to the national honour and dignity, had not our bullying cousins begun to let blood amongst themselves.

Most unfortunately for the nation, the proceedings in Greytown were not suffered to attain any notoriety in this country; the locality was distant and little known, otherwise the public would have made itself heard in reprobation of such scandalous conduct, and probably by interposing have prevented the crowning act of this disgraceful drama, by which we gave up everything at America's dictation, and negotiated a treaty as weak and contemptible as that concluded in 1787. Under a Liberal Government acts like these seem to be quite the fashion; there is, indeed, the utmost liberality in giving up all that a true Englishman holds most dear. Every principle was thrown to the winds in the treaties regarding the Bay Islands and Mosquito. The Mexican question has been shamefully mismanaged; and there can be no doubt that, however much the policy of non-intervention between the Northern and Southern States of America may be supposed to subserve our interests, by permitting us quietly to look on while our powerful and, it must be owned, unscrupulous rival utterly exhausts and brutalizes himself, yet that policy is not an honest and manly one; it does not spring from the true and generous instincts of an Englishman's heart, and therefore its degrading selfishness will inevitably recoil upon us. One result of our present policy is already certain: both North and South are agreed in dislike to England. This might be met with contempt, and the enmity of the whole world treated with equanimity, if brought upon us undeservedly; but it becomes a very different affair when a people feel that it is the result of a narrow and sneaking policy, and one which appears to be chronic on the part of their Government. It has been well said by an able writer, that "A Government in this country is more strengthened in public estimation by timely acts of necessary firmness and prompt decision than they can be weakened by the most rabid and concentrated attacks directed by the leaders of organized assemblies, animated by a zeal for passive endurance of wrong, in feeble dread of the possible results of a vigorous and unflinching maintenance of undoubted and important rights. No true statesman can be regardless of the future dangers and difficulties which are certain to spring from every concession wrung from a weak policy."

A narrative of facts in connection with the policy of England, the United States, and Nicaragua on the

Mosquito question, will be given in a future chapter; in the meantime it is necessary to give a brief description of Mosquito itself. The immediate coast-line, extending from Cape Gracias-á-Dios to Greytown, is for the most part low and uninteresting, although in some places a spur of elevated land reaches quite to the sea, and diversifies the otherwise monotonous aspect by slight cliffy projections or headlands. In the interior, lofty mountains present themselves in two directions: those to the south, rising some 8000 to 10,000 feet above the sea, form the elevated lands of Costarica, while those to the north, which do not anywhere attain so great a height, terminate in a rich gold-bearing ridge, called Chontales, at about the fourteenth parallel. The interval between these mountain-ranges is occupied by the great transverse valley of the Nicaraguan lakes, and extends completely from the Gulf of Fonseca to the Caribbean Sea, the whole intervening land appearing to be of very moderate elevation. Numerous rivers, of more or less volume, intersect the country, but they all have a dangerous bar at their mouth, and are therefore only navigable for small craft. The banks of these rivers are thickly studded with patches of mahogany and cedar. For about twenty miles from their mouths the land is low, but beyond that distance it generally slopes away on savanas, dotted here and there with pine-clumps. The coast from Monkey Point to Cape Gracias-á-Dios is fringed with a series of lagoons lying parallel to the sea, and a canoe might pass from one end to the other of this interior navigation even in the dry season; but in the wet season there is a very respectable channel, and the coast-line then has the appearance of a range of islands. This fact will be of great importance as affording cheap water transport when Mosquito takes its proper position as a cotton-growing country, for which in all respects it is admirably adapted. The nature of the interior may be divided into three heads, for the sake of clearly describing it. (1.) The soil of the high wooded lands is the best, and is everywhere excellent, being either a black mould or rich brick clay. (2.) The low wooded ground is not so good, but is mostly chosen for plantations by the inhabitants from its proximity to their villages. (3). The savana lands are the worst. The soil is light sand, mixed with some rich mould. The swamps, or marshes, are very rich soil, and only require the trees upon them to be cut down to become most valuable for rice. Cotton has been grown everywhere, on the worst land even; the staple was remarkably good. Since the emancipation of the slaves, the plantations have gone to ruin.

From Cape Gracias-á-Dios to Blewfields there are a great many islands and coral cays, but from Blewfields southward the sea is singularly free from any impediment to navigation. The land is clothed to the water's edge with dense tropical vegetation, which gives it a very same appearance; indeed, for miles on either side of Greytown the general aspect is so similar, that it is a difficult matter to distinguish the anchorage from any distance; and ships, in spite of careful navigation, (the sky is overcast for weeks together in the rainy season,) frequently miss it, and, falling to leeward, take days to beat up against the wind and current.* There are no land-locked harbours worthy the name on the entire coast, and only one secure and protected anchorage. At the time of the Discovery, Mosquito boasted three magnificent harbours, namely, Cape Gracias, Blewfields, and Greytown. These harbours, situated at the respective mouths of the three great rivers of the country, namely, the Wanks, the Escondido, and the San Juan, were formed by the enlargement of their outlets into extensive lagoons, having each a deep channel seaward, affording an ample sheltered anchorage. In process of time these harbours silted up, Greytown being the last to succumb. Seventy years ago Nelson used that at Cape Gracias for his squadron; it is now so shallow that only a very small schooner can enter. Blewfields was a favourite resort of the buccaneers, but at present a man-of-war's launch cannot cross the bar at all seasons; while Greytown, in 1860, only carried a depth of eleven feet over the entrance. The immense amount of mud and earth brought down by the rivers readily accounts for this gradual filling up; but the regular action in the case of Greytown has been hastened by an ill-judged interference with the natural causes. Obstructions have been placed in certain positions near the mouth of the river, with

* The currents are governed almost entirely by the winds, which, being prevalent from the north-east, (trade wind,) almost invariably cause a south-going set of the water, often running as much as three miles an hour. An easterly wind has been known to cause a northerly flow, but a southerly wind is sure to turn the tide in the opposite direction almost immediately after it springs up. The above rule holds good to the extent of thirty miles off shore, where a westerly current is met with the greater part of the year.

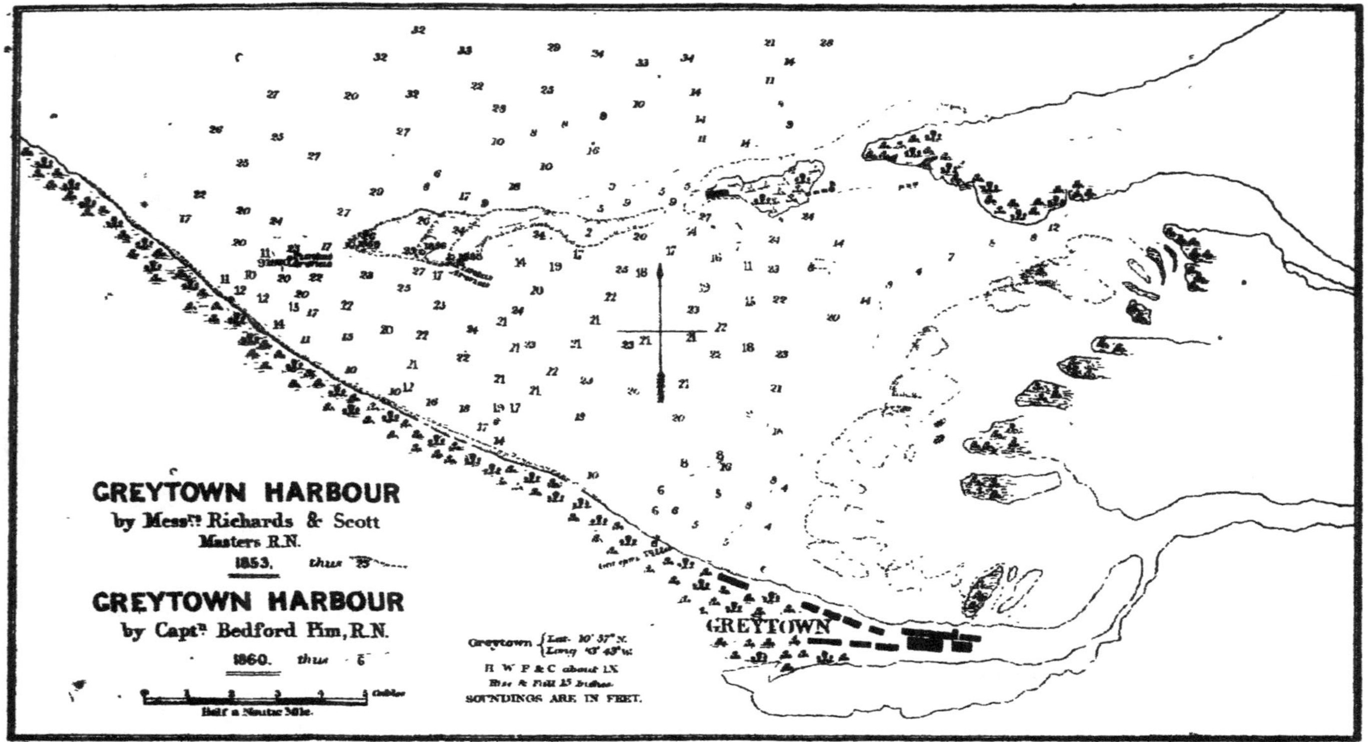
GREYTOWN HARBOUR
by Messrs. Richards & Scott
Masters R.N.
1853. thus
GREYTOWN HARBOUR
by Captn. Bedford Pim, R.N.
1860. thus
Half a Nautic Mile.
GREYTOWN
SOUNDINGS ARE IN FEET.

a view to widen and deepen a favourite channel, but the wishes of the ignorant designers have not been realized; indeed, quite the contrary has been the result. The rapid accumulation of deposit has been startling, and hastened materially the choking up of the harbour. It is very doubtful if any engineering efforts could save it from shortly following the example of its northern neighbours, and becoming a shallow lagoon. In April, 1860, I made a survey of the port, and, after reducing my work to the same scale as the Admiralty chart constructed in 1853, I placed my own plan upon it in red ink; the effect was to show at a glance the encroachments of the land and the difference in the depth of water. The sand-spit, which forms the outer enclosure of the harbour, had grown towards the mainland, and therefore narrowed the entrance two hundred yards; whilst the deepest water I could obtain between the points was only twelve feet, and that not continuous across. This is a very rapid decrease when it is remembered that about two years before, the sailing frigate 'Eurydice' went out of the place without any inconvenience, taking a depth of at least twenty-four feet. The accompanying chart will, however, give the best idea of this remarkable instance of silting up.

As the harbour was too shallow to admit the 'Gorgon,' we had to be content with the roadstead outside,—a by no means pleasant exchange. In the first place, the prevalent wind blows right on the land, making it a lee shore, whilst a swell tumbles in, and renders the anchorage perhaps the most unquiet in the world. For example, I may mention the fact that her Majesty's ship under my command on one occasion rolled so heavily that the cutter, hoisted close up to the davits, dipped under water, and was very nearly dragged bodily away from the ship's side, davits and all; in short, there was a ceaseless motion of many degrees, morning, noon, and night, enough to wear anything to pieces. Our boats suffered the most, as they were very seldom hoisted or lowered without some damage. Fortunately I was able to obtain a house on shore, which was called "Gorgon Villa," after the ship, and where both officers and men occasionally found quiet and rest.

The following remarks on the climate apply chiefly to the Mosquito coast. The heat is never oppressive while the trade-wind blows, but during calms it is sultry and overpowering, although in a far less degree than is experienced in the West Indies. The climate is anything but unhealthy; for during the five months I was stationed on the coast the average sick-list on board her Majesty's ship under my command only amounted to four, while not a single death occurred; and other naval officers of much larger experience express the same opinion. But perhaps a better proof is given by the statistics of health amongst the Moravian missionaries, who have been established at all points of Mosquito for fourteen years, and during that period have not lost one of their number by death, neither has it been necessary to send one of them, man, woman, or child, to Europe to recruit. This last instance is most important testimony, and a stubborn fact in disproof of the repeated allegations made by ignorant persons of the unhealthiness of the country.

The prevailing type of disease appears to be a low form of intermittent fever, chiefly confined to Greytown, which is built upon a swamp; but that it is not of a deadly nature even there, is proved by the fact that our Consul-General has had it several times, without apparently any injury to his constitution. The months in which most sickness is felt are June and July; August also is considered sickly; but much depends upon the constitution and habits of the residents, and many a place has obtained a bad name from the frequent deaths amongst the disorderly, dissipated members of the community. January, February, March, and April, are considered the healthiest months. March and April are the hottest months. The thermometer seldom rises above 82° or falls below 71°; the temperature may therefore be called equable. Thunder is rarely heard between December and April.

Mosquito is at present a rainy country, but the dense tropical vegetation probably causes the annual fall to be greater than in adjacent parts either entirely savana, or nearly treeless; and, doubtless, as the face of the country is cleared, the rainfall will suffer a proportionate diminution, as it has done at Rio Janeiro, St. Helena, and many other parts of the world.

The following is a short monthly abstract of the usual weather met with on the coast:—

January.—Strong breezes from E.N.E., N.E., and N.N.E.; dry weather; occasional showers, principally during the night. Northers may be looked for in this month, but are not common.

February.—Squally weather, wind changes from N. to E. in sudden gusts; this month is sometimes showery, the wind never shifts beyond N. or E.

MARCH.—Strong breezes from E.N.E. About the 20th the equinoctial gale from N. to N.W. may be expected, but it has been known as late as the 7th of April. It is, however, sure to come and blow with very great violence, generally for three days. The rain during the gale comes down in torrents, otherwise March is a dry month.

APRIL.—Light S.E. and S. winds with calms; no rains. In this month the lagoons are very shallow, the river at this season being very low. Great quantities of fish are taken; they come in shoals from the sea, which, owing to the lowness of the rivers, loses its muddy characteristics, and becomes a bright transparent green.

MAY.—Calms; dry weather; winds very light and variable.

JUNE.—Very heavy thunder and vivid lightning, with a deluge of rain; generally calm, but subject to violent squalls and sudden gusts.

JULY.—The same as June, but varied by strong steady breezes from E.N.E. to N.E.

AUGUST.—The same as the two preceding months, with the addition of very heavy squalls of short duration.

SEPTEMBER.—Calms and light variable winds; thunder and lightning, with occasional rains.

OCTOBER.—The northers commence in this month generally about the 15th; heavy northerly or north-north-easterly gales may be expected, with rain and squalls. Northers may be looked for at any time between October and March, sometimes even until April. During a wet north the weather is cold and thoroughly unpleasant, like a November day in England; but should the north be a dry one, it is both healthy and invigorating, and looked upon as a great blessing by the inhabitants.

NOVEMBER.—Similar weather; plenty of rain; sometimes the trade-wind blows uninterruptedly, and the entire month passes without a norther.

DECEMBER.—Passing showers, the trade-wind blowing strongly occasionally interrupted by northers; not veering to N.W. as usual, but remaining steady at N.

SEASONS.

Rainy.	*Dry.*
June.	January.
July.	February.
$\frac{2}{3}$ August.	March.
$\frac{1}{2}$ October.	April.
November.	May.
December.	$\frac{1}{3}$ August.
The rain descends in a perfect deluge, accompanied sometimes by dreadful thunder and lightning.	$\frac{1}{2}$ October.
	Sometimes not a drop of rain falls, but generally in these months the weather is like an English April, except that the rain-drops are heavy tropical ones.

The signs of a coming norther are as follows:—Dead calm, sea smooth as glass, tide very low on the shore; northern horizon banked up with heavy clouds; faint, bluish sheet-lightning. Before the north can come the N.E. trade-winds must be completely killed, to use a native expression; hence the calm. The above phenomenon will give from three to eight hours' warning of the approach of the storm, during which time every preparation must be made, as the gale appears to come on at once and knocks up a tremendous sea immediately. At night the stars shine with great brilliance, just as they do on a frosty night in high latitudes. The longest time a norther has been known to last is three days. The weather is generally clear and dry, parching up everything, but in a wet north the rain descends in torrents.

The following passage from a memorial on the Mosquito shore, prepared by the Council of State for

Jamaica, and transmitted to the Board of Trade and Plantations as early as 1773, might have been written at the present time:—"The climate of the Mosquito shore is milder than any of the West India islands, and the air is more salubrious; the lands are everywhere well watered, and everywhere fertile. The soil is rich in an uncommon degree; the necessaries, and even the luxuries of life, present themselves on all sides; the rivers, lagoons, and sea, abound in excellent fish, and the coasts afford the greatest number of excellent turtle, both for food and the shell, of any country of equal extent in the world. The cotton-tree, cocoa, and vanilla flourish spontaneously, all over the country; indigo too is a native, and seems to be the same with that of Guatemala, which is accounted the best of any. The sugar-cane here arrives at as great perfection as in any of the islands, and of mahogany and sarsaparilla the quantity exported annually is so great as to render the settlements already an object of no small importance to the commerce of Great Britain, no less than 800,000 feet of the former, and 200,000 lb. of the latter, exclusive of 10,000 lb. of tortoise-shell, having been shipped to England in 1769. The banks of the rivers and lagoons are as equally well adapted to the growth of logwood as any part of Honduras, and we have reason to think that there is here enough to supply all Europe."

To this account it may be interesting to add the list of present produce, viz. precious metals, cochineal, hides, sarsaparilla, indigo, hard woods (such as lignum-vitæ, oak, etc.), mahogany, the pencil or Spanish cedar, dyewoods; large forests of pitch-pine, containing much tar; India-rubber, sarsaparilla, balsam, copal, copaiba, sugar, vanilla, cotton, silk-grass, and no doubt many more valuable products, which will become known when the interior is a little more explored; at present it has never been visited by any scientific traveller, although it affords a rich field for the naturalist. For domestic use there is the bark of the red-tree, used as tea by the mahogany cutters, breadfruit, cocoa-nuts, and plantains. The breadfruit requires at least four years from the slip before it bears fruit; a solitary tree has two crops in the year, first from August to October, second in March and April; but if a number of varieties are judiciously planted, there will be fruit every month in the year. The largest breadfruit I ever saw weighed thirteen pounds. Cocoa-nuts are most abundant: the tree bears fruit in rare instances at five years old, but the average is seven years, at which age it produces about one hundred nuts per annum. The cocoa-nut-tree is perhaps the most wonderful production in nature: it affords to man meat and drink, clothes and shelter, and the means of locomotion on the water. There are all sorts of stock in abundance, wild hogs, deer, tapir, maniti, and quantities of turtle, all of which are procured by the natives with little or no trouble.

The best season for shooting wild hogs is June and July, and for deer about December; tapir and maniti are killed on the rivers during the whole year; turtles, the flesh of which is nutritious food, while the shell is an article of commerce, are found in great numbers everywhere on the coast. They lay in June, but continue to deposit eggs until the middle of October. About fifteen days after the eggs are buried in the sand, the young are hatched. Upwards of a hundred are secreted at one time. Unlike the other great turtle depôt, Ascension, both male and female turtles are taken on the coast of Mosquito. A male turtle has never been seen on the sands of Ascension. The flesh of the hawkbill variety is not much esteemed; the shell, however, is very valuable, and known as the tortoise-shell of commerce. This shell is not the upper shield or covering of the turtle, but only the scales, of which there are thirteen; eight of them are flat, and five curved; a large turtle will yield as much as six or seven pounds of scales, sometimes a quarter of an inch in thickness. The turtle is not killed, or there would soon be an end of tortoise-shell, but he is fastened securely, and a fire of grass made on his back; the scales separate at the joints, and are skinned off with a knife. There are many instances of the same turtle being caught a second time, but the outer coating is reproduced in one scale instead of thirteen. It would be very interesting to ascertain how long this scale is in process of formation.

The earliest account of the natives of this part of the American continent is given by Fernando Columbus, son of the great navigator; he describes them "as almost negroes in colour, bestial, going naked, in all respects very rude, eating human flesh, and devouring their fish raw as they happen to catch them." This description cannot be called flattering, and was probably so highly coloured because the inhabitants offered so stubborn and successful a resistance to the Spaniards; at all events, be that as it may, from constant intercourse with the English, the natives of the present day are very different creatures, and quite equal, if not superior, to their neighbours.

The Mosquitos consist of two distinct races, the aborigines and the descendants of the negroes formerly wrecked on the coast. The Valiente, Rama, Cookwra, Woolwa, Tonga, and Poya, aboriginal Indians, are all tributary to the King of Mosquito, and render him a cheerful and willing obedience, the more readily, perhaps, from the unanimous detestation in which they all hold anything of or belonging to Spain. Their numbers are small: probably the total amount of pure aboriginal natives does not exceed 20,000, but some thousands of Creoles, Caribs, and Sambos must be included, making up the population altogether to about 30,000. The Sambo is the result of a large admixture of the negro family amongst the aborigines of the Mosquito shore, the offspring of a number of male blacks wrecked from a slaver very many years ago. This dark element is a prominent feature in the population of the coast; it is now self-supporting, having been much stimulated by a large influx of escaped slaves. All trace of the Indian share in this family has now disappeared, and the woolly hair, thick lips, and flat nose, of the pure African, prevail in all their pristine vigour.

Some writers have mistaken this hybrid people for the aboriginal, or at all events the predominant race, and describing their vices and customs, have occasioned a low estimate to be formed of the Mosquitos. One American writer in particular published a book called 'Waikna,' which he doubtless wrote for "strategical" and diplomatic purposes—Samuel A. Bard (E. G. Squier), formerly *chargé d'affaires* from the United States to Central America. The real possessors of the country are pure Indians, whose king must be of pure blood, and a direct descendant of those Caciques who have ruled the land from time immemorial.

In appearance the aborigines are about the middle height, very swarthy complexion, long coarse black hair, good eyes, and thin lips; the most remarkable feature is the nose, which is sharp, thin, and small, and looks more so from the cheek-bones being high. They do not think little of themselves, as is evidenced by their native appellation, "Waikna," man;* but this conceit is not altogether unjustifiable, for they are brave, warlike, and about the best canoemen in the world. No weather stops them; when a ship's boat could not venture to sea, they go off without the smallest hesitation; indeed they seem to be amphibious. When death occurs, they burn everything belonging to the deceased, and even cut down his fruit-trees; the grave is guarded with the greatest care, but the memory of the departed is not cherished; on the contrary, any mention of him is considered the greatest offence. The wife or wives (polygamy is allowed, although not common) cut off their long hair, from a feeling that no one ought to touch what their lord and master delighted to handle.

* This is a common practice of the aborigines of America, from the Arctic to the Antarctic regions; for example, the Esquimaux call themselves "Innuit," men, *par excellence;* and, travelling southward, the custom exists amongst the Apaches, the Athapascans, and other tribes, until the southern part of America is reached, where it is found amongst the Araucanians.

The men test their endurance by bending down and seeing how many blows they can endure; and many of them suffer a perfect martyrdom of flogging without a groan. Intoxication is common at certain seasons, a custom in repute amongst their forefathers long before the Discovery. The liquor is made from cassava, in the same manner as Cook found the Sandwich and other South Sea Islanders making ava or kava; it is chewed by the women, after boiling the roots; about one-third is chewed, the rest pounded; then hot water and cane-juice is poured upon it, and after two days' fermentation it is ready. It looks like buttermilk, and is sour, but very strong.* Fermented cane-juice, or

* Can there be any philological connection between the American terms "Cassava" or "Kasava" and the Polynesian "Kava" or "Ava," supposed to be derived from the Sanscrit "Kasya" (intoxicating beverages)? Strange to add, preparing an intoxicating liquor from the cassava, or yuka, (*Manihot Aipi*, Pohl,) is also practised in the interior of Peru, where the Indians call it "Masato." Antonio Raimondy, in his 'Apuntes sobre la Provincia litoral de Loreto,' (Lima, 1862, page 132), gives a circumstantial account of it which, from its ethnological importance, may here be translated and ought to be compared with the description of the preparation of kava furnished by Dr. Seemann in his 'Viti,' (London, 1862,) page 327: "In order to get an idea of the way in which this beverage masato) is prepared, it is necessary to enter for a moment one of the great houses of the heathens of Ucayali on the eve of a great festival. On one side are seen several half-naked women seated on the floor around a heap of yucas, and occupied in pealing the skin off them. On the other side is a woman busy in putting the cleaned roots in a pot large enough for a man to fall into. After this has been done, a small quantity of water is put in the pot, the yucas are covered over with leaves, and then boiled. When boiled they are mashed. . . . Advanced to this state they proceed to the most important, and at the same time most disgusting, operation. The women, and in some instances the men also, sit down once more in a circle around the mashed yucas, taking large handfuls of it in their mouths, which they chew without swallowing until completely saturated with saliva and almost become liquid. In this state the filthy mass is spit out, and the operation repeated until the required quantity is prepared.

pine-apple juice, is also in much request: it need hardly be said that each of these drinks is very intoxicating. Amongst the Indians living about the head-waters of the rivers, there are one or two tribes which still preserve the custom of flattening the heads of their children, just like the Flathead tribe in British Columbia; they are much fairer than their brethren inhabiting the low lands of the coast, and some of their women are almost white. They are a slow, stolid race, peaceably inclined towards the English, and no doubt they would afford every assistance to a traveller desiring to explore their country.

The Mosquito Indians have earned a well-deserved character for the scrupulous exactness with which they fulfil their engagements; they will endure any hardship, and work well, if only properly treated. Each village has its head man, who is responsible to the king, to whom all grave matters are referred. There are no regular taxes, but every year canoes, tortoise-shell, provisions, and various valuable products, are presented to him.

Morality, it must be confessed, is not a native virtue: the punishment for adultery was the infliction of a sound beating to the wife, and the exaction of a certain payment from the other delinquent: but a great change

After this a small portion of mashed yuca is mixed and kneaded with the chewed mass and then put into pots, which are covered up till fermentation sets in. The saliva contained in the mashed yuca produces fermentation; changes the starch into sugar, and the sugar into alcohol—a process which, according to the state of the temperature and the existing quantity of saliva, takes place in two, three, or four days. This fermented mass accompanies the Indians on all their journeys. When wishing to prepare from it their disgusting beverage it is dissolved with a little water."

for the better has come over the people within the last few years, owing to the missionary efforts of the church of the United Brethren, or Moravians, which commenced in 1848. Their first station was established in the town of Blewfields, to the population of which, consisting chiefly of so-called "Creoles" with but few Indians, the labours of the missionaries were, with the exception of occasional visits to the more distant settlements, almost entirely limited for some years. Subsequently, however, a footing was obtained on other parts of the coast, and among the pure Indian population. A station which was in course of establishment at Cape Gracias-á-Dios was necessarily abandoned, in consequence of the anarchy prevailing at the time of the transfer of that part of the coast to the Republic of Honduras (1860–61). The stations at present occupied are the following:—

1. *Blewfields*, where a congregation of 198 persons is under the direct care of the missionaries. These are chiefly "Creoles."

2. *Ramah:* 152 persons, pure Indians of the Rama tribe. It is on the Rama Cay in Blewfields Lagoon.

3. *Magdala:* 157 persons, pure Indians, mostly Mosquitos and Woolwas. It is situated in Pearl Cay Lagoon.

4. *Joppa:* 33 persons, Creoles, on Corn Island, about fifty miles north-north-east from Blewfields.

5. *Ephrata:* only two persons under regular instruction, as the station is quite new. It is on the Wounta Haulover, a narrow strip of land, between the main ocean and the Wounta Lagoon. A considerable number

of Indian settlements are accessible from this point. By recent returns there are 542 persons under the care of the missionaries, not including occasional hearers, eight day-schools with 245 scholars, and one school for the training of Indian boys for future usefulness as teachers, etc.

The English language is taught in all the schools. The Indians use various native dialects, but can all understand the Mosquito, the language of the most influential tribe. In this language the missionaries have prepared several elementary works for use in the schools. The labours of the missionaries have been attended with encouraging results. At the four older stations, there are congregations arranged and conducted on Christian principles, with regular divine worship, and the administration of the sacraments, besides those more individual means of instruction which form so important a feature in the missionary system of the Brethren's Church.

As regards that external improvement which is the unfailing result of the diffusion of Christian principles, it is evident that it is by no means lacking among the christianized inhabitants of this coast. Eye-witnesses speak of the village of Ramah as affording a striking specimen of a well-arranged Christian settlement, though its inhabitants were, but a few years since, notorious for their drunkenness and their bloody feuds. Yet progress in respect to domestic habits and the amenities of civilized life must be gradual; and still more must this be the case with the development of an industrious, enterprising spirit, which will lead to a more careful improvement of the resources of the country. In this latter respect something has been done by the planting of cocoa-nuts, and the like. It is also intended to furnish presses, to extract the oil of the cocoa-nut in a more speedy and profitable manner than the rude process employed by the natives, while it is hoped that a small saw-mill may render it possible to make use of the vast quantities of timber in the forests. In these and similar ways, a stimulus may be given to continuous industry, and the fruits of the Gospel, even in temporal prosperity, may be as manifest in Central America, as they have been in South Africa and elsewhere.

The usefulness of the missions on the coast of Mosquito appears to have received a heavy blow from the abandonment of the protectorate of that country by England. In the following extracts the missionaries speak for themselves:—

"Blewfields, March 14th, 1861.

"My position, under the present political circumstances of the country, is peculiarly difficult. Foresight must almost assume the character of prophecy, in order to determine with any degree of certainty what the events of the immediate future may be. Communication is slow and imperfect here. All we can attain to are suggestions and suppositions, which frequently prove futile, almost as soon as they are made. This was very much the case with regard to our settlement at the Cape. The king and the consul entertained no doubt, that all the Indians living north of the present Mosquito boundary would immediately remove within its limits, being quite averse to Spanish rule. Hence we deemed it expedient to commence at Wounta without delay. Now, however, it is pretty clear, that the Indians are determined to hold their ancient possessions, as their former warlike spirit is aroused. If Honduras or Nicaragua undertakes to molest them, they will defend their rights most desperately; and there is little doubt, if the conflicting parties are left to themselves, whose the victory will be. There are some here who believe that the treaty, though ratified, will come to nothing at last.

"By the accounts from the Cape [Gracias-á-Dios] it appears, that the Indians are very sorry that the Gospel is to be taken away from them. Yet it is a question whether it is advisable to endeavour to retain a footing there. At all events Br. Kandler cannot leave at once. The Cape is the central point of the Mosquito Coast, more than one-half of the Indian population being settled to the northward of it, while in the immediate neighbourhood there are numerous settlements.

"Rama, June 4th, 1861.

"Ever since England gave up the protectorate of the Mosquito Coast, I have been apprehensive as to what would become of our Mission. It now appears as if the light which was just commencing to shine was to be trodden underfoot. On the 10th of May, I was alarmed by the report that there was a Romish priest in the place, who had come to baptize the people. I really did not know what to do, as there are still a number not baptized. However, there was present help in Him that is mighty. When the brother in whose house the priest had taken up his lodging came home from his work, the priest asked if he was baptized, to which he replied that he was, and that the people here had a minister, who had come from beyond the great ocean, and wanted no other. Upon this the priest said he was sorry, and went away. Subsequently, two persons went to Blewfields, and were baptized. It is no wonder that the people ran after him, as he said nothing to them about their sins. I fear there will soon be Roman Catholic churches at many places, and I have been told that the priest had said that we should then have to leave the country. What will become of the Mission, and of all the dear people who have learned to read their Bibles?

"June 11th, 1861.

"On my return home, I heard to my grief, that, in my absence, a Spanish priest had been here, baptizing all who came to him. About 150, old and young, including some who have attended our church, where deceived by him. He told the magistrates, that he was sent by the Governments of Nicaragua and Honduras to baptize all the Indians on the coast. Thus we see what measures these republics adopt to ensure their success among these people! But we will trust in the Lord's outstretched arm, which must prevail over His enemies. May He grant us grace and boldness to make known His everlasting Gospel without fear! If we should leave the Cape at this juncture, the priests will suppose we are afraid of them, which I think we ought not to give them occasion to do.

"We are sorry that England has given up the protectorate of the Mosquito Territory. We see that it is better to trust in the Lord than to put confidence in man. The Romish Church in Nicaragua is now doing its utmost to make proselytes, and to destroy our work, if possible. Last week, a Spanish priest was here, sent by the bishop to baptize every one who comes in his way, without any instruction. Here, the people would not go to him, saying that they had a minister already. But at the Indian villages, he called the poor ignorant people together, and, by the present of a large piece of tobacco to each, induced them to consent to his baptism.

"On the 12th and 13th of October, 1861, in the presence and by the direction of her Majesty's Consul, the new system was established in the king's name. There are to be a general and an executive council, of which the king, under the title of Hereditary Chief, is to be the president, with an annual allowance of fifteen hundred dollars. The majority of the members of these councils are either pure Indians or half-breeds. The English laws are to be those of this land. Whether the British Government will insist on payment of the compensation agreed to by the republics of Honduras and Nicaragua, time will show. But I should think England will feel herself in honour bound to compel those republics to fulfil their engagments, according to the terms of the treaty."

"Blewfields, November, 1861.

"On the 12th and 13th instant, the new constitution was

established in the king's name, consisting of a general and an executive council, the king being president of both. The majority of the members are either whole or half Indians. The laws of England are to be the laws of the land. The king, under the title of Hereditary Chief, is to receive an annual stipend of $1500. Whether the English Government will see to it, that this compensation is duly paid by Honduras and Nicaragua, time will show. I should think, however, that England would feel herself bound in honour to compel these republics to fulfil their engagements, according to the tenor of the treaty.

"Three legal members have been nominated for both councils, Mr. Green, myself, and Mr. Booth. Three other officers were likewise chosen, a Secretary, a Treasurer and Receiver-General, and the Chief Justice of the second office: I was urged to accept, and at length did so, though with much hesitation. Mr. Green is shortly expected, and intends to make Blewfields his permanent place of abode. I trust that the carrying out of these plans will tend to counteract the proceedings of disaffected and mischievous people."

"Blewfields, February 5th, 1862.

"As regards the present government, and the political circumstances of this country, it is hard to say what the king's real relation to Nicaragua is. If our interpretation of the treaty is adopted by the British Government, he is still, in some measure, independent, as Nicaragua is not to interfere with internal arrangements, or with the produce of the land; while the king, on his part, undertakes not to sell or cede the territory to any other nation.

"As regards the administration of internal affairs, the advisory members of the council, and particularly the Consul, are to direct the working of the machinery, and, if let alone, all will do well."

"Blewfields, August 9th, 1862.

"In reference to the political state of this poor country, I have but very feeble hopes for good; for the English Government has no interest either one way or the other, which Nicaragua or Honduras, observing, will spare no trouble to turn to their own benefit; they will advance inch by inch, and eventually take it as a matter of course, and England, as explaining it as an arrangement of necessity, will wink at it. I therefore scarcely think that the presence and co-operation of the Consul will avert the blow, for, as her Britannic Majesty's servant, he must adopt the ever-changing views of her Government."

It will now be necessary, before concluding my account of Mosquito, to give a general description of the various settlements of importance on the coast and adjacent islands, namely, at Corn Islands, Pearl Cay Lagoon, Blewfields, and Greytown. There are, besides, several minor establishments, such as Cape Gracias-á-Dios, where numbers of cattle are raised and some commerce carried on, Grand River, and Pearl Cay Islands, whence cocoa-nuts, etc. etc., are exported, and in each place there have been English settlers for many years.

CORN ISLANDS.

The Corn Islands are two in number, called Great and Little; they are both moderately high and very picturesque, the beach fringed with cocoanut-trees, and the high land with avenues of the magnificent breadfruit-tree, whilst orange and lime-trees abound in every direction. A coral-reef nearly surrounds each, and makes it necessary to approach with care and caution. There is a very fair anchorage on the lee side of either island, in about five fathoms water.

The Great island, which, by the bye, simply affords a pleasant walk all round it, and is not, therefore, very great, is peopled by about 200 Creoles and Negroes.

Their language is English, and they have a small portion of land under cultivation; sufficient however, such is the richness of the soil, not only to supply their own wants, but to afford a large amount of stock to vessels calling. Bullocks, pigs, goats, fowls, ducks, turkeys, and a great variety of fruit and vegetables, can always be procured. Cotton of the finest sort was at one time exported in considerable quantities; but since the emancipation of the negroes, effected here as summarily as elsewhere, all commercial enterprise has ceased, if a very small trade in cocoa-nuts be excepted.

The story of the emancipation of the negroes at the Corn Islands is best told in the words of a memorial addressed to the English Consul by the Creole residents of English descent, and a copy of which they placed in my hands:—

(COPY.)

"To James Green, Esq., H.B.M.'s Consul in Mosquito, and agent to his Majesty the King of Mosquito: The respectful memorial of the undersigned, formerly proprietors and the heirs of proprietors of the emancipated slaves of Corn Island,

"Humbly represents,

"That your petitioners have long and patiently laboured under many painful difficulties, the consequence of having been suddenly and unexpectedly dispossessed of their slaves; no notice whatever being given them, to prepare for the event which involved the greater part, to a great extent, in utter destitution, nor has their case been ameliorated by the receipt of a single payment of any part of the compensation promised them at the time of manumission.

"Your petitioners humbly presume that you are already in possession of the well-known fact, that the emancipator of said slaves was Colonel (now General) Macdonald, a British officer, who on the 27th day of August, A.D. 1841, caused them to be assembled on South-west Bay, and did then and there publicly pronounce them free, in the name of H.B.M. Queen Victoria and the King of Mosquito, and at the same time openly declared and proclaimed that the following compensation would be paid the owners, viz.—

"The proprietors of the slaves now emancipated shall respectively receive for each the sum of £25, which will be paid in yearly instalments, with interest thereon, until the amount be fully discharged.

"Your petitioners, some of them British-born subjects, the others the immediate descendants of such, loyally attached to H.M.'s person and government, would further respectfully state, that they were inspired with the most flattering hopes when a British Consul first became resident in Mosquito, and confidently hoped that through such an authority, justice would be speedily, or at least eventually, awarded them. They still hope and expect that this will be the case, and further state that your predecessors in office, Messrs. Christie and Walker, did each, throughout the period of his superintendence, hold out encouraging hopes, that the compensation overdue would yet be forthcoming. The former also settled the rate of the interest above mentioned, at four per cent. per annum, to be paid from the date of manumission to the time that the principal could be fully liquidated.

"Your petitioners therefore earnestly entreat, that as duties are now being levied at this island, and rent being paid the Government for the Little Corn Island, you will please to take into your earnest consideration the expediency of appropriating such part of the same, or other government funds or revenue, as you may deem proper, to the liquidating of the said government debt, so long due to them.

"And your petitioners, as in duty bound, will ever pray.

"March 1, 1853. A true copy attested.

(Signed) "JAMES BOWDEN, Chief Magistrate."

	No. of Slaves.		No. of Slaves
James Bowden . . .	19	Lydia Brown . . .	13
James N. Bowden .		John Hooker . .	5
John Bowden . . .	10	Margaret Hooker .	
Michael Quin . .	39	Susan Hooker . .	
Patrick Quin . .		Amelia Hooker . .	
John Quin . . .		Janette Hooker .	
Catherine Quin . .		Christopher Downes .	2
Mary Quin . . .		Elizabeth Cottrell . .	1
Margaret Quin . .		Eleanor Culver . . .	4
Maria E. Forbes . .	1	Escalona Nansank	1
Eleanor Frances . .	2	Caroline Nansank .	
Joseph M. Nansank .	1	Total, slaves	98

This petition, when I left the coast, still remained unattended to; indeed, I would not give much for the islanders' chance of payment. It is simply a case of petty larceny, and the victims must console themselves with this reflection, that they have plenty of brothers in affliction—to wit, soldiers and sailors who cannot get their prize-money. For—

> "To beg, or to borrow, or even *to get your own*,
> It is the very worst world that ever was known."

I had the curiosity to question the ex-slaves on the matter of their freedom, and found them unanimously of opinion that their condition whilst in slavery was preferable to their present state; it was all very pleasant to lie about in the sun while they were in health, but when sickness or age overtook them, no one cared the least whether they died like dogs or not. The truth is, that the Negro is quite unfit to be left to himself, anywhere out of his own land; when freed from all restraint, he becomes a burden to himself and to his neighbours.

Little Corn Island is chiefly grazing-land, and affords excellent pasturage for herds of cattle, which however are not bred on the island, but imported from Cape Gracias-á-Dios. The channel between the Great and Little Island is about six miles broad, and is deep and safe. About twenty of the Great Corn Islanders generally live on the Little Island to look after the cattle, collect cocoa-nuts, and pick guava, of which great quantities grow wild on the south side, and prove excellent food for pigs. Its scenery is still more pretty than that of the Great Island, and its healthiness is proverbial; the few cases of sickness which occur may be traced to imprudent exposure to the weather. In short, I was delighted with the Corn Islands. Their salubrity and charming scenery, as well as the abundant supply of fresh meat, fruit, vegetables, lobsters, fish, and turtle, which can always be obtained, will make their vicinity to the future railway most valuable to those employed upon the works, whenever change and recreation may be deemed desirable. As a sanatorium, the Corn Islands will be invaluable, and I have already made certain arrangements to ensure their full usefulness.

Great Corn Island is in lat. 12° 13′ N., long. 82° 10′. W. The anchorage is on a sandy bottom in about 5 fathoms, and the water is so clear that all the coral dangers can be plainly seen. The distance from Pearl Cay Lagoon is 34 miles, from Blewfields 38 miles, from Gorgon Bay 52 miles, and from Greytown 82 miles. There is only one shoal of any consequence in the vicinity; it is called the Blowing Rock, and is eight miles south from Great Corn Island.

PEARL CAY LAGOON.

My description of Pearl Cay Lagoon will not be so glowing as that of Corn Islands. In the first place, the anchorage for large ships is a long way off the entrance, owing to the shallowness of the water; the coast is very flat and same, without any prominent feature to distinguish it. The lagoon is very extensive, reaching as much as twenty miles from its mouth; the bar has only eight feet upon it and breaks, except in fine weather; at the spring, there is a rise and fall of two feet, H. W., F. and C. 1h. 45m. The lagoon is full of shoals, averaging but little more than a fathom in depth over its entire extent. The settlement is simply a collection of wooden houses, imported from the "States," and placed in a straggling line along the borders of the lagoon at the opposite extreme from the entrance. The surrounding scenery is most uninteresting; wherever you turn, dense primæval forest meets the eye, fringed at the water's edge by the everlasting mangrove. The inhabitants number about 500; an excellent Moravian missionary, by name Lundberg, dwells amongst them, who acts as magistrate as well as pastor; his church is very pretty, and forms a pleasing addition to the town buildings. All sorts of stock, fruit, and vegetables can be procured here, and excellent oysters abound in the lagoon; but from the distance between the village and the anchorage the place is but very little resorted to. I had heard especially of the cheapness of the fowls, and accordingly purchased six or seven dozen for distribution amongst the hungry squadron at Greytown; but during the long pull off to the ship, for the most part against a fresh trade-wind, a large proportion of my unfortunate live-stock, nearly two dozen, found a watery grave in the bottom of the boat, so that my American friends at Greytown had but a Flemish account of what would have been a most acceptable present to them. The Pearl Cays lie within a few miles of the Lagoon; there are a good many of them, but the principal are Askill, Crawl, Grape, Baboon, Lime, and Water Cays. Three of these have been purchased by a Mr. Thompson (American), one by Mr. Kirkland, and one by Mr. Taylor. The Cays are a favourite resort of turtle, and great numbers are caught in the vicinity. Mr. Thompson has cleared his three Cays and planted them with cocoa-nuts, by which he expects to realize a good income. There is deep water between the Cays, but the navigation should not be attempted without good local knowledge. Mr. Quin, of Corn Island, late pilot of H.M.S. Orion, 91 guns, safely conducted the Gorgon through this dangerous locality.* He probably saved the Government a false keel and some sheets of copper; nevertheless his charge of £6 was objected to, and I received an intimation from the Admiralty that half that sum would be mulcted from my pay, which was accordingly done.

BLEWFIELDS.

Blewfields Lagoon is about twenty miles south of Pearl Cay; it is far more picturesque, but not quite so large, though rather deeper; the anchorage outside also

* H.M.S. Racer had got on shore shortly before our visit, and her repairs at the Havana cost our Government £600.

is much better, and more easily distinguishable, Blewfields Bluff being quite a conspicuous object. The bar is by no means so dangerous; indeed, small schooners drawing seven feet can enter with safety in moderate weather. Like Pearl Cay, there is abundance of stock of all sorts, sufficient for ten times the population. Oysters also are found in profusion. The settlement, which is of course considerably larger than Pearl Cay, is also situated at the top of the Lagoon, at the further extremity from the entrance, and is close down to the edge of the water. The flood-tide only runs three hours; same rise and fall as Pearl Cay, H. W. 1h. 50m. There is a good church and schoolrooms, under the superintendence of Pastor G. Feurig, assisted by two other Moravian brethren, whose influence for good is very perceptible. The inhabitants I should estimate at about 1000 souls,—a very mixed population of Indians, Sambos, Negroes, English, and Creoles. English is almost universally spoken, although, of course, Mosquito is the language of the country. The Lagoon is rapidly filling up; many of the present inhabitants remember, as a large expanse of water, what is now dense mangrove bush. The quantity of mud brought down by the river Escondido is the principal cause of this rapid silting. Large quantities of mahogany grow in the vicinity of the river, principally on the banks of the small tributaries; and it is here that the mahogany trade has, for the present, reached its southern limit, although, no doubt, there are many cuttings on the banks of the Rama River, a few miles south of Gorgon Bay. The houses are all built of wood, the material for which is imported from the States at a very cheap rate, cheaper by far than they could be built for in the country. The king's house is the best in the place, and is a most comfortable habitation; it is substantially built, but plain, and is situated on some slightly rising ground to the southward of the town. His Majesty resides at Blewfields about half the year; during the other six months he travels from one end of his country to the other.

In this place it may not be uninteresting to give a description of the ruler of a country which has attracted so much attention of late years; the more especially as so much misconception appears to exist about him, chiefly traceable to certain American publications. His Majesty then is a Mosquito Indian of pure blood, in direct descent from a long line of regal ancestors. He is rather below the middle height, with a swarthy complexion, though much fairer than the generality of his countrymen; his face is flat, cheekbones high, nose small and thin (a characteristic of his race), hair jet-black and fine, no beard or moustache. His countenance is expressive and intelligent, giving the idea of a good heart; he is thoroughly English in his habits, thoughts, and dress, and having received a first-rate education at Jamaica, and been brought up under excellent tutors, he considers English his proper language; in short, although he may have faults, the impression he makes is that of a thorough English gentleman. His costume is that of a yachting man in the season, and his great delight is in sailing about in a canoe, which he manages with the accustomed dexterity of his countrymen. He is a very active man, not yet thirty, and still in a state of single blessedness; and, what is more, the damsels of Mosquito do not seem likely ever to make an impression upon his heart. I advised him to come to this country, and try his fortune in perhaps the finest matrimonial market in the world.

His mother and two sisters also live at Blewfields, but at some distance from the king's residence. His Majesty introduced me to them; and I found the queen-dowager, a singularly firm and upright old lady, much taller than the generality of her countrywomen. She was very plainly and neatly dressed, as also her daughters, who closely resembled their mother. Th y have not received any education beyond that obtainable in Mosquito, but nevertheless seemed to exercise considerable influence over their kingly relative; indeed, it appeared to me that, although by no means houris, their position was far superior to that of their sisterhood in Turkey. The dresses of the princesses were not remarkable either for elegance or pattern; the puckers or gathers were few and far between; indeed, the ladies appeared straight up and down, like "a yard of pump-water." I thought of the full skirting of our ladies at home, and could not resist speaking, through the medium of his Majesty as interpreter, of the utility and elegance of a certain article of dress much in request in my own country. The youngest princess, however, with charming *naïveté*, remarked that one garment was quite enough in their country, and that the addition of another would be a burden grievous to be borne. I eagerly rejoined that she could not have the least idea of the light bird-cage airiness of the garment in question, if she looked upon it as a burden. After a little more conversation on this interesting topic, upon which I became quite confidential, we adjourned to the king's residence, where a plentiful dinner was served quite in the English style—plates, knives, forks, etc., all of English make.

This was my first introduction to Mosquitian royalty, and I must confess myself pleased with all I saw or heard. His Majesty's residence is a large American lumber house, most tastefully built in the villa style with a capital verandah, and well fitted up. His sanctum contains a very good collection of books by some of our best authors. The grounds are enclosed by a substantial railing, within which cocoa-nut, breadfruit, orange, lime, cacao—indeed, all sorts of fruit-trees flourish with tropical luxuriance and hide the house from the land side. From the water the scene is very pretty. The house, perched on a small plot of rising ground close to the edge of the Lagoon, and backed by the luxuriant foliage, has quite a charming appearance. Several natives of the better class seemed to be always hovering about the vicinity of the house, but the king is seldom attended by any one except his body-servant, a tall, powerful Sambo, and is never addressed as 'Your Majesty,' but by both subjects and strangers as 'King.' I ought to mention that in disposition his Majesty is most quiet and inoffensive, although his power is absolute over his subjects, who implicitly obey his slightest order, as I can personally testify. There seems to be but one feeling throughout Mosquito about their neighbours the Nicaraguans; the detestation is as great as it ever was, and the Nicaraguans will have plenty to do if they attempt in any way to coerce the Mosquitians. The present king, George Frederick, succeeded his father, Robert Charles, in 1848. I had more than one opportunity of observing his character when my guest on board the 'Gorgon,' and can truly say that his good qualities predominate over the bad ones to a great extent.

A description of Greytown has already been given; it therefore only remains to add, that when I left, in April, 1860, the town probably numbered about one hundred houses, with an average of five inmates in each. A noticeable feature in the place is the absence of any sort of church, of any denomination. Efforts, however, were being made to complete a small wooden shanty for religious purposes. Nothing can be said in extenuation of this indifference. Poverty certainly cannot be pleaded—although the place is rapidly declining—for Greytown boasts a good masonic lodge and even theatrical entertainments, each of which are more costly than good church accommodation would have amounted to. The houses are, without exception, of wood imported from "the States," easily taken to pieces; so that I should not be surprised, at no very distant day, if the site of the present town entirely disappeared: it only wants the conviction that the transit at Greytown is played out, to cause a general migration.

The town has never recovered the wholesale destruction caused by Commander Hollins, U.S. corvette Cyane, who first bombarded and then landed his men and burnt it to the ground. Some conception of the atrocity of this

H Sewell Esq R.N del

Vincent Brooks, lith

GORGON VILLA, WITH A VIEW OF GREY TOWN MARCH [illegible]

act may be formed by reading the following quotation from an American author, whose prejudices and party views doubtless made him put the best face on the matter, but who nevertheless was compelled to condemn the act.

"Its (Greytown's) prosperity was much retarded by a dispute with the adventurers into whose hands the transit had fallen, producing an irritation of feeling which resulted in certain alleged insults on the part of the town to an American diplomatic agent, whose belligerent tendencies led him to interfere in matters quite beyond the sphere of his duties. An American vessel of war was sent to inquire into the circumstances of the case. Her commander, acting under improper influences, assumed a most offensive and hostile attitude toward the town, and made various arrogant demands, which were not complied with, whereupon he bombarded the place, and, landing a force of marines, burned it to the ground. The annals of this century furnish no parallel to this wanton and cruel procedure, and it stands a lasting disgrace and infamy to all concerned. It is certain that no such act was contemplated by the American Government; but, as it retained the delinquent officer in its service, and did not formally disavow the deed, it must be held to share the odium consequent upon it."

Viewing the above quotation by the light we have now to guide us regarding American writing, we may put the destruction of Greytown down as a dark deed, deserving condign punishment. One is at a loss to conceive how an officer could be found to perpetrate so cowardly and brutal an act, and how our own Government could allow the matter to pass unnoticed and not *even* demand compensation for the sufferers.

In winding up this general account of Central America, I shall place before the reader, in a tabular form, the areas and populations of the various places described, and the sum total of the whole.

CENTRAL AMERICA.

	Square Miles.	Population.
Isthmus of Panama	34,000	129,000
Mexican Provinces (Yucatan and Chiapas)	92,000	800,000
Costarica	25,000	135,000
Nicaragua	30,000	300,000
Honduras	40,000	350,000
San Salvador	11,400	290,000
Guatemala	60,000	800,000
Belize	9,600	25,000
Mosquito Territory	4,000	30,000
Central America	305,500	2,859,000

Central America therefore contains an area of about 300,000 square miles, and is nearly equal in extent to England and France together. The average population is rather more than nine to the square mile.

CHAPTER V.

SCHEMES OF TRANSIT BY CANALIZATION.—ISTHMUS OF TEHUANTEPEC.—FERNANDO CORTEZ.—PRIESTLY OPINION OF TRANSIT.—THE SPANISH CORTES.—SEÑOR MORO.—SURVEYS AND ESTIMATES.—REGENERATION AND THE IRON-ROAD.—LETTER OF DON JOSÉ DE GARAY.—DECREE OF SANTA ANNA.

I SHALL now detail the various schemes of transit by canal which have from time to time been proposed at and between Tehuantepec and Darien.

In little more than ten years after the first settlement was formed by Columbus, the Isthmus of Panama was successfully crossed by Vasco Nuñez de Balboa (September, 1513), who, rushing up to his breast in the water of the Pacific, took possession of that mighty ocean in the name of his master, the King of Spain. From that period the outline of the Pacific coast, both to the north and south, was rapidly delineated on the charts, and a glance was sufficient to show how narrow a strip of land intervened at more than one point between the two oceans. Hence arose the desire to find a practicable route from sea to sea; and as commerce and colonization increased, doubtless every effort was made by the early conquerors and their followers to discover such an opening, but entirely without success as regards a water passage.* Owing to the extraordinary jealousy of the mother-country, but little has ever transpired as to the nature of the explorations made with a view to transit by the early conquerors; and the first authentic account of the nature of the overland passage from sea to sea was obtained from the buccaneers, from whom that most remarkable man, William Patterson, one of the founders of the Bank of England, gleaned the information which enabled him to propound a project which was the grandest conception, as it was the greatest national misfortune, of the seventeenth century. Patterson's noble project of opening a "highway of nations" was basely and treacherously ruined, and the idea was not revived until after the Spanish-American colonies had thrown off the yoke of the mother-country; then, indeed, a host of plans were formed for joining the two oceans.

Fernando Cortez was the first who gave his earnest attention to the search for a practicable route from sea to sea. In his admirable letter to the King of Spain this passage occurs:—"It is the thing above all others in this world I am desirous of meeting with, on account of the immense utility which I am convinced would result from it." Cortez appears to have concentrated his attention upon the isthmus at Tehuantepec; and so great was his confidence in the belief that at this part of Central America the problem would be solved, that he selected the lands in the vicinity as his portion of the conquered country.

After the death of Cortez, the great advocate of the

* In the town library at Nuremberg is preserved a globe, made by John Schoner in 1520, on which a passage through the isthmus of Darien is carefully delineated.—*King's Wonders of the World.*

Tehuantepec route, the idea of forming a passage from sea to sea across that isthmus appears to have been abandoned; indeed, the jealousy and bigotry of the conquerors seems to have caused a reaction in favour of closing every avenue of approach to the New World instead of opening new roads through it. The learned divine P. Acosta, writing in 1588, says: "I am of opinion that no human power would be sufficient to cut through the strong and impenetrable bounds which God has put between the two oceans, of mountains and iron rocks, which can stand the fury of the raging seas. And if it were possible, it would appear to me very just to fear the vengeance of Heaven for attempting to improve the works which the Creator, in his almighty will and providence, ordered from the creation of the world." It is not a little curious that, exactly two hundred years later (1788), another divine secured to himself the honour of making a water communication from sea to sea at the southern extremity of Central America.

In 1814 the Spanish Cortes authorized the formation of a canal across the isthmus of Tehuantepec in preference to Nicaragua or Panama; but, as usual with that august body, they were just in time to be too late; the revolt of the colonies rendered such an enterprise impossible at that period. In 1842 the provisional President of Mexico, Santa Anna, granted to Don José de Garay the exclusive privilege of using steam locomotive power for transit across the isthmus, and that gentleman caused the most elaborate surveys of the route to be made; but the length of the line, the poorness of the ports at each extremity, and the distracted state of the country combined to deter capitalists from embarking on such an undertaking, and consequently nothing has been attempted. Dampier, Don Augustin Cramer, and the great Humboldt, have at various times spoken in favourable terms of this route. The latter writes, "We cannot doubt that this point of the globe deserves no less attention than the Lake of Nicaragua." The following is a succinct account of the surveys and estimates made by Don José de Garay and Señor Moro:—

"The width of the isthmus, from the Bay of Tehuantepec on the South Sea to the mouth of the river Coatzacoalcos, which flows into the Atlantic, is, according to the survey of Don José de Garay, about 138 miles. This river runs so far up into the country that its source has not yet been explored; but it evidently takes its rise among the same hills where some other large rivers, flowing into the Pacific, have also their origin. The Indians say that it runs from a lake from which the river Ostuta, running in the opposite direction, also derives its waters, but that the lake is difficult of access, and is guarded by supernatural beings. It is to be regretted that Don José de Garay, among his other valuable labours in this part of the isthmus, did not trace these waters to their source, and it is still more to be regretted that the distracted state of Mexico will probably prevent Don José de Garay from receiving any compensation for his services, or for the great expenses he incurred in making this important survey.

"The river Coatzacoalcos falls into the Atlantic Ocean, or rather into the Gulf of Mexico, in lat. 18° 8′ N., long. 94° 17′ W., discharging itself by two separate navigable mouths. The principal entrance has a depth of twenty feet of water on the bar, and within the bar the depth is from six to seven fathoms at low water, where the river is about 800 yards wide, but it is of greater width higher up, before the separation of the two outlets. Its course up to the confluence of the river Malatengo, taking the windings of the stream, is about 160 miles with a fall of about 40 mètres, or about 132 feet; but, taking a straight line in the general direction of the river, which is S.S.W., the distance from the coast to the river Malatengo is about 90 miles, with a depth of water varying from 30 feet, in the lower part of the river, to 6 feet in the higher part, and presenting only two obstacles of any consequence, both of which may be removed without much difficulty.

"Above the junction with the river Malatengo, the volume of the water in the Coatzacoalcos is much less; it begins to take a south-easterly direction, and its declivity becoming more rapid, it ceases to be so well adapted for the purposes of navigation; but the Indians continue the ascent in their canoes and rafts until it divides into two small streams, being a distance which Don José de Garay says may be reckoned at about 90 kilomètres, or about 55 miles, beyond the village of Santa Maria de Chimalapa, which is situated on the Coatzacoalcos, about twenty miles above the junction of the Malatengo, and which village is laid down in the maps attached to Don José de Garay's report. Beyond this village it was not thought necessary, for the purposes of the expedition, to carry the examination and the survey of the river Coatzacoalcos.

"Leaving this river and ascending the river Malatengo, which here flows from west to east for about five miles, is found the Chichihua, a river flowing into it, and coming in a northerly direction from the Mésa de Tarifa, or table-land, which is about 200 mètres, or 656 feet, above the ocean. This is the summit level, where the mountainous chain is interrupted for a distance of about 35 miles, and gives place to an elevated plain, diversified with slightly rising grounds and valleys, from which several rivers flow both to the Atlantic and the Pacific Oceans. Water is abundant, the soil is rich and fertile, vegetation is luxuriant, fine timber grows in profusion, and the climate is mild and healthy.

"In this table-land rise several streams flowing northwardly into the river Chichihua, and through it into the Malatengo, the Coatzacoalcos, and the Atlantic Ocean. Among these streams is the Rio de Tarifa; and close to its source rises the Monetza, which flows into the river Chicapa, and by it passes to the Pacific Ocean, through the great lagoons of Tehuantepec. The distance from the parting of the waters, at the summit level, to the Pacific Ocean, is about 35 miles, of which about 15 miles are occupied by the lagoons.

"These lagoons are three in number, communicating with each other, and extending from east to west for about 35 miles; their depth of water, from the mouth of the river Chicapa to the ocean, varies from 12 feet to 18 feet, with a bottom of mud and shingle. They are in fact natural harbours, and are capable of great improvement.

"It is evident from the preceding brief description of

the country, that the works to be executed in making a navigation on this line, must be the improvement of the river Coatzacoalcos; the ascent to the Mésa de Tarifa, or table-land, from the river Malatengo, being a rise of 525 feet; the canal, or cutting, at the Mésa de Tarifa, or summit level; the descent of 656 feet to the lagoons on the shores of the Pacific; and the improvement of these natural harbours.

"Don José de Garay had the valuable assistance of Señor Gaetano Moro, as engineer-in-chief, under whose direction, with the aid of several talented Spanish officers, a survey of the country was made in 1842 and 1843.

"The time occupied in the survey was about nine months. Señor Moro and the officers who assisted him appear to have made good use of the means they could command: the survey was made trigonometrically, the levels were taken by the barometer; and his Report confirms, in every important particular, the accounts given by the old Spaniards of this part of the isthmus, and the previous surveys of Don Augustin Cramer in 1774, and of Don Tadeo Ortiz and Don Juan de Orbegozo in 1824.

"Señor Moro takes the works on the Caledonian Canal as the basis of an estimate, which he gives as the probable cost of those he contemplates in the present instance; including certain trenches for conveying a supply of water to the canal.

"He gives it, however, with great diffidence, and, as he truly says: 'I have arrived at the most difficult and delicate part of our labours. Dutens, speaking of the

Caledonian Canal, which he visited before its completion, observes, that in a great undertaking of this kind it is impossible to pre-estimate the cost of every part; and so it is; the amount of expense is mostly influenced by eventual causes, by the mode of husbanding the funds, and by the skill with which the engineer conducts the work.'

" Señor Moro sums up his estimate thus:—

	Francs.
Cost of 150 locks, at 200,000 francs	30,000,000
Cost of 80 kilomètres (about 50 miles) of canal at 475,000 francs	38,000,000
Cost of 25 kilomètres (15½ miles) of trench for supplying water, estimated at 10 francs per cubic mètre	10,000,000
Cost of 5 kilomètres, or about 3 miles, of trench, estimated at 15 francs per cubic mètre	3,000,000
Cost of regulation of the river Coatzacoalcos, of the lagoons on the Pacific Ocean, and of the Boca Barra, or entrance to them from the sea	4,000,000
Total, francs . . .	85,000,000
	Or about £3,400,000."

Even supposing the above estimate to be correct, the work would assume gigantic proportions, requiring many years of hard labour, under favourable circumstances and a settled government, to complete it; but while Mexico remains in her present distracted state, any attempt would be hopeless. It is useless to speculate upon what might have been the condition of that ill-fated country had it only been moderately well governed during its forty years of freedom; but the Spaniards appear to have left as a legacy to their revolted colonies all their vices and not one of their virtues, and therefore it is more than probable that no effort to reform the present possessors of the soil can be successful, rendering it necessary before this beautiful country can be restored to civilization, to infuse a very large admixture of new blood. Whether France will be as successful as she has been elsewhere remains to be seen, but every well-wisher of the world's progress must cordially wish her "God speed." If regeneration is effected, there is no doubt the locomotive will be speedily introduced as the surest means of consolidating the good work, and in that case we may hope to see the iron rails across the isthmus at Tehuantepec. There have been Mexicans fully alive to the advantages which would thereby be gained for their country, as the following correspondence will show. I have inserted it in this place, not only because it is intrinsically well worth preservation, but because it contains probably the first concession granted by any of the Spanish-American Republics for crossing their country:—

Memorial of Don José de Garay, soliciting of his Excellency the President of the Mexican Republic the Privilege of opening a Communication between the Atlantic and Pacific Oceans, through the Isthmus of Tehuantepec.

"Sir,—Your Excellency has caused the Mexican public to look forward to the present epoch as one of improvement and gigantic advancement in the career of national aggrandisement.

"No measure can be more fruitful in prosperous results, none more remarkable or more glorious, than that which shall form a junction between the two oceans, without the necessity of doubling that stormy Cape, discovered by a Hollander, and to which he gave his name, which forms the southernmost extremity of the American continent.

"Thousands of ships yearly perform this difficult and tedious voyage, passing twice through the tropics, in the midst of innumerable and imminent dangers.

"The mind is bewildered with the difficulty of embracing, in one comprehensive view, the astonishing consequences that would result from a communication between the two oceans, by means of which, ships sailing from Europe will save 2000 leagues, and those from North America 3100 leagues, in their voyage to the coast of China. What an economy of time and money! And how far will these advantages extend, now that the lines of steamboats established on the high seas have so prodigiously shortened distances!

"A great revolution will take place in the commercial, and even the political, affairs of all nations, the instant America shall open the passage through any of her isthmuses. The epoch which shall see this effected will be more memorable than that of the discovery of this continent; and the name of him to whom the world shall owe this event will be at least as glorious as that of Columbus.

"If your Excellency is ambitious of this glory for yourself and your country, you should now dedicate your attention, and the powerful mind with which you are endowed, to the execution of the enterprise contained in the present representation, and to which is annexed the project I have conceived for forming a communication between the two oceans.

"By this your Excellency will see that I propose to execute this gigantic work in a very short time, considering the magnitude of the enterprise, and I ask not the least pecuniary assistance from Government; and from the commencement I offer to the national treasury a considerable revenue, viz. one-fourth of the transit duties on the line of the route: and these will, after a term of fifty years, belong wholly to the republic.

"What I ask as an indemnification of expenses is certainly not much, when it is considered that it will be necessary to form forts, raise fortifications and other edifices, and open roads or canals; and when it is borne in mind that the indemnification does not consist in any funds of which the Government is at present possessed, but in property to which I am about to create a value.

"The value hereafter of the lands of which I solicit a grant will be the consequence of my efforts, for at the present day they have none whatever.

"The enterprise could not be undertaken by any person for less than what I have solicited, because the magnitude of the works will be such as probably to absorb all the resources arising from what I ask.

"Your Excellency cannot fail to remark two very striking features in my proposition. First, the establishment of the neutrality of the line of transit; this is a point worthy of the magnanimity of the Government, and necessary to interest all nations, in order that the communication may not be seized by any foreign Power, but be ever preserved as the property of the republic. Secondly, that I have not proposed to open immediately a ship canal across the isthmus, because I have seen similar proposals fall to the ground in other parts of Central America and Columbia. Often the desire of carrying into execution a magnificent undertaking is the cause why a lesser one, though highly important, has been neglected.

"Convinced that it has been well said that by 'seeking perfection we lose what may be attainable,' I have resolved to carry the latter into effect, without, however, renouncing my hopes of accomplishing the former. Although a communication by water may not be practicable for the present, this will infallibly take place when the isthmus shall become known from the commerce of the world traversing it, when the advantage of giving to this grand work all the perfection of which it is capable shall be duly appreciated, and when both sides of the Line shall be dotted with rich and populous cities, as will certainly happen in a few years.

"Let this be enumerated among the acts of your Excellency's public life, and your name will not only belong to the glory of your country, but will be identified with the best interests of mankind, and immortalized by an imperishable monument. The whole world will receive incalculable benefits; and what advantages will not accrue to Mexico in particular, when the accomplishment of this undertaking shall make her the centre of universal commerce, giving a vast impulse to the elements of her terrestrial wealth, undeveloped at present, from the little intercourse she enjoys with the splendour and industry of Europe.

"I beg leave, Sir, to repeat that the mind is bewildered in the attempt to calculate the beneficial results that must accrue to Mexico from the facility with which her native products will be exported, and from her becoming the emporium of the commerce of the world, as also from deriving revenues from duties not levied upon the inhabitants of the republic, and from the vast influx of population and capital into the country.

"May your Excellency therefore become the author of these great and numerous benefits to your country, and by acceding to the articles of this memorial, thus sanction the most memorable act of your illustrious and patriotic career.

"Mexico, February 25, 1842.

"José de Garay."

Edict ordering the Opening of the Isthmus, with the Grants therein specified; and Contract between the supreme Government and Don José de Garay.

"Antonio Lopez de Santa Anna, General of Division, Benemerito of the Country, and provisional President of the Republic of Mexico, to all the inhabitants thereof. Know ye:

"That, firm to my purpose of exalting the nation and of rendering the people happy, and, taking into consideration the propositions which Don José de Garay has presented; and considering that no means are so sure and effectual for promoting the national prosperity as that of creating the republic the centre of the commerce and navigation of all countries; and that this must be the consequence of the establishment of an easy and short communication from one ocean to the other; that nature herself offers the means of accomplishing this without opposing any great obstacle, and without the necessity of incurring any vast expense, in the isthmus of Tehuantepec, inasmuch as there the Cordillera dips to such a degree that it may almost be said to disappear; that there are two harbours in those parts, one towards the north and the other towards the south, at a short distance from each other; and that a considerable portion of the space between is transitable by means of a navigable river and a lake; and that the nature of the intermediate ground is favourable for carrying on such works as it may be necessary to undertake, as it abounds in materials for construction: And considering that if up to this moment public attention has not been properly called to this enterprise (which alone is capable of exalting the republic), this has perhaps happened from not having duly calculated its important consequences, or because the possibility of its execution has not been known, or that from a preconcerted idea existing in favour of making a cut to join the two oceans, the advantage of a road or canal destined for the transshipment of goods has been entirely lost sight of, by which the same results might be approximately obtained: And furthermore desiring, if more cannot be done to accomplish what is practicable, but still of the greatest importance to the republic and the world in general, and seeking, by promoting the execution of what is at present attainable, to give an impulse to future attempts on a larger scale, since the opening of a line of communication, by tending to show that it is not difficult to cut across the continent, may hereafter conduce to the undertaking of this great work: Feeling, besides, that in order to encourage the spirit of speculation, it is necessary to make concessions, by which alone enterprise has ever been fostered; and that by this enterprise in particular the nation will obtain revenues which it cannot reckon at present, derivable from foreign trade, and immediately reap the advantages which must result from universal intercourse, when its soil shall become the emporium of commerce, and consequently teem with wealth and abundance when its various products shall become articles of exportation:—Therefore, by virtue of the powers and faculties vested in me by the 7th article of convention, signed at Tacubaya, and sworn to by the representatives of the departments, I have determined to issue the following

"DECREE.

"Article 1.—A line of communication shall be opened between the Pacific and Atlantic Oceans, through the isthmus of Tehuantepec.

"Article 2.—This shall be performed by water, but when this may not be convenient, then railroads and steam-carriages may be used.

"Article 3.—The passage to be opened across the isthmus shall be neutral, and common to all nations at peace with the Mexican republic.

"Article 4.—The execution of this work shall be confided to Don José de Garay, to whom is hereby granted an exclusive privilege to this effect. His obligations and indemnifications shall be as hereafter expressed:—

"*First.*—Don José de Garay shall cause to be made, at his own expense, a survey of the ground and direction which the route should follow, and also of the ports which may be deemed most proper and commodious from their proximity: all which shall be concluded, at furthest, within the space of eighteen months from the date hereof, and the works shall be commenced, at furthest, within the space of ten months next thereafter; and in case this shall not be performed within the time specified, the exclusive privilege hereby conceded to him shall cease.

"*Second.*—The said Don José de Garay shall cause to be made in the ports which he shall select, all kinds of works that may be necessary for shelter and utility. He shall construct in each of them fortresses and warehouses; he shall carry into effect the line of communication between the two ports by means of water, carriage, or railroad, in both cases by means of steam; and he shall establish as many steamboats and trains of steam-cars as shall be deemed necessary, so that there shall be no delay for want of means of transport.

"*Third.*—The grantee shall pay, at a just valuation, for any private property through which the route shall pass, but he shall not demand, on account of public utility, more than a quarter of a league on either side of the line, which is all he can require the proprietors to sell.

"*Fourth.*—The indemnifications which are here accorded to the grantee, and to those who may acquire his rights, are the following:—He shall have the right of collecting the transit duties for the term of fifty years, at the expiry of which time they shall revert to the Government of the Republic; and for sixty years the exclusive privilege of carrying on the transport by steam vessels and railroad cars, fixing equitable rates of freight; but he shall give to the Government, from the time that the line of communication shall be made available, the fourth part of the net produce of the dues that are paid for the right of transit, deducting all expenses of administration, preservation, and repairs. A similar fourth part shall be given by the Government to the Negotiation for a like term, when it shall enter into possession of the before-mentioned transit dues payable on the line of communication.

"*Fifth.*—The Government and the Negotiation may each name their agents to look into the receipts and expenditures during the whole of the time that each respectively shall be entitled to the before-mentioned fourth part of the transit dues. All the unoccupied lands for the distance of ten leagues on either side of the line of communication, road, or canal, are hereby ceded in fee-simple to the Negotiation.

"*Sixth.*—All foreigners are permitted to acquire real property, and to exercise any trade or calling, not even excepting that of mining, within the distance of fifty leagues on either side of the line of transit. That territory shall be the country of all who may come to establish themselves there, subject, however, to the laws of the Republic.

"*Seventh.*—The Government engages to give to the Negotiation every protection and assistance, as well for effecting the survey as for carrying on the works, but the remuneration of the services of the inhabitants of those parts shall be at the expense of the Negotiation. The Government also engages not to impose any contributions or taxes upon the travellers or effects *in transitu*, during the aforesaid term of fifty years, and not to levy upon the Negotiation or its funds any imposts or forced loans.

"*Eighth.*—The Government shall have the right of appointing the custom-house officers which it may see fit, in the ports and in any other points it may choose, on the line of communication, but only for the purpose of recovering the duties of exportation and importation upon articles which do not come and go merely *in transitu*, and for the prevention of smuggling. The Government shall in no case interfere in the collection of transit dues, nor in the collection of freight, lighterage, or tonnage, or of any other class of dues, for none shall be payable by vessels loading or unloading in transit, as long as the line of communication shall belong to the Negotiation. The measures which the Government shall adopt for the prevention of smuggling shall be such as shall cause no embarrassment or delay in the transport of effects across the Isthmus, and particular regulations will be adopted and issued to this effect.

"*Ninth.*—When the works shall be completed they shall be examined by two surveyors, one to be named by the Government and the other by the Negotiation, in order that they may declare whether the terms of the contract have been complied with by the latter; and in case these shall disagree, the surveyors shall nominate an umpire, who shall settle the dispute. No kind of question or difference shall prevent the line of communication from coming into operation as soon as it shall be ready; nevertheless, the Negotiation is always bound to fulfil the contract in every particular.

"*Tenth.*—In case it should hereafter be found practicable to join the two seas by a cut, and that propositions to this effect should be made by any individual or any company, they shall not be admitted during the period of fifty years for which the privilege is granted to Don José de Garay, without his previous consent, or that of those who may have acquired his rights.

"*Eleventh.*—The contract between the Government and Don José de Garay shall be drawn out in writing according to the tenor of the articles forming the basis of this decree, with all the formalities required by law; therefore I command that it be printed, published, and circulated, and duly carried into effect.

"Given at the Palace of the National Government, this 1st day of March, 1842.

"ANTONIO LOPEZ DE SANTA ANNA.
"JOSÉ MARIA BOCANEGRA."

Theorists have advocated a canal from the Gulf of Dulce on the Atlantic, to the Gulf of Fonseca on the Pacific, but, independently of the great disadvantage of traversing two states (Guatemala and Honduras), the nature of the intervening country is so mountainous that it seems surprising that any one could have advanced such an idea; at all events, before a decision can be given, a regular survey must be made. All that is known with certainty is, that the terminal ports are adapted for such an object.

CHAPTER VI.

NICARAGUAN CANAL THE MOST PRACTICABLE.—DON FRANCISCO CASTILLON AND PRINCE LOUIS NAPOLEON BONAPARTE.—EXTRACTS FROM THE FRENCH EMPEROR'S PAMPHLET.—COMMANDING POSITION OF CONSTANTINOPLE.—MASSAYA THE CENTRE OF THE NEW WORLD.—COLONIZATION PROJECT.—PROFITS OF THE UNDERTAKING.—ALL INTERESTS CONSULTED.—COURSE OF THE PROPOSED CANAL.—ESTIMATES.

THE greatest, and, beyond doubt, the most practicable scheme of Central American canalization that has ever been advocated is that passing through Nicaragua, where the comparative facilities for forming a magnificent canal for ships of the largest size admits of no dispute; but if from no other consideration, the gigantic nature of the enterprise and its enormous cost must place it, if not beyond the reach, at all events beyond the inclination, of the money-making capitalists of the present day.

It is admitted by its most zealous friends that ten years must elapse before the canal could be finished; and it must be remembered that it could not be opened and used in sections like a railway, and therefore not one penny could be earned until the whole work had been completed. Is there a capitalist living who would embark in such an undertaking?

The Nicaraguan project has been upheld by many

first-rate men, Baily, Stephens, Belly, and others. In 1830 a company was formed in Holland, under the patronage of the king, for making the canal, but the disturbances in that country broke up the company. Again, in 1835, the project was brought before the Government of the United States, and a resolution of the Senate was passed in favour of it; but the agent sent by General Jackson, then President, to arrange with the Nicaraguan authorities, died on the road, and the matter was allowed to drop. No one, however, has taken so warm an interest in the subject as the present Emperor of the French. It appears that Don Francisco Castillon, envoy to the Court of France, put himself, in 1840, in communication with Prince L. N. Bonaparte, at that time a prisoner at Ham, and proposed to him, in the name of the Nicaraguan Government, to take upon himself exclusively the construction of the proposed canal. Had this offer been accepted, the result might have been that Louis Napoleon would have ruled the destinies of Nicaragua instead of those of France; but, fortunately for the latter country, the captive was not allowed to go. Some very interesting correspondence passed between the Prince and Señor Castillon; and the subject appears to have made so permanent an impression upon the mind of the former, that after his escape from Ham and safe arrival in London, he devoted a considerable amount of time and study to it, and not only wrote a most able pamphlet, but publicly advocated the project at the Institution of Civil Engineers, London.* The pamphlet points out

* *Vide* vol. vi., 1847, p. 427: Excerpt Minutes of Proceedings of the Institution of Civil Engineers.

clearly the manifold advantages of a transit through Nicaragua; and as the arguments apply quite as forcibly now as when the pages were penned, I have considered it advisable to quote the Imperial author's own words.—

Extracts from a Pamphlet written in 1847, *by His Imperial Majesty Napoleon III.*

"There are certain countries which, from their geographical situation, are destined to a highly prosperous future. Wealth, power, every national advantage, flows into them, provided that where nature has done her utmost, man does not neglect to avail himself of her beneficent assistance.

"Those countries are in the most favourable conditions which are situated on the high-road of commerce, and which offer to commerce the safest ports and harbours, as well as the most profitable interchange of commodities. Such countries, finding in the intercourse of foreign trade illimitable resources, are enabled to take advantage of the fertility of their soil; and in this way a home trade springs up commensurate with the increase of mercantile traffic. It is by such means that Tyre and Carthage, Constantinople, Venice, Genoa, Amsterdam, Liverpool, and London attained to such great prosperity, rising from the condition of poor hamlets to extensive and affluent commercial cities, and exhibiting to surrounding nations the astonishing spectacle of powerful states springing suddenly from unwholesome swamps and marshes. Venice in particular was indebted for her overwhelming grandeur to the geographical position which constituted her for centuries the *entrepôt* between Europe and the East; and it was only when the discovery of the Cape of Good Hope opened a ship passage to the latter that her prosperity gradually declined. Notwithstanding, so great was her accumulation of wealth, and consequent commercial influence, that she withstood for three centuries the formidable competition thus created.

"There exists another city famous in history, although now fallen from its pristine grandeur, so admirably situated as to excite the jealousy of all the great European Powers, who combine to maintain in it a government so far barbarous as to be incapable of taking advantage of the great resources bestowed upon it by nature. The geographical position of Constantinople is such as rendered her the queen of the ancient world. Occupying, as she does, the central point between Europe, Asia, and Africa, she could become the *entrepôt* of the commerce of all these countries, and obtain over them an immense preponderance; for in politics, as in strategy, a central position always commands the circumference. Situated between two seas, of which, like two great lakes, she commands the entrance, she could shut up in them, sheltered from the assaults of all other nations, the most formidable fleets, by which she could exercise dominion in the Mediterranean as well as in the Black Sea, thereby commanding the entrance of the Danube, which opens the way to Germany, as well as the sources of the Euphrates, which open the road to the Indies, dictating her own terms to the commerce of Greece, France, Italy, Spain, and Egypt. This is what the proud city of Constantine could be, and this is what she is not, 'because,' as Montesquieu says, 'God permitted that Turks should exist on earth, a people the most fit to possess uselessly a great empire.'

"There exists in the New World a state as admirably situated as Constantinople, and we must say, up to the present time, as uselessly occupied; we allude to the state of Nicaragua. As Constantinople is the centre of the ancient world, so is the town of Leon, or rather Massaya, the centre of the new; and if the tongue of land which separates its two lakes from the Pacific Ocean were cut through, she would command by her central position the entire coast of North and South America. Like Constantinople, Massaya is situated between two extensive natural harbours, capable of giving shelter to the largest fleets, safe from attack. The state of Nicaragua can become, better than Constantinople, the necessary route for the great commerce of the world; for it is for the United States the shortest road to China and the East Indies, and for England and the rest of Europe to New Holland, Polynesia, and the whole of the western coast of America. The state of Nicaragua is then destined to attain to an extraordinary degree of prosperity and grandeur; for that which renders its political position more advantageous than that of Constantinople is, that the great maritime powers of Europe would witness with pleasure, and not with jealousy, its attainment of a station no less favourable to its individual interests than to the commerce of the world.

"France, England, Holland, Russia, and the United

States, have a great commercial interest in the establishment of a communication between the two oceans; but England has more than the other Powers a political interest in the execution of this project. England will see with pleasure Central America become a flourishing and powerful state, which will establish a balance of power by creating in Spanish America a new centre of active enterprise, powerful enough to give rise to a great feeling of nationality, and to prevent, by backing Mexico, any further encroachment from the north. England will witness with satisfaction the opening of a route which will enable her to communicate more speedily with Oregon, China, and her possessions in New Holland. She will find, in a word, that the advancement of Central America will renovate the declining commerce of Jamaica and the other English island in the Antilles, the progressive decay of which will be thereby stopped. It is a happy coincidence that the political and commercial prosperity of the state of Nicaragua is closely connected with the policy of that nation which has the greatest preponderance on the sea."

The Imperial author then proceeds to make a calculation and estimate regarding the nature of the works for the proposed canal and its cost. No useful object, however, would be gained in preserving the mass of figures which he has accumulated. Sixteen years ago the locomotive had not attained the perfection of the present day, and people were then accustomed to reckon distance by mileage. Now time is acknowledged by every one to be the true measure. A passenger would now consider himself deeply aggrieved if the train arrived a few minutes late, whereas, a few years ago, loss of time was not considered of any moment. This revolution in public opinion is due to the locomotive; and this is one of the main reasons why canalization projects do not find favour in the eyes of the people. It was unmistakably the *vox populi* speaking through Robert Stephenson which condemned the Suez Canal project. Had public opinion been in favour of that scheme, the puerile objections and narrow ideas of our Government would have been as contemptuously ignored as they have lately been in the Thames Embankment question.

In the remainder of his pamphlet the Emperor enters fully upon his plan for combining colonization with the Canal undertaking, and the main features of this plan are well worthy the most careful consideration.

"We have stated that the secondary profits of the Canal would arise from the increase in the value of the soil. According to our information, the Government of Nicaragua would cede to the Company all the land lying on the right and left banks of the Canal throughout its entire course, to an extent of two leagues inland, forming 300 square leagues, or about 1,200,000 acres. These 1,200,000 acres are at the present moment worth 1*s.* 6*d.* per acre. The proposed gift by the Government of Nicaragua to the Company is, therefore, now of the value of £90,000. If we deduct from the above number 200,000 acres as probably incapable of cultivation, and

300,000 more that would be required for the service of the Company, producing no income, or as concessions to its engineers, servants, etc., there will remain 700,000 acres to explore and improve. The Canal being accomplished, it will be easily granted that these lands may in all probability bear a value of at least £2 per acre. Let us put it at £1 per acre only, and we shall have a property of £700,000 vesting absolutely in the Company, for we must not forget that the soil is here very fertile; that they frequently have more than two harvests a year; that the indigo produced in this country is better than that produced in the East Indies; that the tobacco is as good as at Havana; that coffee and sugar are easily produced; that the forests are filled with Brazil-wood; that there are mines to work; and finally, that the waste water thrown off the Canal locks would afford power for manufacturing purposes. It is thus evident that, if the Company should limit itself to the disposal of these lands when the Canal is complete, they would derive great profit, were it only by the increase of value; but in our opinion there is a greater advantage to be derived from their retention.

"We firmly believe that it is important to combine with the construction of the Canal the project of colonization, in order that the two undertakings should assist each other, and to enlist as shareholders the mass of emigrants, who annually depart for America, and who, according to the statistical information gathered up to this day, set forth with an average sum of £20 per head.* Thus the shares would be placed in hands most

* We read in the 'Journal des Débats' of the 3rd of May, 1846, that the

interested in the success of the undertaking; for those only who join an enterprise for the sake of investment, and not mere gamblers, ensure the solidity of an undertaking."

"The capital of £4,000,000, which we presume to be necessary for the construction of the Canal, should be divided into 400,000 shares of £10 each. By paying down the value of one or more shares, the emigrant shareholder would be entitled on his arrival in America to such accommodations as would enable him to overcome the first difficulties, necessarily attendant on early steps in colonization. Every emigrant shareholder would receive from the Company twenty acres of land to cultivate as well as the necessary implements for that purpose."

"The 700,000 acres of land would be thus distributed among 35,000 emigrants, and sold to them on the following terms:—Ten years' time would be allowed for the emigrant shareholder to pay to the Company the price of the twenty acres allotted to him, as well as the outlay incurred by the Company in procuring him dwelling, food, and all the accommodations required. The

society formed at New York, the 31st of March, 1784, to assist the indigent Germans in the United States, celebrated on Tuesday last the sixty-second anniversary of its foundation. On this occasion they have published a pamphlet, which states, amongst other things, that the number of German emigrants which arrived during last year in the city of New York alone amounted to 30,567, each of them having an average sum of £20 sterling. Of these emigrants 12,225 arrived from Havre, in 78 ships; 9647 from Bremen, in 77 ships; 3718 from Antwerp, in 25 ships; 2525 from Hamburg, in 24 ships; 1959 from Rotterdam, in 13 ships; and 493 from Ghent, London, and Liverpool, in 5 ships. The greater part have taken their direction towards the Southern States. In 1814 there arrived only 17,999 German emigrants at New York.

payment should be made by annual instalments, and proportionate to the progressive increase of value likely to increase every year in the property.

"So, the whole of the first year having been entirely taken up by preparing and tilling the ground, the emigrant shareholder should not be made liable for any payment whatever during that time. The annual instalments should begin to be paid at the end of the second year, and accomplished in the progressive manner indicated in the following table:—

	Per acre, per annum.		
At the end of the first year	£0	0	0
" " second year . . .	0	1	0
" " third year . . .	0	1	6
" " fourth year . . .	0	2	0
" " fifth year	0	2	6
" " sixth year . . .	0	3	0
" " seventh year . . .	0	3	6
" " eighth year . . .	0	4	0
" " ninth year . . .	0	4	6
" " tenth year . . .	0	5	0
" " eleventh year . .	0	5	6
	£1	12	6

"So every acre of land will procure to the Company, in the course of eleven years, a net profit of £1. 12*s*. 6*d*., and consequently 700,000 acres of land will bring, in the above-stated lapse of time, the corresponding profit of £1,137,500.

"The Company would establish as many villages as would be necessary for the number of colonists. Each village would be erected on the most healthy spots, and in the vicinity of a river. It would be composed of

200 dwellings, each dwelling being appropriated to one family. A village would then cost:

200 dwellings, at £4 each	£800
Maintenance for the first six months, and seed, at £4 per family	800
Church, stores, and schools	280
Casual expenses	120
	£2000

"If we divide this sum by the number of families, we shall find that the outlay will be £10 per family in ten years, to be reimbursed as above stated. Now, let us suppose that in about ten years the Company has established 175 villages, containing 35,000 families: the expense will have been £350,000, which the Company will be reimbursed, by the annual progressive rate. As each of these families has been enabled to buy and pay for twenty acres of land at the progressive rate above mentioned, the Company will have received for 700,000 acres the sum of £1,137,500, from which, deducting £350,000, the outlay for the construction of the villages, there will remain a clear profit of £787,500, exclusive of the interest received on the outlays. We must also remark that the colonists, being shareholders, will have paid £787,500 to themselves in their capacity as a company; thus there would be a perfect amalgamation of interest between the shareholders and the colonists, who would be equally interested in the success of the undertaking. Thus, deducting this sum from the amount of £4,000,000, necessary for the construction of a canal, the capital expended would be about £3,200,000 only, bringing a net profit of £600,000, or 10 per cent. per annum.

"At present, when the colonist goes to America he finds no dwelling, no advance of capital, and often no employment; on our plan, on the contrary, by means of a share, he is sure to find, on arriving in America, a wholesome dwelling, livelihood for six months, fertile lands, and a community already settled. Moreover, a part of the money paid for the purchase of his land would come back to him as a shareholder; and in about ten years his property would not only be freed from all burdens, but he might expect at that period, that both his share in the Canal and his land would be doubled in value.

"Thus our project protects all interests, the capitalist realizes large profits, and the emigrants partake of the benefit, with a moral certainty of future prosperity. This neglected country speedily changes to flourishing towns, its lakes are covered with fleets, and its wealth is increased by the progress of agriculture and commerce.

"Central America can emerge from her present languor only by following the example of the United States, namely, by borrowing from Europe labour and capital for this first object. Independent of the advantages of its geographical position and of the fertility of its soil, the state of Nicaragua presents to European emigrants advantages which are not to be found in the United States. In the north of America, the population settled itself in the beginning on the eastern coast, gradually extending inland. As long as the uncultivated lands were not far from the sea, the European emigrants easily found employment; but now the case is altered, and the great number of foreigners that daily arrive in the United States become, for the following reason, a burden to the nation. The uncultivated lands where adventurers may easily find employment, are three hundred leagues from the coast, and as, in most instances, the emigrants are destitute of means to reach those remote districts, they become in the towns on the coast a prey to indolence and misery. In Central America the reverse would be the case; the indigenous population has settled by preference on the coast of the Pacific Ocean, deserting all that part situated opposite the ancient world, so that when the country is in a position to require colonists and European labourers, they may arrive through the Canal to places already inhabited; and the population will gradually extend from the west to the east, and not, as in the United States, from the east to the west, thus getting nearer to Europe, in proportion as it increases, and offering facilities to the new colonists, till they reach the extreme borders of the country.

"The prosperity of Central America is connected with the interests of civilization at large; and the best means to promote the welfare of humanity is to knock down the barriers which separate men, races, and nations. This course is pointed out to us by the Christian religion, as well as by the efforts of those great men who have at intervals appeared in the world. The Christian faith teaches us that we are all brothers, and that in the eye of God the slave is equal to the master, —as the Asiatic, the African, and the Indian, are alike equal to the European. On the other hand, the great men of the world have by their wars commingled the various races of the world, and left behind them some of those imperishable monuments which, in levelling mountains, opening forests, and canalizing rivers, has a tendency to upset these obstacles which divide mankind, and to unite men in communities, communities in people, people in nations. War and commerce have civilized the world. The time for war is gone by; commerce alone pushes its conquests. Let us then open to it a new route; let us approximate the people of Oceania and Australia to Europe; and let us make them partakers of the blessings of Christianity and civilization. To accomplish this great undertaking we make an appeal to all religious and intelligent men, for this enterprise is worthy of their zeal and sympathy. We invoke the assistance of all statesmen, because every nation is interested in the establishment of new and easy communications between the eastern and western parts of the globe. Finally, we call upon capitalists, because whilst they are promoting a glorious undertaking, they are sure to derive a large profit thereby."

How nearly the Emperor's predictions have been fulfilled, let those bear witness who have watched Walker's career in Nicaragua. Politically his success would have been a great advantage to England, but we co-operated with the United States, to our own injury,—so short-sighted, so ignorant, or so timid, was our Government.

The idea of canalization, if not exploded for ever,

may at all events be looked upon as postponed for an indefinite period; nevertheless it will be necessary to give a brief description of the proposed course of the canal, and also of the amount of money supposed necessary to complete it. Surveys have lately been undertaken under American auspices; but as the following is home-made, and has moreover been well sifted by the late Mr. Joseph Glynn, M.I.C.E., it would seem to be the most reliable.

In the years 1837 and 1838, a survey was made by Mr. John Baily, lieutenant in the Royal Marines, at the request and under the authority of General Morazan, then President of the Central American Republic, for the purpose of ascertaining the practicability of forming a canal, from the port of San Juan del Sur, on the Pacific Ocean, in lat. 11° 15′ N., long. 86° 1′ W., by the Lake of Nicaragua and the river San Juan, to the Atlantic.

The port of San Juan del Sur is narrow at the entrance, but widens within the harbour; it is surrounded by high land, except from west-south-west to west-by-south; the depth of water at the entrance is three fathoms, and its width 1100 yards. Ships can go up for about half a mile; but, as the winds often blow with great violence from the north and north-east, there is sometimes considerable difficulty in making the anchorage.

From this port Mr. Baily took a line of levels; not in a direct course, but diverging, so as to pass between the hills at the lowest point, when it could be done, without widely deviating from a straight line; and in many places he passed through ravines of from 30 feet to 120 feet in depth. Mr. Baily found the ground rise, with a gradual acclivity, from the beach to the distance of 5880 yards, where it attained a height of 284 feet; then for 904 yards it rose rapidly to the summit—615 feet above the level of the ocean. At that point the waters separated; those on the north side of the ridge flowing to the Atlantic, through the lake and the river San Juan, and those on the south side to the Pacific Ocean.

The ground then descended rapidly, and in a distance of 8664 yards the elevation was reduced 295 feet, whence it gradually sloped, with but slight interruptions, for a further distance of 6168 yards, where it joined the river Lajas, along which it ran for 6792 yards, and afterwards discharged itself into the Lake of Nicaragua. The surface of that lake was 128 feet 3 inches above the level of the sea; the whole distance from the South Sea to the lake, by Mr. Baily's track, being 28,408 yards, and his mean course N. 33° E.

The distance, in a straight line, from his starting-point on the sea-beach, to the mouth of the river Lajas, was 20,401 yards, or less than 12 miles; the summit level of the ground intervening between the lake and the South Sea being 488 feet above the surface of the lake. The entire length of the proposed canal would, however, be about 15⅝ miles.

The river Lajas varies in width from 25 yards to 100 yards; the depth of water also varies from one to three fathoms, with a bottom of mud, of a thickness of several feet, as was ascertained by boring.

The dimensions of the Lake of Nicaragua are variously given by different writers; but Mr. Baily seems to have taken some pains to ascertain them correctly, and he states the length to be 95 miles; the breadth, in its widest part, to be about 35 miles; and the average depth of water, according to his soundings, 15 fathoms. These dimensions agree with the map of Don Felipe Bouza.

The length of the river San Juan, with all its windings, from the Lake to Greytown, is 119 miles, with a fall of 107½ feet. There are four rapids, viz. Machuca, Castillo Viejo, El Mico, and Del Toro, extending over about six miles, with broken water running over a rocky bottom. The San Juan is fed by many tributaries, the largest of which are San Carlos and Serapiqui, taking their rise in Costa Rica. The volume of water in the San Juan varies of course in different seasons; at the commencement of June, the lowest stage, about 12,000 cubic feet per second passed from the lake. The greatest rise in the lake ever known was six feet. At high lake, about October, there is probably between 40,000 and 50,000 cubic feet per second, divided at the delta of the river, of which about three-fourths pass out by the Colorado branch, and the remainder by the San Juan.

The whole length of the canal, from the Lake of Nicaragua to the Pacific, is fifteen miles and two-thirds. According to the plan, in the first eight miles, only one lock is necessary. In the next mile, 64 feet of lockage are required. In the next three miles, there are about two miles of deep cutting, and one mile of tunnel, and then a descent of 200 feet in three miles by lockage, to the Pacific.

Sir W^m G Ouseley, del — Vincent Brooks, lith

Thus far of the canal across the Isthmus. The Lake of Nicaragua is navigable for ships of the largest class down to the mouth of the river San Juan (where it quits the lake). This river has a fall of one foot and six-sevenths per mile, to the Atlantic. If the bed of the river cannot be cleared out, a communication can be made either by lock and dam, or by a canal along the bank of the river. The latter would be more expensive, but on account of the heavy floods of the rainy season it is preferable.

The total length of the canal from sea to sea would be little short of 200 miles, viz. 15½ from the Pacific to the lake, 56½ across the lake, and 119 to the Atlantic: total 191 miles.

The estimate is:—

From the lake to the west end of the tunnel	£1,500,000
Descent to the Pacific	500,000
From the Atlantic by canal along the river	2,500,000
4½ millions.	£4,500,000

The Emperor Napoleon proposed to avoid the difficulty of cutting through the Rocky Ridge, by carrying the canal forward through Lake Leon or Managua, to the Port of Realejo, or the Gulf of Fonseca, on the Pacific Ocean. This lake, according to statements made by Mr. Baily, is about 45 miles in length, and 105 miles in circumference; its greatest breadth being about 27 miles. The average depth of water is 10 fathoms, and its surface 28 feet 8 inches higher than the Lake of Nicaragua, with which it communicates by the river

Tipitapa. The length of this river is stated to be 20 miles, and for a distance of 14 miles from the Lake of Nicaragua the water is from one fathom to three fathoms in depth, but beyond this there are rapids, and in a distance of four miles and a half, a fall of 13 feet.

CHAPTER VII.

SPLENDID ATLANTIC HARBOUR.—DESCRIPTION OF DAVID.—AMERICAN SCHEMES OF ANNEXATION.—PRESIDENT LINCOLN'S SPEECH.—AMERICAN AVERSION TO NEGROES.—COAL-PITS VERSUS TRANSIT.—POETRY.—SENATOR POMEROY.—SCHEME CHECKED IN THE BUD.

THE next point of interest as regards canalization is Chiriqui Lagoon, lat. 9° 8′ N., long. 81° 57′ W. This port, or rather series of ports, is beyond doubt one of the finest and most capacious harbours in the world; it may fairly be compared with Rio de Janeiro. From Chiriqui it has been proposed to construct a canal to the river David, which empties itself into the Pacific, and this route has met with warm advocates; but unfortunately David does not afford any port at its mouth, and would require a considerable outlay before it could offer the commonest facilities as an *entrepôt*. I made an excursion up the river some years ago, but cannot regard it as fitted for such a purpose, or as likely to be made so by any expenditure at all compatible with the requirements of modern speculators.

David lies in lat. 8° 23′ N., long. 82° 27′ W., on the left bank of the river of the same name, in a beautiful plain, and is surrounded by the villages of Gualaca, Dolega, Boqueron, and Bugaba, and by mountains of considerable elevation. On the south-west rises the volcano of Chiriqui, a peak 7000 feet high; on the north, the Galera de Chorcha, a flat table-mountain, which, as the first part of its name indicates, has some resemblance to a gallery or corridor; from the top a waterfall descends, over huge blocks of granite, several hundred feet in depth. During the wet season, when great quantities of water are discharged, it is very conspicuous, resembling from a distance a stream of silver, and serving navigators as a landmark in making Boca Chica, the seaport of David.

David has about six hundred houses, built of wood and clay, and generally one story high, and being all whitewashed, they form several neat-looking streets. There is only one church, which stands in the centre of the public square, where also the government offices are situated. The town contained in 1843, according to official statements, 4321 inhabitants; their number is however yearly augmented by immigration. Several French, Italians, and North Americans have settled there, and it is principally owing to their exertions that David has risen within the last fifteen years from a paltry hamlet to a prosperous town. Though the Davidenians are mostly a mixed race, the number of whites is considerable; their employment consists in breeding cattle, agriculture, and commerce. The exports of the place are rice, coffee, sarsaparilla, pearls, hides, turtle-shells, dried meat, and some gold dust. Several other natural productions might be advantageously shipped. The Corpachi (*Croton Eluteria*, Swartz), the bark of which is used in the country against toothache, and is also of commercial value, grows plentifully in the forests;

the Quira (*Platymiscium polystachyum*, Benth.) is found in abundance in the neighbourhood, and the Saumerio (*Styrax punctatum*, De Cand.), producing an odoriferous balsam, a substitute for frankincense in Veraguas, is seen in extensive groves in the adjacent mountains. At present, all the produce has to be carried to Panama; but when a road to Bocas del Toro has been completed, and a direct communication with North America established, many productions which at present are not worth sending, will be exported with advantage.* The climate of David, if compared with that of other parts of the isthmus, is particularly healthy. Longevity is common; few of the cutaneous eruptions so frequent in other districts of the Isthmus are experienced; the common fever of the country being the predominant disease, and even this malady is only prevalent during the change of season. The climate is annually improving; if we may believe the tradition of the country, the rainy season a hundred years ago was most violent, making it necessary to navigate from house to house in canoes.

The intervening land is of gradual ascent, but the central ridge is of such a height as to render cutting or tunneling in that vicinity for a canal a very questionable proceeding. M. Hellert examined the route, and found it to present the most formidable obstacles; the locality however possesses many and great advantages, so much so indeed that the Federal Government have fixed upon it as the best place for the deportation of their surplus coloured population; and it will not be at all surprising

* The prospectus of a company desirous of making this road was issued some years back in London, but the undertaking fell to the ground.

if this act eventually leads to the formation of a rail or tramway from sea to sea. Mr. Wheelwright found coal of tolerable quality in the vicinity, and the entire line of country, unlike Panama, offers every inducement for colonization. There is one great objection to the construction of a railway, and that is that the Republic of New Granada, of which this is a part, has given the *exclusive* right of transit through its territories to the Panama Railway Company; but it is not a trifle, as we all know, which will deter the Federal Government if it sets its heart upon an object. And as the subject cannot but be of great interest to England, it has been thought advisable to introduce in this place President Lincoln's speech, and the programme of the first effort at colonization and—*Transit!*

SPEECH OF PRESIDENT LINCOLN ON THE NEGRO QUESTION.

A deputation of coloured men waited upon the President on the 14th of August, 1862, to hear his views upon their position. "After a few preliminary observations, the President informed the deputation that a sum of money had been appropriated by Congress and placed at his disposition for the purpose of aiding the colonization in some country of the people, or a portion of them, of African descent, thereby making it his duty, as it had for a long time been his inclination, to favour that course. 'And why,' he asked, 'should not the people of your race be colonized? Why should they leave this country? This is perhaps the first question for proper consideration. You and we are a different race. We have between us a broader difference than exists between almost any other two races. Whether it is right or wrong I need not discuss, but this physical difference is a great disadvantage to us both, as I think your race suffer greatly, many of them, by living with us, while ours suffer from your presence: in a word, we suffer on each side. If this is admitted, it affords a reason why we should be separated. You, here, are free men, I suppose. (A voice: 'Yes, Sir.') Perhaps you have long been free, or all your lives. Your race are suffering, in my opinion, the greatest wrong inflicted on any people. *But even when you cease to be slaves, you are yet far removed from being placed on an equality with the white race. You are cut off from many of the advantages which the other race enjoy. The aspiration of man is to enjoy equality with the best when free; but on this broad continent not a single man of yonr race is made the equal of ours.* Go where you are treated the best, and the ban is still upon you. I do not propose to discuss this, but to present it as a fact with which we have to deal. I cannot alter it if I would. It is a fact about which we all think and feel alike, I and you. We look to our conditions owing to the existence of the two races on this continent. I need not recount to you the effects upon white men growing out of the institution of slavery. I believe in its general evil effects on the white race. See our present condition,—the country engaged in war; our white men cutting one another's throats, none knowing how far it will extend,—and then consider what we know to be the truth. But for your race among us there could not be a war. Although many men engaged on either side do not care for you one way or the other, nevertheless I repeat, without the institution of slavery and the coloured race as a basis, the war could not have an existence. It is better for us both, therefore, to be separated. I know that there are free men among you, who, even if they could better their condition, are not as much inclined to go out of the country as those who, being slaves, could obtain their freedom on this condition. I suppose one of the principal difficulties in the way of colonization is, that the free coloured man cannot see that his comfort would be advanced by it. You may believe you can live in Washington or elsewhere in the United States the remainder of your life, perhaps, more comfortably than you can in any foreign country. Hence you may come to the conclusion that you have nothing to do with the idea of going to a foreign country. This (I speak in no unkind sense) is an extremely selfish view of the case. But you ought to do something to help those who are not so fortunate as yourselves. *There is an unwillingness on the part of our people, harsh as it may be, for you free coloured people to remain with us.* No; if you could give a start to the white people, you would open a wide door for many to be made free. We deal with those who are not free at the beginning, and those whose intellects are clouded by slavery. We have very poor material to start with. If intelligent coloured people, such as are before me, would move in this matter, much might be accomplished. It is exceedingly important that we have men at the beginning capable of thinking as white men, and not those who have been systematically depressed. There is much to encourage you. For the sake of your race you should sacrifice something of your present comfort, for the purpose of being as grand in that respect as the white people. It is a cheering thought throughout life that something can be done to ameliorate the condition of those who have been subject to the hard usages of the world. It is difficult to make a man miserable while he feels he is worthy of himself, and claims kindred to the great God who made him. In the American revolutionary war sacrifices were made by men engaged in it, but they were cheered by the future. General Washington endured greater physical hardship than if he had remained a British subject, yet he was a happy man, because he was engaged in benefiting his race, in bestowing something on the children of his neighbours, having none of his own. The colony of Liberia has been in existence a long time. In a certain sense it is a success. The old President of Liberia, Roberts, has just been with me,—the first time I ever saw him. He says they have within the bounds of that colony between 300,000 and 400,000 people, or more than in some of our old States, such as Rhode Island or Delaware. They are not all American colonists or their descendants. Something less than 12,000 have been sent thither from this country. Many of the original settlers have died, yet, like people elsewhere, their offspring outnumber those deceased. The question is, if the coloured people are persuaded to go anywhere, why not there? One reason for an unwillingness to do so is, that some of you would rather remain within reach of the country of your nativity. I do not know how much attachment you may have towards our race. It does not strike me that you have the greatest reason to love them, but still you are attached to them at all events. The place I am thinking about for a colony is Central America. It is nearer us than Liberia—not more than one-fourth as far as Liberia—*and within seven days' run by steamers. Unlike Liberia, it is on a great line of travel—it is a highway.* The country is a very excellent one for any people, and with great natural resources and advantages, and especially because of the similarity of the climate with your native land,—thus being suited to your physical condition. The particular place I have in view *is to be a great highway from the Atlantic or Caribbean Sea to the Pacific Ocean;* and this particular place has all the advantages for a colony. On both sides there are harbours among the first in the world. Again, there are evidences of very rich coal-mines. A certain amount of coal is valuable in any country, and there may be more than enough for the wants of the country. Why I attach so much importance to coal is, it will afford an opportunity to the inhabitants for immediate employment, until they get ready to permanently 'settle' in their homes. If you take colonists where there is no good landing, there is a bad start, and so also where there is nothing to cultivate, and with which to make a farm; but if something is started, so that you can get your daily bread as soon as you reach there, it is a great advantage. Coal land is the best thing I know of with which to commence an enterprise. You have been talked to on this subject, and told that a speculation is intended by gentlemen who have an interest in the country including the coal-mines. We have been a mistaken all our lives if we do not know that whites as well as blacks look to their self-interest, unless among those deficient in intellect. Everybody you trade with makes something. You meet with these things here and elsewhere. If such persons have what will be an advantage to them, the question is whether it cannot be made of advantage to you. You are intelligent, and know that success does not so much depend on external help as self-reliance; much, therefore, depends upon yourselves. As to the coal-mines, I think I see the means available for your self-reliance. I shall, if I get a sufficient number of you engaged, have provision made that you shall not be wronged. If you will engage in the enterprise, I will spend some of the money entrusted to me. I am not sure you will succeed. The Government may lose the money, but we cannot succeed unless we try; we think that with care we can succeed. *The political affairs in Central America are not quite in as satisfactory a condition as I wish. There are contending factions in that quarter; but it is time all the factions agreed alike on the subject of colonization.* To your race they have no objection. Besides, I would endeavour to have you made equals, and have the best assurance that you should be the equals of the best. The practical thing I want to ascertain is whether I can get a number of able-bodied men, with their wives and children, who are willing to go when I present evidence of encouragement and protection. Could I get a number of tolerably intelligent men with their wives and children, I think I could make a successful commencement. I want you to let me know whether this can be done or not. These are subjects of very great importance, worthy of a month's study of a speech delivered in an hour. I ask you, then, to consider seriously for yourselves, for your race, for the good of mankind, things that are not confined to the present generation, but as

> "'From age to age descends the lay,
> To millions yet to be,
> Till far its echoes roll away
> Into eternity.'"

The chairman of the delegation briefly replied that they would hold a consultation, and in a short time give an answer.

The President said, "Take your full time. No hurry at all."

The delegation then withdrew.

Senator S. C. Pomeroy had, by request of the President, organized a system of coloured emigration to Central America. The Government proposed to send out the emigrants in steamships, and provide them with all the necessary implements of labour, and also sustenance until they can gather a harvest.* With the concurrence of the President, the following advertisement was issued:—

"TO THE FREE COLOURED PEOPLE OF THE UNITED STATES.

"The hour has now arrived in the history of your settlement upon this continent when it is within your own power to take one step that will secure, if successful, the elevation, freedom, and social position of your race upon

* The Federal Government has abandoned the negro colonization scheme *for the present*, the Ministers of the Central American Republics having protested against its being carried out in *their* country.

the American continent. The President of the United States has already signified his desire to carry out fully in the letter and spirit of the late Act of Congress the desire of the National Legislature, which made an appropriation to facilitate your emigration and settlement in some favourable locality outside of these States; and at his request I have consented and agreed with him to aid you in organizing this emigration, and in selecting a locality that will be valuable and attractive to your people in itself, as well as give the promise to you and to us that it shall be a suitable location for a great, free, and prosperous people. I now address you as one awake to this momentous revolution in American history, alive also to your interest in this conflict of arms, whereby you are led to hope that in this unsettling of established institutions your people may go free. This then is the hour for you to make one earnest effort to secure your own social position and independence, by co-operating with those who now reach out their hands to aid you. I ask you to do this by the pride you may have to make *another exhibition* to the world of the *valour, heroism, and virtue of the coloured race;* by the love you may have for your struggling and oppressed people now among us, as well by the hopes you may indulge of making smooth and prosperous the pathway of coming generations.

"I propose on the 1st day of October next (1862) to take with me 100 coloured men as pioneers in this movement, who, with their families, may equal the number of 500 souls, and for whose benefit the appropriations in the Acts of Congress referred to were made.

The President will provide us the means of transportation and the protection of the settlement. Being familiar with organizing and settling the early emigration to my own State (Kansas), I indulge the hope that that experience may be made serviceable to you. I am in earnest for the welfare of your people, present and prospective. I want you to consider this an auspicious period for you. If this travail and pain of the nation becomes the birthday of your freedom, let us plant you free and independent beyond the reach of the power that has oppressed you. Consider this as an opening by the wisdom of Divine Providence, when you are called of God to go with me to a country which your oppressed people are soon to receive for their inheritance.

"I propose to examine, and if found satisfactory and promising, to settle you at Chiriqui, in New Granada (with the approval of the Government), only about one week's sail from Washington, D.C. All persons of the African race, of sound health, who desire to take with me the lead in this work will please send their names, their number, sex, and ages of the respective members of their families, and their post-office address, to me, at the city of Washington, D.C. No white person will be allowed as a member of the colony. I want mechanics and labourers, earnest, honest, and sober men; for the interest of a generation, it may be of mankind, are involved in the success of this experiment, and with the approbation of the American people, and under the blessing of Almighty God, it cannot, it shall not fail.

"S. C. POMEROY,

"United States Senate."

CHAPTER VIII.

PANAMA THE NARROWEST PART OF THE ISTHMUS.—FAVOURITE LOCALITY FOR A CANAL.—M. NAPOLEON GARELLA.—HIS PROJECT.—FRENCH MISSION OF CIVILIZATION.—SAN BLAS ROUTE.—FAILURE OF CANAL SCHEMES. —A DESCENDANT OF MONTEZUMA.—DESCRIPTION OF THE NATIVE TRIBES. —AN HISTORICAL PUZZLE EXPLAINED.

More attention has been attracted to this portion of the Isthmus than to any other part, because it offers the *narrowest* impediment to joining the two seas. Of the various projects proposed, perhaps that of connecting the two rivers, Chagres and Rio Grande, by a short canal, and then deepening their beds, has been the most favourably received. The line has been thoroughly examined, but the nature of the country did not come up to expectation, and the plan was consequently abandoned. The French Government under Louis Philippe manifested the most decided predilection for the Panama route, and caused it, in 1843, to be minutely surveyed by M. Napoleon Garella. He proposed to start from the little bay of Vaca del Monte, twelve miles west of Panama, and cross over to Limon Bay, two miles and a half east of Chagres, the summit to be tunnelled through (at least three miles from end to end). He estimated the cost at £5,000,000, the canal to be twenty-three feet in depth, and forty-six feet in width. Monsieur Napoleon Garella winds up his report in the following words:—

"It belonged," he says, "to the French Government, which has taken the initiative in so many purely scientific expeditions, to put itself at the head of a movement that will lead to the execution of a work which concerns the whole world, to place this question in its true light, and to bring the point into public discussion among the nations interested in it.

"Without the pretension of having laid down a perfect plan, I have, I believe, sufficiently fulfilled the object of the mission with which I had the honour of being charged. The possibility of the junction of the two oceans at the Isthmus of Panama, appears to me now beyond a doubt, and I hope that those who peruse my work will participate in that opinion. The time has arrived for executing this important work; and France, which has taken the initiative in the real exploration of the Isthmus, owes it to herself, to her interests, and to the mission of civilization which she has filled so long among nations, to take also the initiative in the measures to be proposed for securing its accomplishment."

No one would attempt to deprive M. Garella of the merit which belongs to him, but it is much to be regretted that he has endeavoured to monopolize the credit due to others, especially that of Captain Lloyd, whose observations he freely avails himself of; indeed this section of the Panama route has been thoroughly examined by competent persons, English, French, and American,—Lieutenant Strain, U.S.N., Captain Lloyd, Mr. Stephens, Dr. Cullen, Mr. Wheelwright, M. Hellert,

Admiral Horatio Austin, and a host of others, to whom the world is deeply indebted, and who have carried out their explorations in the teeth of hardships and dangers enough to daunt the most intrepid. All the routes proposed for a canal in this vicinity passed over or near the present line of the Panama Railway, and if laying the iron road proved so difficult, some idea may be formed of the obstacles there would have been in the way of the construction of a canal.

There remains yet another route to describe in this neighbourhood, and which, if judged by the narrowness of the intervening land, seemed to offer the best chance of any scheme yet proposed. That route is at the very shallowest part of the Isthmus, and would but little exceed thirty miles across. The Atlantic terminus would be at San Blas, and its Pacific at Chepo; the latter place *might* be made into a port, there being anchorage between the mouth of the river and an island off its mouth, called Chepillo; and the former could also be used, but the intervening land is said to be very difficult. Several attempts have been made to explore this route, but the natives offer the most determined opposition to any examination of their country; for although only a few miles from Panama, they have never been conquered, and maintain their independence to this day. Mr. Oliphant, who has lately been up the river Chepo, is inclined to believe that this is the real point for a transit. He was within twenty miles of the Atlantic, and saw no obstacle in the shape of high land. He could not however ascertain the height of the country, from the cause stated above. Mr. Wheelwright made the attempt some years ago, and was received with much hospitality and kindness; but although the Indians are as much attached to the English as they are inveterate against the Spanish race, they positively refused to permit him to proceed. Another gentleman was told by one of the chiefs, with whom he was on friendly terms, that if he attempted to cross the country he would be the first to drive an arrow through him. At present the knowledge which might be gained would not be worth the risk attending the attempt.

The following extract is of too much interest to need any excuse for its insertion in this place:*—

"The Indians who at present inhabit the Isthmus are said to amount to about ten thousand. They are scattered over Bocas del Toro, the northern portions of Veraguas, the north-eastern shores of Panama, and almost the whole of Darien, and consist principally of four tribes, the Savanerics, the San Blas Indians, the Bayanos, and the Cholas. Every tribe speaks a different language, and they not unfrequently wage war against each other.

"The Savanerics occupy the northern portion of Veraguas, and appear to be most numerous in a district situated a few days' journey from the village of Las Palmas. One of their chiefs has adopted the pompous title of King Lora Montezuma, and pretends to be a descendant of the Mexican emperor. Almost every year he sends some ambassadors to Santiago, the capital of Veraguas, to inform the authorities that he is the legitimate lord of the country, and that he protests against

* Dr. Seemann, 'Voyage of H.M.S. Herald,' vol. i. pp. 317–22.

any assumption on the part of the New Granadian Government. Although no credit can be attached to the belief that King Lora is a descendant of the great Montezuma, yet there is reason to suppose, and future investigations may tend to corroborate the supposition, that his subjects are a distant branch of the great family of Anahuac. A direct intercourse still existed, at the time of the Discovery, between the southern portions of the Mexican empire and Veraguas. Little golden eagles, the national emblems of Mexico, are frequently met with in the tombs of the district, and chocolate is still the prevalent drink. Such facts are indeed quite important enough in themselves to draw upon this tribe the attention of the ethnologist. Unfortunately no European has as yet had time to study, and the Spanish inhabitants are too indolent, and, it may be added, too much prejudiced against the Indians, to be ever able to draw correct conclusions, or to make proper use of the rich ethnological materials scattered around them.

"The Manzanillo or San Blas Indians inhabited the north-eastern portion of the province of Panama. They occasionally visit Portobello and the neighbouring villages, and live almost in constant feud with the Bayanos. They are probably the same tribe which came in conflict with Columbus's crew during his fourth voyage of discovery, when, unlike most savages, they exhibited no fear at the discharge of the cannon. The thunder of man probably appeared to them but insignificant when compared with the terrible tornadoes so frequently visiting their coast. All, however, must remain a matter of conjecture until we know more, or, to speak plainly, until we know something about them. At present our knowledge of this tribe is merely nominal, and of its language we are ignorant.

"The Bayanos inhabit the district about the river Chepo, and are a martial people, who, up to this time, have preserved their independence, jealously guarding their territory against the white man. Their dislike to Spaniards and their descendants is intense, and strongly contrasts with their friendly disposition towards the British, a feeling entertained since the days of Dampier and Wafer.* Annually British vessels touch at the northern coast for the purpose of trading; and it is probably from that source some of the Bayanos have obtained a smattering of English. Their cacique has frequently paid visits to the British representative at Panama, yet there the friendship ended. The Consul, on asking permission to show the same mark of attention to the chief, was told that no European was allowed to enter their country, and if the Consul should attempt such a journey it would cost him his life.

"The Cholo Indians are one of the most widely diffused tribes of tropical America, extending, as they do, from the Gulf of San Miguel to the Bay of Choco, and thence, with a few interruptions, to the northern parts of the Republic of Ecuador. We can follow them all along the coast, from lat. 2° 0′ to 8° 30′ N., recognizing them by their peculiar mode of raising their habitations upon posts six or eight feet above the ground. The fact that the Cholos have such a wide

"* Observe the close resemblance between the Bayanos and the Mosquito Indians.

range, explains an historical puzzle. When reading of the discovery of Peru, how the Spaniards gradually pushed southwards along the shores of America, everywhere inquiring after the empire of the Incas, and even obtaining information of the city of Cuzco, we are at a loss to explain how the discoverers could understand the stories related to them, how the two parties could make themselves intelligible. Even the best historians have not explained this puzzle. But the fact that the same language is spoken from San Miguel to the northern boundaries of Ecuador, where the Quichua commences, and that it was familiar to the Spaniards before starting on their expedition, renders the proceeding intelligible. We now comprehend how the existence of the empire of the Incas could be known on the banks of the Churchunque, how Balboa could receive intelligence of the llama and other productions of Peru, and how the barks of Pizarro could collect information from the lips of natives, who never before had beheld the face of a white man."

CHAPTER IX.

GULF OF DARIEN.—ROUTE FROM CALEDONIA BAY TO SAN MIGUEL.—DR. CULLEN.—MR. GISBORNE'S EFFORTS.—TAKEN PRISONER BY THE INDIANS.—SUCCEEDS IN CROSSING TO THE PACIFIC.—SUFFERINGS OF LIEUT. STRAIN AND PARTY.—RESCUE BY LIEUT. FORSYTHE, R.N.—COMMANDER PREVOST'S JOURNEY.—VALUABLE PRECEDENT.

SEVERAL plans have been proposed, and various routes have been well surveyed in Darien, which appears to have been that part of the Isthmus the great Humboldt was inclined to look upon as the most favourable for a canal. In the first place, a cut was proposed from Port Escoces or some point in Caledonia Bay, on the Atlantic, and proceeding in a south-westerly direction, to terminate in the Bay of San Miguel, in the Pacific; a distance of about thirty-nine miles. Attention was first directed to this route by Dr. Cullen, in 1850, who averred that he had repeatedly crossed the Isthmus at this point, in which respect much controversy has arisen. The correctness of Dr. Cullen's survey was questioned by Mr. Lionel Gisborne (Assoc. Inst. C. E.), who subsequently surveyed the route, on behalf of Messrs. Fox, Henderson, and Company, but who did not at first succeed in crossing from one side to the other, and when he did, only sufficiently examined it to be able, in his opinion, to pronounce on the practicability of the scheme. He reported favourably of the capabilities of Port Escoces and Caledonia Bay, on the Atlantic, as also of the entrance into the so-called Darien Harbour, on the Pacific, from the Gulf of San Miguel, by the Boca Chica. He proposed following the Savana and its tributary the Lara, and thence cutting a canal over the summit-level, which he estimated at only 150 feet, to the Caledonia river. This project might be executed either with or without locks. The following is that gentleman's report to his employers:—

"To Messrs. Fox, Henderson, and Brassey.

"Gentlemen,—Having made arrangements with Sir Charles Fox to ascertain the practicability of an interoceanic navigation for the largest ships, at all times of the tide, across the Isthmus of Darien, between Port Escoces on the Atlantic and San Miguel on the Pacific, and having made such preparations as I could in this country, I sailed with my assistant, Mr. Henry C. Forde, on the 2nd of April last, from Southampton to Cartagena, where we arrived on the 1st of May. Here we completed our arrangements, chartered the schooner 'Veloz,' sailed for Port Escoces on the 12th of June, and anchored in that port on the 15th.

"At Cartagena we obtained information which fully confirmed what we had been led to expect from the little we gathered before leaving England,—that no strangers had been allowed to visit the interior since the buccaneers assisted the natives in repelling the Spaniards nearly two hundred years ago; that it was in vain to think of obtaining from these jealous savages permission to enter their territory; and that to do so without their permission was hazardous in the extreme. Yet as it was generally supposed that the summit-level between the two oceans was near the Atlantic coast, and it was therefore important to ascertain whether that was the fact, we determined to make the attempt. From the schooner the Cordilleras appeared to run in an unbroken range. We landed on the morning of the 17th of June, and crossed this range without any obstacle, ascertaining the lowest point visible from the seaboard to be 276 feet high.

"Beyond this point we followed a small stream, which led us to a larger river flowing from the south-west, in a semicircular sweep towards the north. A flat plain extended to the south-west, in the direction of the Gulf of San Miguel, as far as the eye could reach; looking over the tops of the trees from a bluff about one hundred feet high, which we ascended for the purpose, we obtained an uninterrupted view for at least six miles in that direction.

"We followed the course of the river to the north until dark. Early on the following morning two Indians in a canoe came in sight, who, upon perceiving us, instantly landed and fled to the woods. Proceeding on our journey, we met, a few hours afterwards, a woman and two children (one an albino), from whom we were unable to derive any information. We had scarcely passed her when a canoe suddenly appeared with five well-armed Indians in it, who made us understand that we were to follow them, which we thought it prudent to do.

"They led us, fortunately, along the course of the river, which gradually assumed a more easterly direction, winding among the hills that overlapped each other, until we reached a village at its mouth in Caledonia Bay. We were thus singularly assisted in our object by the discovery of a passage through the range of the Cordilleras, which had been heretofore supposed to be unbroken. Here an Indian, who spoke a little English, and seemed a principal man in his tribe, questioned us as to our object in entering their territory. Thereupon a meeting was held of the chief men, who detained us as prisoners. After several hours, and with great difficulty, we prevailed on them to allow us to return to our vessel, on the condition, however, that we should set sail instantly, and upon the understanding if we were again caught in the interior, more summary measures would be adopted. Five or six Indians accompanied us to

Port Escoces, about five miles off (where our vessel was lying), and they remained until the afternoon, when we were well clear of the coast.

"Our great object had, however, been obtained in finding that the Cordilleras, which appeared from the sea a continuous range, had an intervening valley, and that the summit between the two oceans must be in the centre of the Isthmus, if not nearer the Pacific coast.

"It had also been ascertained that Port Escoces, though rather small for the terminus of a great ship navigation, would make an excellent harbour of refuge, and that Caledonia Bay, as far as I had an opportunity to examine it, was most admirably calculated to serve the purposes of a harbour to the contemplated undertaking.

"We now sailed for Navy Bay, and thence crossed the Isthmus to Panama, where we arrived on the 25th of June. Here we hired a small schooner of twelve tons burden, sailed on the 27th for the Gulf of San Miguel, and arrived in the night of the 29th at Boca Chica, the entrance of Darien Harbour. We proceeded on the following day to the examination of the Savana river. At its mouth we found it two miles wide, narrowing for seven miles above to a width of half a mile, and skirted by hills from two to three hundred feet high, running within a mile or two of its banks. The depth of the river varies from nine to six fathoms at low water; and soundings gave us a soft muddy bottom. From this point to the junction with the river Lara, the depth diminishes till the bottom becomes level with mid-tide. The tide rises for five miles further up the Savana to a fall of about two feet over a stratum of rock crossing the stream diagonally N.E. by E. at a dip of 60°. The same class of rock appears both at the bottom and the sides. The course of the Savana beyond tidal influence is tortuous.

"On the morning of the 2nd of July we began our land journey to the north-east in the direction of Caledonia Bay. For the first two miles the country was level and less overgrown than on the Atlantic side, which made our progress comparatively rapid.

"We then crossed a range of hills which we ascertained to be 100 feet high. After passing a valley in which was the confluence of two small streams, we crossed a second range of 130 feet high, forming the summit between the Savana and Caledonia rivers; at the foot a stream flowed nearly due east. We followed it for two miles, which led us to a larger one, the course of which we traced. At this point a clear view to the north-east, towards Caledonia Bay, showed a flat plain with no intervening hills. . . . Our commanding view, for at least six miles, from an elevation of 100 feet, was perfectly conclusive with regard to the few miles seen and not actually walked over. We therefore accepted the admonition of a footpath and a bridge formed by the trunk of a tree placed across the river at this point, that we were again in the territory of the Indians into whose hands we had fallen at Caledonia Bay, and that our object being accomplished, it was unwise to incur further risk from the Indians by walking over these six miles, thinking it best for the success of the undertaking to retrace our steps at once.

"On mapping our route, I found that the point I [of my map] was too high up the Savana river for the shortest junction between it and the Caledonia. We therefore ascended the river Lara, which ran in a more easterly direction; the tide carried us up six miles, the width narrowing from 300 feet to 30 feet. Some falls of a few inches each are caused by a rock of the same character as that of the Savana; its course is very tortuous; for the five miles I examined beyond tidal action the bottom was uniformly rock, and it became an insignificant stream. After mapping the direction, I feel confident that its source is the confluence of the small streams found in the valley between the two ranges of hills previously mentioned.

"The gravel banks in the Savana and Lara rivers are composed of the detritus of igneous and stratified rock. The latter is the same as that forming the falls on both rivers; its dip being from 60° to near 90°, and its strike varying from north-east to south-east.

"The general character of the country is that of a flat plain, subject to inundation at high tides for a considerable distance out, and covered with mangrove wood, whose high interlacing roots growing out of soft mud, render walking impossible. Beyond tidal influence the banks rise five to ten feet above ordinary water-level, and are covered with the finest timber I have seen on the Isthmus,—cedar, mahogany, ebony, lignum-vitæ, cuipa, palms, and other trees.

"On the 9th of July we returned to San Miguel. This bay is naturally divided, by a promontory and a chain of islands, into a roadstead and a magnificent harbour. Captain Kellett's unpublished chart, supplied by the Admiralty, shows only a part of the former. I have made a survey of the remainder, and the general features are represented on my maps, as also those of Darien Harbour. I did not examine Boca Grande, as I understood from the natives that the navigation through it is rendered dangerous by rocks, and as Boca Chica, on account of its depth and position, is far more advantageous.

"I do not think it is possible to exaggerate the merits of this part of the Isthmus as the terminus of a great ship navigation; it requires but an examination of the map to be convinced of this fact.

"We returned to Navy Bay, and sailed for England on the 24th July, where we arrived on the 17th instant.

"On Map No. 1, I have shown in red colour the topographical facts which have been ascertained by personal investigation, with sections of the portions traversed. From this it will be collected that the harbours of San Miguel and Caledonia are both excellent as the termini of a ship navigation on the largest scale, with Port Escoces as a harbour of refuge, should circumstances occur to render its use necessary; that the Savana river has six fathoms or upwards in depth at low water, for a distance of seven miles from its mouth, the effect of the tide reaching up the Lara tributary eleven miles above this, or eighteen miles from Darien Harbour, leaving a distance of thirty miles to Caledonia Bay, *which is the actual breadth of the Isthmus between the tidal effect of the two oceans*; that the summit-level is ascertained to be 150 feet, and is formed by a narrow range of hills, having a gradually rising plain at their foot on each side. There is every reason to believe that a more detailed examination of this division of waters will result in a considerably lower summit being found; but this, under the circumstances of the section, is not such an important point as might at first be supposed, the narrowness of the ridge making the cubic quantity through it very small compared to the excavation through the plains; so that, should the hills depress into the actual level of the plains, the estimate will not be materially affected. The bulk of the work to be done is in the plains themselves, and the cost will be proportionate to the cross-section adopted, or, in other words, the depth and breadth of the navigation required. The question, therefore, resolves itself into what are the necessities of commerce as to an inter-oceanic water communication.

"I do not consider it necessary to enter into the merits of this question. My instructions are to design a navigation capable of passing with security at all times the largest vessels navigating the two oceans, not with a view to a local coasting trade, but for the accommodation of the whole maritime world.

"There are two methods of accomplishing this object:—

"1st. To make a cut of sufficient capacity to form an uninterrupted navigation (without locks) from sea to sea.

"2nd. A navigation with locks on a scale suitable to the object in view.

"There can be no doubt that the carrying out of the first proposition will comply in the fullest sense with the requirements of all classes of vessels, and, when completed, will best supply the want of a natural connection between the oceans. Its execution offers no engineering difficulties, and no chance of future failure; it is simply a question of cubic quantity of excavation dependent on the dimensions of the cross-section.

"Many large merchantmen and men-of-war draw from 24 to 28 feet of water, and oceanic steamers measure 350 feet over all, with a breadth of 70 to 74 feet across the paddle-boxes. Ship-building is not at a stand,—on the contrary, the size of vessels is rapidly on the increase; in such an undertaking it is therefore reasonable to forestall progress by a timely concession to it. I propose to make a cut 30 feet deep at low tide, 140 feet broad at bottom, and 160 feet at low water's surface. Such a cut carried from sea to sea is not larger than the trade of the world requires, and will form a permanent, safe, and rapid mode of transit.

"On the Pacific the tide rises twenty-three feet and on the Atlantic it is scarcely appreciable. Mid-tide is on a level, or nearly so, in the two oceans, so that there will be a current both ways dependent on the ebb and flow of the Pacific. This current will not exceed three miles an hour, and will act most beneficially, not only as a scour to prevent deposit, but as an assistance in the transit of vessels. It will secure the passage being effected in one tide, and prevent the passing of vessels going different ways, as the direction of the trade will be influenced by the ebb or flow of the Pacific tide. The material to be excavated through is chiefly rock (not expensive to quarry), so that this current will not wear away the banks, nor will the wash of passing steamers cause injury; it also affords security against any interruption to the navigation from slips, and reduces the cost of maintenance to a nominal sum. This rock is a stratified shale with thinnish beds, easy to get, though sound, and will form an admirable side-lining to the navigation dispensing with the necessity of any artificial protection. The fact of its existence is one of the most favourable features to the undertaking as regards permanence and certainty of success.

"I estimate the cost of this design at £12,000,000. It must be remembered that no project has ever been before the public which embraces anything like the objects attained by such an uninterrupted navigation. All other propositions have but local importance, and look to their profits from local trade; this one is adapted to every ship afloat, and seeks a return from the trade of every country. Its completion will make a change in the carrying commerce of every Pacific port; and as a railway makes its own traffic, so will this work, most certainly, greatly increase the commerce between the distantly separated countries which steam power is only now beginning to reach.

"This is the design which, after mature consideration, I confidently recommend for adoption, and it is almost with regret that I feel it my duty to submit any other, so sure am I that it is the only one which will satisfy the requirements of commerce.

"My second proposition necessitates two levels joined by a series of locks.

"I adhere to the cross-section of cut recommended in the previous design, as well as the fact of the navigation being open to the largest vessels at all times of the tide.

"A tidal canal, supplied on the upper level at high water, would be a very imperfect navigation, and one-third more expensive than the design I am about to submit. I estimate the cost at about £7,000,000. It would involve all the disadvantages of a canal, and offer many obstacles to be guarded against, such as the arrangements for draining the country on each side, without the risk of strong currents and shoals formed by deposit, and increase the time of transit considerably, by the small speed attainable by steamers in such a class of navigation. I cannot recommend it for the purposes intended.

"It has been before mentioned that the Savana and Caledonia rivers run into two extensive plains. They are uninhabited, and the land is uncultivated. It grows, however, fine timber, which, if means of transit were at hand, would be of considerable value. During the dry season, neither of these rivers, could, near their source, supply the water required at a summit-level of a navigation on the scale contemplated; during the wet season, again, they discharge a large volume of water which, in an ordinary canal, would cause trouble and expense to regulate, and prevent accumulations of deposit. Under these circumstances, I propose placing an embankment across both these rivers, making the embankments long enough and high enough to raise the water at their back 90 feet above low tide in the Pacific. This will flood both plains up to the range of hills which forms the boundary of their catchwater basins. Through the summit a cut is to be made of the same cross-section recommended in Design No. 1, but with 40 feet depth of water, so as to allow 10 feet to be drawn off the lake for lockage, or a rise of 10 feet to catch flood waters and prevent, too rapid a current in the tidal entrances to the harbours. All the valuable timber in the lake must be cut previous to the water being let in, so that an easy means will be afforded to convey it to the harbours for shipment. From Caledonia Bay to the embankment, a cut will have to be made of the cross-section, adopted in the other design. The Savana is navigable up to the point where the embankment is to cross.

"The rise of 90 feet will have to be overcome by locks placed in the side of one of the ranges of hills against which the embankments terminate, and which are composed of rock; weirs will also be provided to discharge surplus waters.

"It is a serious undertaking to raise a large vessel 90 feet, without much loss of time.

"I am fully prepared to meet this difficulty, and propose that the locks should be 400 feet long from mitre to mitre, and 90 feet wide between the gate quoins. Each lock to have a lift of 30 feet, to be overcome by wrought-iron gates. The large supply at the summit level does away with the usual objection to a high lift wasting water. There will be no difficulty in constructing the locks and gates of the dimensions proposed; stone, lime, and sand of excellent quality, are obtainable in more than one place on the line of country to be traversed.

"Three locks will thus be required in each embankment, and I have estimated for two sets at each end; the second set to be 300 feet long and 50 feet wide, with 22 feet of water on their cills. Thus, four vessels can be passed into the lake at the same time, and the larger locks only used for those adapted to their size.

"For a navigation requiring the use of locks, I can submit this design with confidence. It possesses the facilities of deep still-water lake navigation, without the disadvantages attendant on the use of a canal. The concentration of lockage in two places will save time. Great facility is also offered in the execution of the work, by its not being spread over a large area and only a small portion of it below tidal level. The estimated cost is £4,500,000; it is only about one-third of that set down for an uninterrupted cut from sea to sea, but the disadvantages are very great; locks are decidedly objectionable in an undertaking of this magnitude and mercantile value. The best studied plans, carried out in the most perfect manner, cannot guard against accident or neglect, which may stop the whole transit for months. Delay and risk there must be, when such large machinery is worked, and there is no doubt shipowners would sooner pay a higher toll to pass directly from sea to sea, than run the risk and incur the delay of lock navigation.

"This question is not one on which a hasty opinion should be formed, nor must the decision be biassed by the disparity in the cost of the two measures. The real point is, which is of the greatest value to the mercantile community? A far-seeing thinker cannot doubt that the level cut is the only one which will comply with the requirements of the world.

"In framing the estimates, I have calculated wholly on imported labour, making a liberal allowance for the diminution of work to be expected in a tropical climate, and the extra wages necessary to induce parties to emigrate. This portion of the Isthmus of Darien is, without doubt, in one of the most healthy districts. Neither Mr. Forde nor I suffered in the least from the climate until our return to Panama, notwithstanding we were often for days together in the same wet clothes without a blanket to cover us at night, and living on bad provisions.

"The reason of this comparative salubrity, is the absence of swamps or overflowings of the river-banks out of the range of the tide, and the general dry character of the surrounding district.

"I have purposely abstained from entering into any detail of the works contemplated, or the arrangements for carrying them out. My object has been to give a concise view of the facilities of the Darien route, the facts elicited by the examination of the country by Mr. Forde and myself, and the best means of carrying out a project which has for centuries occupied the attention of Governments and mercantile men, without much advance towards its completion. I cannot conclude, however, without again earnestly recommending for adoption that design *which will, without locks, at all times, permit the passage of the largest vessel.*

"I remain, Gentlemen,

"Your obedient servant,

"LIONEL GISBORNE, C.E.*

"41, Craven Street, Strand,
"London, 28th August, 1852."

Lieutenant Strain, of the United States Navy, was unable to find the routes and passes laid down by Mr. Gisborne; and although he ultimately succeeded in crossing from the Atlantic to the Pacific coast, it was only after wandering in the valleys of the Chucunaque and the Savana for nearly three months, during which, the sufferings and privations they endured proved fatal to many of his party. The account of the trials and difficulties they bravely encountered is very interesting:—

On the 19th of January, 1854, Lieutenant Strain, of the U.S. corvette Cyane, landed from that ship in Caledonia Bay, Darien, with a party composed of twenty-eight officers and men, supplied with ten days' provisions. Previous to setting off on the journey, which they hoped would not be of longer duration than a week at most, an arrangement was made with the cacique of the Indians, from whom permission was obtained to explore his country, and some of the na-

* Mr. Gisborne afterwards succeeded in crossing the Isthmus of Darien. He started a short time before the ill-fated American expedition, under Lieutenant Strain, and in five days reached the opposite side. There is no doubt, however, that all the labour, hardship, and suffering in this locality, has been thrown away as regards canalization. Mr. Gisborne is since dead, and therefore I have abstained from making any comment on his work.

tives were ordered to accompany the Americans as guides. This, it afterwards appeared, was the plan of the cacique to dispose of his present visitors, and at the same time to deter future interlopers from manifesting any disposition to put their foot upon the soil of Darien. The guides were directed to conduct the ill-fated party into the depths of the forest and there leave them, and these instructions were only too faithfully followed. The subsequent sufferings of Strain and his companions are almost beyond belief. They wandered hither and thither, without any clear idea of their whereabouts, strange to say, while one after the other lay down and died. The narrative of their trials is heart-rending, but they appear to have emulated the glorious conduct of our own Franklin, in his celebrated journey across the Barren Grounds, in displaying the most heroic courage and fortitude. For sixty-three days these poor men wandered about without a particle of food beyond the roots and berries they were enabled to collect, when, on the 17th of March, Strain himself was rescued on the Pacific side of the Isthmus by Lieutenant Forsyth, H.M.S. Virago, who had been sent to look after him, and render any assistance in his power to the party. Strain instantly turned back with his English deliverers, and six days afterwards (the 23rd of March) had the joy of discovering his lost shipmates, a happiness participated in, to the fullest extent, by Lieutenant Forsyth and his companions.

Six of the American expedition left their bones in Darien, the rest slowly recovered; but Lieutenant Strain did not long survive the fearful shock to his constitution. His body lies buried on the line of the Panama Railroad, near Monument Hill.

The expedition under Captain Prevost, in 1853, after attaining an altitude of about 1200 feet, discovered no indications that they had even then reached the summit. Similar attempts were made, about the same time, by parties under Colonel Codazzi and Captain Joureiguiberry, with results equally unsatisfactory. All these researches seem to demonstrate that the Sierras Lloranas extend in an unbroken chain, from the Bay of San Blas, westward to the Gulf of Uraba or Darien, and the decided hostility of the Indians is a matter on which all explorers agree.

The following is the official journal of Commander Prevost, and is full of interest, besides being a valuable precedent as regards the daily progress in cutting through the primæval forest:—

"*December* 16*th*, 1853.—(Full Moon.) 8 P.M. Weighed and steamed from the anchorage of Taboga, near Panama, shaping a course to pass inside the Pearl Islands. 11. Sighted Pacheca, the northernmost of the Pearl Islands. Daylight, off the Farallon Ingles.

"*Saturday*, 17*th*.—8 A.M. Entered the Gulf of San Miguel, steering mid-channel between Points Brava and Garachiné, to avoid the Buey Shoal, which extends some distance south of the former. The tide or current was strong against us; general soundings from 6 to 8 fathoms, which deepened as we approached Punta Patino. Passed through the Boca-Chica Passage at low-water spring-tides; lowest cast 7 fathoms. Entered the harbour of Darien, a magnificent sheet of water, and at 2.30 P.M. anchored in the mouth of the Savana river.

"*Sunday*, 18*th*.—8.15 A.M. Discovered the ship dragging her anchor; let go small bower and got steam up; brought up outside the river in Darien Harbour, with 48 fathoms on each anchor. 10.30. Low water. Weighed and proceeded up the river. In picking up a berth, the ship grounded on the soft mud-bank off the right side of the river Savana; laid out kedge, let go small bower, and waited for the tide to flow. 3 P.M. Ship floated, steamed to an anchorage in mid-channel, and moored with swivel, 36 fathoms on each anchor. We were shortly afterwards visited by the authorities from Chapigana, a village situated about 8 miles distant on the south bank of the Tuyra, containing about 150 inhabitants. These persons, viz. the Gefe Politico and Governor of the province, Don Manuel Borbina, the Alcalde, and Messrs. Hossack and Nelson, Scotchmen, gave us every information in their power of the route we were about to take, and obtained for us all the native assistance we required.

"*Monday*, 19*th*.—About noon a party in the cutter and gig, with a canoe for the Indians, left the ship fully armed and equipped, with fourteen days' provisions.

"The latitude and longitude of two principal points being given, viz. Fuerte del Principe, lat. 8° 34′ N.,* long. 77° 56′ W., and Port Escoces, lat. 8° 50′ N., long. 77° 41′ W., I deemed it better to work out our route as a course and distance, and cut our road accordingly, rather than trust to the uncertainty of the published maps, which appear to differ materially from each other. The survey made by Mr. W. Haydon, acting second master of this ship, shows the course followed by the boats as far as the islands 'Fairfax' and 'Eliza,' which we reached at 3 P.M., and were joined by two more native guides (hunters) in a small canoe, who promised to accompany the expedition as carriers. Beyond this, the Savana forms a reach about 3 miles long in a N.N.W. direction. Its western bank is entirely lost among small islets and other streams running into it, forming a long, shallow mud-bank, the channel being apparently on the eastern side, where, at half-tide, we found 5 fathoms. At 3.45

* "The positions of these places are, according to Mr. Gisborne's recent survey (as laid down in his MS. map), also adopted in an Admiralty Chart, just published, Fuerte del Principe, lat. 8° 44′ N., long. 78° 8′ W., and Port Escoces, lat. 8° 51′ N., long. 77° 36½′ W."

P.M. we were abreast of a point opening into a straight reach, and beyond it a conspicuous hill was visible, which our guide named 'Periaki,' estimated by us at about 300 feet in height; further than this there were no hills. Following this reach about 3 miles, the river suddenly narrowed to 60 yards, taking a sharp turn towards the N.E., bringing Periaki before us; thence the turns of the river became sharp and tortuous, our soundings giving only one fathom, and the banks consisting of mangrove-trees and swampy land. 5 P.M. Reached the mouth of the Lara, the Savana running N.N.W. about 30 yards wide, its turnings sharp and stream sluggish; about one mile above this, the eastern side began to assume banks, with large trees, the western side still swampy. 5.30 P.M. Abreast of Matumaganti, a small stream on the W. bank. A mile above this, our guide pointed out a spot on the same bank, said to have been in former days the Spanish settlement of Fuerte del Principe; the absence of forest trees, and the presence of brushwood and young shrubs, was the only indication we could perceive. A short distance beyond this, as the sun had gone down, we were glad to stop for the night at an old rancho on the western bank, the boats now only just afloat in the middle of the stream.

"*Tuesday, 20th.*—Taking advantage of the flowing tide, we passed a small stream on the W. bank, by our guide called 'La Villa.' This was about a mile from our rancho; and half a mile higher up we were stopped by falls and rocks crossing the river diagonally in several places. We had now ascended the river about 22 miles from its mouth; the tide appears to flow as high as this point, but only for half an hour; this obliged me to land the party here, and unload the boats. In addition to a tent, a large rancho was provided on the E. bank of the river, and the stores and provisions were left in charge of Mr. Hornby, midshipman, with a petty officer and twelve men, all well armed. During this short detention I ascended the river, accompanied by Mr. Kennish, a volunteer, in a piragua, which had to be carried over the various falls abounding at this point, called by our canoemen Point Chepo, some Indians of that tribe having once settled there. Alternately walking along the banks and poling in the canoe, we ascended with some difficulty about 3 miles, when the river became so winding, shallow, and blocked up with fallen trees, etc., that we were obliged to return. We were told that in the month of July we could have ascended two days' journey until we reached its source. Its banks assumed a more perfect form, and the débris collected on the overhanging branches of the trees gave evident signs of the height and rapidity with which the stream runs during the floods of the rainy season. On my return to Rancho No. 1, I found all our party equipped and ready for a start, with the exception of the two native volunteers of the previous night; their hearts had failed them, and they remained behind with their countrymen, the huntsmen.

"Mr. Kennish had orders to steer N.N.E., compass in hand, and myself and Mr. Inskip, acting-master, with small axes to mark the trees, the latter carrying also a compass to check Mr. Kennish. Lieut. Moore and Mr. Gordon, mate, measured the road. We left No. 1 Rancho about 2 P.M. on the 20th, and on

"*Wednesday*, 21*st*, we were able to start early, cutting our way through the bush. Halted at a large cuipa-tree, upon which we cut 'Virago,' and commenced measuring with a line, one chain in length, which we continued until we returned south again. Many monkeys were seen, and some shot; they made a savoury meal for our guides.

"Not far from Virago tree we discovered the remains of a well, and near it several pieces of earthenware jars, etc., said by our Indian interpreter to be the work of some Indians. Encamped this night at Rancho No. 3, estimating our distance at nearly 3½ miles from the boats.

"*Thursday*, 22*nd*.—At our first halt a native climbed a tree, whence he saw over the dense forest 'a white space like a river, but no hills.'

"The largest watercourse we crossed to-day, with but little water in it. All the guides, with Pedro (interpreter), exclaimed it was the Lara. Encamped at Rancho No. 4, having travelled over 219 chains, 2¾ miles, at 80 chains to the mile. While the rancho was being built, I returned about three-quarters of a mile to examine what I supposed to be a river we had passed on our left hand, but it proved only a small stream. The cutting this day was heavy. As yet we have seen neither snakes, tigers, nor any ferocious animals.

"*Friday, 23rd.*—Our work did not commence as early as usual; the cutting was through thick underwood and stunted shrubs, which made it more difficult to get ahead. The supply of water was less plentiful. Soon after noon a tiger (jaguar) approached very close to us, but quickly made off. Two turkeys were shot. Tracks of the wild hog, and also of a large animal called the tapir, were seen near the streams.

"Encamped for the night at No. 5 Rancho, having progressed 208 chains. From a tree level land was seen ahead, but no mountains.

"*Saturday, 24th.*—We struck on a considerable river flowing S.E., and built our 6th Rancho on its other bank, making this day 249 chains. We here missed the fine leaves of the palm, which appears never to grow in wet, swampy land, but in its place is found another species, with thorns, by no means so useful. A fine deer passed close to me to-day, and many birds of beautiful plumage were seen. Pedro, our Indian interpreter, said Indians came up this river, for he saw bamboo-trees, etc., cut through, which otherwise would have obstructed the passage of a canoe.

"*Sunday, 25th.*—The river we were encamped near, though at present containing but little water, is evidently a rapid stream when the freshes come down. Here we had the first intimation of being in the territory of the Indians of the interior, three shots during the day being distinctly heard to the northwestward, which our natives immediately said were fired by Indian hunters.

"*Monday, 26th.*—Our road lay through low, swampy, unpleasant ground, as on the other side of the river, for about half a mile, then over several streams to undulating ground from 50 to 60 feet high, on which the wood was more open and breeze very pleasant, leaving higher ground sometimes on our left, at others on our right. On the slope of a pleasant hill we encamped for the night at No. 7 Rancho, having gone 185 chains. On the summit of this hill one of the officers climbed part of the way up a tree, and saw a similar hill N.N.E., so that we were crossing over a range of hills varying from 50 to 60 feet high, running in a N.N.E., direction; this being the highest land we have yet been on.

"*Tuesday*, 27*th.*—Some rain fell during the night, but not sufficient to annoy us. Pioneers started first, as usual, passing over the same kind of undulating hilly ground for 36 chains, which brought us to a nice stream running to the eastward. Here we fell in with the certain tracks of Indians for the first time, pronounced by Pedro to be the bare feet of men, a child or children, and a dog, both towards the east and west; the most recent towards the east. The trees were the finest this day I have yet seen, and well grown; the mahogany, fustic, caoutchouc, and the tree of which the natives make their canoes, most abundant. We met also the wild lime, which quite perfumed the air; also several most brilliant flowers of the fuchsia kind. At the foot of the last of the hills, 125 chains from our starting-place to-day, we came to the largest river we have yet seen, running pretty rapidly to the eastward, two feet deep. It had more water in it than at our 6th rancho, though its bed was not near so deep. After crossing this, the ground became swampy, the road was soft, and the day far advanced, so that after crossing three other streams flowing eastward, the palm disappearing, and our way becoming more swampy as we proceeded, we determined not to attempt to cross it that night. After a slight examination we therefore retraced our steps to the first high ground, which was across the largest river; turning a short distance off the road, we selected a rising ground and, though nearly dark, by the united exertions of all hands, we soon had a rancho built, No. 8; distant from No. 7, 125 chains.

"*Wednesday*, 28*th.*—George Julier and an officer ascended a tree this morning. From the summit of the hill, near our rancho, the former reported a mountain and a range of hills across our path, apparently about six miles off, with a few small risings of the ground between them and us. He also saw a gap in the range away to the right, bearing about E. The latter reports 'hills running in a direction about W. by N. ½ N., and E. by S. ½ S.' Those to the right of our N.N.E. course seemed the highest, and the nearest about six miles distant; those ahead about eight miles; those to the left further off, and not so high; saw what he thought was a gap, bearing about N.; could not see the gap. Julier spoke of the foliage of the tree he was in, shutting out the view in that direction.

"The pioneers started alone this morning, as it was thought most prudent to find a road through the swamp, before bringing up the provisions, etc. On we went, compass in hand, cheerfully retracing our steps of yesterday, in hopes of overcoming the difficulty we had met in the soft black swamp about three-quarters of a mile distant. Steering the same course, N.N.E., we pushed through, sometimes knee-deep in water, at others nearly the same in black mud, but in a swamp with rather a hard bottom; this, together with the fact of trees growing in it, without brush or underwood, gave us hopes it would not continue.

"Three hundred yards of this disagreeable travelling brought us at last to *terra firma:* the heavy cutting commenced, and we advanced on level ground, nearly half a mile, when we once again found the palm and other dry-soil shrubs and trees; monkeys also began to chatter, and we, in high spirits, hastened on to reach the Cordilleras. The falling sun, however, reminded us it was time to rejoin our shipmates, who were waiting anxiously at No. 8 Rancho. We arrived about five o'clock, having advanced our road about a mile beyond the swamp. This day we again fell in with the tracks of the Indians,—their marks cut on a tree, but not recent, apparently intended to mark a spot we called the Tiger's Den, an open space of about ½ an acre, thickly covered with a species of wild grass. This space we supposed had some time or other been cleared for the cultivation of maize or other Indian food. Here, too, we saw the clear sky for the first time since leaving the boats,—11 days,—so dense was the forest we had cut our way through.

"*Thursday, 29th.*—Some were employed throwing a bridge across the river, improving the road, etc.; others measuring the height of the adjoining hill and tree whence Julier observed the surrounding country: while the remainder accompanied me to reconnoitre the banks of the river; following its course in a S.E. direction for about a quarter of a mile, we came upon a rancho. There were some marks of a canoe having ascended the river as high as this hut during the summer season, but only an Indian eye could detect them.

"Mr. Inskip, with a party of our native guides, was this afternoon occupied in throwing bridges across the streams, and otherwise improving the road already cut before us.

"*Friday, 30th.*—The pioneering party left early, to continue our road-cutting; the remainder had directions to join us as soon as the petty officer and his party returned with provisions. Retracing our steps, we soon reached the point we had left off at on the 28th; from No. 8 to the swamp, 1¼ mile; distance across swamp, ¼ mile; length of road cut beyond, ½ mile. The nature of the forest became quite changed: instead of the small underwood, we came on almost impenetrable thickets of the prickly palm or aloe, rather more than six feet in height, through which we with great difficulty cut our way for ¾ of a mile. The total absence of all underwood, together with the thickly spreading roots of large trees, and the rich nature of the soil, made one fancy that the whole of this belt of land had been once under cultivation. At last we came to a small gorge between two hills (that on our right about 30 feet high), through which ran a small mountain-stream, due N. This gave us all great joy, as we at once believed it to be the Caledonia. In its bed we found stones, the streams hitherto met being generally over a bed of soft clay. On the right-hand hill we encamped for the night, making our No. 9 Rancho distant from No. 8, 283 chains.

"*Saturday, 31st.*—Started this morning as usual, the pioneers ahead, in high spirits, believing we had entered the Cordilleras, and that we should soon be rewarded with a sight of the sea, more anxiously looked for by us, than ever was the Pacific by Nuñez Balboa.

"Having reached more undulating ground, we lost the prickly palm which had so delayed our progress, crossing two mountain-streams flowing W.N.W., which evidently joined that of yesterday, then ascending a hill, about 30 feet high, from whose summit, being partially clear of trees, we fancied we saw the sea. Descending the side of the hill covered with large stones, evidently washed by water, we came upon a noble river flowing swiftly towards the E.S.E., so suddenly that the foremost woodcutter almost fell into it; another certain proof of the density of this forest. This discovery, however, quite puzzled me: the size of the river, 100 feet broad, apparently too deep to ford even at this time of the year; the rapidity of its current, nearly 3 miles an hour; with its fine banks, plantations of bananas and plantains, were all certain signs of its being the Chuqunaque, which, by the Spanish charts and other public maps, we ought to have left some distance to the eastward, steering the course we had done from the Savana.

"We pushed on towards the westward, along the banks of the river, to a more open space, distant 10 chains, where there was evidently a ford. Here we determined to build our 10th rancho; but, being early in the day, we followed on another quarter of a mile, hoping to meet some huts or a village, but without success. We returned to our first halting-place on the river, and encamped for the night at No. 10.

"*Sunday, January 1st*, 1854.—By measured distance we had advanced nearly 20 miles in a straight line from our point of starting on the Savana, near La Villa. If former reports are to be relied on, this must place us only a short distance from Port Escoces. Still, knowing the difficulties we had to contend with, I hesitated to give the order to go forward, until the return of a party sent in search of the Indians. To accomplish the examination of the country on the other side of the river, our pioneers crossed early by the ford, not more than two feet deep, cutting our way through a plantation of bananas and plantains, which were growing wild.

"Crossing several steep but small quebradas and broken ground, cut up by small streams emptying themselves into the main river, we reached the foot of a hill about 80 feet high, covered with fine timber, over which we crossed; then a steep descent to a mountain-torrent or small river, flowing N.W., another tributary, and a very considerable one in the rainy season. Reaching the summit of another hill, about 120 feet high, the view became rather open and clear towards the N.W.; turned in that direction, and while resting sent our native guide, Maria, up a high tree on the brow of the hill. He reported a distant view of the sea to the N.W., with hills on his right, and the river we had left in the morning winding its course from the westward, as far as he could see. In consequence of this report we altered our course to N.W.; descending steeply the other side of the hill we had just mounted; crossed several mountain-streams in the same direction, and reached a high point whence, from the highest tree, we discovered a river at its foot, with a rapid descent leading to it, and found it about 90 feet broad, flowing from N.N.E. to S.S.W., along a valley 105 chains distant from No. 10 Rancho.

"The day being far advanced, we thought it prudent to retrace our steps, and reached No. 10 a little before sunset. Messrs. Inskip and Gordon had returned without having fallen in with Indians, having followed the course of the river 3½ miles, which they found to continue its north-westerly direction, varying but little in size, depth, and strength of current. Its banks were steep and precipitous, and at least 300 feet high.

"From the nature of the country we had passed over this day it was agreed that each officer and man should carry his own four days' provisions, and that the remaining provisions, with all unnecessary clothing, stores, etc., should be left at No. 10 Rancho, as a depôt for the advancing party to fall back upon, in charge of an armed party.

"Having made all necessary arrangements, and given my final instructions to the party to be left in charge of No. 10, we only waited for daylight to cross the river, hoping to see the Atlantic, and return in safety.

"*Monday, 2nd.*—We left early, fifteen in number, including four native guides. We soon reached the beautiful river of yesterday, and followed its course for 80 chains, sometimes in its bed, about knee-deep in water, at others cutting our road along its banks, clothed with fine overhanging trees, until it became tortuous, winding away in a more westerly direction, when we ascended its eastern bank, and cut our road over several small hills with quebradas between them, through which ran a stream towards the main river. Striking this river again, we crossed it, flowing then more easterly. Here we came upon a rancho, being built on the W. bank. Some of the party declared they heard the axe at work, which ceased immediately we approached; 100 yards further along, on the opposite bank, was another Indian hut, but apparently deserted; near it a tree almost chopped through, the marks very fresh. We observed also a curious hole, which appeared to us like a grave; but our native guides said it was made by the conejo, or wild rabbit.

"Continuing our N.N.E. course, we crossed over a high hill, and on our descent struck another river flowing to the N.W. Ascending then along a ridge for 25 chains, we encamped for the night at No. 11 Rancho.

"*Tuesday, 3rd.*—The early part of this day we had climbing enough, crossing several deep ravines, whose steep and slippery sides caused many a tumble. We, however, cut our way through in a N.N.E. direction, and about noon reached the summit of a hill, estimated by us at 800 feet high. Even from here we could see nothing of the surrounding country, so dense was the forest, until George Julier mounted a high tree, when, on his right, or to the eastward, he saw a three-peaked mountain, very distant, and hills in our course not so distant. Not long after this, having descended considerably, we came to a river, flowing N. by W., which cheered us on, concluding it must eventually fall into the Atlantic. We crossed this, having travelled 144 chains from No. 11, and ascending gradually over high undulating ground, we came at last to a spot, whence there was so abrupt a descent, 45 chains from the last river, that we could almost see the surrounding country.

"As sunset was fast approaching, and we were still some distance from water, we had to turn our attention to the selection of a spot for encamping. The descent into the valley beneath was too perpendicular to attempt, so we followed the ridge downwards, 25 chains, which brought us to another river in a most picturesque situation, flowing S.W. Here we built our 12th and last rancho. Total distance measured 26 miles and 14 chains from Rancho No. 1.

"*Wednesday, 4th.*—Although finding ourselves in the centre

of the Cordilleras, and, I believe, within a very few miles of the object of our search, yet having already exceeded the limit of my stay, it became my duty to rejoin the ship without delay—still feeling confident that, had time and our provisions allowed us, we should have eventually reached the Atlantic shores, and that easily, by following one of the several rivers or streams which appear to exist in this range of hills, forming certain passages to the sea.

"We now retraced our steps to the river we had crossed yesterday flowing N. ½ W., and leaving one-half of the party there with directions to build a rancho for the night if we did not return before 2 P.M., we pushed on, following its course to ascertain, as best we could, in what direction it ran; and when we came upon it again, a magnificent sight was before us. Precipitous rocks, causing a fall of at least 150 feet in something less than a quarter of a mile, in which even at this season was a beautiful waterfall and several deep pools, finding their way through, not over, the masses of rock around them; the richly-clothed hills, verdant with the finest forest trees; and, above all, the perfect solitude, perhaps never before broken by civilized man, made us feel ourselves already repaid for our labours. Our guide thought it too precipitous to follow; so we ascended one of its overhanging hills, and from its summit commanded a view tolerably clear towards the S.W., over an apparently level country, but too distant to distinguish its true nature.

"The passage which the river might take towards the N.E. was very indistinct. Descending from this point at a very sharp angle, we came again upon the river, flowing southwesterly, which we followed until it took a turn W.S.W., between hills rising very high on both its banks, when, finding it very difficult to proceed, we returned to the remainder of the party, feeling sure it did not run through the passage we had supposed it did the previous night. Many fine fish were seen in it, which Macao told us were only found near the sea-coast. Having plenty of daylight, we passed on to No. 11, which we found undisturbed, and the fire still burning.

"*Thursday, 5th.*—Started off at early dawn, hoping to reach our depôt, No. 10 Rancho, in good time, to rest and enjoy a fresh and cooked meal, half allowance of pork with biscuit having been our mountain fare. Returned to Rancho No. 10 by our old road without meeting anything worthy of notice, except that in wading through the river as before, we missed our mark for crossing over the hills; and following the stream lower down, it gave evident signs of soon emptying itself into the main river.

"We reached the river Chuqunaque, and crossed it by the same ford, when, arriving at the rancho, to my utter astonishment and dismay I found all the party gone, as well as all our provisions and stores; and there was every appearance of the hut having been ransacked. Our native guides searched in vain for traces of an Indian attack, or even of their footsteps. Rancho No. 9 was soon passed; and in Indian file we came to the swamp, and there plainly distinguished the marks of Indian feet. Still we were undisturbed, and had reached within a quarter of a mile of No. 8 Rancho, when, in taking a short turn in the road, to my horror I came suddenly upon the bodies of three of our shipmates, Thomas Hyde and James Perkins, R.M.A., and Henry Windsor, A.B., lying dead in the pathway.

"At No. 8 Rancho we found the few stores and provisions left there untouched; the Indians had not advanced so far; still we were liable every moment to the same unseen attack, had such been their object. Our only resource appeared to me to push on to the boats by forced marches, taking every precaution as we went along to prevent a surprise. My fears for the safety of those left at Rancho No. 1 were not allayed until we reached No. 6, where we found a day's provisions, letters from the ship, and a note saying a strong party had left that rancho only a few hours previous to our arrival. The moon lighted us to No. 5, where we arrived about eight o'clock.

"*Friday, 6th.*—As soon as we could distinguish the bushes we were on the march towards the boats, which we reached about eleven o'clock, and found all well.

"*Saturday, 7th.*—About two A.M. we reached the ship, much refreshed in body, but sad in heart and spirits. So toilsome was our journey that we spent fifteen days in performing a distance little more than twenty-six miles, having to force our slow and laborious path through forests that seemed to stretch from the Pacific to the Atlantic shores. The trees, of stupendous size, were matted with creepers and parasitical vines, which hung in festoons from tree to tree, forming an almost impenetrable network, and obliging us to hew open a passage with our axes every step we advanced."

Although Captain Prevost and his party did not accomplish their object in reaching the Atlantic, yet for a first attempt it was eminently valuable. Success is rarely, if ever, grasped at once; the fickle goddess requires to be wooed; and, especially in undertakings like that of Captain Prevost's, patience is as requisite a quality as indomitable perseverance; it could hardly be expected that a body of sailors, totally unused to bush-work, should have penetrated even so far as they did. I think, therefore, every one will admit that although success did not crown the efforts of this gallant party, yet such a consummation of their hopes was richly deserved. The loss of life cannot be attributed in the least degree to any indiscretion; it was simply the result of a mistaken notion on the part of the Indians that the men were Spaniards, against whom and their descendants, in common with all the independent aboriginal tribes, the most undying hatred is manifested.

Their course was no doubt too far to the north, and they were unable to rectify this error from their inability to determine the exact position day by day, owing to not having observed for latitude and longitude; for let people say what they like, the compass in some localities, such for instance as that the party was traversing, is as likely as not to deviate, and that too in a manner to defy corrections. Regarding the distance traversed, there is no question about that, for it was accurately measured mile for mile; indeed the whole journey affords a most valuable precedent for future guidance in undertakings of a like nature: when the experience gained will prove of great assistance.

Captain Prevost's party consisted of himself, four officers, two volunteers and servant, eight seamen, and seven Indians, assisted by a midshipman and a boat's crew of twelve men,—total altogether, thirty-six. The above expedition stands alone as the only *real* effort sanctioned by the English Government for the purpose of finding a transit route from sea to sea.

It is curious to reflect how studiously we naval men are taught "how *not* to do it;" for example, during the surveying service of the 'Herald'* throughout the Bay of Panama and in its vicinity, many opportunities occurred of exploring the land intervening between us and the Atlantic, and I can personally testify that there would have been no lack of volunteers. I remember once, when the Alcalde of Cupica told us that the canal of Raspadura, mentioned by Humboldt as completing the water communication from sea to sea, was still navigable, and that he could point out favourable localities over which he thought a great canal could be constructed, how anxious we were to make an exploration of the country; but our captain was far too careful an officer to risk going beyond his instructions, and therefore all our energies were directed to the survey of the coast-line,

* See, for further information, Dr. Seemann's 'Voyage of the Herald,' vol. i. pp. 221–8.

much, it appears, to the chagrin of Mr. Lionel Gisborne, who says in his book, 'Darien in 1852,' how glad he would have been of some information regarding the magnificent Gulf of San Miguel, but that the tracings of Captain Kellett's surveys lent by the Admiralty did not conduct him beyond the entrance.

I have been thus particular in noticing all the features and inserting all the remarks on this part of the Central American Isthmus, Darien, because it is *the only* locality towards which English efforts(!) have been *officially* directed. It is painful to think how other nations must have laughed at the noisy squabbles and indecision which have characterized our transit attempt. The only silver lining to the cloud is the journey of Commander Prevost, which plainly shows what might have been done by an organized system of research.

CHAPTER X.

CANAL BY THE RIVER ATRATO.—PASSAGE OF A CANOE FROM OCEAN TO OCEAN.—FAILURE IN LONDON TO FORM A CANAL COMPANY.—MR. KELLEY'S PROJECT.—DIFFERENCE OF LEVEL BETWEEN THE TWO OCEANS. —LETTER FROM ALEXANDER VON HUMBOLDT.—APATHY ABOUT TRANSIT IS DANGEROUS TO COMMERCE AND FREEDOM.—PRESENT FRENCH EFFORTS.

THE remaining projects take one starting-point, namely, the river Atrato, which is ascended for some distance and then quitted for one of its affluents, the Naipipi or Truando for example, whence it is proposed to cut a canal to Cupica Bay or Kelley's Inlet, near the Bay of Panama. Other projectors prefer continuing along the Atrato until its shallows are reached, and thence cutting a canal to the deep waters of the San Juan, which empties itself into the Pacific at Point Chirambira. This last was Humboldt's favourite project, and this is the point where the passage from sea to sea has actually been made, as described by him in his 'Travels.' It appears that the *padre* of the district in 1788 induced his Indian converts to cut a trench between the head waters of the San Juan and the upper stream of the Atrato through the ravine De la Raspadura, and that he actually passed from ocean to ocean in a canoe during the rainy season. The cut is about three miles in length and has been neglected of late years; but I was informed by the Alcalde of the place, when I was surveying about Cupica in 1847, that he had himself paddled through the cut. The total distance from sea to sea, from the mouth of the San Juan to the mouth of the Atrato, is about 225 miles.

As regards the shorter route, in 1845 an attempt was made in London to form a company to promote this undertaking, and in the prospectus they then issued the localities are thus described:—"The entrance, on the Atlantic side, will be from the Gulf of Darien, by the great river Atrato. This river runs inland, almost due south, for 52 miles, to its confluence with the river Naipipi, which branches off to the westward for 35 miles. Here it is proposed to cut a canal, the length of which will only require to be about 5 miles, to the river Cupica or Tupica, which runs westwardly for 13 miles, to the port of Cupica on the Pacific side; the total distance will be 105 miles, of which 100 miles will be river navigation."

"It is well known that the rivers Atrato and Cupica are navigable for vessels of considerable burden, almost their entire distance; as also the river Naipipi. With the aid of powerful steam-dredging machines, therefore, they will be rendered navigable for vessels of the largest dimensions."

The promoters of this company failed to obtain the concessions they solicited from the New Granadian Government, and therefore the effort fell to the ground.

At a later date (1854–5) an American gentleman, named Kelley, entered warmly into this matter, and spent large sums of money in regular surveys and explorations. As Mr. Kelley's efforts at canalization have been most systematically carried out, and his surveys and estimates contain some sound information, a few extracts are inserted in this place.

"The line will proceed direct south from the Bay of Candelaria, up the Atrato to its junction with the Truando, lat. 7° 15′ N., and long. 77° 8′ 32″ W.,—a distance of 67 miles 1436 yards,—whence it will diverge by the Truando to the south-west, and terminate at Kelley's Inlet, lat. 6° 57′ 32″ N., and long. 78° W.,—a distance of 63 miles 1216 yards. It will thus have a total length of 131 miles 892 yards from sand-bar to sand-bar, with a minimum width and depth throughout, of 200 feet and 30 feet respectively.

"The difference in the height of the tides at the two extremities of the proposed route, has been ascertained to be, at the entrance of Kelley's Inlet in the Pacific, 12 feet 6 inches at spring-tides and 10 feet 11 inches at neap-tides; while the tidal rise at the mouth of the Atrato never exceeds 2 feet at any phase of the moon."

Colonel Lloyd estimated the mean level of the Pacific at 3·52 feet above that of the Atlantic; and more cently, M. Garella fixed it at 9·54 feet. Now, from a series of careful observations made in 1855 by Colonel Totten, the engineer of the Panama Railway, in Navy Bay, on the Atlantic side, and the Bay of Panama, on the Pacific, it results that the difference, if any, is exceedingly trifling. Colonel Totten says in his Report, "Although my observations make the mean level of the Pacific from 0·14 to 0·75 feet higher than the mean level of the Atlantic, this is probably owing to local circumstances alone. We may therefore state that there is no difference between the mean levels of the two oceans."

The winds are periodical, blowing from the south from March to September, and from the north from September to March. During the whole year it is calm from six P.M. to ten A.M., when a light wind breeze begins, which increases to a breeze at noon, and gradually dies away.

A Summary of the Estimated Cost of the Canal and Appurtenances.

Works at the mouth of the Atrato	$50,800
Excavations under water in the Truando	1,360,000
Excavations at the confluence of the Truando and Canal, including coffer-dams and pumping	40,000
Excavations between confluence, as above, and Pacific (excepting tunnel). The quantities are all called rock; the excess by these measures being allowed, for grubbing and clearing, at $⅞ per cubic yard	77,883,994
Tunnel at $2, being $10 for heading, etc.	25,403,840
Harbour and Kelley's Inlet	150,000
Lighthouses	35,000
Piers	20,000
Depôts (Pacific)	50,000
Depôts and hospitals on line	35,000
Depôt and hospital, Townsend's Junction	15,000
Depôt at Turbo, and improvements necessary	70,000
Executive department, twelve years	180,000
Engineering department	562,000
Medical department	120,000
Pay department	140,000
Commissary department	260,000
Quartermaster's department	150,000
Supplies for ditto	550,000
Twenty-five pumping and hoisting engines, for the work in the great cut	1,250,000
Contingencies, 25 per cent.	27,081,408
	$135,407,042
If the rock is estimated at $1, this would be, with contingent allowance, about extra	10,000,000
Say, £30,000,00	$145,407,042

The following letter from the great Humboldt to Mr. Kelley on this his favourite point for the junction of the two oceans, cannot fail to be read with interest.

(*Translation.*)

"It is with the deepest satisfaction, Sir, that I made myself acquainted, during your too short stay in Berlin, with the sound and extensive series of measurements and levels which, by your direction, have been executed, since the beginning of January, 1855, upon the course of the great Rio Atrato and its affluents on the west, by an able engineer, Mr. William Kennish. This survey and those previously undertaken by your orders, and to which my learned friend Mr. Alexander Bache, Superintendent of the Coast Survey of the United States, had already drawn my attention, are so much the more deserving of regard, since you purpose to have examined with the same precision the pass from the port of Cupica to the Rio Naîpi (Naipipi), and the points situated above the mouth of the Truando, which are all very important in the solution of the vast problem of an oceanic canal.

"The great number of charts and sections on a large scale in your possession, furnish all the elements necessary for judging of the possibility of establishing a communication between the two oceans, by the mouths of the Atrato, the Rio Truando, and a canal leading to the Pacific Ocean. It was on account of his not having made so thorough an examination of the mountainous country between the Gulf of San Miguel and Caledonia Bay, that Mr. Lionel Gisborne's plan of 1852 could not be carried out. The ignorance he was in as to the localities, and the absence of measurements of altitude, led to the unfortunate issue of the courageous expedition of Lieutenant Isaac Strain.

"The great object to be attained is, in my opinion, a canal which would unite the two oceans, without locks and without tunnels. When the plans and sections can be placed before the public, a free and open discussion will elucidate the advantages and disadvantages of each locality; and the execution of this important work, which interests the civilized nations of the two continents, will be entrusted to engineers who have successfully distinguished themselves in similar enterprises. The Junction Company will find subscribers among those governments and citizens who, yielding to a noble impulse, will take pride in the idea of having contributed towards the execution of a work worthy of the intellectual progress of the nineteenth century. More than fifty years ago I earnestly expressed the same opinion, and I have incessantly laboured in the propagation of those geographical views which tend to prove the practicability of establishing commercial communications, either by canals, (with or without either stop-gates or locks), or by means of railroads uniting opposite coasts, and rivers flowing in contrary directions.

"I was the means of obtaining, through General Bolivar, the exact geodesic survey of the Isthmus of Panama, and I was the first, from information found in the archives of the Viceroyalty of Mexico, to lay down in my Mexican atlas the course of the two rivers, the Huasacualco and the Chimalapa. I pointed out the proximity of the almost unknown port of Cupica to the sources of the Rio Naîpi and to the waters of the Atrato, and also the existence, with which Europe was unacquainted, of a very small navigable canal, 'excavated' in 1788, under the superintendence of a monk, the priest of Novita, by the Indians of his parish, in order to unite the waters of the Rio de la Raspadura, an affluent of the Rio de Quito (Quibdo), to the waters of the Rio de San Juan de Chirambira.

"I think nothing more dangerous to the extension of commerce and to the freedom of international relations, than to inspire an aversion to all future investigation by an absolute and imperious declaration, that all hope of an oceanic canal must now be abandoned. I expressly described, in my 'Political Essay on New Spain,' (compare vol. i. pp. 202–248, with vol. ii. pp. 95–145, 2nd edition,) the immense work of cutting through the mountains an open channel for the Desague of Huehuetoca, which was executed by the Spanish Government at the beginning of the seventeenth century, and I have too much faith in the powerful means afforded by the present state of civilization, to be yet discouraged.

"The important communications for which I am indebted to the courtesy of Colonel Augustus Codazzi, and to the exceeding kindness of M. Pastor Ospina, Minister of the Interior at Bogotá, have made me fully aware, that the line from Cupica to the Rio Naîpi presents a series of elevations; in directing this passage to be levelled, you will therefore be rendering a further service to geography. Captain Robert Fitzroy, R.N., whose name is justly renowned among navigators, in his 'Memoir on the Isthmus of Central America,' says: 'Of all the comparatively well-known routes, it has been shown, that the Atrato and the Cupica line seems the most suitable for a canal, and the Panama route for a railway. The officer who recently surveyed Cupica (Lieut. Wood, R.N.) states, with respect to the land between it and the Naîpi, that he set out one morning from Cupica at eight o'clock, walked with native guides to the Naîpi, bathed in the stream, and reached his ship (the 'Pandora') at noon.'* The most elevated ground was, in his judgment, 300 to 400 feet. (Journal of the Royal Geogr. Soc., vol. xx., 1850, part ii. p. 178.)

"Receive, my dear Sir, etc.,

(Signed) "ALEXANDER VON HUMBOLDT.

"Berlin, January 27, 1856."

Finally, it appears that at this moment certain French gentlemen have taken up afresh the idea of a canal from Caledonia Bay to the Gulf of San Miguel. Two expeditions have already been sent out, headed by the engineers Messrs. Bourdiol and De Champeville, and the geologist M. De Puydl. The second expedition was accompanied by the Abbé Amodru, who, it appears,

* The following quotation from Dr. Seemann's official Narrative of the Voyage of H.M.S. Herald, as I well remember, clearly expresses the feeling on board that ship at the time :—

"Captain Kellett and Lieutenant-Commander Wood . . . after walking several hours, came to a river, which they *supposed* or were told flowed into the Atlantic; if such was really the case, it might afford facilities for constructing a canal. . . . Captain Kellett never spoke on the subject, probably because he was not certain whether the river reached actually flowed into the Atrato; and that portion of his journal relating to Darien is unfortunately wanting. . . . The land around the Bay of Cupica is hilly; but how far in the interior the country has the same character we had no means of ascertaining."—Vol. i. p. 221.

was well received by the Indians, a number of whom brought to him their children for baptism. The accounts of a practicable passage were so encouraging that a third expedition is in course of preparation, which, like the others, is to enjoy the protection of a French man-of-war.*

* *Vide* Proceedings of the Royal Geographical Society, vol. vi. no. 111; Pim's 'Central American Transit Route,' p. 77.

CHAPTER XI.

PANAMA RAILWAY.—PRELIMINARY EFFORTS.—THE NEW-GRANADIAN CHARTER.—MAKING THE RAILWAY.—THE COMPANY CHARGES WHAT IT LIKES.—CONCESSION OF LAND.—THE COMPANY'S I O U.—THE HALF-WAY BRIDGE.—CHEAP YET EFFICIENT WORKING OF THE LINE.—EXORBITANT RAILWAY FARES.—PROFITS.—PANAMA AND ASPINWALL.—COLONEL AND MRS. TOTTEN.

If all the schemes of canalization have failed, this has not been the case with railway projects. The Isthmus of Panama has been successfully spanned by the iron road, and the locomotive now makes its daily journey from sea to sea, through the primæval forest.

I have seen some of the greatest engineering works of the day,—for example, the railroad over the Sœmmering, and the Dom Pedro Secundo line at Rio Janeiro,—but I must confess that when passing backwards and forwards on the Panama Railway, standing on the engine to obtain a good view, I have never been more struck than with the evidence, apparent on every side, of the wonderful skill, endurance, and perseverance, which must have been exercised in its construction.

In 1848, three American merchants, Messrs. Stephens, Aspinwall, and Chauncey, turned their attention to the Isthmus of Panama, with a view to constructing a railway across it. The former of these gentlemen, well known in the scientific world for his writings on Central America, devoted himself to a preliminary exploration, and proved the feasibility of the project. Having satisfied himself of this fact, he returned to his partners, and they conjointly entered into a formal contract with the Government of New Granada, for the *exclusive* privilege of constructing a railway across the Isthmus. The following extracts give the main features of this contract:—

Extracts from a Contract for the Privilege of constructing an Iron Railroad from one Ocean to the other, by the Isthmus of Panama.

"Article 1.—The Government of New Granada concedes to the Company styled the 'Panama Railroad Company,' their representatives or assigns, the exclusive privilege of establishing an Iron Railroad between the two oceans, across the Isthmus of Panama.

"Art. 2.—The privilege conceded to the Company by the preceding Article, to establish an Iron Railroad, shall continue forty-nine years, counting from the day of the completion of the road and its being opened to public use. Nevertheless, said privilege shall terminate before the expiration of the said forty-nine years, if before their expiration the Government shall have redeemed the privilege by virtue of the right and power reserved in the following terms:—

"At the expiration of twenty years, counting from the day in which the Railroad shall have been completed and opened to public use, the Government may redeem the privilege for the benefit of New Granada, by the sum of five millions of dollars, to be paid as the whole amount of the indemnification. If the privilege should not be redeemed at that date, it shall continue in force ten years still longer, at the end of which the Government may redeem it, by paying two millions of dollars.

"In order that the Government may avail itself of the right thus reserved to it of redeeming the privilege, it shall notify the

Company of its intention to redeem it at least one year before the day of the expiration of either of the three periods above expressed.

"Art. 3.—The sum to be paid to the Company for the redemption of the privilege in either of the three cases mentioned in the preceding Article, *is to be in specie*, in American dollars, without any reduction, it being well understood, that in all other cases in which mention is made of dollars in this contract, it is of American dollars, without any deduction.

"Art. 4.—The Company shall, after the redemption of the privilege, remain in possession of the lands conceded to it gratuitously and perpetually by the eighteenth Article of this Contract.

"Art. 5.—The Railroad from ocean to ocean shall be completed within six years, counting from the expiration of four months after the present act of concession shall have been approved by the Congress of the Republic; and the fact of its completion shall be verified before the Governor of Panama, on the request of the Company, by a statement drawn up on both sides, after discussion between it and the agent or agents of the Executive Power, commissioned to that effect.

"Art. 6.—During the time of the continuance of the exclusive privilege conceded to the Company, or persons engaged in the enterprise, for the establishment of the Iron Railroad from one ocean to the other, *the Government of the Republic engages neither itself to make nor to grant to any other Company whatever, under any title whatever, the power to establish another Iron Railroad on the Isthmus of Panama*; and it is equally stipulated, that during the period of the existence of the said privilege, the New-Granadian Government shall have no power to undertake, itself, nor to permit any other person to undertake, without the accord and consent of said Company, the opening of any *maritime canal* which may communicate with the two oceans, across the said Isthmus of Panama.

"Art. 9.—The exclusive privilege is also granted to the Company for forty-nine years:—

"1st. To use the ports situated at the two extremities of the Railroad, required for the anchorage of vessels, and for the landing and shipping of goods which are to pass over the said road.

"2nd. To use the ports situated at the two extremities, and for the free deposit of all effects and merchandise admitted for transit across the Isthmus by means of the Railroad established by the Company. In virtue of said privilege, the Company *may levy such duties of transit, warehouse, and toll*, as it may judge proper to establish, in compensation for the use of the lines of communication, the means of transportation, the ports, passages, warehouses, and establishments of all kinds belonging to it.

"Art. 15.—In consideration of the difficulties of the enterprise, and of the direct and indirect advantages which the Republic is to derive from it, various concessions of land are made to the Company, on the continental part of the Isthmus, comprised within the limits which the provinces of Panama and Veraguas had, on the first day of January, 1819. The Government of the Republic concedes therefore, gratuitously, to the Company, in the terms expressed in this Article:—

"1st. The lands which may be necessary for the establishment of the line of Railroad in its whole extent.

"2nd. All the lands which it may require for the establishment of ports and places for landing and embarking, dry docks, places for lighterage, warehouses, stations, inns, and, in general, for all the necessary purposes of the construction and service of the Railroad.

"Art. 16.—Although according to what is expressed in the preceding Article, the Company has no right to vacant lands on the islands adjacent to the Isthmus of Panama, the Government nevertheless binds itself to concede to the Company all the vacant land which may be on the island of Manzanillo, in the Bay of Limon, provided the Company consider it proper to extend the work of the Railroad to said island, so that one of the extremities terminate on it.

"Art. 18.—Concession is moreover made to the Company gratuitously, and in perpetuity, of one hundred thousand fanegadas of vacant land in the provinces of Panama and Veraguas, within the limits indicated in the first part of the fifteenth Article, which may be increased to one hundred and fifty thousand, if such extent be found disposable in the two provinces above mentioned, so that the Government can pronounce them vacant; and the Company shall have liberty to select them, in the continental portion of those provinces, wheresoever it may judge most proper, it being stipulated, however, that wheresoever they may be selected on the line of the road, or in its vicinity, intervals shall be exactly left, in which the Government of the Republic may make concessions or sales of land for other establishments, such as it may choose to form on said line and its vicinity. The hundred thousand fanegadas of land, or any other extent less than a hundred and fifty thousand fanegadas, which may be found disposable as vacant, and thus granted to the Company, may be used for encampment for workmen, fields for cultivation, pastures for beasts of burden and cattle, or for cutting wood from them for the construction of the road, or for fuel; and in general, for establishments of any kind facilitating industrial operations undertaken by the Company, especially those tending to colonization.

"Art. 19.—The vacant lands which are granted to the Company by the eighteenth Article of the present Contract are given to it in full ownership; and the Company may dispose of them freely during the period of the privilege, and after the termination of said period, or of the redemption of the said privilege.

"Art. 30.—The Executive Power shall at all times determine what foreign nations may be permitted to transport their correspondence across the Isthmus of Panama by the Railroad; but in all cases in which the mails of foreign nations are permitted to pass by the Isthmus of Panama, all the contracts or pecuniary arrangements for their transportation by the said Railroad shall be made by the Company, and all the pecuniary proceeds of such contracts and arrangements shall go into the funds of the Company as a branch of its profits. In compensation for this privilege, the Company obliges itself to transport by the Railroad, free of charge, all the mails of New Granada, and moreover, to pay to the Government of the Republic five per cent. on all the sums of money which it may receive in virtue of said contracts and arrangements, whether such sums proceed from contracts which the Company may enter into with foreign governments, or from the general regulations which it may establish for the carrying of the correspondence of nations which may not have entered into special contracts with it.

"And it is also stipulated:—1. That whatever may be the profit which the Company may receive by virtue of such contracts and arrangements, in no case shall it on this account pay to the Government of New Granada less than $10,000 per annum. 2. That this payment shall be over and above the three per cent. of the net profit of the enterprise to which New Granada is entitled; and 3. That the power of the Company to enter into such contracts or pecuniary regulations shall not be opposed in any manner to the contracts or arrangements which now exist between the Republic of New Granada and any foreign nation or nations for the transportation of mails on the Isthmus of Panama.

"Art. 35.—Foreigners who may form establishments on the vacant lands conceded gratuitously to the Company shall be exempt from all forced contributions, and from tithes, on the interior consumption of their productions, during the space of twenty years from the date of the formation of such establishments. They shall be entitled to letters of naturalization, so soon as they solicit them, provided they fix their residence in the territory of the Republic; they shall be exempted from military service during the twenty years after the formation of their establishments; and they shall not be required to serve in the army, except in case of invasion of the country by a foreign nation.

"Art. 51.—In the collection of the duties and costs of transportation fixed by itself, the Company engages to effect always with care, punctuality, and celerity, and without exception as to national character, the transportation of travellers, cattle, goods, merchandise, and materials of all kinds which may be confided to it, all of which shall be transported without any diminution of tariff prices, except such as it may allow in favour of nations which are now bound or which may hereafter become bound, by means of public treaties entered into with New Granada, to guarantee positively and efficaciously to this Republic its rights of sovereignty and ownership over the territory of the

Isthmus of Panama and the perfect neutrality of said Isthmus, to the end that the free transit from one sea to the other may never be interrupted or embarrassed; but notice is expressly given, and in effect it is here especially stipulated, that New Granada, Granadians, and their property, shall enjoy all the benefits and advantages which any other nation whatever may obtain by virtue of the provision in this Article.

"Art. 55.—The Company engages to pay to the Republic of New Granada three per cent. annually of the net profits of the enterprise, in the same proportion in which they are distributed in form of dividends to the shareholders, without however bringing into the account, in payment of the said three per cent., any deduction for the general advantage of the capital of the association, or for any sum which the shareholders may desire for a reserve or sinking-fund. It is stipulated that, for the recovery of this duty, the Government of New Granada shall, as well as the shareholders of the enterprise, look to the accounts produced and liquidated in the general assembly of the Company, which accounts the agent of the Republic is to examine, and he may make observations with regard to them in the same manner as any shareholder; but he is to have no power of interfering in the administration of the Company. Besides what is stipulated in the present Article, it is also agreed that the payment of the said duty of three per cent. shall be made at Bogotá, Panama, or New York, according to the order of the Government of the Republic.

"Art. 57.—The present privilege cannot be ceded or transferred to any foreign government, that is, to any government existing out of the New-Granadian territory, under pain of forfeiture of the privilege by the mere act of attempting or carrying into effect such cession or transfer; and although it may be attempted or carried into effect, it will be and from this time is declared absolutely null, and of no force or effect.

"Art. 61.—All the legislative acts, decrees, and agreements, by which, in former years, various privileges have been conceded for the opening of the intermarine communication by the Isthmus of Panama, are irrevocably annulled. Consequently, only the Panama Railroad Company has the right and the obligation to construct a railroad from one ocean to the other, by the said Isthmus, in conformity with the stipulations of the present Contract, which is the only one which remains in force on the subject, between the Government of the Republic and said Company; since, by this clause, not only all the acts, decrees, and agreements above mentioned, but especially all the contracts and stipulations which formerly existed between the said Government and the said Company, or the individuals in whose rights it has been substituted, are annulled.

"Art. 62.—The present Contract, divided into two chapters, and extending to sixty-two articles, shall be submitted to the approbation of the Executive Power of the Republic, and that being obtained, shall be presented by him to Congress; the consent and approbation of which are required, in order that, receiving the force of a law, it may be carried into effect. In faith of which, the Commissioners on either side, that is to say, Victoriano de Diego Paredes, in the name and under the especial authority of the Government of the Republic, and John Lloyd Stevens, as Vice-President and General Commissioner of the Panama Railroad Company, in the name and by the especial authority of the said Company, have prepared two copies of the present Contract, both of the same tenor and form; and in evidence thereof, they sign and seal them with their respective seals, in Bogotá, the fifteenth day of the month of April, in the year of our Lord one thousand eight hundred and fifty."

Pending the ratification of this contract a company was formed at New York. A large and experienced party of engineers had been sent down, early in 1849, to make a complete survey, and soon after triumphantly announced the entire practicability of the project. The Pacific terminus was selected a little to the eastward of the city of Panama, quite clear of the suburbs, and the Atlantic at Navy Bay, sometimes called Colon, but now named Aspinwall, after one of the chief promoters of the Company.

The work commenced in January, 1850, and was finished on the 28th of January, 1855, having occupied five years in completing. The nature of the country through which the line of road had to be carried, was calculated to strike the hardiest speculator with dismay. The first thirteen miles from the Atlantic led through deep swamps covered with jungle, full of reptiles and venomous insects.* Further on, the line ran through a rugged country, over rapid rivers, and all sorts of impediments, and after passing the summit descended rapidly to the Pacific. The climate also was sultry, beyond almost any other part of the world, while, during the wet season, the rains descended in a perfect deluge; moreover, to crown all, the resources of the country were found to be *nil*, or nearly so, and consequently everything, especially labour, had to be imported. Despite all these obstacles, the undertaking was commenced, and, under the able superintendence of Colonel G. M. Totten, one of the boldest and grandest enterprises of modern times successfully completed.

The total length of the road is 47 miles 3020 feet; it runs on the right or easterly bank of the Chagres, as far as Barbacoas, where it crosses the river by a bridge 625 feet in length, 18 feet in breadth, and 40 feet above the mean level of the river, This bridge is of wrought iron, and is exactly midway between Aspinwall and Pa-

* "In all muddy places, down to the verge of the ocean, are impenetrable thickets, formed of mangroves, chiefly rhizophoras and avicennias, which exhale putrid miasmata. . . . Myriads of mosquitoes and sandflies fill the air, while huge alligators sun themselves on the slimy soil. . . . To destroy these dreaded swamps is almost impossible."—*Seemann's Voyage of H.M.S. Herald.*

THE BRIDGE OVER THE CHAGRES

Vincent Brooks lith

nama; and it is not a little singular that the bridge thrown across the Nile between Alexandria and Cairo is also exactly halfway; in other words, both the great isthmus transits of the world are intersected at half their length by a large river. The Barbacoas bridge is of six spans, built of boiler iron, with a top and bottom chord two feet in breadth and one inch in thickness, joined by a web of boiler iron nine feet in height at the centre, and seven at the ends. The rails are laid on iron floor-girders, three feet apart, and the whole structure is supported by five piers and two abutments twenty-six feet wide and eight feet in thickness, increasing in the proportion of an inch to the foot down to their foundations, which are constructed of piles and concrete.

The highest point of the line is 37¾ miles from the Atlantic, and is 263 feet above the mean level of that ocean. The maximum grade on the Atlantic slope is one in ninety; on the Pacific descent it is rather more, viz. one in eighty-eight.

Of the road 23⅞ miles are level, and 28⅝ straight, but there are some very abrupt curves. There are no less than 134 culverts, drains, and bridges of 10 feet and under, and as many as 170 bridges from 12 feet span to 625 feet span.

The line is only a single one, but there are four very commodious sidings, viz. one at Gatun, 7½ miles from Aspinwall, one near Barbacoas, 22 miles, one at Matachin, 30 miles, and one at the summit, 37 miles.

Experience has proved that there is no difficulty in keeping the line in order at a reasonable expense, but, on the contrary, that it continues in better condition than similar works in northern latitudes, where the climate appears to have a more injurious effect than within the tropics.

Stations occur every four miles; the house is the residence of the track-master, who, with ten labourers, has charge of the intervening mileage. The road is kept in perfect order by these men. There are twelve track-masters and 120 labourers in the employ of the company, solely to look after the security of the line. Their wages are—track-masters, three dollars per diem; labourers, sixty cents.

The staff of the company is not very extensive; the civil engineers, with their assistants and managing clerks, constituting the greatest expense. The strictest economy consistent with efficiency is practised: for example, there is an excellent locomotive shop at Aspinwall, in which the engineers and stokers, when not at work on the railroad, are employed; and it is said that the business done in effecting the necessary repairs for steamers calling at the Bay almost supports the engineering staff and working locomotive expenses of the company.

A substantial telegraph is established between Aspinwall and Panama. There are twenty-six posts to the mile, constructed in the following manner:—a scantling, four inches square, of pitch-pine, is encased in cement, moulded in a cylindrical form, tapering towards the top, and sunk four feet in the ground. I was assured that when once dry these posts would last for ages; the cost of each was five dollars, about £1 sterling.

They have the appearance of hewn stone, and are quite an ornament along the line.

The total expenditure of the Panama Railway Company amounted to 7,407,553 dollars, or rather more than £1,500,000 sterling, which is very nearly £32,000 per mile, an expense, by the bye, below the average of our English lines, which is £34,638 per mile. Very few undertakings have paid better than the Panama Railway. A return of fifteen per cent. to the shareholders is acknowledged, but there is reason to believe that in reality there is a much larger profit; and this is not to be wondered at, when it is remembered that the company have a monopoly of transit, and charge exorbitantly; for example, the passage-money is £5. 4*s.* 2*d.*; children under twelve years of age, half price; under six years, quarter-price. There is only one class, so that each passenger has to pay the same. The transit occupies about four hours, the distance is forty-seven miles and a half, and the fare therefore 2*s.* 2¼*d.* per mile, the most expensive travelling in the world. At the same time the working expenditure is very moderate; the fuel, for instance, is entirely wood, and sufficient for the whole journey there and back is procured for two dollars and a half, or 10*s.* This I can personally testify, having traversed the line both ways on the engine. The charge for freight is on the same high scale as the passenger traffic. Take, for example, live stock: cattle, by passenger train, owner's risk, twenty-five dollars each, the same exactly as a passenger; sheep by passenger train, owner's risk, twelve dollars and a half each, the same as a child under twelve years of age.

Mr. Oliphant's description of the scenery is so good, that I transfer it to these pages at length:—

"When once the deadly swamp is passed, nothing can exceed the beauty of the vegetation through which the line passes. Palm-trees of many varieties weave their broad leaves into thick screens, to shut out the sun; tufts of bamboo are interspersed with heavy trees whose branches support gigantic orchids, and whose stems are concealed amid a mass of purple convolvulus and divers brilliant parasites. To one only accustomed to see a thickly populated and highly cultivated country traversed by railways, and familiar with tropical jungles only when they are penetrated by the devious little paths of the woodcutter or the hunter, this dash through the virgin forest at the tail of a locomotive is very imposing, and presents, with unusual force to the mind, the important change which steam is destined to effect on the face of nature."

The above is a brief description of the *only passage* at present in use across Central America. The outlay for the construction of the road was no doubt very great, and arose partly from the entire novelty of the work (it was the first real tropical railway), and partly from the extreme paucity of labour. Men were brought to the locality in great numbers from China, India, Africa, and almost every nation in Europe, tempted no doubt by the very high rate of wages.

There is no question of the unhealthiness of that portion of the Isthmus over which the railway runs; but of all the labourers the Chinese lost the greatest number; for besides those carried off by disease, a strong suicidal tendency developed itself amongst this singular people, and it was not uncommon in the morning to find half-a-dozen bodies suspended from the trees in close proximity to the road. In spite, however, of every difficulty, the railway was completed in five years; and in spite of the great expense the undertaking has proved by far the most remunerative enterprise of modern times. From the report of the company to the Legislature of New York, it appears that although only in part opened, the road had paid, up to January, 1855, in the form of dividends, fifteen and a half per cent. on its stock, besides the interest on its bonds.

For the year ending January 1st, 1856, it appears from an official statement published by the directors, that the gross earnings of the road were 1,166,552 dollars; expenses, repairs, interest on bonds, etc., 395,345 dollars; leaving a net profit of 771,237 dollars, out of which were paid two semi-annual dividends of six per cent., equal to twelve per cent. for the year, with 133,165 dollars, or three per cent., undivided surplus. The earnings for the year were fifteen per cent., against twelve per cent. estimated.

For the year ending January 1st, 1857, the gross earnings of the road were 1,459,525 dollars; expenses, repairs, interest on bonds, etc., 530,252 dollars; leaving a net profit of 929,273 dollars, out which were paid two semi-annual dividends of six per cent., equal to twelve per cent. for the year, with 344,216 dollars, or about eight per cent., undivided surplus. *The net profits for the year were therefore twenty per cent.*

These earnings, it should be remembered, have been

made on a divided travel; the transit route, *viâ* Nicaragua, carrying very nearly one-half of the passengers between the seas. And moreover it must be borne in mind that the Panama Railway depends upon transit *alone*—I mean passengers and freight passing from ocean to ocean—for its profits, the local traffic and trade not being worth mention, inasmuch as the line does not approach any main road or avenue of commerce; in fact, it runs through the primæval forest throughout its entire length, and is simply a bridge between the Atlantic and the Pacific, and not in any respect a centre towards which the products of the surrounding country naturally flow. In proof of this, I will just enumerate the various abodes of men on the line, and extract from my journal a few remarks on each settlement.

Leaving Aspinwall, we crossed from the island (Manzanilla) to the mainland, if the swamp deserves the name, the connecting link being a solid embankment, with a sluiceway intersecting it. The mangroves appear impenetrable on each side. Gatun is the first settlement; it is seven miles from Aspinwall, and situated on a little stream of the same name, which is close to its confluence with the Chagres, and crossed by a bridge of ninety-seven feet span. A wooden house and a few huts, with a very limited clearing, the population certainly under a hundred, make up Gatun. It used formerly to be a stopping-place for the *bongos*, or native boats, and certainly throve in those days, but the rapidity of the locomotive has taken away the native breath, and the glories of Gatun may be reckoned of the past. Bugio Soldado is another settlement also established on the banks of the Chagres; it is composed of reed and cane huts, and is eight miles beyond Gatun, population about fifty. This place was the favourite residence of J. L. Stephens, the great Central-American traveller, and President of the Railway Company. Then we have Buena Vista. About twenty-five rude huts form the village, which supplies a good proportion of labourers for this part of the line; number of souls say one hundred. Barbacoas is quite a small settlement, numbering about thirty inhabitants; the locality is interesting from the noble bridge which here spans the Rio Chagres, exactly halfway between Panama and Aspinwall, viz. twenty-three miles and three-quarters; and also because "barbacoas" is a general term for Indian suspension bridges, with us a modern invention, but known well to the Asiatics and Americans from time immemorial.

Up to this station the line has been confined to the right bank of the river; it now runs along the left bank for about eight miles, when river and rail separate, one turning northward, the other south-eastward. The next collection of huts is Baila Mona, forty-five inhabitants. Gorgona, a large village, and probably containing three hundred, is fast dwindling away. Then comes Matachin, about one hundred and sixty people. Here the trains pass each other by means of commodious sidings. Near the summit there are the faintest remains of what was once the largest assemblage of habitations on the line; it was called Culebra, and was the railway terminus in 1854, just twelve miles from Panama; the distance required a whole day to overcome, on mules which struggled through the mud like ships labouring in a heavy sea. At Culebra the inhabitants do not number more than forty. Paraiso (Paradise) is the last native village worthy of mention; the huts are just as rude as those on the other side of the summit; the people, I should think, would not exceed, all told, fifty souls. Paraiso is a curious instance of comparative value. I should have been much more inclined to call Sheerness Paradise than the specimen just alluded to.

I have now enumerated the Isthmian settlements: adding to their numbers the men employed as platelayers, etc., it will be seen that the entire population does not exceed 1500. There is not a road in the locality, and only one mule-track from Chorera, skirting as it were the district of Panama. The local traffic and trade therefore may be put down as next to *nil.*

The wide difference between Panama and Aspinwall is very observable; as regards the former, it struck me that it might perhaps be a shade cleaner than when last visited ten years before, but in a commercial point of view it can scarcely be said to have improved at all; the same indolence still prevails, houses and public buildings are falling to decay, and all the enterprise so characteristic of olden times appears to have departed. This may probably be accounted for by the fact mentioned above, that the railway entirely avoids the city, and that the terminus is some distance outside the walls; all merchandise therefore passes through the country without in any way affecting the prosperity of the city, and five-eighths of the passengers do the same. Panama on the Pacific has been for centuries the chief city of the Isthmus, while Chagres on the Atlantic has only been looked upon as a mere port of entry; but now the order of things is reversed, the glory of the Queen of the Pacific is departed, while the Anglo-Saxon city on the Atlantic takes a high position in commerce. The site of Panama has been once changed. In 1512, when the Spaniards first arrived, they built upon the site, and took the name, of an Indian town then in existence. The place was so named from the abundance of fish in the vicinity; Panama in the Indian dialect signifying "much fish." In 1521 the town was raised to the dignity of a city by royal charter. In 1670 it was sacked and reduced to ashes by Henry Morgan, and subsequently rebuilt on its present site.

"The city of Panama lies in lat. 8° 56′ 56″ N., long. 79° 31′ 12″ W., at the foot of the Cerro de Ancon, a little peninsula connected towards the west with the mainland. It is divided into two parishes: that within the walls, the city, is called San Felipe; that without, the suburb, Santa Ana. Panama differs considerably from the other towns of Spanish America: its high buildings, tiled roofs, numerous churches, and massive walls, give it an air reminding one, at first sight, of a European town; on a closer inspection, however, the peculiarity of the old Spanish style becomes evident. San Felipe, the best and most regularly-built part, is surrounded by walls and watch-towers, which are at present rather dilapidated; the fortifications are irregular and not strong, though the walls are high, the bastions having been constructed at various times, as the menaces of pirates and other enemies have suggested;

the most modern seem to be those on the eastern and southern sides, erected in 1778. The city has four gates, two opening towards the sea, two towards the land; the traveller coming from Chagres enters by the western one, which was formerly strongly defended, and connected with the main entrance by means of a drawbridge. The principal streets run from west to east, and are crossed by others extending from north to south, from sea to sea, preserving a current of air, which greatly adds to the salubrity of the place. The streets are paved and regular, but rather narrow, seldom exceeding more than fifty feet in breadth; the pavement for foot passengers is covered by the balconies of the houses, and a person may walk almost all over the town, during a shower of rain, without getting wet.

"The population of Panama is composed of three races, the Caucasian, the American, and the African, and the numerous shades and varieties produced by their intermixture. Any man, whether black, brown, or white, may hold the highest office in the state. The whites are sadly in want of moral principle—probably the result of their religion—and steadiness of purpose, for which the enervating climate may account; but they are hospitable to strangers and generous to the poor and needy. The negroes are treacherous, thievish, and extremely indolent; they work one or two days, and then cease until necessity compels them to resume their occupation. "Only fools and horses work" is one of their favourite sayings, and is the principle on which they act. Slavery has long ceased to exist. The character of the half-castes is, if possible, worse than that of the negroes; they have all the vices and none of the virtues of their parents; they are weak in body, and more liable to disease than either the whites or other races; when they intermarry with their own shade they may have children, but these seldom, if ever, live to grow up.

"The population of the canton of Panama in 1823 was nearly 11,000; in 1843 it was less than half, and now it is about 10,000, by far the greater proportion being of the coloured races. There are a few public buildings deserving of notice,—the cathedral, and some of the convents. The ruins of buildings formerly devoted to religious purposes cover one-half of the superficial area of the city, a strong proof of the wealth and bigotry of the inhabitants in former times; none of the convents are now in use. The Jesuits' college is the finest ruin in the town; it was commenced in 1739, but was not completed in 1773, when the Jesuits were expelled from Spanish America, and it has never been finished; it is two stories high. The church attached to it, which is in tolerable repair, is used for theatrical exhibitions, rope-dancers, etc. etc. Most of the private buildings of San Felipe are constructed of stone, those of Santa Ana of wood. They are two stories high, surrounded by balconies, and have tiled roofs, the violence of the rains not permitting the use of flat ones. All have large doorways, sufficiently spacious to admit a person on horseback. The halls are small. Near the staircase is a door leading into the courtyard, and to the stables, the bathroom, and the well. In most houses the lower story is let to shopkeepers, spirit-sellers, and tradespeople. The first floor is inhabited by the servants, and the upper, the most salubrious, by the landlord and his family. All the apartments are large and airy; the drawing-rooms are generally thirty feet long, twenty-four feet broad, and twenty feet high. The floor is either of wood, brick, sandstone, or marble. Every room has one or more folding doors, opening towards the balcony; the wings have a shutter, supplying the place of windows. Sometimes a piece of glass is inserted, but regular windows do not exist, and will probably never be introduced; they prevent a free current of air, an indispensable condition in so hot a climate. Besides the doors, there are, higher up, smaller apertures, mostly in the shape of stars, by means of which a further reduction of the temperature is produced. The walls are from two feet to two feet six inches thick; they are decorated with pictures, crosses, figures of saints, etc., and are generally whitewashed, which, though depriving them of that aspect of comfort by which our papered rooms are distinguished, makes them look cool, and prevents them from harbouring centipedes, scorpions, and other noxious animals. The balconies are from four to five feet wide, protected from sun and rain by the projecting roof, and abundantly provided with flower-pots containing roses, balsams, and carnations. In a shady corner stands the filtering-stone, and several earthenware jars containing water, about which there is a degree of cleanliness not observed in any other part of the house. The furniture, which is very simple, is mostly imported, either from Europe, North America, or China. In all the rooms are hammocks, in which the Panamians, and the inhabitants of the Isthmus in general, may be seen swinging themselves for hours in succession."*

The following observations on the prevailing winds and weather in the neighbourhood of Panama are the result of some experience, and have been carefully collected.

During the first three months of the year the weather is beautiful, with a bright clear sky and, almost without intermission, fresh northerly winds. In April there are frequent calms, and when there is wind it is for the most part light; although it generally prevails from the north, yet southerly airs are by no means uncommon; the north wind dies away in squalls accompanied by rain, thunder, and lightning. The weather in May is much the same as that of the preceding month, except that the coming wet season makes itself more felt; occasionally there are fresh squalls from north-east and south-east. The rainy season fairly sets in at the beginning of June. Squalls and heavy rain constantly alternate. Strong breezes from the south prevail during the day, but at night light winds from the northward (the land wind) generally clear up the weather, and towards the end of the month as much as a week of sunshine may be experienced. July, August, and September are wet months, but the rain seldom continues more than twenty-four hours; it however descends in a perfect deluge, and I have known the streets of the city of Panama so completely flooded that the boys amused themselves by swimming round the plaza. The prevailing

* Dr. Seemann's Voyage of H.M.S. Herald, vol. i. pp. 289–293.

winds are from the southward, with squalls. Towards the end of the latter month there is generally an equinoctial gale from the south, lasting the best part of a week without cessation. In October south winds begin to take off, and are often alternated by land breezes from the north; the weather begins to clear, and indicates the approaching end of the wet season. The intervals of fine weather increase in November, and towards the end of the month the dry season may be said to have fairly set in. South winds now become faint, while puffs off the land often clear the sky. December is calm, as a rule, but in the first part of it gentle south winds blow, while at the latter end norths are frequent, and fine weather may be said to be established. When the wind from either the north or the south continues fresh at Panama for more than twelve hours, it is certain to amount almost to a gale at the entrance of the bay, at Punta Mala for example. A south wind brings in a long heavy swell, which breaks with great force against the reef; otherwise the anchorage is not on the whole insecure; its great fault is the distance ships must anchor from the landing-place.

Aspinwall is indeed a contrast; there Anglo-Saxon energy is visible on every side. The bay is usually crowded with shipping, and the wharves heaped with merchandise; and this, be it remembered, on a site that ten years ago was a gloomy swamp, infested with snakes and alligators. On the 29th of February, 1852 (leap year), I must not say the first stone was laid, for the place is built only of wood, but a city was founded by Don Victoriano Paredes, Secretary of State for Foreign

Affairs of New Granada, and by him named Aspinwall, as a just tribute to one of the railway promoters. The town or city is quite New England in the style of its buildings, dazzling with whitewash, and brilliant with its green *jalousies*. The usual American hotels, with the customary bars, flourish luxuriantly: the Howard, City, and Aspinwall Hotels seem to be the best; the charge is 12*s*. 6*d*. per diem; but very fair accommodation can be obtained at a much lower rate. I would, however, recommend the too confiding Britisher to come to an understanding about the terms in the first place.

There are now about 3500 inhabitants, and the place is rapidly increasing in population and wealth. The houses are built upon an island, called Manzanilla, of very limited extent, not more than a square mile at the utmost. It has been ceded in perpetuity to the company by the Government of New Granada, and it is leased for building lots to individuals, no doubt very profitably. Every effort is made to increase the available space by bringing down trucks of rubble and tumbling it into the sea, whenever the locomotive has any spare time from ordinary duties; by this means not only will considerable ground be gained, but the wharves will be brought out into deeper water; one, indeed, has been constructed about three hundred yards in length by nearly fifteen in breadth. At the head of this wharf there is a good reservoir, containing many thousands of gallons of rain-water, caught during the wet season, and which is sufficient for the supply of town and shipping. The island of Manzanilla, being of low coral formation, does not possess any springs, and the wells which have been dug produce water too brackish for use. There are several other piers, most of them roofed over, and all conveying the idea of careful construction and great strength. The freight warehouse of the railway company is a sight well worth seeing; it is a substantial stone building, with three tramways running into it from the wharf; inside are piled up a miscellaneous collection of merchandise from all parts of the world, viz. boxes of dollars, bar silver, gold ore, bales of Peruvian bark, ceroons of indigo and cochineal, hundreds of bags of coffee, cacao, sarsaparilla, copper ore, thousands of hides, oyster-shells, barrels of salt provisions, flour, cheeses, and biscuit, Manchester goods, and many other products too numerous to mention.

The company's mess-house is one of the neatest and pleasantest establishments it has ever been my fortune to visit. Some cocoanut-trees, tastefully distributed around, give it quite a picturesque aspect; whilst its situation close to the beach, and to windward of the city, is enviably cool and enjoyable. So much for out of doors: within the hospitable walls, the eye is delighted by the neatness and order everywhere evidenced; indeed, he is a lucky man who can secure an introduction to Colonel Totten, who is the presiding chief not only in the mess-house but over the entire transit. I was particularly struck with the thoughtful care bestowed by that gentleman and his amiable lady on the comfort and happiness of those employed on the Colonel's working staff, and therefore under his immediate superintendence; they messed together just like the officers of a regiment, with the exception that

Mrs. Totten always graced the table with her presence, and infused a degree of domesticity into the "mess-house" which I must confess went far to disperse my previous notions about American society. I gladly take the opportunity now afforded me of tendering my sincere thanks to Colonel Totten and his staff, not only for their kindness to me personally, but also to the officers of the 'Gorgon,' who were provided with free passes over the railroad, and thus had an opportunity of visiting Panama, and of obtaining a sight of the Pacific after a manner strongly in contrast to the toilsome and laborious journey of Vasco Nuñez de Balboa.

Although Aspinwall is in the territory of New Granada, it has a separate municipal government vested in American residents, for the most part connected with the railway company.

The following steamship lines run from the termini of the Panama Railway:—

1. The Atlantic and Pacific Steam-Ship Company (New York and Aspinwall).

2. The Pacific Mail Steam-Ship Company (Panama and San Francisco).

3. The Central American Line (Panama, Costarica, Nicaragua, San Salvador, Guatemala).

4. British Pacific Steam Navigation Company (Panama, Buenaventura, Ecuador, Peru, Bolivia, and Chile).

5. The Royal Mail Steam-Packet Company (Southampton, West Indian Islands, Aspinwall, Greytown, Blewfields).

In addition to the above, there are lines of sailing

vessels and screw-steamers running between Europe and Aspinwall.

There is a good lighthouse on the point, not built up at great expense and unnecessary solidity, after the English fashion, but raised upon a strong iron framework, well calculated to withstand the action of the sea.

Unfortunately, the harbour accommodation at each terminus is very indifferent. At Aspinwall the bay is quite open to the "northers," the scourge of the coast. On the 31st of December, 1854, a "norther" destroyed the wharves and wrecked every vessel at anchor, except the American steamer 'North Star' and the mail steamer 'Derwent," which got up steam and left the anchorage just in time. The northers are of periodical occurrence, and cause great damage. An account, for instance, has only just been received, describing considerable disasters to the shipping this year. The Royal Mail steamer 'Avon,' while lying at Aspinwall with two anchors down, was driven ashore early on the morning of the 22nd of November, 1862, by a norther, and the heavy rollers setting into the bay. The crew were landed by means of a line thrown from the ship to the shore, and so passed along it through the surf, *which was running over the railway up to the houses.* The United States brig of war 'Bainbridge' also dragged her anchors and drove towards the beach, having thrown overboard her guns and stores, and cut away her masts. The 'Bainbridge,' however, did not go ashore, as her anchors brought her up close to the reef after the crew had left her. The American Mail steamer 'Ocean Queen' succeeded in getting out, but with the loss of

Sir W^m G Ouseley del

Vincent Brooks lit.

EASTERN SUBURB OF PANAMA

RAILWAY TERMINUS ON THE RIGHT

paddle-box, and other damage; as also did her Majesty's ship 'Jason.' The Royal Mail steam-ship 'Tamar,' with the outward mails per Atrato, arrived at Aspinwall on the 23rd of November, but could not communicate in consequence of the boisterous weather and heavy sea.

The Bay of Panama cannot by any perversion of the term be called a port; it is simply an open roadstead; and at certain seasons not particularly safe. The steamers are obliged to anchor some miles from the shore, and passengers, goods, and supplies have to be transshipped in a small steamer and lighters; and this can only be done at certain times of tide, for the rise and fall is great, and the water very shallow near the shore. In bad weather there is considerable uncertainty and danger, and sometimes disembarkation is delayed a considerable time.

The following extract is from 'A Statement to the Public,' drawn up by a committee of the passengers on the steamers 'Illinois' and 'George Law,' adopted at a meeting of said passengers, and ordered to be published, June 16, 1856:—

"On the arrival of the 'John L. Stephens' at her anchorage at Panama, the passengers were placed on board a small steamer, and a lighter filled with baggage, to be conveyed to the shore, distant about five miles. The number of passengers was about 750, about 500 of whom were crowded on the steamer, and the residue on the lighter. Both vessels were filled beyond their capacity, and in the event of an ordinary accident the results must have been fearful. Shortly after embarking, the rain poured down in torrents, which continued up to the time of landing—nearly two hours. The passengers in the lighter, mostly women and children, being wholly unprotected, were drenched to the skin, while those in the steamer fared but little better."

Close to Panama there are two small islands, Flaminco and Perico, which dominate the city and anchorage of Panama. The possession of these islands would command the transit route. About twelve years ago, when I was serving in the Bay of Panama, they were offered for a small sum to our Government, but of course declined, probably from fear of bringing the Americans about our ears. The United States, however, fully alive to their importance, did their best by occupation to secure possession, and it is more than rumoured that the purchase has now been effected, thus enabling that enterprising nation to *command* the monopoly of the transit from sea to sea.

CHAPTER XII.

NICARAGUAN TRANSIT LINE.—BULWER-CLAYTON TREATY.—COMMANDER FEAD'S SKILFUL SEAMANSHIP.—SCHEMES OF THE ACCESSORY COMPANY. —BOMBARDMENT OF GREYTOWN.—A LIBERAL GOVERNMENT.—THE COMPANY FORGET TO PAY.—THE BATTLE FOR TRANSIT.—AMERICAN EFFORTS TO HOLD THE ROUTE.—CORRESPONDENCE.—DAMMING THE COLORADO.— SAN JUAN DEL SUR.

IT must not be supposed that the Panama transit has always held the undisputed monopoly of the passage from sea to sea; on the contrary, long before it was completed, a formidable rival route was opened and in full operation. It commenced at Greytown; passengers were forwarded by steamer up the river San Juan and across Lake Nicaragua, whence a ride of about thirteen miles across the intervening land carried them to the Pacific. The profit to be derived from opening up a short route for the thousands of Californian immigrants wending their way in a steady stream to that golden land being manifest, attention was turned to the water communication of Nicaragua; and it was soon ascertained by certain sharp Americans, that although it could *not* be made available for a great ship-canal, yet it could be easily adapted for passenger traffic *under cover* of forming a ship canal from ocean to ocean.

The Nicaraguan scheme of a great ship-canal has

always held a high position in public favour: it has been warmly advocated, especially by the Emperor of the French, and the idea appears to have taken a firm hold upon the mind of all classes of the natives of the republic, as a certain means of benefiting themselves and their country. There was not, therefore, any difficulty in obtaining a charter for such an object, and one was accordingly procured by Messrs. Vanderbilt and White in 1849. On the 19th of April, 1852, a convention, guaranteeing the neutrality and independence of any exclusive control by any nation of the proposed canal, was signed at Washington by John M. Clayton and Sir Henry Bulwer. This treaty between Great Britain and America, entered into from a desire "to consolidate the amity which now so happily subsists between the two Powers," by the settlement of all questions connected with the proposed route from the Atlantic to the Pacific by the river San Juan and over or about the Lakes of Nicaragua or Managua, or either of them, is also expressly stated to apply in principle to other modes of transit across Central America, whether by railway or otherwise, which may be at any future time constructed.

The first article of this convention was as follows:-- "The Government of the United States and Great Britain hereby declare that neither the one nor the other will ever obtain or maintain for itself any exclusive control over the said ship-canal, agreeing that neither will ever erect or maintain any fortifications commanding the same or in the vicinity thereof, or occupy or olonize, or assume or exercise any dominion over Nicaragua, Costarica, the Mosquito coast, or any part of Central America; nor will either make use of any protection which either affords or may afford, or any alliance which either has or may have, to or with any state or people for the purpose of maintaining or erecting any such fortification, or of occupying, fortifying, or colonizing Nicaragua, Costarica, the Mosquito coast, or of any part of Central America, or of assuming or exercising dominion over the same." The second article enacts that in case of war between the two countries, the canal is to be neutral territory, and not to be molested by either of the belligerents: and that this inviolability is to extend to such reasonable distance from each end of the said canal or pass as may be hereafter determined. The third article provides that parties contracting to construct such canal, after having obtained the consent and authority of the local government interested, shall be protected by the contracting Powers against any unjust detention, seizure, or any violence whatsoever. Fourth, Great Britain and America to use all their influence to induce the local governments to erect two free ports or harbours at each end of the canal. Fifth, when complete, the canal to be guaranteed from interruption or seizure, but conditionally only that all shall be fair, and no unjust favouritism of one nation over another be shown by the company. If the company should transgress this wise and equitable regulation, each of the Powers may adopt such measures or seek such redress as may be deemed advisable: six months' notice being previously given to other guaranteeing states. Sixth, other Powers to be invited to form this compact.

It now only remained to raise the money for making the ship-canal; a company for that purpose was formed at New York, called the "Pacific and Atlantic Canal Company," and a deputation, consisting of Messrs. White and Vanderbilt, came over to England to arrange with British capitalists for the concession of half the Nicaraguan shares; but beyond a vague promise from the principal capitalists,—that if, after a proper survey of the proposed route, and the exhibition of a reliable estimate of the probable cost, the project should appear feasible, they and others would be happy to assist in effecting so great and desirable a work,—nothing was done in this country. The New York company dispatched Colonel O. W. Childs, favourably known in the States as the engineer who effected the enlargement of the Erie Canal, assisted by several young men, to make an accurate survey of the Nicaraguan route; but, as said the 'Times,' the strenuous advocate of the Nicaraguan scheme, however high the estimation in which Mr. Childs may be held in America, in this country nothing less than "a report, confirmed by Government engineers," will induce British capitalists to embark in a project of which the random, hap-hazard estimates, as given by friends and opponents, vary from three to ten millions sterling! The 'New York Herald' affirmed at the time that there was no real intention on the part of the New York company to enter seriously upon the work of a ship-canal; and that their veritable and sole object was, so to improve the transit to California by the San Juan river, as to render it a preferable route to that by way of Chagres. In this the 'New York Herald' was not far from the truth, as is evidenced by the date and terms of the respective charters obtained from the Nicaraguan Government. The first was signed on the 27th of August, 1849, and ratifications exchanged with amendments on the 9th of March, 1850. It granted the exclusive right to construct a *ship-canal*, and to control and manage it for eighty-five years.

Art. 5. The Company agrees to pay the State 10,000 dollars on ratification, and 10,000 dollars per annum until the completion of the canal; also 200,000 dollars of stock.

Art. 6. The Company agrees to pay out of the income of the canal, for the first twenty years, 20 per cent. of the net profits after deducting the interest of the capital at 7 per cent.; and for each year afterwards 25 per cent., after deducting the said 7 per cent.; and during the twelve years allowed for construction, the Company is to pay 10 per cent. of the net profit, without any deduction of interest, of any route, whether rail, carriage, or other means of communication, which the Company may establish.

Art. 12. The State grants the right to take from all public lands all wood, stone, lime, or timber, and to use such portions of public lands as may be required for houses, wharves, docks, and stations.

Art. 27. The State makes a free donation of land contiguous to the river San Juan, of eight sections, each six miles long by six broad; the colonists on said lands shall be exempt for ten years from all public services or taxes, but shall be subject to the laws of Nicaragua.

No attempt was made to construct a canal, and probably no such idea was intended, as the second charter was obtained on the 14th August, 1851. It authorized the Pacific and Atlantic Canal Company to graft upon their body another company, to be called the "Accessory Transit Company," "with the sole object of facilitating the construction of the maritime canal;" and it expressly stipulated—

"Art. 8. That the charter should become null whenever the primary one of 22nd of September, 1849, should expire or be forfeited."

Under this new charter the real objects of the canal-scheme cropped out; the projectors opened a transit, and strained every nerve to overshadow Nicaragua, and get under their immediate influence and control that magnificent country, whether by fair means or foul was a matter of indifference. In 1852 the line was opened most successfully; and as its manifold advantages over the Panama Transit became known, thousands of emigrants wended their way to California by the new route. The passage was effected as follows:—the ocean-steamer could at that time enter the harbour of Greytown, whence passengers embarked on board the river steamboats, vessels drawing three feet at most (precisely similar to those in use on the Mississippi), and proceeded up the river San Juan as far as the Castillo Viejo Rapid. Here they changed boats; light carriages conveying them on a tramway from the foot to the head of the rapid, where they re-embarked, and made the rest of the journey to San Carlos at the head of the river. At this place there was sometimes another change to the lake steamer which ran between San Carlos and Virgen Bay, on the north-western shores of the Lake Nicaragua. Here the final disembarkation took place, the passengers crossing on mules to the Pacific over a well-made road, thirteen miles in length, extending to the beach of the small port of San Juan del Sur, where the largest ocean steamers can approach quite close to the shore to receive their freight and passengers. Although there were no less than six changes, this route speedily became very popular; the charges were comparatively moderate, being some pounds less than the cost *viâ* Panama, while often two days in time were saved, to say nothing of shortening the sea-voyage on either side the Isthmus.

The healthiness of the climate, the beauty and variety of the scenery, the superiority of the ports at each terminus, the abundance and cheapness of the provisions, the gain of about two clear days in time, and the much cheaper rate of fare, could not fail to attract the public to the Nicaraguan route in ever-increasing proportion; nevertheless, the Accessory Transit Company was not destined to reap the fruit of this largely remunerative traffic. Unfortunately for the shareholders, there seems to have been quarrelling and heartburning from the very commencement of the undertaking. The project, if the 'New York Herald' be right, originated under false pretences. The Accessory Transit was announced to be an accessory and necessary adjunct to the Pacific and Atlantic Canal, and brought into operation, it was alleged, solely with a view to forward that gigantic scheme; but it is needless to say that nothing was ever done towards even the commencement of a canal, and at an early date that fiction, having played its part, was allowed to die out. As might have been expected with such antecedents, rival parties soon sprang up and came to loggerheads in the Company itself; and an impression got abroad that one section was trying to depress the market-price of the stock, so as to buy in, get a majority of shares, and thus obtain the control. However, be that as it may, it is certain that an unscrupulous policy characterized the proceedings of the Company, and it was not long before their actions began to attract public attention. In the first place, the agents and captains of the steamers connected with the "Accessory Transit Company" refused payment of the port-dues at Greytown; they had for some time cavilled at the harbour regulations, which enabled the properly constituted authorities to levy tolls for the purpose of maintaining the requisite order and discipline, both ashore and afloat,—a matter of vital importance, when it is considered with what a lawless rabble the municipal officers often had to deal. The instance to which I allude was that of the 'Prometheus,' when, to the usual application for the payment of the port-dues, a most positive refusal was given: Mr. Vanderbilt, the head of the company, being, it is said, on board at the time, so that the refusal did not emanate from an ignorant servant of the company, but directly from one who was fully cognizant of the importance of the step he was taking. However, this wilful violation of law was not allowed to pass unnoticed or unchecked; the authorities appealed to the captain of an English man-of-war, H.M. brig Express, then in port, on the plea that the town being within the Mosquito territory, with the Mosquito flag* flying over it, and the country under British protection, it was his duty to defend them from spoliation. Commander W. F. Fead felt the justice of the claim, and the consul approving, action was at once taken.

It is with great pleasure that I take this opportunity of drawing attention to the manner in which Commander Fead performed his duty; indeed, the admiration of *all* parties was elicited by his skilful management. He got his *brig* under way, and manœuvred her in so masterly a manner, that the *steamer* found it impossible to escape; and to the chagrin of the defaulters, the port dues were exacted to the uttermost farthing before the vessel was allowed to proceed on her voyage. Commander Fead died soon after; his death, it is supposed, being hastened by the treatment he met with from the Admiralty. It is due to the memory of a true Englishman to state that a more gallant officer, or a better seaman, it would have been hard to find anywhere; yet in spite of his well-known character and services, his act was disavowed with the most nervous haste, and he was removed from the station as quickly as possible.

The following extract from the 'United Service Journal' will show the course taken by the authorities. "H.M. steam-frigate Arrogant, corvette Calypso, and brig Express were in the harbour of Greytown on the 19th of January, 1852. The 'Arrogant' had been dispatched

* The Mosquito flag is formed by the English Union Jack in the upper canton; the remainder alternate blue and white horizontal stripes, with a crown in the lower canton.

by the Admiral of the West Indian Station, with assurance to Commodore Parker that the British Government entirely disavowed the acts of the Consul and the captain of the 'Express,' *in the exercise of any authority whatever in connection with the Mosquito Government* or interfering in any way with foreign commerce at San Juan (Greytown). The most friendly feeling existed between the officers of the ships of both countries. Salutes were exchanged on the 16th, on the Commanders visiting each other's ships. Commodore Parker was highly complimented by Captain Robinson hoisting the American ensign during the salute. It was returned by the 'Albany,'* with the British ensign at her main."†

The mere fear that Mr. Vanderbilt would "tell his big brother" was quite sufficient to scare the English Government into adopting the measures they did; measures, it must be admitted, not at all calculated to add to the prestige of the country, or to elevate themselves in the estimation of the naval service.

Thus the Accessory Company failed in their attempt to ignore Greytown; but from this period may be dated the most bitter hatred between the townspeople and the employés connected with the Transit Company. And here I must explain that Greytown is situated on the right-hand or mainland going in, and the company's buildings, stores, etc., on the opposite side of the

* Commodore Parker had his broad pendant on board the U.S. steam frigate Saranac; he does not appear to have condescended to return the salute himself, but delegated that duty to the 'Albany,' a sloop of war.

† United Service Journal, 1852, part i., page 442.

harbour, on Punta Arenas, and that one channel from the river San Juan runs close to the town, and another skirts the shore of the Company's sand-spit. In the bitter rivalry and hatred of the contending parties, each did their best to *improve*, as they said, their respective channels, by driving piles and placing timber-dams in certain positions; and with such vigour was this *improvement* carried on, that the natural process of silting up was hastened to such a degree, that the port may be said to have been almost destroyed in consequence. At the same time the antagonism was not confined to the water, it raged with equal fury on land; and so far did the Company carry their hatred, that their employés were forbidden, on pain of dismissal, from even visiting Greytown, and consequently they were forced to reside on the point opposite.

The main object of the prime mover or movers in these transactions was probably to cause the commercial downfall of Greytown, and the construction of a place of business, which would ultimately become a town, on their own locality, Punta Arenas. It is easy to understand the large amount of money which might have been realized by the conversion of their sand-spit into town lots; but "when rogues fall out, honest men come by their own," and in this case the rogues overshot their mark, and after a variety of vicissitudes lost their transit and their hold on Nicaragua altogether. Had they succeeded in maintaining the route, and in gradually acquiring possession of the adjoining district, England would indeed have had cause to rue the day. The failure of the Accessory Transit Company to monopolize the Nicaraguan Transit has been of immense political importance to this country.

We now come to one of the darkest pages in the history of this distracted country, and one which stamps indelible disgrace upon all connected with it; I allude to the bombardment and destruction of Greytown. I have narrated above the hatred which existed between the townspeople and the Company, and how the former compelled the latter to pay the port dues. This constituted offence number one.

The second occurrence was after this wise. About the end of 1853 the captain of a river-steamer shot the *patron* of a native bongo, while their respective vessels were passing on the San Juan, merely because the *patron* used some coarse expressions towards him in the brief conversation which usually ensues upon two vessels meeting. It was reported at the time that Mr. Borland, American minister to Nicaragua, who was then on his way home on board the steamer, instigated the captain to commit the deed; but be that as it may, it is certain that the passengers and crew of the steamboat, at Mr. Borland's instance, resisted the authorities sent on board to arrest the murderer. The American minister afterwards went on shore at Greytown; he was speedily surrounded by a mob, and while attempting to address the excited citizens, one of his own countrymen threw a bottle at him, which struck and wounded him on the head. This constituted the second offence for which the United States demanded reparation and damages.

The third and last case brought against the unfortunate townspeople was as follows. Mr. Scott, the Company's agent, lodged a formal complaint against the authorities of Greytown for harbouring and refusing to give up a man in the employ of the Company, who was alleged to have committed several petty thefts, none of which, however, could be proved before the proper magistrates.

For the above three *heinous crimes* the Government at Washington determined to exact retribution, and Commander Hollins, in the U.S. corvette Cyane, was dispatched to the locality to conduct the business. He arrived at a time when the harbour was entirely unprotected, the only vessel with a pendant flying being H.M. schooner Bermuda, two guns and thirty men, Lieutenant Jolly commanding. Commander Hollins, after setting forth the high crimes and misdemeanours of this wretched trading town, demanded an indemnity of 25,000 dollars, which being refused, the authorities never dreaming of the result, he brought his broadside to bear upon the houses, and for six hours continued to fire shot and shell into the place. Strange to say, this warm cannonade did not do so much damage as was expected, and Commander Hollins decided to consummate this monstrous abuse of force by burning the town. He accordingly landed a body of about fifty men, who marched with colours flying and their officers at their head, accompanied by Mr. Fabens, the American consular agent, into the town, and there deliberately set fire to the houses, which being entirely of wood were soon consumed. The English Consul's house fell with the rest, "the flag that's braved a thousand years the battle and the breeze" being trampled under foot amidst every indignity; the Mosquito flag, with the English time-honoured union jack quartered in the upper canton, sharing the same fate.

The bombardment commenced about 10 A.M. on the 13th July, 1854; the men were landed with all the appliances for firing the town at 4 P.M., and by 6 o'clock on the same evening nothing remained of Greytown but a heap of smoking ashes. Thus upwards of 500 peaceable and inoffensive inhabitants, in less than twelve hours, found themselves houseless and destitute by this unqualified act of villany, and, to make matters worse, the rainy season was at its height. The feelings of Lieutenant Jolly, R.N., and of the officers and men of the 'Bermuda,' may be better imagined than described; but the former did not consider himself justified, with the handful of men at his disposal, in taking any steps beyond an indignant protest; indeed, with the above-mentioned fate of Commander Fead, H.M. brig Express, before his eyes, I think he deserves the good opinion of his countrymen for doing what he did. The case was one, thank God! of so exceptional a character amongst civilized nations, that it required more than an ordinary man to deal with it.

The destruction of property amounted to nearly £1,000,000 sterling, against £5000 demanded, and of course ruin was entailed on a number of individuals. It is painful to go on with this subject, but duty compels me to add that the Cabinet at Washington took upon itself the responsibility of this cowardly action, and therefore it followed as a matter of course that the

English Government hushed up the matter as quickly as possible: no reparation has ever been made by the United States in any manner or shape.

A complete light has been thrown upon the motives of the principal actors in the Greytown tragedy, by the publication of a letter from Mr. Joseph L. White, a leading member of the Accessory Transit Company. It appears that the American consular agent at the time of the bombardment, Mr. Fabens, and Mr. White, subsequently quarrelled; hence the publication of part of the correspondence of the latter, which shows up the whole transaction, and completely silences the allegations made by certain American journals, and the excuses of the American President in his message of the 4th December, 1854.

"Office of the Nicaraguan Line,
"New York, June 16, 1854.

"Captain Hollins, commanding the corvette 'Cyane,' leaves on Monday. You will see by his instructions, which I have written on the margin, that it is intended his authority should not be so exercised as to show any mercy to the town or people.

"If the scoundrels are soundly punished, we can take possession, and build it up as a business place, put in our own officers, transfer the jurisdiction, *and you know the rest.*

"It is of the last importance that the people of the town should be taught to fear us. Punishment will teach them. After which you must agree with them as to the organization of a new government, and the officers of it. Everything now depends on you and

Hollins. The latter is all right. He fully understands the outrage, and will not hesitate in enforcing reparation.

"I hope to hear from you that all has been properly executed.

"I am, etc.,

"J. L. WHITE.

"To Mr. J. W. Fabens,
"Consular Agent of the U.S. at Greytown."

The above letter sets the matter in its true light. A great and useful project had fallen into the hands of unscrupulous speculators, who considered no means too vile to compass their greedy ends; and when their crafty efforts to raise the value of their possessions failed, they decided on the destruction of Greytown as the only obstacle in the way of the realization of their wishes. But, in spite of the deep-laid plots and carefully-planned schemes of these men, an avenging Providence overtook them, and instead of the accomplishment of their hopes, they soon found that they had only succeeded in putting another nail into the coffin of their transit. They did not long enjoy immunity; punishment was following closely on their heels, and the destruction of the Company soon followed.

The directors appear to have been emboldened by their success at one end of the transit, and determined to try their hand at the other extremity. They entirely *forgot* their stipulation to pay a certain percentage to the government of the country for the concession which had been granted to them; and when their memory was jogged regarding this fact, they declared that they considered the republic of Nicaragua sufficiently unsettled to justify the non-fulfilment of their engagement. At the time this declaration was made Rivas was President, but he had at his elbow General Walker,* who was a man not at all disposed to bear the conduct of the directors, fellow-countrymen though they were, so patiently as the head of the republic would have done. Accordingly, the chairman of the Company at New York was peremptorily notified, in November, 1855, under a clause of the charter, to appoint commissioners to settle the matters in controversy with Nicaragua. The Company replied, enclosing an opinion of their legal adviser, maintaining that the matter had passed from their hands. Such an answer was justly deemed an evasion; and two clever lawyers, Edmund Randolph and A. P. Crittenden, having carefully examined the charter of the Company, gave it as their clear and decided opinion that it had been forfeited. It was not, however, until the following August that any decisive action was taken; then the commissioners appointed to investigate the indebtedness of the Company reported that the dues amounted to more than 400,000 dollars.

* It was not without mature deliberation that Walker took the steps he did in the Accessory Transit question. He was disgusted with the conduct of those engaged in the matter. The character of Walker has been much misrepresented in this country. He was, in reality, an earnest, straightforward man. The following, from one of his letters, depicts the principles upon which he acted:—"Without the aid of religious sentiments and religious teachers there can be no good government, for the fear of God is the foundation of all social and political organization. In God I put my trust for the success of the cause in which I am embarked, and for the maintenance of the principles I advocate. Without His aid all human efforts are unavailing; but with His divine assistance a few may triumph over a legion."

Some payments had been made, and, deducting all these, there still remained a debt of upwards of 350,000 dollars,—a sum much more than the value of all the property on the Isthmus. As the Company failed to appear, judgment was given against them by default, and all their property seized. In the meantime, Messrs. Garrison and Morgan entered into negotiation with the Nicaraguan Government for a new charter, which was granted directly the old one was forfeited. The working of the line was not so much injured by these transactions as might have been supposed. Messrs. Morgan and Garrison became the possessors of all the steamers, wharves, stations, etc. etc. belonging to the old Company, and continued the conveyance of passengers and freight across the Isthmus. The late owners, however, true to their combative instincts, determined to fight out the matter, and a feud commenced, like the famous one between the Hudson's Bay and the North-West Companies, although with a very different result—the Transit rivals being very much in the condition of the Kilkenny cats at the termination of the contest. Mr. Vanderbilt, the prime mover in the "Accessory Company," enlisted the services of a man named Spencer, who appears to have been both clever and daring. He was sent to join the Costaricans, then at war with the Nicaraguans, led by Colonel Walker; and very shortly, by the energy and dash of himself and Colonel Cauty (an Englishman), succeeded, not only in capturing all the Transit steamers, but in obtaining possession of every one of the important posts on the river. By this means the transit once more fell into the power of the "Accessory Company," but as a commercial undertaking there was an end of it; and as no attempt was made to run the steamers, the line fell to the ground. One effect of the breaking-up of the line was the withdrawal of Colonel Walker from Nicaragua. He was dependent upon the Transit for men and munitions of war; and when the main feeder of his army was thus cut off, he had no other course but to succumb. The annihilation of the Transit was not the only result of the proceedings I have related. The destruction of the navigation of the river San Juan may also unquestionably be traced to the lawless and violent passions of the leaders in this faction fight. Obstructions were placed in the river, in the bitterest spirit of hatred and rivalry; and the laws of nature, in the silting process common in this region, were thus hastened to their fulfilment. For example, a steamer is blown up, sunk, or piles placed in the channel; in an incredibly short space of time detritus collects around the wreck or the obstruction, and an island appears where formerly the main channel existed. Probably there is not a reader but will feel that the utter ruin which has fallen upon those connected with the "Accessory Transit Company," *née* Pacific and Atlantic *Ship Canal* Company, has been richly deserved.

As regards the surviving steamers of this miserable Company, their owners appear to have been true to their colours to the last. I saw some of the vessels, and was told by those on board that they found it impossible to get their wages, and therefore held possession in the hope of disposing of them, and thus paying themselves. One, the 'Laura Frances,' was sold, and became a New-Granadian vessel of war. The sum she fetched proved just sufficient to remunerate those who had navigated and conducted her for so long. Another, the 'Cass Irisarri,' was on the Lake ready for use, but there were no bidders: she is probably there still.

It is painful to contemplate such a record of fraud and violence as I have just given. Here was an enterprise which, if only properly conducted, was calculated not only to confer every blessing upon the natives of the country through which the line passed, but to prove perhaps the most remunerative undertaking of the present day. Yet we find the project swamped in a sea of intrigue, falsehood, and dishonesty, and stained with the perpetration of a crime unparalleled for atrocity in the annals of modern times,—one which would cover with shame even uncivilized savages. The San Juan Transit route appears now on the point of being played out. The shallowness of Greytown harbour, as well as the river, seem to offer, unless at a great outlay of money, such an obstacle to the reöpening of the line, as will effectually prevent its reorganization. Nevertheless, the well-known wonderful *paying* qualities of such an undertaking have brought various speculators into the field; and a Mr. Stebbins, of New York, obtained the necessary authority to commence operations. The following is a copy of this authorization, and also an extract from a letter of President Martinez, showing his sentiments regarding a transit through Nicaragua:—

"Managua, 28th Dec., 1857.

"Sir,—I have received orders from my government to say to you that, having constantly received from the company of which you are president, the most vehement desire to comply with its engagement to this government, and having manifested to Mr. Irissari, Minister Plenipotentiary of Managua at the Court of Washington, the most lively interest for the fate of this country, the Transit shall be opened to the operations of the company, although before the prefixed time, as soon as the company shall be in a situation to act.

"This good disposition is the result of a conviction that you and your associates have the same interest as my government, namely, to impede the piratical expeditions of filibusters; and with such powerful interest it is not just to the whole world any longer to deprive them of the benefits which the route across the Isthmus offers. It has been sensibly painful to us to keep it closed, and nothing but the obligation of natural protection could induce us to close it,—a necessity which has disappeared through the co-operation of the said company and the asserted policy of your government, which has known how to repress the vandalism which Walker had banded together.

"In making you the present manifestation, I have the honour to subscribe myself,

"Your very obedient Servant,

"ROSALIO CORTEZ.

"To the President of the Company of the Transit,
"Don H. G. Stebbins, New York."

Extract from a letter from President Martinez, dated 31st of December, 1857, written in reply to a congratulatory letter from the president of the company to Martinez on his elevation to the Presidency of Nicaragua:—

"I shall be rejoiced that friendship may be well cemented, and that the commerce across this Isthmus, far from being interrupted, or from producing us the evils they formerly caused us, may be the foundation of happiness for this country, and for the company which has acquired or has the right of transit.

"Tomas Martinez.

"To Mr. H. G. Stebbins,
"President of the Canal Company, etc., New York."

Nothing but uncertainty prevails in this quarter, in spite of the various announcements of the intentions of the company. There is no doubt of the earnest desire of the United States to reopen the route in American interests, if only to check British trade and enterprise in the Pacific; nevertheless, it is my opinion, backed by recent information from the locality, that the San Juan River Transit requires *too much money* to open it permanently. Of course, it is diplomatically of importance to the United States to keep a hold on the country; and accordingly, the matter is not allowed to rest.

"San Juan del Norte, or Greytown, Nicaragua,
"June 18, 1862.

"There is once more a chance of the re-establishment of the transit from ocean to ocean up this river. An influential company has been organized in New York to carry out this object, and has obtained a favourable charter from the Nicaraguan Government. The company has paid to the government the amount stipulated, and received in return all the property belonging to the old Transit Company. The chief engineer, Mr. Walter Campbell, is here, preparing to receive the vessels (now on the way), with new boats for the river, coal, lumber, etc. He has selected a spot on the town side of the harbour for the company's depôt, and has received from the owners of the land deeds of title at the *nominal value* of one dollar. Agents are at work repairing the steamer 'Virgin' on the lake, and the short road on the Pacific side, and gangs of men employed at different places on the river, cutting wood for the steamboats. The chief engineer considers the opening up or widening and deepening the mouth of the harbour an easy matter.

"There is a strong feeling in California to support an opposition line to the Panama; and it is said that the United States Government will give such a one an active support.

"An English company should join this Central American Transit Company, and carry the mails and passengers for British Columbia, New Zealand, and Australia across this way: their interests need not clash. This route, when opened, always beat the Panama line in time, and it can be put in thorough order for one-tenth what the Panama road has cost.

"I am glad to state that this country has entirely recovered from the impoverished condition into which it was thrown by the filibuster invasion.

"The exports from this port (estimated to be one-third of the whole state) in 1861 amounted to 310,306 dollars, including 83,592 dollars gold from the mines; and the imports of merchandise to 285,798 dollars, and in specie, to balance, 24,508 dollars.

"The exports for the first four months of this year have been 112,311 dollars, and the imports to 94,605 dollars, leaving a balance in favour of the country of 17,706 dollars.

"The condition of this town has but slightly changed since its surrender to Nicaragua. The governor and other officers sent down by the government were wisely selected, and, instead of any difficulties being thrown in their way by the inhabitants, every disposition has been shown to assist them."

"San Juan del Norte, Nicaragua, July 18, 1862.

"Last mail I informed you that there was a prospect of the re-establishment of the Transit Company here, and I have now to add the arrival from New York of both men and material. Workshops have been erected, lighters built, and a steamboat for the river commenced.

"The general agent of the line, Mr. Raymond K. Weed, is superintending the repairing of the road and bridges on the Pacific side; and the chief engineer, Mr. Campbell, has just gone to the lake to put the finishing stroke to affairs there. Both these gentlemen are indefatigable in their endeavour to get the line open by the beginning of October, as, under the contract with this government, the company must convey 500 passengers across this Isthmus during that month. The company pays to the government 1 dollar 50 cents, or 6*s*., head-money on each adult passenger."

There is no question that could the transit be opened at a moderate outlay, and the integrity of the line guaranteed by one or more of the great Powers capable of keeping it open in spite of any political disturbance, it would prove a great boon to the world, and be most remunerative to the projectors. The prevailing idea at Greytown is, that if the Colorado branch of the Delta could be dammed across, the water would be forced to seek a passage to the sea through the San Juan branch, and by means of its greatly increased volume, soon scour away the obstructions which at present close the navigation. The following will give an idea of the nature of the Delta:—

"The Colorado diverges from the San Juan in lat. 10° 50′ N., and after running in a south-westerly direction falls into the sea in lat. 10°46′N., forming a dangerous bar. This river abstracts from the main stream a considerable quantity of water; the opening from the San Juan being 1200 feet wide, and having in the deepest part nine feet of water at the lowest state of the river. From measurement of this section, carefully taken at two different periods in May, when at the minimum, and in July, when much increased with freshets, it appears from calculation that at the first period the loss of water from the river was 28·178 cubic yards per minute, and at the latter observation as much as 85·840 cubic yards. The main current being thus suddenly weakened, the motion of the water through the San Juan becomes sluggish; and the natural effect is, that deposits of sand and mud are formed, which gradually augment when the movement of the water is feeble. Trunks of trees, and other floating bodies grounding on these, small islets are formed by successive aggregations, which soon become covered with rank grass, reeds, and other herbaceous plants of rapid growth. A great number of these mounds have been thus raised, and the progress of formation is continually going on."*

Meanwhile, every month finds the river shallower and shallower, while valuable time has been thrown away in trying to organize a grand ship-canal. M. Belly has spared no pains in that matter, and has obtained a liberal concession from the Government of Nicaragua; but his scheme appears to have fallen to the ground. His agreement was to pay 200,000 francs on or before the 1st of September, 1859, and having failed to do so the charter was annulled. Had he contented himself with the resuscitation of a transit on the simple and cheap form of the late attempt, he might, at the early period he commenced, have been in time to keep the San Juan navigable; and there is no doubt the most liberal concession would have been given to him, and he would then have had the satisfaction of reopening the route in French interests,—a consummation which, no doubt, would have been very agreeable to his Imperial master as well as to the natives of the country, who, in common with the rest of the world, cannot fail to have observed the deservedly high position France has attained in public opinion under the present *régime*.

* Survey of the river San Juan by Mr. Bailey.

Before closing this chapter, it will be as well to give a brief account of San Juan del Sur, the Pacific port of the late transit. In England we have but a vague notion of the place; indeed, in the search for it made by Sir Edward Belcher, it is doubtful if he found it. He says: "We quitted our anchorage on the 20th. My principal object at this moment was to seek for and examine the port of San Juan, which spot I had been informed that a Mr. Bailey (employed by the Government of Central America) had selected as the point where the projected canal or railroad through Nicaragua should communicate with the Pacific.

"On the 3rd, by dint of perseverance, we reached the Bay of Salinas, but had not observed anything like a river or *port*. As we could not fetch Salinas, I beat up to a position where we observed a flag displayed, rockets fired, and a number of men and women in holiday garb collected; and it being Sunday, we anchored for the day. The surf was too heavy to attempt landing; therefore we could neither fix our position satisfactorily, nor obtain information about San Juan, although I strongly suspected this to be the spot. Every nook was narrowly examined, but without success; therefore I am satisfied that Sunday's position, before noticed, was the port in question."*

M. T. de Lapelin, *capitaine de frégate* in the French corvette 'Brillant,' was more successful. The following is a translation of the pith of his observations:†—

* Belcher's 'Voyage Round the World,' vol. i. pp. 179–182.

† 'Reconnaissance Hydrographique des Côtes Occidentales du Centre-Amérique,' pp. 50–54. Paris, 1854.

"Approaching San Juan del Sur, the coast rises a little, and the hilly ridges of the land lose the uniformity which distinguishes them towards the north, becoming serrated in the direction of Salinas Bay. The hills are thickly wooded, and descend almost perpendicularly to the water's edge; the cliffy projections jutting into the sea, and forming between their points numerous small indentations or bays.

"The entire coast is steep, too, and it is only close to the shore that bottom is obtained in twelve to fifteen fathoms.

"It is difficult to make out San Juan del Sur from the similarity in the configuration of the coast; but when the weather is clear, the bearings of Momobacho, Ometepe, or Orosi will prove an unfailing guide.

"The American agent's house at San Juan del Sur is in lat. 11° 15′ N., long. 86° 1′ W. The prevailing winds are from the N.E., or right off the land, and commonly attain considerable force, sometimes suddenly changing to east, or N.N.W. During the winter the west and south-west winds sometimes blow with violence. The anchorage outside the port is in eight to ten fathoms, sand and broken shells, at about half a mile from the points.

"The port itself is open to seaward, and, except with winds from that quarter, the landing is good; but in all weathers the points afford sufficient shelter for small vessels."

In the following chapter will be found some account of my journey up the river San Juan, across the Lake of Nicaragua to Granada, and thence to Managua, from which it is hoped the reader will glean some idea of the interior of Nicaragua, and especially its water communications.

CHAPTER XIII.

START UP THE COLORADO.—LEAF'S ISLAND.—LAURA FRANCES.—DELTA OF SAN JUAN.—SAN JUANILLO.—SEREPIQUI.—COLONEL CAUTY.—WRECKS ON THE RIVER.—CASTILLO VIEJO.—FORT SAN CARLOS.—LAKE STEAMER.—SAN MIGUELITO.—VOYAGING ON THE LAKE OF NICARAGUA.—SPECIMEN OF CARIB WORK.—GRANADA À DEMI.—OTTER'S MULE.—INTERVIEW WITH MR. WYKE.—MANAGUA.

MONDAY, *January* 16*th*, 1860.—At 1 o'clock in the morning, I was up and stirring; mosquitoes abundant. At 2 the Carib canoemen were down at the house (Gorgon Villa); and my friends Sewell, Otter, and Devereux went with me on board the 'Laura Frances.' We found that the fires had been lit soon after midnight, but it was half-past seven before the stokers could raise sufficient steam to leave Greytown Harbour. The 'Laura Frances' is an American river-boat, of about one hundred tons, and seventy-five-horse power; she draws three feet, and will steam six knots. She belonged to the American Atlantic and Pacific Ship Canal Company, but was at present held for their wages by her crew, viz. Mr. Dickson, clerk or supercargo; Mr. G. F. Holton, captain; Mr. Carman, mate and pilot, and two deck hands. The engineers and two stokers were hired for the occasion. When the company was in full operation, the wages of the above were nearly as follows:—Captain, seven dollars per day; mate, two dollars and a half per day; clerk, four dollars and a half per day; engineer, four dollars per day; head fireman, one dollar and a half per day; second fireman, one dollar per day; two deck hands, one dollar each; cost of coals *per diem*, about twenty dollars; wear and tear, seven dollars and a half per day; total cost per day, fifty dollars. The 'Laura Frances' cost 13,000 dollars, and sold for about 5000 dollars.

My arrangement with the owners of the 'Laura Frances' was as follows:—She was to take my canoe and party across the bar of the Colorado,—the San Juan branch being too shallow to ascend,—and up the river as far as the Machuca rapid; for which service I agreed to pay 100 dollars, and supply the boat with five tons of coals. After that I should have to make the best of my way in the canoe, which was 25 feet long by 3 feet 9 inches wide, and which, it was said, would attain great speed when propelled by our sturdy Caribs, Isaac Perry, Joseph Simon, John Peter, Joseph Manuel, Cæsar Brown, and Robert Pike.

On leaving the harbour we experienced the usual Greytown swell, which almost brought the little river-boat to a standstill, and it was two hours before we rounded the point and shut in the Gorgon and Sabine. The coast is low and monotonous. There are a few shanties between Punta Arenas and the Colorado. I remarked that the swell decreased considerably as we neared the river. At half-past eleven we crossed the bar through a nasty surf, least water seven feet; but, with the exception of a little damage from one sea, which struck us fair on the port quarter, and poured in a huge wave across the deck, we escaped scatheless. The bar is in the shape of a semicircle, which is the case with all the bars which I have seen off the mouths of rivers in Central America. Before crossing we had a good view of Tortuga, a hill which shows like an island, and is a most useful mark for this part of the coast, the sight of it at once convincing the navigator that he is to leeward of Greytown. The entrance to the Colorado is two hundred feet in width, and as much as five fathoms in depth inside the bar. The banks of the river are low, and covered with a dense jungle, abounding with reptiles. At 2.15, about ten miles from the mouth, we came to a shoal stretching right across the river, having from four to six feet over it. This was the shallowest water we had yet passed, never having found less than ten feet before: great quantities of grass grow in the river, the blades being in many places seven or eight feet in height. From 2.30 to 4.30 we encountered many difficulties from shoal water, but by the latter time we were clear of it, when at a distance of five miles from the apex of the Delta; up to this point the river makes several sharp turns and has a strong current. At 5.30 we passed the hut of one of the most daring of the filibusters, named Moore, but he now follows the peaceful occupation of shingling. After leaving this hut behind us the apex of the Delta appears in sight, with Leaf Island off its point, and one or two small islands between. The distance is eighteen miles to the mouth of the Colorado, and sixteen to Greytown.

Both point and island are cleared and cultivated, although a great portion of the latter has been lately washed away by the rising of the river (December, 1859); at which period Mr. Leaf's house and much property was destroyed.

A rise of the river in December is most unusual, *October being the month for floods.* Between January and May it is at the lowest; for instance, the 'Laura Frances' got on shore on the Machuca rapids on the 27th of January last year, and remained there until the following 8th of July.

At 6 o'clock we reached Leaf's Island, about a mile beyond the apex, passing houses on each bank; but half an hour later, about three miles above Colorado, the 'Laura Frances' got aground, and remained fixed all night close to the left bank; the river quite shallow right across. During the day little was seen worth remarking; the land was everywhere low, flat, and monotonous; the right bank was the highest, but for miles no banks at all could be discerned, the water being bounded by swamps, covered with the most luxuriant grass of the same nature as lower down, the feeding-ground of the manati. We did not however see any of those animals, and only a few alligators, cranes, macaws, parrots, and iguanas. Thus ended our first day; as regards distance, we afterwards found we could have done more by paddling in the canoe. The grounding of the 'Laura Frances' gave me more time and opportunity for examining the apex of the Delta, with a view to forming an opinion as to the practicability of damming the Colorado, and by that means forcing the water, which now uselessly escapes to the sea, into the San Juan branch to act as a scour. I cannot say that I found much encouragement in the prospect before me; the surrounding land is very low, and is so loose and friable, as to be almost of the nature of a quagmire, and therefore easily displaced by a more than ordinary rush of water; indeed, during the freshets, the outline of the river-banks is repeatedly altered, even the large island guarding the apex does not escape; and there is no doubt that the whole of it will disappear in time, and the *débris* lend a helping hand to silt up the San Juan. Every sign seems to be in favour of that arm becoming at no distant period a mere driblet, while the Colorado will increase in volume, and become the main stream of the river. Considering therefore the unstable quality of the ground, the great size and immense solidity of such a dam as would be required, and the swampy nature of the country through which the water would have to be forced,—the San Juan branch, be it remembered, being anything but straight; on the contrary, winding and curving sharply in its course; I am of opinion that, even supposing the dam could be constructed, the stream, instead of scouring, would simply spread over the swampy Delta, and ultimately divide itself into a hundred little rivulets. The cost of these river operations would be enormous.

At 7 A.M. (after sticking on the sandbar twelve hours) we managed to pick our way into deeper water, and about an hour afterwards reached the San Juanillo,—an insignificant stream, which, after leaving the river, takes a small curve and empties itself into the San Juan branch a few

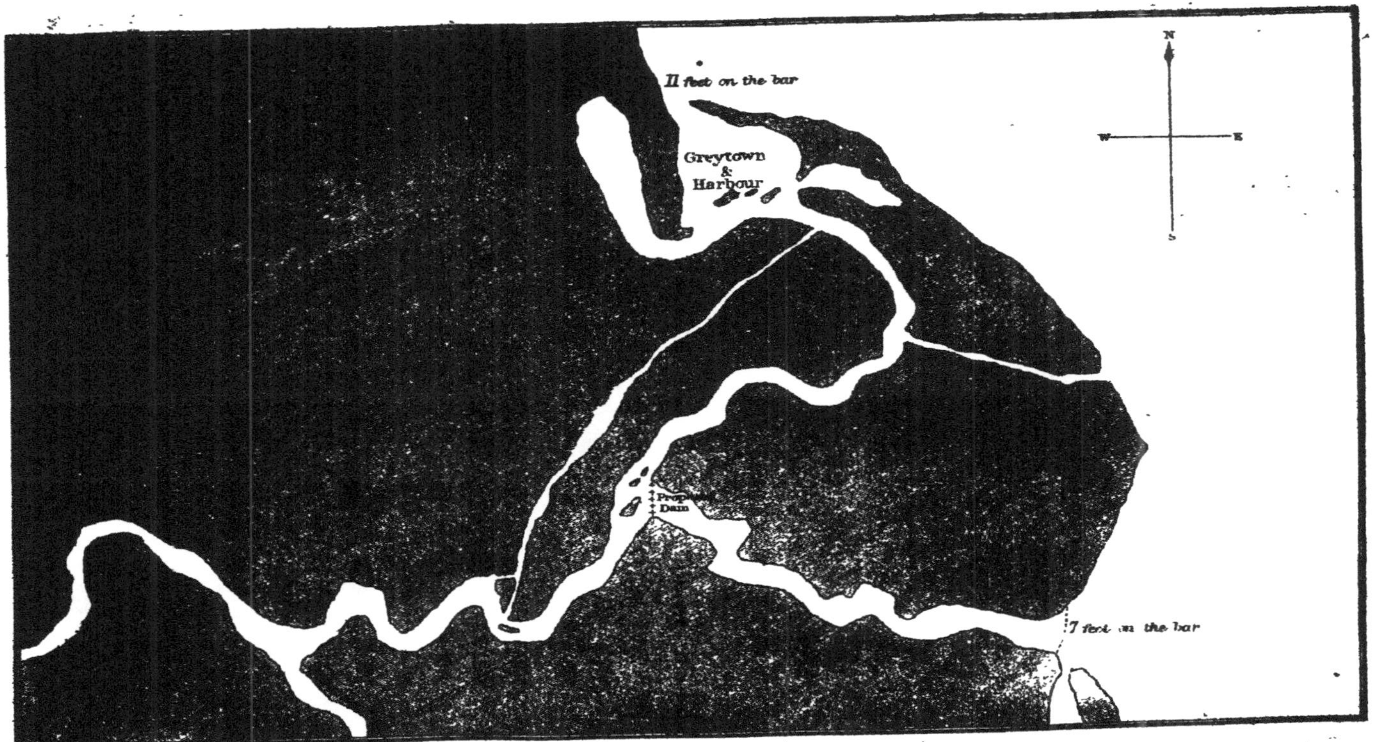
N
W
E
S
11 feet on the bar
Greytown
&
Harbour
Dam
7 feet on the bar

miles above Greytown. It is very narrow and very shallow, and the entrance is almost hidden by a small island. About a quarter of a mile above it the river takes a bend (*vide* plan), and it is proposed to cut a canal from the bight of this bend through the intervening land to the San Juanillo. This idea seemed to be more feasible than the damming proposition; that is to say, it might be done for very much less money; and as the course of the San Juanillo is more direct than that of the San Juan, the water might be kept within bounds by the aid of a few groups of piles driven judiciously at prominent points: however, a careful survey of the stream must be made before a decisive opinion can be given, and this I had not time to effect either going or returning. The distance by the San Juanillo to Greytown would be about eighteen miles. Here I observed the first appearance of rock, in the shape of a few boulders on the point.

Abreast of the San Juanillo is a very nice little plantation, belonging to a Mr. Wolf; this is the usual resting-place for a smart canoe at the termination of the first day from Greytown. The house is one of the best on the river; the clearance is about five acres, and, like all the rest, only planted with vegetables and fruits, for which a ready sale was always obtained during the halcyon days of the Transit. The river in this vicinity is dotted with islands, but the banks continue low, nowhere more than ten feet above the water. At 9, arrived at the widest part of the river, which is here from three to four hundred yards across, with rocks right over, having from four to five feet upon them. This is the first cropping out we have seen, nothing hitherto but mud, if a few loose stones at the bend above the Juanillo be excepted. At about 10 passed the wreck of a transit steamer, called the Wheeler; she is the first of a series of wrecks, extending as far as the Toro rapids. At this place we overtook the canoe carrying the Costarica mail; all the crew were quite naked, poling their boat along by main force against the current. At 10.30 arrived at the mouth of the Serepiqui, about a hundred and fifty yards wide, and very shallow; about a mile below we passed close to the position carried by Captain Lock, R.N., in 1848. The battery has quite disappeared, overgrown in fact by the jungle; only a few stones and a rusty old gun, visible at low river, mark the place.

It was at the mouth of the Serepiqui that the Costaricans, led by English and American officers, inflicted so disastrous a defeat upon the filibusters, in December, 1856. The clearance which they had occupied and partially stockaded was not yet overgrown with underwood, and the remains of the camp were still visible. Walker's object in posting these men (about sixty) at the mouth of the river was to check any attempt on the part of the Costaricans to seize the Transit vessels, and thus cut off his supplies of men and munitions; and no doubt, if those entrusted with this important post had performed their duty effectually, Walker might, in all human probability, still have been President of Nicaragua. The manner in which the post was taken deserves relating: it was due entirely to the infusion of English and American intelligence into the counsels of the Costaricans, who, at that time, were doing their utmost to expel

Walker from Nicaragua, from the fear that his example might induce some enterprising American to try his hand upon their State. The originator of the plan for the capture of the garrison at the Serepiqui and the ultimate seizure of the river steamers was Mr. George F. Cauty. At first no attention was paid to his suggestions, but upon the arrival of an agent of Mr. Vanderbilt, a Mr. Spencer, the project was adopted. It was decided to avoid the Serepiqui altogether, and to cut a path through the woods to the San Carlos, descend that river, and thus take the garrison from the rear. This was accordingly done; a working party was advanced through the woods before the main body, and when it arrived at the San Carlos, rough boats were hurriedly dug out from single trees for the transport of the soldiers. The Costarican Government gave Mr. Cauty a commission as captain, and that gentleman appears to have been the life and soul of the party; he had been a sailor, and his nautical knowledge must have stood him in good stead in the construction of craft to convey the men down the river. On the 2nd of December, 1856, 250 men, under Colonel Bareillet, a French officer, and Colonel Blanco, a native, started across the mountains, and on the 7th reached the San Carlos; on the 12th they embarked on board five dug-outs and three rafts constructed by Captain Cauty, and on the 17th reached the confluence of the San Carlos and San Juan with only one day's provisions remaining. Here the party nearly came to grief, from the quarrels of the leaders as to who was commander-in-chief; this was settled by Cauty, who decided that Spencer, the American, was to be the chief.

Accordingly that worthy started with half the force on the 13th, on the evening of which day he arrived in rear of the doomed camp; here they were obliged to lie hidden for the night, the rain descending in torrents. Next morning at daylight a rush was made on the garrison, which, being quite off its guard, was of course overpowered in no time. The commander of the filibusters fought well and received many wounds, but it was of no avail; the surprise was complete, a number of men being in the water bathing at the time of the attack. All the garrison were killed except twelve, two of whom were made prisoners; the remainder swam across the stream and escaped. This success was vigorously followed up, the expedition proceeding down stream to Greytown, where it obtained possession of all the river-boats which happened to be in the port, four in number, without firing a shot, thus virtually sealing Walker's doom.

It requires local knowledge to appreciate the bravery and dash of this brilliant little campaign. First cutting through the primæval forest between thirty and forty miles, over swamps, cactus, and other tropical impediments, then felling trees and shaping them into canoes, and lashing others together for rafts with the long tendrils of the wild vine, and finally embarking 125 men, with arms, provisions, etc., upon such frail contrivances, to float down a rapid and comparatively unknown stream, and attack a daring enemy,—is no common action, and deserved well of the country.

But to resume my narrative. At 11.45, passed the narrowest part of the river, not fifty yards across, about seven miles from the Sérepiqui; at this part of the river there are no plantations, and only a hut here and there, used by the gatherers of sarsaparilla. We observed a canoe full of Greytown negroes, busy fishing; on their road home these fellows steal all the plantains they can get, from the plantations lower down; a ready market, and no questions asked, awaiting them at Greytown. Heavy tropical showers and a broiling sun alternated during the day; but a capital pilot-house on deck afforded first-rate shelter from both. Passed the 'Nicaraguan' mail canoe; the natives, stark naked, poling their boat against the current; they were streaming with perspiration, and are alternately washed by heavy rain and then baked by the sun, for days together,—a dog's life, I should think; nevertheless they seem actually to thrive on it. At 2 P.M. passed the Moreno Grande, or great whirlpool, which whirls with considerable force, and at high river is very dangerous; we go through it with a good head of steam, without much difficulty. This whirlpool is about thirteen miles from the Serepiqui; here the banks are a little higher, and a red clay takes the place of the mud lower down, and besides appears partially stratified and more indurated; indeed two or three cliffy projections in this vicinity give quite a picturesque appearance to the otherwise same scenery of the river. From this position the hill of San Carlos can be seen; it is one of the prominent river-marks, and valuable as such to the navigator. The banks even here, although much higher than lower down, are flooded at high river, as the driftwood sufficiently proves. A little after 5 P.M. passed San Carlos Island, which is opposite the mouth of the river of that name; its width is about two hundred yards, and its current quite two knots an hour. It was here that a curious disaster befell the Costarican force sent down to reinforce the vanguard, which had operated so successfully against the Serepiqui garrison, as narrated above. It appears that the troops, numbering about 400, were descending the San Carlos on rafts and dug-outs similar to those constructed by Captain Cauty, when one of the captured steamers sent by their friends to assist hove in sight, paddling and puffing up stream: this sight, so strange, indeed supernatural, to the ignorant Costaricans, caused quite a panic amongst them; a number in their fright jumped overboard, and in endeavouring to reach the shore were drowned. From San Carlos island, the river winds almost in semicircles, for two or three miles. When dark, we still pursued our way, and steered between the shadows of the trees, in the middle of the stream. The current was very strong off Companion Island, but the 'Laura Frances' went over it well, and reached Mr. Emmons's plantation at the foot of the Machuca rapids at 8.30, where the steamer was secured for the night, and her part of the contract fulfilled. We went to bed early, after paying the hundred dollars to Mr. Dickson, and fortunately slept well,—as we had plenty of work before us. From Leaf's Island to Machuca usually occupies two days in a canoe; we have therefore gained one day in time, and avoided considerable exposure, by employing the steamer.

The following is an itinerary of the distances from point to point on the river, between Greytown and the Machuca rapids:—

	Miles.
From Greytown to the mouth of the San Juanillo . .	2·310
Mouth of the San Juanillo to the divergence of the Toro	1·690
From divergence of the Toro to the Colorado	11·530
From Greytown to Colorado	15·530
Colorado to the sea	18·000
From the Colorado to the San Juanillo	5·494
From San Juanillo to the Serepiqui	8·036
From Serepiqui to San Carlos Island	25·040
From San Carlos to Machuca rapids	17·499
From Colorado to Machuca	56·069

Wednesday, January 18th.—This morning we were up and away the first thing, leaving the 'Laura Frances' before 6. It took us thirty-seven minutes to get over the Machuca rapid, paddling in the deep water, and poling in the shallow; the bottom was rocky, with not more than a depth of 2½ feet right across. The rapid is marked by the wreck of a river steamer, named the 'Oras,' around which a quantity of trees and *débris* have collected, now almost covered with vegetation, and which will soon become a permanent island—not improving, by any means, the navigation of the channel. A quarter of a mile ahead of the 'Oras' lies the wreck of the 'Catalina Maria,' also doing its part to obstruct the river.

The strongest current over the Machuca rapids is about seven knots an hour, and is called by the natives Infiernito (small hell). The average rate is between four and five knots per hour. A road has been cut on the river's bank for passengers to walk round, but it is now nearly destroyed, for the most part by the crews of the bongos, who have wantonly cut up the bridges for firewood, when any amount of fuel might have been picked up all around.

At 6.45 passed Machuca Island, and about 8 came to the foot of Las Balas, and in little more than half an hour got through, impelled by ten sturdy paddles, for we all worked with a will. By 10 we had left the Mico rapid behind, and made fast to the bushes for half an hour, to eat our breakfast, which consisted of biscuit and cheese, washed down by sherry and water. Our stopping-place was at the mouth of a creek called San Bartolomeo. Soon after leaving, we passed another wreck, 'Henry Bulwer.' I should think it would be worth while to collect the machinery of the various vessels left here to rot.

At 10.15 rounded Punta Gorda, where the current runs very strongly, and then sighted Castillo Viejo, which is a very conspicuous landmark, and perhaps the most important position on the river. There are two rounded conical hills, on the right bank, commanding the rapid, and upon the one nearest the water the old castle, captured by Nelson, is a prominent object.

Unfortunately for the defenders, the hill behind commands the one on which the fort is situated, and this was taken advantage of by Lord Nelson, who battered and ultimately captured the fort from that vantage-ground; it is called Nelson's Hill to the present day. This is not the fortification described by our great naval hero as having been taken by boarding. At 11 we landed at the foot of the rapid, while some soldiers, guiltless of any outward sign of their profession, dragged the canoe through the rushing water, and secured her safely in the placid river above, which is here 200 yards in breadth. The rapid extends right across the river; it has a fall of five feet, and runs about eight knots an hour. In the meantime on shore I made the acquaintance of the commandant, Colonel Manuel Arguello, a *quondam* filibuster, who, having quarrelled with Walker, made his peace with his countrymen, and now holds office under the native Government. The Colonel, who was lame from a bullet in his leg, was very civil to us, and gave us a couple of fish at parting, for which I pressed upon his acceptance a bottle of rum. At this place the transit passengers disembarked, and were transferred to another steamer above. A very cheap light tramway was used in the intervening space between the landing piers, by means of which the travellers and their luggage were quickly conveyed from one vessel to the other.

Castillo cannot properly be called a rapid, as there is a decided fall of some feet, causing the water to boil and tumble in a dangerous manner at its foot, so much so indeed, that a canoe would be instantly swamped if she got into it; in fact we had to cross from Point Gorda, some distance lower down, with every care and precaution.

From Castillo to the foot of the Toro the scenery maintained the same monotonous character, becoming low, and overgrown with grass, just as it was about the delta. Toro proved the largest rapid and was the most trying part of the day's work, although the stream upon it did not exceed four knots; but by a little after 4 the canoe was above it, and in the Agua Muerte, or dead water, viz. with a current of only one knot against us.

Here we stopped for a few minutes while the Caribs cut some light spars for a mast and sprit, so that we could make sail across the lake. It is a wonder that the Spaniards did not select this rapid for the site of their fort, because, in a strategical point of view, it is far superior to any place below; for instance, the rapid is straight for several hundred yards, consequently a well-directed fire would destroy the attacking force long before they could return a shot. At the head of the rapid the Savolo river empties itself, and at its mouth a family of Indians are living, consisting of two women and two men. One of the latter boarded us, and volunteered the information that he was the lieutenant of the tribe and his brother the king: he was a powerful man, and very fond of grog. We saw the family mansion as we passed, but had not time to inspect it. The wreck of a steamer, called the 'Central America,' close to, was perhaps the cause of the location. At 4.30 stopped at a deserted house, and made a capital dinner on the fish given us at Castillo, and some coffee afterwards. The rest quite set us all up; and as mosquitoes were plentiful, I determined to push on all night to reach Fort San Carlos, on the lake, twenty-seven miles off. Just at sunset we passed another wreck, the 'Matapa.' During the whole night (there was no moon, and it was very dark) the men worked splendidly at the paddles; it was impossible to sleep, so we four took watch and watch, one looking out, another steering; and thus the dreary night passed on, occasional showers wetting us to the skin. Steering was much preferred to looking out, for the banks were so low that the canoe often ran into the long grass before the look-out could give warning; and I can bear witness to the aching pain in the eyes occasioned by peering into the darkness hour after hour. So painful was this watching, and the constrained position in which we were obliged to sit, that it is probable we should have made fast to the bank had there been one; but thrusting the canoe as far as possible into the long grass we could find no footing, and therefore landing was out of the question.

Thursday, January 19*th*, 1860.—At 3 this morning we were close to the fort, but the Caribs objected to going there while it continued dark, because the valiant commandant had a playful habit of firing at boats approaching without giving them any warning; and having already succeeded in killing a few innocents, our men preferred sitting patiently on their thwarts, in the pouring rain, and waiting for daylight. The canoe was pushed well into the grass, and we were prevented moping over our wet and cold plight by the vigorous attacks of thousands of mosquitoes, which made our faces, hands, and feet like plum-puddings, long before daylight enabled us to push boldly across to the fort. Here we found the current was certainly not more than a knot an hour. Fort San Carlos is the place described by Nelson in a sketch of his life written by himself for Dr. M'Arthur in 1799. He says: "In January, 1780, an expedition being resolved upon against San Carlos, I was chosen to direct the sea part of it. Major Polson, who commanded, will tell you of my exertions: how I quitted my ship; carried troops in boats a hundred miles up a river which none but

Spaniards, since the times of the buccaneers, had ever ascended. It will then be told how I boarded, if I may be allowed the expression, an outpost of the enemy, situated on an island in the river; that I made batteries, and afterwards fought them; and was a principal cause of our success."

The fort is situated on the left bank of the river, at the point where it escapes from the Lake; the land is low all round, and cleared to the extent of perhaps 2000 yards. The island that Nelson describes as having boarded is not in the vicinity of San Carlos, as many suppose; it is just below Castillo Viejo, and merely an outpost of that fortification. The old fort built by the Spaniards is in ruins, and overshadowed by the luxuriant vegetation. There are three guns mounted and ready for service; but the place could offer no resistance to men-of-war boats well manned and armed. It is a dirty, sickly hole, with dirty inhabitants, and everything dirty about it; doubtless, in the hands of the Spaniards it was different, as the remains of paved streets and ruined houses testify. I ought to mention that this fort also fell into the hands of the Costaricans, and principally through Captain Cauty, who was made colonel for his services on the occasion. It appears that after securing the steamers and the fortified positions on the river, it was determined to add San Carlos to the conquests; and accordingly, a party of picked men was placed on board the 'Virgen' Lake steamer, one of the prizes, which, with the usual Transit signal flying, steamed as close to the fort as her draught would allow. The garrison had not the least idea that she contained enemies; and Captain Gruder, the commandant, according to his wont, came on board to see what he could pick up. He was at once secured; and being convinced that Captain Cauty and a body of men were in the rear of the fort, having forced their way through the swampy thickets during the night, he determined to surrender, and accordingly did so without firing a shot.

Here we were asked for our passports by a ragged sentry, and a show made of searching the canoe; but I objected strenuously to this proceeding, and it was not persisted in. At that early hour the commandant was asleep, but I marched off to his house, woke him up, and having gone through the form of calling on him, and presenting a note of introduction in lieu of a passport, I lost no time in clearing out of the filthy place, and pulling on board the 'Cass Irissari,' a Lake steamer, belonging to the late company, and at present held by the captain and engineer in payment of their wages. The captain's name was Slocum, and the engineer's was Place; the latter was at Granada, but the former received us very civilly, and gave us free permission to use his cook-house to prepare our breakfast, etc. Our right-hand man, Perry, during my interview with the commandant, managed to replenish our nearly exhausted larder; but he reported that provisions of any sort were exorbitantly dear. While the breakfast was getting ready under the guidance of the aforesaid Perry, we poured the waters of Lake Nicaragua over each other, and were much refreshed thereby. After a good breakfast of eggs and milk,—the former twopence halfpenny each, the latter one shilling per bottle,—we once more embarked in the canoe, and made sail, to voyage from one end to the other of the Lake, a distance of ninety miles. The water is shallow off San Carlos; indeed, in the dry season, six feet is about the deepest obtained. By steering direct for the island of Solentinane (800 feet high) the best water is found. I was disappointed in getting a good view of the scenery, owing to thick weather; lofty islands dotting the sides and centre of the Lake could, it is true, be discerned, but they had a ghost-like appearance through the mist, and did not present any striking or remarkable feature; the peaks of Madera and Ometepec were just visible. Ometepec is thickly inhabited, and is the only island on which there is a volcano; it is 5050 feet high, and Madera 4190. It is a very curious circumstance, that throughout America, and pretty generally in other parts of the world, the vicinity of volcanoes is chosen for settlement, and moreover is thickly inhabited. Ometepec and Madera are joined together by a narrow isthmus, densely covered with wood; a great deal of produce is raised here. The water of the Lake, instead of being clear as crystal, was a dirty yellowish-green, with lots of sharks and alligators cruising about: sailors surely ought to be free from their bitterest enemy when in fresh water. The wind was light and puffy, which made the canoe very uncomfortable, for in this species of craft it is necessary to be always on the *qui vive* to keep her balanced; so the body is in perpetual motion, seesawing backwards and forwards. At 1.30 passed Bagueta. The coast was low and swampy at first starting, but as we drew away from San Carlos it began to rise, and as far as the eye could reach it seemed to undulate towards the interior, while the dense forests gave way to savana, here and there dotted with trees, giving quite a park-like appearance to the scene. At 2 o'clock arrived at San Miguelito, the Lake terminus of my proposed temporary line. It is simply a collection of substantial huts (some of them with an upper story) perched upon some rising ground, with savana land stretching away inland as far as the eye can reach,—a most beautiful scene.

The country in the vicinity is favourable for a road. It is slightly undulating, and without any impediment in the shape of hills worth speaking about. The depth of water in the bay is amply sufficient for the near approach of Lake steamers; in short, the place seems well adapted for the Lake terminus of the railroad. Everything was very dear, and, there being little inducement to stop, we once more sailed, after buying a couple of fowls and some oranges. I had been armed with a letter of introduction for Señor Montenegro, the alcalde of the place, but he was away. The Spanish American natives always imagine that every white man, and especially every Englishman, must be a doctor; I was therefore much bothered for medicine; but as that commodity was scarce, I contented myself with ministering to one old woman, who was very ill. I obtained a few soundings, both going into and running out of the bay, with a marked fishing-line and an American bootjack (iron) tied to the end of it for a sinker. There was nine feet close to the beach. At 3 o'clock the canoe was well away from San Miguelito; and as the breeze had freshened, we went along at a spanking pace, or to use the Carib expression, "she ripped," and soon wetted us through. In half an hour Pedronal* was passed, the next inhabited place to San Miguelito; it consisted of three huts, and is merely a cattle rancho. The scenery of the savana land is an agreeable change after the monotonous river-banks. At this part of the Lake the beach is low, but not swampy, with no sign of mountains. The land rises to one or two hundred feet, covered with grass. I saw a few cocoa-nuts,—a tree which seldom thrives inland, or even out of sight of its beloved sea.

As we sailed along, the weather became more and more squally, and the canoe shipped a good deal of water, which we had to bale out as fast as possible. Passed some solitary huts, and at 6 o'clock stopped at one, called Cocito, which may be known by its being opposite to the islands of San Bernardo and San Bernadito, in line; the former is 347 feet in height. The bay in which we landed was small and sandy, and Perry soon had a large fire alight and dinner preparing, after which we tried to sleep, but sand-flies, mosquitoes, occasional rain, and the dread of alligators, which are both numerous and audacious, kept most of us awake. At a little after midnight we paddled out into the breeze, and hoisting sail made good progress. At Cocito prices are more reasonable; fivepence for a fowl, for instance. The rancho was filthy, and barely sheltered the inhabitants from the weather; vermin of all sorts rioted in undis-

* In this locality gold has lately been discovered.

turbed enjoyment. An amiable young herdsman was paying his addresses to one of the young lady inmates. Our appearance, and almost forcible entry into the place, did not appear to disconcert the pair, who were speechless with happiness, rolling their great black eyes about in the most approved manner.

Friday, Jan. 20th, 1860.—At daylight this morning we found ourselves off the Chontales Islands, and observed a change in the scenery, the land rising and swelling into hills and mountains towards the northward. The magnificent mountain of Alto Grande was right ahead. It is 3149 feet in height, and is an excellent mark for the voyager. Every one in the canoe was wet through. Passed the landing-place at the commencement of the road leading to the mines of Chontales, and also saw the mouths of three small rivers. The whole of this fertile coast is quite uninhabited, not even a hut to be seen; it is one vast natural pasturage and meadow-land.

At 9.30 A.M. came in sight of the three Cays, where the bongos and canoes keep away for Granada, which is on the opposite side of the Lake. At noon we arrived, and disembarked to stretch our limbs and discuss some biscuit, cheese, and wine for breakfast, after which we pushed out boldly into the Lake under sail, steering straight for the hill of Granada, 4480 feet. When fairly away from the lee of the islands we caught it, and for five weary hours went through a course of fresh-water navigation such as I trust I may never see again. To use the Carib expression, it was one constant "rip," the canoe tearing through the water, scooping such quantities inboard that we were obliged to bale without intermission. Any awkwardness would have been fatal: we had to sit with the immovable firmness of a North American Indian, and try to imitate his stoical indifference; but it was a hard trial, for we all felt it was a matter of touch and go. Had the canoe filled and capsized, not even the admirable Carib canoemen could have righted her with such waves running, and then the sharks would very speedily have made short work with us. It is surprising how soon the waves rise on fresh water; a very little wind makes the water ripple violently in a few minutes, and the strong breeze we experienced caused a high, irregular, topping wave, far worse than would have been met with on the ocean. I can only say that I shall never despise a fresh-water sailor again. At 5 we ran the canoe through a bad surf on the beach, close to the old fort at Granada, and of course she instantly swamped. This was no more than might have been expected; but in addition to having all our things wet through, we were much provoked by a number of natives standing on the beach, who, instead of assisting us, stood by and laughed, for which I anathematized them in my very best Spanish. After some hard work we got the canoe up the beach, and the luggage placed in safety, fortunately without any loss in the surf. We then had to walk about half a mile inland to the city of Granada, or rather that part of it where the only hotel is situated; here, in less than half an hour we found ourselves and our wet traps fairly installed, with the prospect of a dinner, night's rest, and dry clothes. At this hotel I had the pleasure of becoming acquainted with Colonel Cauty. The dinner and night's rest came in good time; and although neither viands nor accommodation was anything to boast of, yet we were only too thankful after our late hardships and imminent danger to get what we could. I do not suppose that any one of my party will, to the day of his death, forget his first cruise on fresh water; and had my friends not been the best of good fellows, physically and mentally, I do not believe they could have stood it. We had been five days on the journey of 230 miles, of which three days and nights at least were spent in hard labour, constant anxiety and watchfulness, with little or no sleep, meals taken anyhow, without shelter of any sort, and therefore alternately wetted to the skin and broiled by the sun. As to the Caribs, they were used to it, but their performance deserves record. They paddled without intermission for nearly eleven hours, during which the canoe was propelled over all the rapids, viz.:—

	Miles.
From Machuca to Las Balas rapids	3·056
From Las Balas to Mico rapids	2·256
From Mico to Castillo Viejo rapids	5·702
From Castillo Viejo to Toro rapids	9·469
Total length of rapids	20·483

After which, with only a rest of two hours to cook our food, these men resumed their paddles, and completed the remainder of the journey to Fort San Carlos, reaching there before daylight next morning.

	Miles.
From Toro rapid to Fort San Carlos	27·228
From Machuca to Fort San Carlos—total distance paddled in twenty hours	47·711

Who will say that they were afraid of work, when they

keep up continuous labour, requiring very great muscular exertion, for the space of twenty-two hours, with the intermission of only two hours for cooking and eating, and when during that time they covered a space of forty-seven miles of river against an average current of two knots an hour at least? Of a feat like this, as most Europeans would call it, these men think nothing; and Perry, the head man, told me they often worked much harder at mahogany cutting. Before going to bed, I called upon Mr. Thomas, Mr. Goussin, and Colonel Vega. The daughters of the latter favoured me with some popular airs on the guitar, while their father placed all that he had "*muy á la disposicion de usted.*"

Saturday, January 21st, 1860.—We were all too tired to make an early start to Masaya; in fact, a night's rest was absolutely necessary; consequently we decided not to start until the afternoon, and so avoid the hottest part of the day. There are regular times for setting off on the journey,—either very early in the morning or late in the afternoon,—and the muleteers will not deviate one jot or tittle from the "custom of the country," although, for our parts, the sun's rays would scarcely have struck us as a very great hardship after the late exposure. A friend at Greytown supplied me with the following memoranda for guidance in travelling through this part of Nicaragua.

"Leave Granada for Masaya at 5 A.M. or at 4 P.M.; the distance is twelve miles, and ought to be ridden in two hours and a half. Sleep at Masaya. From Masaya to Managua it is twenty-four miles, which ought to be ridden in four hours and a half. Start very early. From

Managua to Matiares (a small village) it is eighteen miles, about a three hours' ride. Matiares to Nagarote, fifteen miles, requiring two hours and a half. Nagarote to Pueblo Nuevo, twelve miles, a two hours' ride. Pueblo Nuevo to Leon, twenty-one miles, about four hours on the road.

	Miles.	Hours.
Distances:—Granada to Managua	36	7
Managua to Leon	66	11½
Total distance	102	18½

"Time requisite, three days at least.

"Silver will be required, principally small change."

In the meantime we made a short tour of inspection. The streets about the *plaza*, which is situated near the centre of the city, are roughly paved, inclining gently towards the middle of the road from either side, and thus forming a central gutter. The pavement for foot passengers is raised about eighteen inches above the road, and is very narrow; indeed, it requires some little navigation to enable two people to pass: an English lady would want the entire footpath to herself, but here crinoline is as yet unknown; it therefore does not so much matter. At a short distance from the plaza the streets are left in a state of nature, being sandy in the dry and muddy in the wet season. It was impossible not to be struck with the stagnation all around. It is true that the time of our walk was the hour of *siesta*, but I have never observed in any Spanish town, even at that lazy period of the day, such stillness as was the case at Granada. Indeed the town has suffered a heavy blow, from which it may possibly not entirely recover; only a few houses are slowly rising from their ashes, and those of quite a common order of architecture, showing, as I conceive, a sort of accepted, if not contented degeneracy. Poor Granada! it is one of the oldest cities in the New World, having been founded by Cordova in 1562. I fear it has now arrived at *el último suspiro.* The population does not now exceed 8000, or at most 10,000 inhabitants. The houses of the wealthier classes are of adobes,* and appear to be very comfortable and well adapted to the climate. They are seldom more than one story high, and are built in the form of a square, generally upon a stone foundation, having a *patio*, or courtyard, in the centre, upon which all the rooms open. The *patio*, when neatly laid out with flowers and a fountain, has a most charming effect; between it and the rooms there is a railing and broad pavement, over which the tiled roof is made to extend, so that the inmates can walk all round under shelter in the heaviest rains; the windows are not glazed, but protected with iron bars; and the rooms are guiltless of ceilings. There are commonly two massive gateways, and the kitchen is

* Jarvis, in his 'Scenes and Scenery in the Sandwich Islands,' makes the following remark on adobes:—"These bricks, no doubt, are of precisely the same make and pattern as those required of the children of Israel by their Egyptian taskmasters. Indeed, the resemblance between a group of Hawaiians making the bricks, and the implements employed by them, are strikingly similar to a hieroglyphical painting some 4000 years old. . . . *Adaub* was the Egyptian word for this kind of brick, and it is still used by the Copts, etc. Doubtless the Saracens derived it from the Egyptians, and carried it into Spain; thence it went into America, and from America to the Hawaiian islands. Continuing westward, it may arrive at the land of its birth."

generally detached from the main building. The ventilation is perfect, and the houses all seem delightfully cool. The huts of the poorer people are mere mud and plaster, badly thatched, and can scarcely be called weather-proof. To this cause, and to their careless habits, may be fairly ascribed the sickness which so often exclusively visits the lower orders in this very healthy country. Most of the churches are in ruins, and priests appear to be at a discount. The work of destruction by Henningsen commenced on the 21st of November, 1856, and eight churches were more or less destroyed, viz. the Jaltaba, the Mercedes, the parochial church in the plaza, the San Sabastian, the Guadalupe, the Esquipulas, the San Juan de Dios, and the San Francisco. It is impossible to walk about Granada without a deep feeling of sorrow for its wretched condition, and a longing desire to aid in the regeneration of the country generally; but I fear this can only be effectually accomplished by the gradual substitution of a new race in place of the present Spanish element. It is curious to observe, no matter in what part of the world they have set their seal, how wickedly and selfishly the Spaniard has used the power which the Almighty permitted him to enjoy. In his own country this is not less a fact; and I remember being particularly struck with the stagnation in the city of Granada,—one of the most ancient cities of the Old World,—a year or two ago, when I was rambling amongst the ruins of the Alhambra. Granada in Spain is just as much behind the time as its namesake in Nicaragua. I am sure that Montesquieu ought to have said that

"God permitted that Spaniards (not Turks) should exist on earth, a people the *most* fit to possess uselessly a great empire." At 3.30 P.M. the mules were at the door, and we started, accompanied by an American dentist, who was making money by tooth-drawing. He was a very gentlemanly person, and quite won upon all of us. He told us that the teeth of Nicaragua were sadly out of order. Our guide was an extremely disagreeable-looking fellow, and did not belie his looks, for soon after starting I had occasion to ask him a question, which he did not choose to "intiende" (understand), so I determined to stop that sort of conduct at once, and, seizing him by the collar, told him that if he did not "intiende" every word I said to him, and that right sharply, I would break every bone in his body. I had no more trouble with our worthy guide. Our saddles gave us great discomfort; in the first place, they were of the rudest form of construction—little better, indeed, than pack-saddles—with a sheepskin or pillion thrown over the wooden excrescences; and in the next place, our late repeated duckings had made our skins tender, like a washerwoman's, so that we lost a considerable amount of cuticle in a very short space of time. We did not reach Masaya without some amusement. Otter, "of ours," dismounted to pick up a spur, and upon attempting to get into the saddle again, the mule dealt him a kick which sent him flying into the bush. However, no bones were broken, and after a good laugh we pushed on again, arriving at Masaya a little after 7 o'clock, having been three hours and a half on the road, —if road it could be called, being merely a cutting through the bush to the width of about ten or fifteen feet. The country is flat the whole way to the Gulf of Fonseca; indeed, it is said that nowhere does the road attain a greater height than sixty feet. We passed a good many plantations, a few of which were devoted to indigo. The owners are again, but very slowly, turning their attention to agriculture. Indigo used to be one of the chief sources of wealth to Nicaragua. Its production was carefully attended to, with the most lucrative results; indeed, Nicaraguan indigo commanded the highest price in the European market. The cultivation has, of course, much fallen off in consequence of the late civil wars, but it can be resumed with advantage now that peace is restored apparently on a firm basis. The few plantations I observed seemed to me to be very carelessly tended and managed, perhaps owing to the blight of poverty which appears to have fallen on this beautiful land.

This part of the world would be a perfect Paradise to the small capitalist who would be content to settle down for a few years, and cultivate one or more of the many highly remunerative products of Nicaragua. If the blessings of a good government only prove to be at last permanently secured, this magnificent country would offer the finest field for enterprise in the world. At Masaya we put up at a sort of inn, the master of which was so lazy that he could hardly be induced to get out of his hammock and make money. Our supper consisted of olla-podrida, tasajo, beans, bread, and coffee. Liquids were produced, but did not find a sale, to the host's evident disappointment and disgust. He could not understand sobriety in an Anglo-Saxon. Our beds were hides stretched on frames. There is an indescribable harshness about this style of couch far worse than a plank, to say nothing of the tendency of the material to harbour all sorts of vermin.

Sunday, January 22nd, 1860.—At 4 this morning we turned out, and after swallowing a very nasty muddy cup of coffee, mounted our mules, and rode on for Managua. Our lazy host did not forget, however, to charge us nine dollars for the miserable accommodation he had vouchsafed us. Of course our limited stay at Masaya; and the fact that it was dark when we entered and dark when we left, prevents my giving any detailed description of the place. I could only make out that it was an assemblage of adobe-built houses grouped round the plaza, which was large, and had a decent-sized church in one corner. Masaya is essentially an Indian town, and celebrated for its hammocks and grass *alforjas*, or saddle-bags. The filibusters did not injure this place. Just before daylight we rode through the Indian village "Indiri," three miles from Masaya; and three miles further on, we saw extended before us a large expanse of black cinder, thrown up by the volcano of Masaya, situated close on our left. From the highest part of the road at this place we caught a glimpse of the Lake of Managua, a pretty peep of scenery. The road was otherwise monotonous throughout, being merely a cutting through the dense underwood, with not a single habitation near it, in consequence, it is said, of the total absence of water in the dry season. We jogged along without adventure of any sort; but when more than halfway Otter's mule began to show signs of exhaustion, and his respect for it was so great after its display of prowess yesterday, that he could not be induced to apply any corrective; so, after awhile, he got off to lead it, when the animal evinced unexpected signs of recovery by trotting off very briskly, and leaving its master to enter Managua on foot. This was no joke, as the weather was piping hot, and the road dusty. Exactly at noon (eight hours from Masaya) we rode into Managua, which is merely a large scattered assemblage of huts: there is a plaza, and one principal street of adobe-built houses, with earth or brick floors, as in Granada and Masaya. The plaza contains the church, barracks, and government house, over which the Nicaraguan flag was flying; it is very simple,—blue, white, blue, in perpendicular bars. The streets are unpaved, and the place has altogether a most impoverished and woe-begone appearance. A few soldiers were lounging about in the plaza, close to their barracks, and on the whole were very fair specimens of military for this part of the world. Managua has for some time been fixed upon as the capital, and Congress meets here; the President also has a residence facing the plaza. This step was found necessary, in order to put an end to the bitter rivalry between Leon and Granada for the honour of being the seat of government; this rivalry was within a hair's breadth of destroying the Nicaraguan nationality altogether, at the time when Anglo-Saxon aid, as represented by Walker, was called in. The town and neighbourhood contains about ten thousand inhabitants; the houses are built quite close to the Lake, but that inland sea does not seem in much request for commercial purposes. I did not notice a single vessel upon its waters, and the bongos and canoes hauled up on the beach were the very rudest specimens of naval architecture I have ever seen in any part of the world, without any exception whatever.

After a short rest at the *fonda*, or inn, which we found of considerable proportions and well filled, mostly with Americans who had come here on transit business, I proceeded, under the guidance of a native, to call upon Mr. Wyke (our new minister to the Central American States) to fulfil the object of my journey, namely, to put him in possession of the latest and most important information on the subject for which he had been sent out to this part of the world. I informed him of the present value of Greytown, as illustrated by the chart of my late survey, and that it was more than probable that it would soon become a lagoon, like Pearl Cay or Blewfields; I also pointed out the reasons why the port and river were probably used up for transit, therefore the object of retaining it within the Mosquito territory no longer existed. It had been my good fortune to discover the capabilities of a bay which, I proved by means of my sketch survey, was admirably suited in every respect for the Atlantic terminus of a railroad, which would traverse Nicaragua from end to end, and thus offer the means of restoring that country to a place among the nationalities by turning its geographical position to some account. As it would take some five or six years to complete such an undertaking, in the meantime, by simply crossing the country instead of traversing it from end to end, a transit route might be opened in two years. The immense political and commercial importance such an independent line would be to England no one could doubt, and I am bound to say, Mr. Wyke appeared struck with the project, and admitted its importance; but I have no hesitation in adding that his spirit was troubled at my presence, and that he made no scruple in telling me that he would far rather have been without the information I had brought. I must confess to bitter disappointment, having made the toilsome journey to Managua with the utopian idea that any Englishman, especially an accredited minister, would do what he could for his country's benefit; and particularly anxious that England should at least reap the advantage of the proposed transit, if not possess the entire control.

At Mr. Wyke's urgent request, I did not call upon the President, so that I cannot describe that dignitary, but I have heard that he is a very agreeable and intelligent personage. At the *fonda* we fared well, though not sumptuously, and failed altogether to obtain a dish of the Lake sardines, which are said to be delicious and to resemble our whitebait; but we were favoured with some first-rate cacao, the national beverage, or more properly speaking, food of Nicaragua, for it can hardly be said to be served up in a liquid state. Of all places in the world this state produces the best cacao, and it may literally be called the wealth of the country, as, when not employed in bringing in gold and silver by its exportation, it is used as small change by the people, and it is to this day, as it was at the time of the conquest of the country, a legal tender. The *Theobroma Cacao* (from the Greek, signifying "food for a God," and the Aztec name of the tree) seldom attains thirty feet in height; the beans are contained in pods, something like the shape of the outside covering of a very large broad-bean; as many as thirty beans are often found in the pod. The tree is very tender, and when young has to be carefully protected from the powerful rays of the sun; it is then shaded by the plantain, but another tree of rapid growth is planted alongside it, and as soon as its branches afford the requisite protection, the plantain is removed, and the cacao-tree left to its permanent protector, called "Madre de Cacao," mother of the cacao. At the end of seven years the cacao begins to bear, but does not reach perfection until fifteen; it continues productive about thirty-five years. One man can tend a thousand trees and harvest the crop. Capital is required to begin a plantation, but when once fairly started the return is excellent; a thousand trees will yield twelve hundred pounds per annum, which would fetch in the market at the lowest estimate £300; deduct for the labourer £20, and other expenses, say £30, total £50, leaving a clear annual profit of £250. A *hacienda* of ten thousand trees is not particularly large, and that will yield £2700 per annum when once started.

CHAPTER XIV.

LEAVE MANAGUA ON THE RETURN JOURNEY.—LAVA FIELD OF MASAYA.—ABORIGINAL FAIR.—GRANADA AND MONS. JULES THEVENET.—LOS COCOS.—MORE RIPPING.—COCITO AGAIN.—CASS IRISSARI.—BEAUTIFUL SCENERY.—DESCEND THE RIVER.—EMMONS PLANTATION.—SAN JUAN BRANCH OF THE DELTA.—ARRIVAL AT GORGON VILLA, GREYTOWN.—ASTONISH THE NATIVES.

SATURDAY, *Jan.* 23*rd*, 1860.—Early astir this morning; finished my correspondence with "our minister," and after sending it off, with a message that I should call before leaving, went down to the Lake to bathe in its discoloured water; better that than none, for really the people at the inn were so stingy of *the* element that there was no other method of washing. In their abhorrence of water, the Spanish Americans, in all parts of the continent, seem to be unanimous. I remember the unmitigated astonishment of the natives upon seeing me bathe in the different streams, when I was journeying through the Andes, some time ago, particularly at Loja, where such a crowd collected, that I had to borrow a cloak under the shadow of which to undress, and then take to the water in my trousers; the ladies by far outnumbering the male spectators.

While I was bathing, Sewell took my letter to Mr. Wyke, and informed him that I should make a parting call before leaving, to which that gentleman replied that he was engaged, and feared he would not be able to see me. On returning to the *fonda*, I there found Mr. Eden, attaché to our minister, who informed me that Mr. Wyke would not be engaged; however, I cut this Gordian knot of diplomacy, by sending one of the young officers down to "our minister," with a P. P. C. card.

Whilst making my adieux to Mr. Dimitri, the American minister, who was standing at the gateway of the inn to see us off, and thanking him for several little attentions and acts of hospitality, my mule started off, allowing me only to put one foot in the stirrup; by great exertion however, I succeeded in perching myself on the animal's stern, like the boys one sees on the donkeys at Hampstead; but the creature began to kick and plunge in so violent a manner that not even a negro could have kept his seat, and consequently, after a short struggle to get into the saddle, I was thrown over its head, and, to the great amusement of all present, deposited most ingloriously in the middle of the road. I did not however escape so well as my friend Otter, for my wrist and heel were sprained, and I was much shaken. Mounting again, and giving a gentle reminder to my mule, it was very curious to observe the manner in which all its vivacity and spirit seemed to depart, as it broke into the usual ambling trot, flapping its ears, lazily and naturally, just as if it were quite incapable of dislodging its rider.

At 10.45 A.M. we were fairly *en route*, Otter riding the guide's horse, a very lean *tame* Rosinante, while the guide mounted Otter's *lame* mule, which had to carry our baggage, and two portmanteaus slung over his back in addition. The cunning brute was however probably acquainted with its present rider, and knew better than to play any sort of tricks. At half-past three we arrived at Masaya without any adventure, merely stopping a few minutes on the road to pick up some cinders discharged from the hill or volcano of Masaya, called by the natives Infierno—hell. It is about twenty miles from the Lake of Nicaragua, and six from Masaya. The volcano is still active; there was an eruption so lately as 1859, but hardly deserving the name; that of 1670 was very severe, the flood of lava extending many miles. The high-road from Granada to Nicaragua passes over this lava-field, and the traveller cannot fail to be struck with the singularity of the irregular black expanse before him. Except in colour, it reminded me forcibly of a vast floe of hummocky ice, dotted here and there with bergs, such as I have often seen in the Arctic regions. Arrived at Masaya, we had time before dark to look around us. Masaya is inhabited almost entirely by Indians, who are most industrious. They have a considerable trade in hats, mats, cordage, hammocks, saddles and bridles, shoes, and almost every article of domestic use. We were in good time to see their daily fair, an aboriginal custom. The plaza was crowded with people, bringing every conceivable article of produce which the country affords, and which they spread out for sale. The scene is a singular one; and for its animation, and the eagerness of the natives to do business, is quite equal to an Anglo-Saxon market. The population of the town and suburbs may be about

15,000. There are very extensive plantations all round the town, and a large amount of *Agave*, or silk grass, growing in the vicinity, from which the cordage, hammocks, etc., are manufactured. The great drawback to Masaya and the neighbouring country is the want of water. This necessary of life has to be fetched from the Lake of Masaya by the women, by the slow and toilsome process of carrying jars of the precious fluid on their heads and backs. There have been several foreign proposals to bring the water into the town, but nothing has as yet been done; the natives are helpless, being puzzled by the fact that the lake whence they draw their supplies is without any outlet, and the surface of the water is between 400 and 500 feet below the level of the surrounding country. After making a few trifling purchases, and staring at a man who was to be executed in a few days, and who was quietly walking about in the plaza, dangling his chains, we returned to the *fonda*, where dinner was prepared, I must say in a better style than before, partly owing to the exertions of a Mr. Wassmann, whose acquaintance we made, and who was very kind and attentive. We slept without mosquitoes, fleas, or bugs, for a wonder, but their absence was more than made up for by ticks, which at this season swarm in the bushes, especially in the roadside, and stick to the person like leeches, but, unlike the latter, instead of dropping off when full, they bury their heads in the skin, and if allowed introduce their entire body under the cuticle, where they deposit their eggs. The negroes are very expert in extracting them from the flesh: it is of importance to withdraw them intact, otherwise a painful sore will result. Plentiful ablution is tne best remedy; they dislike water as much as the bipeds. If the insect is removed at once, no inconvenience is felt; twenty-four hours' delay does the mischief.

Tuesday, June 24th, 1860.—Had a decent breakfast, with little more to pay than we had been let in for at our first visit; we therefore mounted our mules in a much more contented frame of mind than when leaving here last. At 9 we set off, weather very hot and roads dusty; but thanks to Mr. Wassmann, who took the trouble to start us by a different route than the one we came by, we had a very pleasant ride; the track, winding over higher ground, gave us some very pretty peeps of the two lakes and the Chontales Mountains. The most noticeable feature on the road was the number and gigantic size of the cotton-trees; they form quite a foreground in Nicàraguan scenery, and seem to domineer over the surrounding vegetation. At 1 P.M., we arrived in Granada. During our absence the canoe had been taken to a place called the Cocos, which is somewhat sheltered, whereas Granada is on a dead lee shore, with very heavy surf, sometimes preventing boats from starting for days together. Any delay would have been great a inconvenience to me, as I was anxious to catch the mail due on the 29th. In the afternoon I had a long chat with Colonel Vega and Señor Gusman, both of whom were much struck with my project, and promised their hearty co-operation. They both assured me that a permit from the Government to make the preliminary survey, from Monkey

Point to the Lake of Nicaragua at San Miguelito, was unnecessary, and that I might commence as soon as I pleased. However, I left instructions with Mr. Wassmann to get a written permit, and send it to me at Greytown, as soon as possible.

Having arrived so early, I was able to get a better view of the city, or rather what is left of it, than when we first arrived. Everywhere ruins and dilapidations stared me in the face, even in the plaza; the most noticeable building was occupied by soldiers, and very respectable military specimens they were, especially the officers, one of whom was a most dashing-looking young fellow, and very courteous. Granada was founded on the site of an aboriginal town; it formerly ranked next to Leon in extent, population, and commerce, but since the independence, the frequent recurrence of civil wars has, little by little, shorn it of its fair proportions, until at last General Henningsen put the finishing touch to it in 1856, and it is now certainly in a deplorable condition. The centre of the town is about half a mile from the little bay on the lake, which is the port of entry, and affords some slight shelter from the prevailing trade-winds,—not enough, however, as I have mentioned above, to enable a boat or canoe to land in smooth water, when there is a strong trade-wind. The church, so gallantly defended by the filibusters, is a short distance from the city, on the road to the lake; I examined it with great curiosity. The walls yet standing were absolutely riddled; it is a wonder the garrison did not perish to a man; nothing but Walker's timely arrival saved them. In olden times Granada was the *entrepôt* of an immense commerce with the surrounding provinces. It is related that two hundred years ago, as many as eighteen hundred mules from San Salvador and Honduras entered the city in a single day, laden with hides, cochineal, and indigo; and on another day, nine hundred mules laden with silver. But, as it is out of the present line of transit, it is probable that its ancient greatness is gone for ever. There will however always be a considerable population in its vicinity, if only to take advantage of the richness and fertility of the surrounding soil. The great sight at Granada is the chasm which extends about halfway round the city; there is not even a tradition about it, but no doubt it was caused by an earthquake. The natives say it is so deep in some places that no line ever made could reach the bottom, but generally its dimensions average 50 feet in depth, varying from 5 to 500 feet in width.

The commerce of Granada is carried on in bongos, which are very primitive specimens of naval architecture; in fact, the bongo is simply a rudely-constructed barge of from eight to ten tons, the after-part boarded in, for the accommodation of passengers; this covering extends about one-third the length of the vessel; the remainder is quite open, with thwarts for the pullers to sit upon. The crew generally consists of twelve men and the *patron;* these men eat, drink, and sleep on their respective thwarts. The cargo is made up of about 100 seroons of indigo, or 500 hides, or eight tons of logwood, with a miscellaneous stock of sundries, which the crew dispose of on their own account. The generality of the bongos have only one mast, upon which a huge lug-sail is hoisted. All the top hamper is of the clumsiest description, and the sail is so badly made that it looks like a large bag: the oars are simply rough spars, with a round piece of deal nailed on to the end. As may be imagined, the bongo is not easily moved; in the wet season, for example, the average passage up the San Juan alone is fourteen days; they are often three weeks from Granada to Greytown: but then it must be remembered that the value of time is not yet understood in this country.

The *bogas*, or boatmen forming the crew of a bongo, are quite an institution of Nicaragua; they are perhaps the hardest-working men in the world. Their powers of endurance are most remarkable: for days together they exist in a perfect state of nudity, exposed to sun and rain, living on plantains and jerked beef, and sleeping at night, without any covering from the damp air or rain, on the thwart on which they sit all day tugging at the oar, yet they always seem contented and happy; their pay is eight dollars, about 35*s*., per month, and what they can make by the sale of their home produce. It must be admitted that they are not bound by any very strict notions of *meum* and *tuum* if they come across a chance, and therefore it is always as well for the traveller to be on his guard when meeting with these gentry on either lake or river.

In the slight curve forming the Bay of Granada, the bongos are unladen; they are kept hauled up on the beach for the most part, but some, rather heavier than others, remain at anchor close up to the old fort. There are neither wharves nor jetties. The fort is semicircular, and no doubt at one time was very strong; it is now in ruins. Granada is about a hundred feet above the

Lake; the streets run at right angles to each other. I did not see a single shop-window; nothing seemed to be displayed for sale, except liquors,—unlike Masaya, where there was a goodly display, and a strong trading spirit. A Jamaica negro, who kept a grog-shop at the lower part of Granada, hailed me as a countryman, and as he did not claim me as a brother, I let well alone, and did not correct his geographical mistake. My Caribs put up at the establishment of this gentleman, and I believe met with good treatment. At the inn where we took up our quarters, and which, by the bye, is the only one of any pretension in the place, we met with the kindest attention from both host and hostess, especially the latter, who exerted herself to send up some dishes curiously and wonderfully made. There was a regular *table d'hôte*, at which several of the better class of inhabitants dined; our host was a Frenchman, and his wife a native of Chile, a very pretty woman, and, like the rest of her countrywomen, fond of her cigarette and a swing in the hammock.

Wednesday, January 25th.—Having settled our accounts, which, on the whole, were reasonable, we left Granada at 7 A.M., having waited nearly two hours for the arrival of the mules; the lazy *arrieros* never hurry themselves on any account. As mentioned above, I had left orders with Perry, our excellent head-man, to take the canoe to a place called Cocos, at the head of the Lake, where there was good shelter, and whence we could depart in almost any weather; accordingly, we made our adieux, mounted, and pushed on for Cocos preparatory to embarking. Our course lay along the borders of the Lake, and our ride would have been a delightful one but for the dust, which, at this season of the year, is nearly knee-deep. We were accompanied by M. Jules Thevenet, a French civil engineer employed on the usual business—transit. We had met him first at Masaya, and the whole party voted him a particularly nice fellow; so, finding that he was unable to get any means of conveyance to Greytown, I offered him a passage in our canoe, which he gladly accepted. We passed two or three ranchos, a considerable number of cattle, and the usual amount of cotton-trees; the distance from Granada to the Cocos is about eighteen miles, quite a level road. When nearly halfway, we had to cross an arm of the Lake running some distance inland, thus forming a lagoon; the water was not very deep, being only up to the mules' bellies, but it was covered with green slime, very thick and dirty, and said to teem with alligators. The ford was at least a quarter of a mile across, and when about the middle I was startled by a cry behind, and turning, expected to see one at least of the party in the jaws of an alligator; the noise, however, was simply a wail from Devereux, who had dropped his naked sword into the slimy water, and fancied it gone for ever; but after groping about a little, he was so fortunate as to recover his weapon, which was sticking upright in the mud. There was not one of the party who did not rejoice when he found himself on the opposite side of this detestable stagnant pool, where an enterprising alligator might have taken a bite, or even a whole leg, from any of us, without a moment's warning.

Our faithful Perry met us hereabouts, and told us all was ready for a start; he rode on in front, showing off his horsemanship, and pointing out the best road. At eleven arrived at Cocos, which is a small village, containing about one hundred inhabitants. Here we found the canoe half drawn up out of the water, with all her gear neatly stowed, and ready for a start; while on the beach a roaring fire was blazing away, and a good meal of stewed meat and vegetables was ready for us. It was a wild scene, but a very enjoyable one; a smile even gleamed upon the grim visage of our guide and muleteer, who gladly accepted some of the good cheer, before turning round to take his beasts back to Granada. While making our repast, the crew packed up the traps; everything had been nicely dried and folded, so that we really seemed to start fresh; indeed it would be impossible to speak too highly of the excellent conduct of our Carib crew: brave, hard-working, always cheerful, they quite won upon us, and I believe, if we had unfortunately got into a row with the Nicaraguans, they would have stuck to us through thick and thin. It was amusing to hear the contemptuous way in which they spoke of the natives, and to see the distant manner which they preserved towards them. The Caribs must not be confounded with the negroes; they are quite a different race, and vastly superior.

Started at 12.30 for Greytown. Cocos is protected by a low marshy island, and is a very respectable harbour for small craft; it appeared to me in every respect a better site for a town than Granada. There is quite water enough for the largest bongo, and the port has the great advantage of being well to windward, so that it can be entered and left at any time; for it must be remembered that the prevailing wind is from the north-east (the trade-wind), which, not being obstructed in its passage from the Caribbean Sea, blows with almost as much force as it does on the ocean. I am surprised that the bongos do not discharge their cargoes here: by doing so, much time and labour would be saved, while a good deal of uncertainty and risk would be avoided. Half an hour after starting, passed the mouth of the Tipitapa, which joins the two lakes; it seemed broad, but is, I understand, too shallow even for a canoe at this season; I observed a few houses on the eastern side. The Lake of Nicaragua is connected with that of Managua by the river Panaloya or Tipitapa, which runs into the former at lat. 12° 10′ N., long. 85° 50′ W.; it is N. 25, E. 15½ miles from the circular fort at Granada. Its exit from Managua is at lat. 12°15′ N., long. 86°03′ W. The width of this communication varies from 150 to 600 feet; its total length, including windings, is about 20 miles, but it is only navigable for canoes. There are several small villages in its vicinity.

The canoe was very deep with our extra passenger, M. Thevenet, and his baggage, but we got well under the weather side of the Lake by half-past four, and could then look forward to smooth water for the rest of the voyage. We had plenty of "ripping" this afternoon, so were all well washed, and looked out sharp for a resting-place; but no sandy bay was to be seen, and we should most probably have had to push on without sleep or food, had not the quick-eared Caribs heard voices, and on pulling in, discovered a bongo, from the *patron* of which we learnt that we were quite close to a landing-place in a little island: this we had no difficulty in finding, and soon had a fire lit and dinner cooking. Our camp was only just big enough for our party; but where will not mosquitoes penetrate? They soon invaded us by legions.

By a process which seems inevitable to the traveller, provided he has money to squander, he finds his luggage increase, stage by stage, on his journey, and most certainly we were not exempt on the present occasion; but in our case we had reason to rejoice, for among our purchases were several hammocks, which we now produced, and hanging them up to the trees, found our selves very respectably located for the night. Our new beds not only kept us off the wet earth, but elevated us above any hungry alligator who might be prowling about. The only fault to be found with a hammock is, that being made of open network, it offers no opposition to the onslaught of the mosquitoes, which riot unchecked over your entire body, from head to foot.

Thursday, January 26*th.*—At daylight we left our encampment, but very little refreshed by our sojourn there. Of the white portion of the party not one had closed his eyes, but the Caribs, I suppose, had "hides of toughest leather," through which the mosquitoes could not thrust their proboscis. The characteristic scenery of this northern shore of the Lake is savana land, undulating away into the interior. Thousands of people might follow pastoral avocations in this favoured region without jostling one another; and I could not help feeling what a glorious immigration-field might be opened up in Nicaragua. The country may be divided into three districts, offering every inducement the mind of man can desire. The first district would be the Chontales Mountains, teeming with gold and other precious metals and minerals: this may be called the cold zone. The second district would be included between the mountains and the lakes, a vast agricultural country, which may be termed the temperate zone; while the third district would be the strip of land between the lakes and the Pacific, prolific in all the products of the tropics, the *tierra caliente*, or hot lands, of the Spaniards,—in other words, the torrid zone. What a thousand pities there are not a few Anglo-Saxons settled in this magnificent country; how soon it would then take its well-deserved position among the nations! Only two miserable ranchos were observed; the coast-line is almost uninhabited. As far as I could judge in running along the land, I should say that there was not a single impediment or engineering difficulty to be met with on the entire shore until reaching the vicinity of our last night's bivouac, where the existence of a rocky spur would probably compel a slight *détour* or cutting. We had a good deal of paddling, owing to the lightness of the wind; but as the day advanced it increased, and our Caribs lost no time in making sail, and enjoying their favourite pastime of "letting her rip," when, as usual, we were speedily wet to the skin. At 10 we passed a very low point about twelve miles beyond the Three Cays, or starting-point for Granada, when the wind came right ahead, and we had to recommence paddling. After an hour's work we reached a small sandy bay, into which we joyfully steered the canoe, and landing, had a fire alight and breakfast cooking in no time; an hour and a half's rest, with an excellent meal, set us all up, and the Caribs resumed their paddles with a good will. At 12.30 we were under way again, the sun striking down with full power upon us and no mistake,—sufficient, as the saying is, to scorch the brains of a brass monkey. It was not very long before every sign of the thorough drenching we had just undergone by the "ripping" process disappeared, and we found ourselves in the opposite extreme, *dry* indeed; however, before we had fairly commenced growling, down came the rain, so we were constrained to laugh, for really there was no pleasing us; we did not like "ripping," we growled at the sun, and abused the rain. What was to be done? We passed several rivulets, or *esteros;* they were of inconsiderable breadth, and we could not observe any current at their mouths. The alligators might be numbered by hundreds in this vicinity, which seems a favourite resort of theirs; they constantly rose close to the canoe, and as soon as they saw her, sank again in their indescribably noiseless manner. We did not succeed in killing any; the bullets seemed to glance off their scaly hides. We constantly passed numbers of trees growing in the water, the branches of which were thickly crowded with young shags and cranes: a tree covered with these white birds has a most peculiar effect, unlike anything I had ever seen before. At 4.30 we reached the Chontales Islands, upwards of twenty in number, and none of them higher than forty feet. Great quantities of wild ducks were swimming about in the various channels. We were nearly two hours before we were clear of the islands. I had hoped to have reached Cocito (the lovers' abode) before dark, but was disappointed, and it was not until 9 o'clock and a great deal of groping about, that the canoe grated upon the beach of that place.

After landing I went up to the hut, which certainly was the filthiest specimen of architecture it has ever been my fate to see; the young lovers were at home, busy spooning and scratching themselves in a corner. Perry soon bought all we required, fowls, eggs, etc., and our supper was speedily under way; in the meantime each individual of our party was stretched at full length, with his feet to the fire, enjoying a sound nap, in spite of the mosquitoes. I, however, tempted by my evil genius, invaded the hut and took possession of the only bed, a sort of wattled bunk covered with a bull's hide, and with a lump of wood for a pillow. The vermin, however, were in legions, almost enough to drag one's body to the ground, so that at 11, when I was roused up to supper, I was in a pretty state; but I almost felt that I had been justly punished for so summarily disturbing the love-sick Juan and his charmer, both of whom had retreated outside the hut when I took up my quarters within. After supper, we all lay down again on the sand; there were no trees to which the hammocks could be suspended; but it is needless to say we slept soundly, quite regardless of either large or small reptilia.

Friday, January 27th.—At 3.30 A.M., we were again under way in the canoe, after swallowing a very refreshing cup of coffee. My most emphatic advice to the traveller in this part of the world is, whatever you do take care of your store of tea and coffee; the value of either of these most refreshing beverages in tropical climates cannot be overrated. The weather was not pleasant; there was a chilly, drizzling rain, wetting us through, and making us shiver with the cold. A little after 6, made sail, which is always a delight to the Caribs; and in this instance, as the "ripping" could not make us wetter, besides driving the canoe twice as fast as when paddling, we all rejoiced. 7.25, passed Pedronal and ran across the bay to San Miguelito, "ripping" all the way, arriving at that place at 8.30. Landed and went to the house of Montenegro, where Perry cooked the breakfast, which we discussed without sauce. Saw the man whose wife I had doctored on the road up, and learnt that she was quite recovered, for which the *grateful* husband said, "Dios á lo pagar" (God will pay you). However I thought I might just as well make him useful, so giving him money, told him to get some eggs, but the lazy fellow would not stir; and I was fain to take back my money and send one of my own men. Just as we were starting, the same man came to me in the coolest manner, saying that his wife might possibly be taken ill again, and would I give him some of the same medicine as before?—to which I replied in so emphatic a manner as rather startled my friend.

Alligators are numerous about San Miguelito; I saw a very large one on the beach, and just before we arrived, a lad had been bitten in the knee by one, which tried all it could to drag him into the water. At 10.30, left San Miguelito, and soon passed through the islands, after which we had to paddle well to windward, and then make a good stretch right to the entrance of the San Juan; the wind at times was north, and quite fresh, and we shipped a good deal of water, sufficient to keep us constantly employed baling. I should not have been surprised to have found myself wet-footed by the time I reached the ship. It is surprising how, almost simultaneously with the freshening of the breeze, the Lake becomes rough, with quite heavy toppling waves, big enough to make our run from San Miguelito a very hazardous one, deep-loaded as our canoe was. A small open boat or canoe therefore ought to keep as near the shore as possible, for in less than a quarter of an hour after the wind rises, the waves become quite formidable. A Ryde wherry would be the craft either for the Lake or the Mosquito Coast. The coast from San Miguelito to San Carlos is very low, with many bays intervening. The entrance to the San Juan is well marked by a curious tree of gigantic size on the Point, after rounding which the fort and huts appear in sight.

At 3.30 arrived on board the 'Cass Irisarri,' to the great delight of every one. Perry was soon at work cooking, and we all enjoyed a good meal and some egg-nog, and then lay down for a real sound sleep on the deck. The 'Cass Irisarri' seems a good solid steamer, and fit for Lake service; she might be very useful for surveying purposes, about which I had a long conversation with her captain. There is a stern wheeler lying close to, but sadly out of repair. I obtained a good deal of information from Captain Slocum (of Newport,

Rhode Island) about Nicaragua. He fervently wished me success in my Transit project, and hoped I should have need of his vessel, which he told me belonged to himself and the engineer; his late masters, the Transit Company, having quite forgotten to pay the considerable arrears of wages due to them. A perceptible rise and fall, caused entirely by the wind, is often observed on the Lake, to the extent of a foot even; of course, there is a very great difference in the height of the water in the wet and dry seasons. Mr. Baily says as much as six feet six inches has been observed; but this, of course, varies according to the nature of the season.

Saturday, January 28th.—To look at the canoe this morning made one feel quite queer, the gunwale was so close to the water: some more weights had been put into her, and any unprejudiced sailor would have pronounced her unsafe; but we had no choice, and therefore simply made arrangements for throwing overboard the least valuable of our possessions in case of necessity. The fact was, we had brought more baggage with us than was needful. I had left a good many things on board the 'Cass Irissari' to lighten the canoe for crossing the Lake; and well it was for us that this precaution had been taken, otherwise I believe we should have foundered, when in the gale off Granada. Now, however, we were loaded like a sand-barge.

This morning we woke up like giants refreshed, showing how comparative one's idea of comfort is; the deck of the steamer was as good as a feather-bed, as far as we were concerned. We had a good view of the Lake scenery, and now that we have had some experience of it, feel disposed to pay a just tribute of admiration to its beauty and variety. At 8, bade good-bye to the Lake, and began the descent of the river, which is rather narrow and shallow at its commencement, and broken up by one or two islands. It is about 200 or 300 yards across, and the shores are densely wooded. The fort commands about 1500 yards. The guns are sheltered by a light shed—a very good protection from the weather, and which might be copied with advantage by more civilized countries. The fort itself might be held by resolute men for some time, but its present possessors could be ejected without much trouble. The ascent of the river might be rendered impossible for a foe, but the sites chosen for defences are certainly not the best that could have been pitched upon.

The San Juan is full of islands, some of them nearly a mile in length. At 10, passed the lagoon of Medio Queso, "half-cheese." Saw a monkey, and made a note of it, because the amount of animal life observed has been very trifling. After passing Isla Grande, at 11.30, the current became very perceptible, and the canoe made rapid way through the water,—very different from our progress against the stream. Soon after we started, the rain began to come down, and will do so now, in all probability, during the rest of the journey. At 12.20 we passed a creek on the left, which takes its rise in the hills, away in the interior, and must therefore be a pretty long stream. Passed some bongos, one of which was freighted with a black colonel, who hardly condescended to look at us. At 10, arrived at the head of the Toro rapids, the rain descending in torrents. Curiosity led us to land at the mouth of the Savolo to examine the Rama king's habitation, and it proved well worth our while. It was merely a roof, supported by uprights; the inhabitants consisted of two old women, two men (all of a large size and fat), three wild "warries" secured to stakes, some very fierce dogs, and young birds just taken from the nest; also a tame plantain bird, tied by its leg to a stick, and which I bought to present to Alice, Colonel Cauty's niece. The whole scene was a very queer one, every article of the rudest description. After staying about half an hour, we pushed off into the rapid, and soon left the Ramas far behind. This tribe has never been conquered by the Spaniards; the king, in broken Spanish, made us understand that he hated the Nicaraguans and loved the English: from the long pull he took at our bottle, I suspect that rum was at the bottom of his affection.

Arrived at Castillo at 3.30, and called upon Colonel Arguello; he introduced us to a very pretty woman, his wife, who did not appear on our way up. She complained of the dulness of the post, and having nothing to do but to smoke; whereupon I at once tendered a cigar. Colonel Arguello, a strikingly handsome white man, improves on acquaintance; he is intelligent and gentlemanly; under his guidance we went all over the ruins of the castle, which does not belie its external appearance; if anything, it is worse inside. A couple of filibuster field-pieces, lying on the ground, constitute the effective armament of the place, and the fortification might be taken, before these guns could be prepared for service. The breach made by Nelson, his tactics, etc., were kindly explained by the Colonel. Castillo Viejo, or Old Fort, bears date from the earliest period of the Spanish rule; it was thoroughly reconstructed in 1747 by the governor-intendant of Nicaragua and Costarica. On the 29th of April, 1780, it surrendered to Nelson. The fortified island of Bartola, situated three miles below the fort, is the locality alluded to as having been *boarded* by our great naval hero. The castle withstood a protracted siege before it was taken, and the comandante, Juan de Ayssa, with his garrison of 228 men, was allowed to march out with all the honours of war, in compliment to his brave defence. Since that period it has often changed hands, both from foreign attack and during revolutionary movements; it was first taken by an Englishman, and it never afterwards withstood a siege until an Englishman was the commandant. The story of the last assault I will repeat, as narrated to me. Colonel Cauty, the same officer whose gallantry and enterprise has been mentioned in connection with the Serepiqui and San Carlos, was in command; he had with him thirty-two officers and men, and had just time to construct a one-gun battery at the foot of the castle, when the Filibusters, under Colonel Titus, made their appearance. Cauty held the post of honour in the lower battery with eleven men, while Colonel Montes de Oca was stationed above in the castle with twenty men. The struggle was a most obstinate one. On the evening of the first day, Colonel Cauty was compelled to retire into the castle,—in good order, however, and taking the gun with him; when mustered inside, the besieged found themselves reduced to twenty-two, one-third of their number having been killed or wounded. For three days the little band resisted each and every one of the vigorous onslaughts made upon it. Colonel Titus then tried what negotiation would do, and it was arranged that the fort should be given up if assistance did not arrive within twenty-four hours; a messenger was at once sent off with pressing demands for assistance, and just half an hour before the expiration of the time named seventy-five riflemen arrived, who charged the besiegers so suddenly, and with so much vigour, as to compel them to beat a hasty retreat. The filibusters however returned to the attack with their force augmented to 500 men; but the garrison having been strongly reinforced, they could make no impression on the place; and one of their steamers having blown up, whereby a hundred of their number were severely injured, all further attempts were given up, and the river San Juan, as well as Greytown Harbour, finally cleared of Colonel Titus in April, 1857. On the 1st of May following, Walker was compelled by the allied Central Americans to leave the country; and thus Nicaragua was once more left to itself.

We had landed well above the rapids, and the canoe was eased through by the soldiers, without risk: eleven men out of a twenty-five-feet canoe, of course lightened her so much, that she ran no risk in taking the rapid. As I was anxious to make the best of my way to the ship, I did not remain one moment longer than necessary, and by four o'clock we were once more paddling down stream. On approaching the broken water of Las Balas, Mico, and Machuca, respectively, our hearts were in our mouths; but our trusty Caribs knew their work. On approaching the rapids, each man paddled gently, reserving his strength till quite close to the boiling, turbulent water, when, at a signal from Perry, the whole of the men, with a wild shout, dug their paddles deep into the river, and gave the canoe such an impetus, that she seemed to fly; one of the crew, named Manuel, sang with a measured cadence, the Caribs keeping their stroke in time. Every now and then Manuel would give a wild yell or shout, and all hands flinging their paddles with a twirling motion high into the air, caught them as they fell with great dexterity, and striking the water with the flats sent a cloud of spray over the canoe. This bit of wild pantomime seemed to infuse a sort of demoniacal strength into all hands; for a moment all was spray, noise, and shouting, during which the canoe rushed over the rapid like a mad thing.

Las Balas, Mico, and Machuca having thus been passed in safety, we soon arrived at Mr. Emmons's house, where we had left the 'Laura Frances' on our way up; at 5.10 we were at the landing, and gladly made our way with all speed under shelter from the pouring rain. Mrs. Emmons soon had a hot dinner ready for us, to which we did ample justice. The contrast between the interior of a native house and that of an Anglo-Saxon settler is wonderful. Mrs. Emmons had her house as neat and clean as possible, everything in its place; poor thing, she seemed born for better things than living in an amphibious state on the banks of the

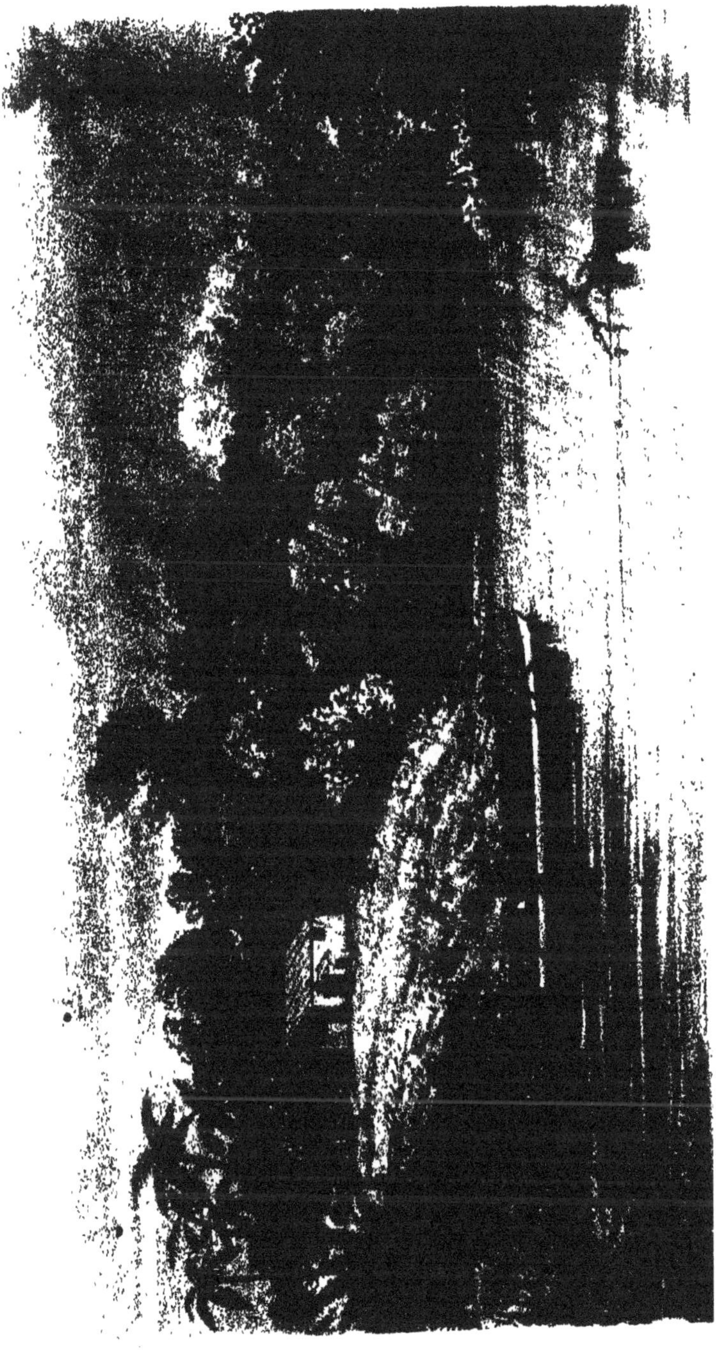

San Juan; she was ladylike and educated. Her husband had hoped to realize a rapid fortune, and he would, no doubt, have been successful in doing so had the Transit continued, but with its downfall his hopes were destroyed. We had some tapir for dinner; it was like tough beef, and it would take, I should think, some time to acquire a taste for it. We bought some of the meat to take *home* with us, but it was never cooked; the smell was so strong that it was unanimously determined to throw it away. Mr. Emmons told me that neither himself nor family have had a day's sickness since coming here; and he confirms my opinion that a clean, airy house, and a plentiful use of water over the person, is the secret of maintaining health in this climate.

Sunday, Jan. 29th.—After a few hours' sleep I roused up the party, shortly after midnight, and then—stowing a good cargo of provender, in the shape of coffee and solids, like Major Dalgetty, to be ready for a heavy day's work—we pushed off into the stream from the foot of the Machuca at 1.30 A.M. The rain was pouring down in bucketfuls, of course wetting us to the skin in a few minutes. Several bongoes were passed, but there was only time to get a sleepy, indistinct answer to our questions as the canoe shot by. At 4.0, passed the river San Carlos, and at 6.15 got safely through the Moreno Grande, or great whirlpool, at which we most fortunately arrived soon after daylight; it would have been dangerous to have got into the whirl during the dark hours. At 8.30 passed the Serepiqui, our spirits rising, in spite of our hunger, and drenched, cramped position, as we rapidly shortened the distance between us and Gorgon Villa. At 10.30 passed Leaf's Island, and soon after, the Colorado, leaving it on our right. Continuing down the San Juan, the current proved sufficiently strong to be a material help, but we had some difficulty from the sand-shoals, reaching right across the river. In several places the men had to jump out and drag the canoe over these shallows. We landed once for five minutes at a plantation, and got some plantains. Just as our journey was coming to an end, I killed a small alligator, about two feet long, and Sewell shot a crane, both with bullets. I mention this circumstance, as these creatures proved the sum total of our game bag during the whole fourteen days of our absence.

The following are a few notes on the San Juan arm of the delta. The stream is not stronger than one knot per hour; the banks are for the greater part low and swampy and difficult to reach, being thickly covered with long coarse grass, everywhere growing in profusion; on the swampy lands of this river it is so abundant as completely to hide the line of demarcation between the water and the river-bank. The trees average a distance of about fifty feet from the edge of the grass. The whole of this arm of the delta is exceedingly shallow; as mentioned above, we had repeatedly to haul the canoe, which certainly did not draw two feet, over the many sand-bars which obstruct the passage. The bongos in this season have, in military phrase, "to cut their way through." There are a great number of low alluvial islands, covered with grass, but only a few of the largest have any trees growing upon them. Perry, our padron, assured me that he had never ascended the river in the dry season, and found it in exactly the same state; in fact, that the silting up and increased difficulty of the navigation was very perceptible year by year; judging by the high-water marks, not only the islands, but a considerable portion of the land is under water during the wet season.

After passing the divergence of the Toro and the mouth of the San Juanillo we came in sight of the 'Gorgon's' mastheads towering high above the low intervening land, and soon after, paddling through, or, rather, grating over the shoals which separate the two channels running into the harbour, Greytown in all its glory opened to our view. As we shot past Colonel Cauty's house, there was a visible commotion, waving of handkerchiefs, etc., young Mrs. Cauty evidently supposing that her husband was with us; she was however, poor thing, doomed to disappointment. Just before 3.0 P.M. we paddled up to Gorgon Villa in true Carib style, to the great astonishment of the Greytownians; I do not mean from our wild mode of approach,—to that they were well accustomed,—but at the rapidity with which the voyage to Managua and back had been accomplished; the most experienced of the inhabitants having assured me, when starting, that it was quite impossible to do the journey in the time I proposed!

It was with very enjoyable feelings that we crossed the threshold of "our villa." My steward had provided a repast fit for a king, to which we lost no time in doing ample justice. I am happy to say that no one was at all the worse for the hardships and exposure to which we had all alike been subjected.

I cannot close my journal without paying the warmest tribute to my white companions; the service cannot produce finer young fellows: may the best of good fortune attend them, wherever they go! M. Thevenet, our guest, proved himself the jolliest of Frenchmen; not a murmur escaped him, although of course he was exposed to the wetting, drying, scorching, hunger, and thirst, just as much as any of us. Regarding the Caribs, they behaved splendidly; I have mentioned above their performances, which, I think, will bear looking into for endurance and hard work. I am not partial to the negro,—his sloth and insolence irritate me; I do not see the joke of his lying under a cocoa-nut-tree, basking in the sun, while I have to get bread by the sweat of my brow. But these Caribs are a very different race; though black as the ace of spades, they are eminently industrious, thrifty, and intelligent, and I should be as glad to meet one of my canoe crew as I should to meet an old shipmate. A white man, it is said, is brother to the negro, but you could not insult a Carib more than by hinting at *any* relationship between himself and the African.

The following is an abstract of the above journey, showing the number of miles travelled:—

	Miles.
In steamer 'Laura Frances'	100
In canoe on river	167
In canoe on lake	210
On mules	100
Total	577

Total absence, fourteen days, or an average rate of forty-one miles and a quarter per day.

CHAPTER XV.

PROPOSED RAILWAY THROUGH HONDURAS.—DIRECTION OF ROAD.—PUERTO CABALLOS.—BAY OF FONSECA.—ESTIMATES.—HONDURAS INTEROCEANIC RAILWAY CHARTER.—FAILURE TO FORM A COMPANY.—COLONEL STANTON, R.E.—VON TEMPSKY.—WHY IS 'MITLA' WORTHLESS?

THE project for railway communication through the state of Honduras must now be considered. The principal promoter is a clever American, and the subject has been before the public some eight years, but without any beneficial result, except, perhaps, to the projector. In describing the line, I shall adhere as much as possible to his own words.

The proposed railway commences at Puerto Caballos, on the Atlantic, in lat. 15° 49′ N. and long. 87° 57′ W., and runs nearly due south across the continent to the Bay of Fonseca on the Pacific, in lat. 13° 21′ N. and long. 87° 35′ W. Its total length, from anchorage to anchorage, is said to be 148 geographical miles, equal to 161 statute miles. It lies wholly in the state of Honduras, whose territorial right and sovereignty over it has never been called in question. Starting at Puerto Caballos, it pursues a course a little east of south, across the plain of Sula, until it strikes the Rio Ulua near the town of Santiago; thence it follows the valley of that river, now called the Humuya, to its very source in the plain of Comayagua.

At the southern extremity of this plain there is said to be a *slight elevation*, which constitutes the "summit" between the Atlantic and Pacific. Here the sources of the Humuya interlock with those of the Rio Goascoran, which stream flows through its proper valley into the Bay of Fonseca.

The Atlantic port is thus described by Lieutenant Jeffers, U. S. Navy:—

"Puerto Caballos is a good harbour, of great capacity, sufficient depth of water, and easy of entrance and exit. Situated at the base of the hills, there are neither marshes nor swamps to affect the healthfulness of the locality, which is sufficiently extensive for the formation of a large city."

To *confirm* the evidence of a responsible naval officer, the projector brings forward the testimony of the master of a schooner, named the 'George Steers,' who winds up his account by stating, that—

"A gentleman, resident on this coast, and of great experience in the winds and weather hereabouts, informed me that some time back he was voyaging in a *dory*,* when the sky, swell, etc., gave unmistakable evidence of a 'norther,' and compelled him to make Puerto Caballos for security. Here he rode out in perfect safety one of the most furious 'northers' he had ever witnessed."

The magnificent Bay of Fonseca, the western terminus

* A *dory* is a small canoe hollowed out of the trunk of a single tree.

of the proposed road, is beyond dispute the finest port, or rather "constellation of ports," on the entire Pacific coast of America. It is fifty miles in length, by about thirty in average width, perfectly protected, and contains two or three large islands, offering inner ports with ample water, and admirable sites for towns and commercial and manufacturing establishments of all kinds. The three states of San Salvador, Honduras, and Nicaragua, touch upon it. Honduras, however, has far the largest front on the Bay. The port of La Union, in the subordinate bay of the same name, is the principal port of San Salvador. Its trade lately amounted to something over 500,000 dollars, and the revenues to about 100,000 dollars. The principal port of Honduras is Amapala, on the island of Tigre. It is a free port, and is rapidly advancing in importance; its population and trade having doubled within the last few years.

In calculating the cost of the proposed road, it must be remembered that nearly all the materials necessary for its construction, as well as for its economic working after it shall have been built, are to be found, in the greatest abundance, on the line of the road. Timber, stone, cattle for draught, and a large supply of available labour, may be obtained in the country itself, which is also capable of furnishing the amplest supplies of provisions. Lying in a valley parallel, and not transverse, to the watercourses of the country, the amount of excavation and embankment on the line is comparatively slight. No tunnels are required, and there are no cuttings in hard rock. Moreover, the climate is such as to admit of the uninterrupted prosecution of the work for the entire year,—the rains, during what is called the rainy season, never being so heavy as to interrupt operations.

Detailed estimates made, in view of these circumstances, by competent engineers, give the following aggregates for a road 161 miles in length, with a single track of six feet gauge, on a road-bed 22 feet wide in excavation, and 16 feet in embankment.

Summary of Cost.

Preliminary expenses	$90,000
Extinguishing titles to land	50,000
Earthworks and excavations	1,932,000
Bridging	608,750
Culverts and passages	161,000
Superstructure	1,347,400
Stations, wharves, etc.	407,000
Equipment and rolling stock	355,000
Engineering contingencies, 30 per cent.	1,415,345
Total	$6,436,495

This gives an average cost per mile of not far from 40,000 dollars.

It will be said that the opening of the Honduras route will induce great competition, on the part of routes already established, leading to considerable reductions in rates, and consequent diminution of revenue. These rates are at present exorbitant, and should be reduced. To effect such reduction is precisely one of the grounds upon which the promoters of the Honduras route base their appeal to the public support. They are confident that the saving of time, and consequent saving of expense, in running steamers and transporting passengers, would enable the Honduras route to sustain the severest competition, while paying a fair return on the capital invested.

Putting the prices to be charged on passengers and freight at *two-thirds* of the prices now charged on the Panama road, we have the following summary of the estimated annual business of the Honduras road:—

Summary of Revenues.

50,000 passengers at $17	$850,000
$80,000,000 precious metals, at ¼ per cent.	200,000
English and American mails	150,000
72,000 tons express freight at $13⅓ per ton	266,000
100,000 tons general freight at $22 per ton	2,200,000
Commerce of Central America, 2 per cent. on $6,000,000	120,000
Local travel and trade	50,000
Gross Total . . .	$3,836,000
Estimated expense of working road	600,000
Government of Honduras	50,000
Net Total	$3,186,000

Charter of the Honduras Interoceanic Railway.

"The State of Honduras concedes to the said Company the exclusive right and privilege of constructing a route of communication by water or by railway, across and through its territories, between such points and by such lines as it may find feasible and proper, and the right of making free use of such ports, rivers, lakes, waters, lands, and natural materials, as may be convenient or necessary for such purpose, under the conditions hereinafter provided.

"The Company engages to conclude the surveys within three years, and to complete said route or road within eight years from the date of the ratification of this contract.

"At the expiration of seventy years, this Charter and the privileges which it concedes to the Company shall revert to the State; and the State shall have the right to purchase the road, its dependencies and appurtenances, at a just valuation.

"The Company shall have the right of free passage over and through the lands alike of the State, of towns, and individuals, for all purposes connected with the construction and working of the proposed route or road, and also the right of occupying and holding any portion of the said lands for the space of two hundred yards on each side of the line of the road, and also such other lands as may be convenient or necessary for the construction of station and engine houses and other dependencies of the road, without the payment of indemnity, except in case the land thus occupied shall belong to individuals, in which case the Company shall be entitled to occupy and hold them upon the payment of such indemnity as may be agreed upon with the proprietors.

"The State concedes to the said Company the right to take, free of any charge or indemnity, from any of the public lands or forests of the State, all the wood, stone, lime, timber, and other natural materials, which they may require for the construction or use of said route or road; and if the Company shall require any of these materials which may be found in or upon the lands of individuals, it shall be at liberty to take the same upon paying the owners thereof such price as may be agreed upon.

"The State binds itself to facilitate and aid, in every possible way, the engineers, contractors, employés, and labourers who may be occupied in the explorations and surveys of the route, and in the construction of the works of the same; and to this end stipulates that it will not require from the citizens of the State who may be in the employ of the Company, a rendition of the civil and military service imposed by the constitution of the State, except in case of great public emergency.

"The Company shall have the right to purchase, in the vicinity of the proposed road, an amount of the public lands of the State not exceeding five thousand caballerias, at the rate of twenty dollars the caballeria, to be paid in the stock of the Company at its par value; and the State makes a free grant to the Company of four thousand caballerias, situated in the district known as the Coast of Lean, and on the coast of Truxillo, and extending to the limits of the State. And all these lands shall be held by the Company in conformity with the laws of Honduras, with the reservation to the State of the exportable mahogany.

"It being the object of the concession of lands by the State to encourage the establishment of colonies within its territories, it is stipulated that such establishments shall be colonies of Honduras, and the settlers in consequence shall be subject to the laws of the State in like manner with native-born citizens, and shall enjoy the same rights and privileges in all respects; but nevertheless they shall be exempt for ten years from all kinds of taxes and contributions, and all public service except with their own consent. Each colony shall have at least fifty inhabitants, but every individual shall equally enjoy the same rights and privileges as soon as he shall be established in the country, whether in a colony or otherwise.

"Considering that it is important that artisans and workmen shall be encouraged to establish themselves in Honduras, to facilitate the works of the proposed route or road, therefore the Supreme Government agrees to concede to such foreigners fifty acres each of the public lands of the State, wherever the same may be found, provided that they shall declare their intention to settle in Honduras, and to become citizens of the same. But to be entitled to such concessions, such persons must have worked in the construction of the route or road herein proposed, and have obtained from the Company a certificate of their services and ability; and upon presentation of the same to the Supreme Government, it shall designate the place where they may establish themselves, and where they shall be put in possession of said lands. To artisans who may come into the State with their families, seventy-five acres each shall be granted; but the number of such concessions shall not exceed one thousand.

"When the route or road herein contemplated shall be established and in operation, the Company engages to pay to the State the sum of one dollar for each person over ten years old who may be transported over the same through the State, or from sea to sea; and upon persons passing from point to point within the State, payment shall be made as hereinafter provided.

"Signed, sealed, and delivered, in the City of Comayagua, this twenty-third day of June, in the year of our Lord one thousand eight hundred and fifty-three.

"Justo T. Rodas. L.S.
"Leon Alvarado. L.S.
"E. Geo. Squier." L.S.

The great *fact* against this project is that it has utterly failed in inducing capitalists to engage in the work with any energy or zeal. It will be seen by a reference to the date of the charter that the matter has now been ventilating for nearly ten years, without the least real progress having been made, and therefore there must be something wrong. I am inclined to think that an objection is taken to the nationality of the projector, for there is no denying that the idea forces itself upon the minds of Englishmen more and more every day, that, as a body, the citizens of the United States are not scrupulously honest nor very particular about truthfulness, and therefore projects emanating from them are naturally looked upon with suspicion. When will Americans, instead of glorying in being "*smart*," find out that honesty is the best policy? I have no personal knowledge of either the route or the projector; but I was assured when in Central America, by those capable of giving a just and impartial opinion, that the scheme is impracticable; and I have since learned in this country that if the proposed line ever meets with supporters, one of the first things to be done will be to have a reliable survey made. Colonel Stanton, R.E., C.B., with a detachment of sappers, has examined the line, and reports "that the harbours are unexceptionable, and that the road can be constructed without any *sharper* curves or *heavier* gradients than are to be found on existing lines over which locomotives work without difficulty." This report cannot be said to be encouraging. Locomotives "work without difficulty" over the Sömmering, for example; yet all Europe knows the engineering difficulty and expense of making a railroad over that ground. Von Tempsky, in his 'Travels,' gives the following remarks on this subject:—

"How the steam 'locomotives' will get over the *little hills* of the interior of Honduras, is a problem that American enterprise alone can solve. But there are no mountains in this hemisphere over which the stars and stripes may not culminate, especially if carried before the footsteps of the heroic Squier, as was his wont to have them carried on his first journey, as Yankee envoy, through Nicaragua and other States, when a standard-bearer rode ahead, displaying to the wondering natives the star-spangled banner, unfurled, and leading the van of the calvacade." ('Mitla,' by Von Tempsky, p. 428.)

For this piece of satire I observe in the "Bibliography" of Squier's 'Notes on Central America,' "'Mitla,' by Von Tempsky—*worthless*."

CHAPTER XVI.

MY OWN PROJECT.—THE SURVEYING SERVICE.—PALMETTO AND ROCKY CAYS.—THE RAMA RIVER.—PACIFIC PORTS OF NICARAGUA.—REALEJO.—SAN JUAN DEL SUR.—NATURE OF THE COUNTRY.—PROBABILITY OF AN EASY GRADIENT.—IMMIGRATION TO NICARAGUA.—MOSQUITO A COTTON-GROWING COUNTRY.—A BLACK MACADAM.

I SHALL now proceed to lay before my readers my own project for interoceanic communication. I have mentioned how my attention first became attracted to the subject by the peculiar nature of the service upon which I had been employed for some years, and how it was riveted upon my mind by subsequent events in my professional career, becoming, in fact, a labour of love to devote my mental and physical energies to its development. Very shortly after taking charge at Greytown as senior naval officer, I became convinced that the value of that port, both in a commercial and political sense, was departing. I think my survey proves, that unless from some unforeseen physical convulsion, or the most vigorous and judicious application of large sums of money to improve the navigation of the river San Juan and the harbour of Greytown, the means of transit in that direction will soon be closed; but if any concurrent testimony is required, this is given with great weight by the action of the inhabitants themselves. These good people with unflinching faith stuck to the smoking ruins of their town after its complete destruction by Commander Hollins, and with indomitable energy set to work to rebuild their houses directly the United States commander would permit them to do so. The town soon arose from its ashes, and the Transit speculation being then at its height, increased in a rapid ratio, because it paid well. But of more avail than the guns and torches of the United States was the silting process going on in the port and river, and which was hastened in its destructive effect by the bitter rivalry and evil passions of the contending factions. The accumulation of detritus has now so filled up that arm of the delta which empties itself into the harbour, as well as the entire port and entrance (over which there is only eleven feet), that the ingress of vessels of any size is impossible except at high floods, and transit is now struggling for its life. The consequence is that the inhabitants are constantly leaving; indeed, last June not more than 200 remained, and that number would have dwindled down to less than fifty, had not large quantities of india-rubber been discovered, the gathering and exporting of which just sufficed to keep the trade alive. Thus, what cannon and conflagration failed to do, nature's work on the harbour and river is accomplishing; and therefore I think it will be acknowledged that poor Greytown is going downhill, the desertion of the inhabitants attesting the fact that "the house is falling."

Having after careful consideration made up my mind that the time had gone by when any practical and remunerative road across Central America could be opened *viâ* Greytown, I determined to look elsewhere for a Gate to the Pacific, and I must confess that an attentive study of the Atlantic coast-line was not calculated to give me much encouragement; for, where the semblance of a port showed itself, there high mountains intervened; and where the land appeared low, there the coast-line offered nothing but an open exposed anchorage, without any sort of shelter. However, one point there was, which held out some hope of its being made available as the Atlantic terminus of a railroad; for, be it at once said, I never have given any consideration to canal schemes, for reasons which I detailed in a paper read before the Royal Geographical Society after my return from a visit to the Isthmus of Suez, with my friend the late Mr. Robert Stephenson, M.P.* Regarding the point to which I have alluded, it certainly appeared on the chart as only a small projecting headland; but many years' experience in the surveying service convinced me that on this account alone I need not despair. By the above remark I do not mean to imply that our hydrographical work is badly done,—on the contrary, it will bear comparison with that of any nation in the world; but what I do mean to say is that our surveying operations are undertaken with a view rather to delineate a large extent of coast-line than to investigate a smaller portion of it in a thoroughly complete manner, and therefore many important features are unavoidably overlooked; this, for example, was my own experience in the survey of the Bay of Panama, under Captain Kellett,

* Proceedings of the Royal Geographical Society, vol. iii. p. 177.

in H.M.S. Herald, 1845–51. In this instance every energy was bent upon putting in the coast-line, while the nature of even such places as the magnificent Gulf of San Miguel was left uninquired into; and this at a time when the Isthmus of Panama was attracting the attention of the civilized world, as the spot where the necessities of commerce demanded a short cut from one ocean to the other. I do not intend to animadvert upon the little result of the expedition of the 'Herald' and 'Pandora.' Our chief was an officer who did not consider himself justified in exceeding his instructions one jot or tittle, and he acted accordingly; but I cannot let this opportunity pass without pointing out to the public the unsatisfactory way in which their work is done, whereby they lose the *real return* for their large outlay. Better have 20 miles of coast mapped, the interior explored, the commerce and resources throughly investigated, and the facts stated plainly to our merchants, than 200 miles of mere beach re-surveyed and placed on the charts. I hope soon to see the day when Captains in the Royal Navy will be enjoined and directed to encourage and assist young officers, by every means in their power, in making any explorations or investigations which the nature of the service will permit. Such a cutting through of the Gordian knot of red tape which enchains the noble profession to which I am proud to belong, will not only add immensely to the enterprise and intelligence of the rising generation, but at the same time be the means of bringing to light new fields of commerce for our merchants, and new facts for our better guidance.

The opinion I had formed that adequate shelter might be found under the lee of the point mentioned above, and which is named Monkey Point on the charts, was strongly confirmed by local accounts of the place. Mr. Michael Quin, of Corn Island, told me that it was the best-sheltered bay on the entire coast, and was of capacity sufficient to make a perfect harbour; it was therefore with no small curiosity that I approached it on the first opportunity which occurred for making the necessary examination. It was an exciting time, as, having a fine breeze, I determined to work the old 'Gorgon,' a paddle-wheel tub of a craft, drawing eighteen feet water, to her anchorage under sail. As we approached, the two islands off the point showed themselves, and rounding these the ship shot up to an anchorage in 4½ fathoms water in a very fine bay, where shipping would be as well sheltered from the heaviest of northers as if moored in Portsmouth Harbour. It must be borne in mind that the northers are the only winds about which the navigator need entertain any dread on this coast; every anchorage from one end of Mosquito to the other is more or less exposed to northerly gales: this practical proof therefore of the existence of first-rate shelter was in my humble opinion a most important discovery. At this visit I had simply the opportunity of testing the capabilities of the Bay, by taking her Majesty's ship in under sail; but on a subsequent occasion I experienced the admirable nature of the shelter afforded by running in during heavy weather, when the transition from the rough sea outside to the smooth and quiet of the anchorage proved the excellence of its shelter.

Finding that the Bay was not named on the charts, I considered I was fairly entitled to christen it after the first man-of-war which had really found out its value, and consequently called it Gorgon Bay. The easternmost end, Monkey Point, is in lat. 11° 36′ N., and long. 82° 45′ W., thirty-eight miles due north from Greytown. The southern extremity, or point itself, is a small rocky headland, thickly covered with trees. At the distance of three-quarters of a mile from the mainland, and in a southerly direction, there is an island called Palmetto, and still further off (about four hundred yards) there is an islet, for it is too small to call an island. Palmetto is about eighty feet high, thickly covered with trees, and with a steep rocky face seaward; its entire circumference is about one mile, and it is fringed with rocks for about fifteen or twenty yards all round. At a rough estimate I should say that it contains about two hundred acres of land fit for cultivation. The small cay is not more than a quarter the size of the larger, and hardly any of the soil on it can be cultivated. It is about forty feet high, with a few straggling trees and silk-grass. While Palmetto is pretty regular in its outline, the smaller cay is almost divided by a deep indentation on its landward side, which might be turned to good account in the construction of a dock. All that would be necessary would be to join the cay to Palmetto by a breakwater, the material for which is in abundance all round, while native labour, almost amphibious in its nature, is plentiful and cheap. Dock accommodation would then be provided equal to any emergency. By connecting Palmetto with the mainland, the capacity of the Bay would be largely increased; for a swell rolls in between the cays and the point whenever the trade-wind is well to the eastward, and this renders it prudent for vessels to anchor further off than they otherwise would. The cost of such a breakwater would be trifling, and the steamers might lie alongside, and so discharge their cargo and disembark their passengers into the railway carriage itself. The mainland is thickly wooded, and rises to an average height of about 150 feet. The eastern end of the Bay is cut up by several rocky projections, forming little indentations, or coves, in most of which excellent fresh water is found. In the north-western part there is a sandy beach, nearly a mile long: here the land is low, but it is effectually drained by a rivulet at one extremity, and a small river at the other, up which I went in the dingy some four or five miles, until it became shallow and intricate. Off the mouth of the small river there are two more cays, both of diminutive dimensions, but capable of being turned to useful account. The remainder of Gorgon Bay is for the most part sandy beach, which continues as far as Little Monkey Point, where the land takes another turn and forms a similar indentation, but without affording any adequate shelter. This second bay may be said to terminate at Rama river, about eight miles S.W. of Monkey Point. The Rama* is the southern boundary of the Mosquito

* The Rama river "has five feet water on the bar, but it generally breaks. This river is reported to flow upwards of eighty miles, and is navigable to a considerable distance by the canoes of the Rama Indians, whose settlements reach far in the interior. There is also a small village just within the mouth on the right bank. The Rama Indians were formerly

reservation, according to the terms of Sir Charles Wyke's late treaty. It probably runs in an E.S.E. direction; but this is simply conjecture, as no scientific exploration has yet been made: all that I have to guide me in this belief is that the neighbouring rivers under analogous circumstances, for example, the Escondido, pursue such a course, and take their rise in the broken range of the Cordillera, which does not, as far as can be judged from the sea, anywhere intercept the view to the westward, that is towards the Lake of Nicaragua.

All the information which I possess about the Rama river is derived from native accounts, and the observations of Mr. Carman, mate of the 'Laura Frances;' from the former I learnt that the stream is sluggish, and that the nature of the land is undulating, with a good deal of savana in the vicinity. Indians constantly pass between the river and San Miguelito, on the Lake of Nicaragua, and therefore their account ought to be correct. The latter confirms the above statement, particularly as regards the strength of the current; Mr. Carman went up the river prospecting, having been led to believe that gold could be picked up on its banks in any quantity. He found the stream deep and slow, and he told me he had particularly noticed that nothing remarkable in the shape of hills was observable in any direction. The party with which he was connected took no pains to ascertain the course of the stream, nor the height of the extreme point reached. Their object

very numerous, but in 1820 they were said not to exceed 500, and they pay tribute to the King of Mosquito. They are considered mild, inoffensive, and faithful, and are most expert in the management of their canoes." ('West India Pilot,' 1861, vol. i. p. 253.)

was gold; and as it did not drop into their pockets, they returned to Greytown. I place reliance on the statement of Mr. Carman regarding the absence of hills of any magnitude, because the very nature of his occupation would compel him to study the topography of the country, and therefore it is not likely that he can have made any mistake in this matter. I have been thus particular in relating all the information I have gathered about this river because, as I shall presently show, it will probably play an important part in the project I shall soon lay before my readers; before doing so, however, it will be necessary to give some description of the hydrography of Gorgon Bay. It so happened that I was pressed for time, and therefore my survey was by no means an elaborate one. The work was necessarily rough — a mere sextant sketch; but Mr. Armstrong and myself satisfied ourselves as to the real capabilities of the bay. We found by our soundings that it was free from shoals or rocks of any description; that the bottom shelved very gradually towards the land; that the holding ground was excellent, a tenacious mud; and that the landing was unexceptionable. Moreover, the point and adjacent country offered very favourable conditions for settlement, the soil being of first-rate quality, free from swamps, and only requiring clearance to enable the trade-wind to blow over every part, without meeting any obstacle to obstruct the free ventilation of the houses. I have already mentioned the abundance of good wholesome water, and I do not know what more could be wished for, in the formation of a thriving place of business; a practical proof of the value of the anchorage may be adduced from the logs of the steamers belonging to the Royal Mail Packet Company, the directors, with the sanction of the Post-Office authorities, having ordered their captains to anchor there when conveying the Greytown and Blewfields mail.

An essential point in the construction of a transit route is, that the terminal ports should be good ones. I have shown the capacity of that on the Atlantic side, "Gorgon Bay;" and before describing the manner in which I propose to connect the two oceans, I will take my reader to the Pacific, and point out what terminal accommodation is to be found in that direction. Nicaragua possesses on this side two harbours of the most unexceptionable character, besides one or two minor ports, more or less useful; of the former, Realejo and a portion of the Gulf of Fonseca are the localities to which I allude; of the latter, San Juan del Sur affords the best anchorage, and has been long used for transit purposes. The Gulf of Fonseca has been briefly described in the last chapter; but as it is not intended to approach it, there will be no necessity for any further account. The harbour of Realejo is the Pacific terminus of my proposed interoceanic communication. I am sorry that I cannot give a description of this beautiful and safe port from English *official* sailing directions. I fear such do not exist, at all events I have been unable to find any; however, the omission has been well supplied by French surveyors,* and what with a translation

* 'Reconnaissance Hydrographique des Côtes Occidentales du Centre Amérique,' pp. 42, 46. Paris, 1854.

of some of their remarks, a short account written by the English Consul for Belcher's 'Voyage round the World,' the admirable sketch of Sir William Ouseley, and the Admiralty chart, I do not despair of conveying to my readers some idea of the nature of this first-rate Pacific terminus.

"The little town of Realejo, which gives its name to the port, is six miles from the inner anchorage. It serves as an *entrepôt* to Chinandega, a pretty town, containing 4000 or 5000 inhabitants, and which divides with Granada all the commerce of Nicaragua.

"Realejo has a population of about 1200, mostly employed in attendance on the shipping or carrying on the commerce of the port, which has greatly increased in importance since it became a calling-place for steamers running between Panama and San Francisco.

"The port of Realejo is formed by the *estero* of the same name, and that of Doña Paula, into which fall the rivers Realejo and Telica; it is sheltered from wind and sea by the islands Asserradores and Cardon, also by the promontory of Castañon, between which there are two channels leading into an inner basin, having soundings from five to nine fathoms, and which is surrounded by low land.

"The perfect tranquillity of the anchorage offers facilities for every kind of repair; there are even beaches, upon which, as it were upon a natural gridiron, vessels may be placed; the only real inconvenience is the distance from Realejo, and the necessity of tiding there in the conveyance of merchandise.

"Of the entrance, one passage, Barra Falsa is be-

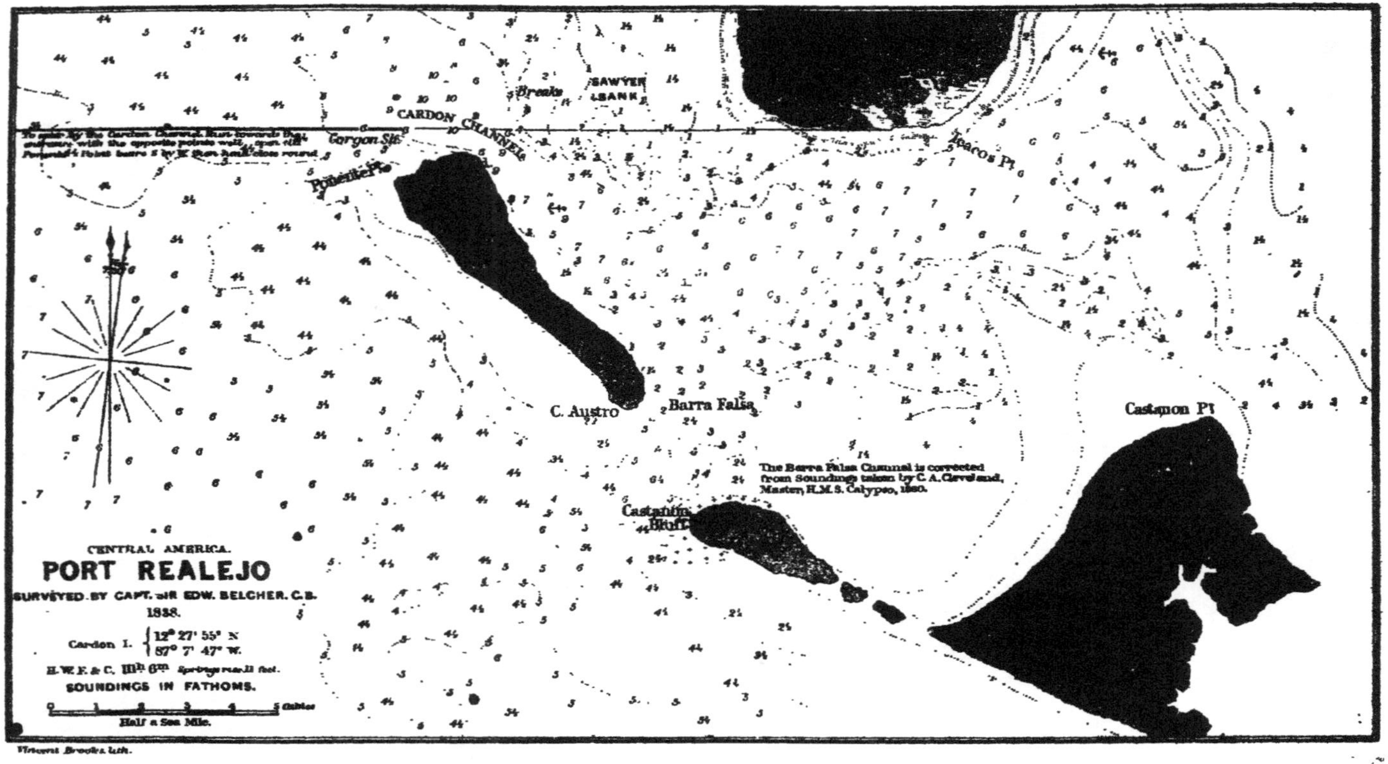
CARDON CHANNEL
Gorgon Sh.
Breaks
SAWYER BANK
Icacos Pt.
C. Austro
Barra Falsa
Castanon Pt.
Castanon Bluff
The Barra Falsa Channel is corrected from Soundings taken by C. A. Cleveland, Master, H.M.S. Calypso, 1880.
CENTRAL AMERICA.
PORT REALEJO
SURVEYED BY CAPT. SIR EDW. BELCHER. C.B.
1838.
Cardon I. 12° 27' 55" N. 87° 7' 47" W.
SOUNDINGS IN FATHOMS.
Half a Sea Mile.
Vincent Brooks lith.

tween the south end of Cardon and Point Castañon, its greatest breadth hardly exceeds three cables, its least one. This channel ought only to be navigated with a pilot.

"The safest as the deepest channel is that of Cardon, between the island of the same name and Asserradores."

In Belcher's 'Voyage round the World,' vol. ii. p. 307, the harbour is thus described:—

"Cardon, at the mouth of the port of Realejo, is situated in lat. 12° 28′ N., about long. 87° 12′ W. It has two entrances, both of which are safe, under proper precaution, and in all weathers. The depths vary from two to seven fathoms, and good and safe anchorage extends for several miles; the rise and fall of tide is eleven feet, full and change three hours and six minutes. Docks or slips therefore may easily be constructed, and timber is readily to be procured of any dimensions. Wood, water, and immediate necessaries and luxuries are plentiful and cheap. The village of Realejo is about nine miles from the sea.* Its population is about a thousand souls; the principal occupation of the working males is on the water, loading and unloading vessels. . . . One branch of the river, Doña Paula, takes a course towards Leon and is navigable to within three leagues of that city."

Although Realejo will be the Pacific port of the transit, yet as a measure in the interest of the shareholders it will probably be necessary, in the first place,

* This distance is no doubt due to the dread the Spaniards entertained of the buccaneers in the seventeenth century, who sacked the original city, then containing 15,000 inhabitants. These daring freebooters even built a fort in the harbour, the ruins of which may still be seen.

to use the port of San Juan del Sur for that purpose, because a temporary line to that place could be opened for traffic in one-third the time requisite to complete the railroad from ocean to ocean. I have therefore considered it advisable in this place to introduce a small plan of the anchorage, taken from "Côtes Occidentales du Centre Amérique (Nicaragua). Carte des atterrages de Salinas de San Juan del Sur au Cap Elena, dressée d'après les ordres de M. le Contre-Amiral Bonard, commandant-en-chef la station des Côtes Occidentales d'Amérique, par MM. Boucarut, lieutenant de vaisseau, et Lefèvre, aspirant. Corvette la 'Constantine,' commandée par M. Huguet de Majoureaux, capitaine de vaisseau. 1859."*

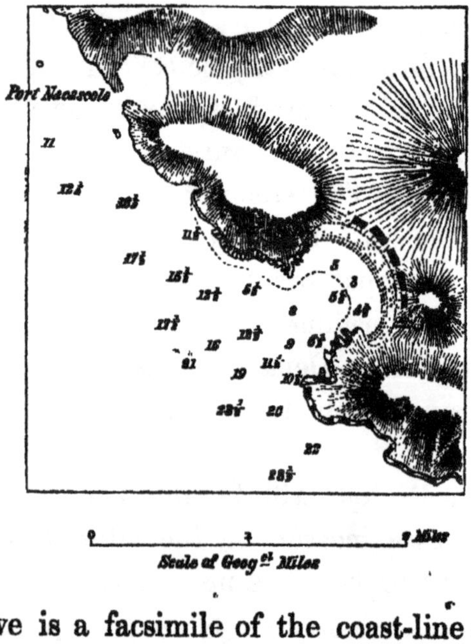

The above is a facsimile of the coast-line delineated by the French surveyors; but I have altered the scale to

* Dépôt des Cartes et Plans de la Marine, 1860, No. 1953.

English miles, made the longitude to correspond with our own by reducing it to the meridian of Greenwich and changed the soundings from French mètres into English fathoms.

This interesting little port is almost unknown to the seamen of this country; indeed, even now the community at large appear to be doubtful of its existence. I have heard it gravely questioned whether there ever was such a place, and the voyage of H.M.S. Sulphur has been relied on to prove that even a surveying vessel had failed to give a plan of it to the world. This, as I have shown above, in the case of San Miguel, is not an isolated instance. Nevertheless I cannot help mentioning, in proof of the accuracy of English surveys, that at the point where the work of Captains Barnett and Belcher touched, close to San Juan del Sur, the one coming from the Atlantic, the other the Pacific, there only existed a difference of 32″ of latitude and 10″ of longitude, although each was quite a distinct expedition, having no connection whatsoever. I trust the sketch taken on the spot by Sir William Ouseley,* and the French plan of the anchorage, will be sufficient proof that a veritable port really exists. There never would have been any doubt on the matter had our information been derived from reliable sources; but it has now become a settled belief with Europeans, that American accounts must be received with caution, the old-fashioned term Munchausen having been superseded by the new appellation, an Americanism.

* The frigate in Sir William Ouseley's sketch is the famous 'Merrimac,' which lately made such havoc in Hampton Roads and was afterwards destroyed at Norfolk, Virginia, to prevent her from falling into the hands of the Federals.

Having now given an account of the means of ingress and egress, the Gates as it were of this part of the New World, I will proceed to describe the route which I hope, ere long, to see in use as a great highway of nations. I mentioned above that I did not contemplate the joining together of the two oceans by means of a canal. That such an idea is a great *conception* cannot be denied; but in my opinion it would practically be one of the greatest failures of the age; it would in reality be a return to the stage-coach travelling of a former period, for time, not distance, has now become the true measure of space; and it must be borne in mind that for a *sailing vessel*, the time occupied from England to India would be *longer*, *viâ* a canal through Nicaragua, than it would be by a voyage round the Cape of Good Hope. However, it is of no use pursuing this theme, as I believe even the French at Suez have at last opened their eyes to the fallacy of canalization as a means of transit.

My proposal is to connect Realejo and Gorgon Bay by means of "the iron road;" the trains running from alongside the wharf in the one port, to a position close to the ocean steamer in the other, thus embarking and disembarking passengers and freight, with an ease and rapidity far superior to the accommodation afforded either at Suez or Panama, where it is necessary to reach the shore in boats, take the train, and re-embark in either small steamers or barges, before the transfer from one ocean steamer to the other is completed. To construct a railway from the Atlantic to the Pacific, by the route I have designated, would require some four or five years to finish; but it would not be necessary to wait until then before a passage from sea to sea could be effected. The completion of the section, from the Atlantic to San Miguelito, would suffice for the immediate opening of a temporary line, as from there passengers and goods could be conveyed by steamer, across the Lake of Nicaragua, to Virgen Bay, whence a fine macadamized road, thirteen miles in length, well bridged and levelled as much as possible, has already been constructed to San Juan del Sur, on the Pacific. There would be several changes, it is true; but still those changes would not be so many as the passengers make on the River San Juan transit, which nevertheless at one time attracted more than half the traffic from the Panama Railway, and proved perhaps one of the best-paying undertakings of the day.

I shall now describe the nature of the country, over which the railroad would pass; and in doing so, I shall divide the line into five sections, and treat each separately.

The First Section, commencing at the Pacific side, would be from Realejo to Leon, the ancient capital of Nicaragua. The country is most beautiful, disclosing a constant succession of fresh views; everywhere palms and flowers, oranges and plantains, line the road, which runs through a perfectly *level* country the entire distance, except close to Leon, where the land is slightly undulating. The road is excellent; even the heavy ox-waggons and tropical rains having failed to cut it up. The distance from the wharf in the port of Realejo to Leon is about seventeen miles, and there is not a single engineering impediment the whole way; the soil is a black loam, about six feet in depth.

The Second Section would be from Leon to Managua, a distance of forty miles. The road here would pass over ground, not, it is true, so continuously flat as the preceding section, but nevertheless of so favourable a nature, that probably not even a single cutting would be required. This portion also is extremely fertile, and more thickly populated than the first section, the line running through the small towns of Pueblo Nuevo, Nargorote, and Matiares, the latter in lat. 12° 14′ N., long. 86° 43′ W.

The Third Section is the shortest, only fifteen miles, and extends from Managua across the river Tipitapa. Here again nothing but a level country presents itself; but, unlike the previous portion, it is almost uncultivated, chiefly from want of water, the Lake of Managua being the only certain source whence that necessary element can be drawn. It need hardly be said, however, that the infusion of a little enterprise, with even a rude system of irrigation, would speedily convert this space into a series of cultivated fields and valuable plantations. Crossing the river Tipitapa would of course involve a bridge, and this would be the first occasion for such a structure; at the same time it would be but a small specimen, as a point might be chosen where the stream is only of inconsiderable breadth.

The Fourth Section would closely border on the eastern shore of the Lake, from the river Tipitapa to the hacienda of Pedronal, or the village of San Miguelito, an average distance of eighty miles. Pedronal would probably be the Lake terminus; but that cannot be stated with certainty until the last section is marked out. The principal feature in this part of the proposed route would be the number of small streams which must be crossed, and over which it would be necessary to construct bridges: of these at least eleven, perhaps fifteen, would be required; but their dimensions would not probably in any case exceed a single span. In other respects the line would run over an undulating savana country, requiring no clearance, and for the most part low and level.

The Fifth Section.—We now come to the last and most difficult part of the undertaking, viz. from about Pedronal to Gorgon Bay, the Atlantic terminus,—a distance of seventy-three miles. This portion has never been scientifically explored, much less surveyed, and, as stated above, I have only for my guidance the native reports, Mr. Carman's account, and certain physical facts, such as the regularity and force of the trade-wind on the Lake of Nicaragua, corresponding to its action in the Caribbean Sea; thus showing that no high land intervenes to obstruct its uninterrupted passage from one ocean to the other; and, the elevation of the Lake itself, which is only 138·3 feet above the Atlantic. These facts may be taken for what they are worth; but for my own part, after some practical acquaintance with both sides of the section, I am inclined to think that no engineering impediment of any importance will be met with in the interior; in point of fact, that an easy gradient might be marked out over the entire distance.

I have now endeavoured to give a plain practical description of the nature of the country over which

I propose to construct a transit route. It will be seen that 152 miles of that line will be laid down over ground offering no impediment whatever to the engineer; and that the only difficulty rests with the remaining portion, a difficulty which will vanish, like all other imaginary obstacles, directly it is grappled with. The entire length of the line, 225 miles, will be best understood by the reader, if I compare it with some familiar distance in our own country, such, for example, as that between London and Darlington, on the Great Northern Railroad, and which is accomplished by the slowest trains in less than twelve hours.

Gorgon Bay, the Atlantic terminus of the new route, would speedily attract a large population to its shores, and I propose to make it a free port, open to the commerce of the whole world, and untrammelled by any narrow regulations calculated to restrict its full usefulness. With the commencement of the town-buildings a church should be erected, and schools established, then, with the blessing of the Almighty upon the undertaking, there can be no fear for the result. By spreading out the basis of the project in this manner, and founding it upon a rock, to what may it not aspire? Every mile the iron road penetrates into the country will be a positive gain to civilization; while those strong moral and religious feelings inherent in every Englishman, and which more than anything else have elevated Great Britain to her present pitch of greatness, would be fostered and encouraged, instead of, as is too often the case in foreign lands, dying out altogether. Thus, by beginning in the way I have indicated, there would be

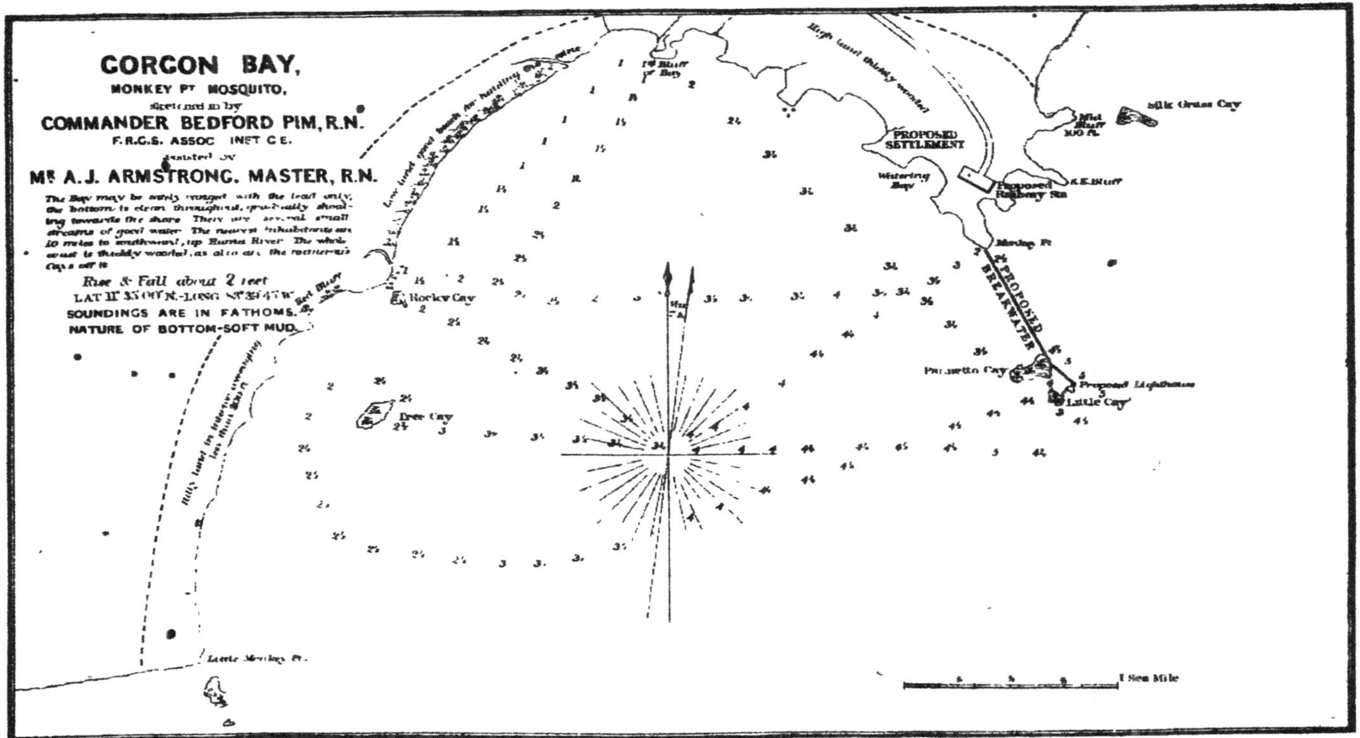

Vincent Brooks, lith.

every hope, from the example of the new-comers, of forming the new community upon the best and purest principles and of thoroughly reclaiming the aboriginal Indians, instead of irretrievably demoralizing them. I am as morally certain as man can be, that the misfortunes and misery brought upon all connected with the Greytown Transit resulted entirely from their dense moral blindness and utter want of truth; and I think, with such a lesson before us, it would be an act of insanity not to take every precaution to prevent the proposed settlement falling into a similar Slough of Despond.

To make my railway project succeed beyond the mere twenty per cent. which it will return to the shareholders, it is necessary to encourage immigration to this favoured land by every legitimate means. The republic offers land to the colonist on easy and advantageous terms; and besides, when a Company is formed to carry out the transit, it will have many extensive allotments to dispose of. But perhaps of more practical value than either of the above considerations, is the fact that the entire Atlantic terminus is already secured: it is the absolute property of the writer of these pages; and he can only say, that so convinced is he of the vast importance of a good start to any embryo community, that he has dedicated the first plot of ground for church and school purposes; and hopes to see this small beginning, this thin edge of the wedge, split to pieces the anarchy and confusion, bloodshed and robbery, ruin and devastation, which have characterized beautiful Nicaragua for the last forty years.

I have given a full account of the climate in a former

chapter: now for the soil. I think it is impossible to exaggerate the value of the land, both of Mosquito and Nicaragua, if only for agricultural purposes. As regards Mosquito, I do not hesitate to say, that it is, both from position and adaptability, the finest country for the growth of cotton in the entire world. Some description of it will be found in a preceding chapter; but as I did not then especially enlarge upon the many advantages it possesses for the growth and export of that valuable product, I will do so in this place. The entire strip of land, 150 miles in length, now appertaining to the King of Mosquito, is for the most part low, and possesses a soil of exuberant fertility. It is ventilated from one end to the other by the prevalent north-east trade-wind, which blows with some force, and carries with it those saline particles from the sea, without which it is useless to attempt the cultivation of some kinds of cotton,—the Sea Island for example. Moreover the land is so formed that it rises inland with a gently undulating slope,—another point of great value to the successful growth of the plant. In short, soil, atmosphere, and indeed all the physical requirements necessary to the cultivation of millions of bales of cotton, here reach the highest perfection. Moreover, when it is borne in mind that along the coast of Mosquito, and on the numerous islands adjacent to it, the plant is not an annual as in the United States, but, on the contrary, a shrub which yields year after year a steady crop, requiring little care or attention to bring to maturity, it must be admitted that a field is offered in this locality highly remunerative alike to cultivator and consumer; and, what is of great importance, the staple would be obtained from a country which, from its proximity to England, could successfully compete with the South-grown cotton of the United States, and thus, as far as human means can do so, render us independent for the future.

I wish it to be distinctly understood that in this matter I am not venturing upon any theory: the statements I have made above are matter of fact. I have myself seen the cotton shrubs,—I might almost say small trees,—both on the islands and the main, the remains of the plantations abandoned in 1848, when the emancipation of the slaves was *summarily and without the least notice* decreed by the Government. The cotton is of the finest quality, and its cultivation might be resumed on the largest scale, particularly as there is no reason to fear any lack of labour, as the Carib labourers, whom I propose to introduce for the construction of the railway, will bring with them their wives and children, who are as hard-working and industrious as their husbands and fathers, and would, I am convinced, undertake the care and culture of the plants. When it is remembered that, in six months from the date of sowing, a crop might be gathered and sent to Lancashire, I think it will be acknowledged that here is the solution of the difficulty, which is now absorbing the attention of high and low, rich and poor,—I mean, a cotton-famine.

Perhaps some explanation of my remark about the proximity of Mosquito will be necessary in this place. The first glance at a map of the world would not satisfy the casual observer on this point; New Orleans and the Cotton States of America appearing to be much nearer

England. But such is not the case, and for this reason—the Gulf Stream bars, as it were, access to New Orleans by the direct passage, for it runs with such force between the Bahamas and Florida that sailing vessels at all events would not attempt that course on their outward voyage, but rather make a detour and pass either between Cuba and Hayti, which is not quite prudent, or between Hayti and Puerto Rico, which is safer. If, then, from either of these two points of departure the distance is measured on the map, it will be found that Mosquito holds a more favourable position than New Orleans; and not only so in actual distance, but the navigation itself is far less hazardous, on account of rocks, shoals, currents, and the hurricane track. Ships bound to Mosquito could make a clean run from the Mona passage, with almost an impunity from any danger, and quite out of the path of those destructive storms, which, while they devastate the West Indies and the places bordering on the Gulf Stream, have never yet been known to visit the Mosquito Coast. In the exportation of cotton, the above favourable circumstances would act beneficially in two ways:—first, in a decided diminution of the cost for freight, as compared with that now paid between New Orleans and Liverpool; and secondly, in the lesser rate of insurance which would be demanded on ships voyaging to Mosquito, because the navigation would be more safe than that encountered in following the boisterous "stream" through the Gulf of Mexico. This, I take it, is the real point at issue, in determining in what direction we shall fix our attention for obtaining a future supply of cotton. Quantity and quality being equal, there is no doubt, cost of freight would turn the balance in favour of that locality which can transfer its bales from the plantation to the hands of the consumer at the cheapest rate. And here I ought to mention that Mosquito stands unrivalled for her means of inland transport. Intersected by numerous rivers running at *right angles* to her coast-line, the easiest means is thus afforded, by which loaded flats or barges could bring the produce to the sea; while an inland system of lagoons, extending *parallel* to and but a short distance from the ocean, would enable the planter to forward his bales for shipment from any part of the country at the cheapest possible rate.

With all these advantages, why should not Mosquito compete successfully with New Orleans? And she will do so at no distant day: the only fear I have is that it may not be in English hands, or even in English interests.

Having now sketched out a future, easily attainable and quite within the reach of Mosquito, I will proceed to show how and in what manner the land bordering on either side of my proposed highway of nations may be turned to good account. In the first place, it cannot be too clearly pointed out that the transit I advocate must, from its very nature, be totally unlike that at Panama, which has neither roads intersecting it, nor local traffic. Nicaragua, on the contrary, in addition to the healthiness of the climate and the choice of temperature which is afforded by the diversity of its surface, occupies a grand commercial as well as geographical position, such indeed as no other country can command. Native produce pours in from the north and from the south, while foreign commerce would constantly arrive from the east and from the west and find here an *entrepôt* on both the Atlantic and Pacific. Directly the highway is opened, the commerce of San Salvador, Guatemala, and Honduras on the north, and Costarica on the south, must concentrate within this favoured state as it did of yore.

As mentioned above, the country between Gorgon Bay and the Lake of Nicaragua has not been sufficiently explored to permit me to enter into details regarding its capabilities; but enough is known to enable me to point at all events to one well-known article of export which may be obtained in any quantity, I allude to mahogany.* This valuable tree here attains a con-

* The mahogany-tree flourishes between the 11th and 23rd parallels of north latitude; it attained to great perfection in Cuba, Hayti, Jamaica, Puerto Rico, and the Bahamas, but the supply from that quarter is now becoming scarce. On the Mainland, the Honduras, and Mosquito, mahogany is deservedly held in high commercial favour; and as regards the southern part of the latter country, vast supplies still exist, which can be easily and cheaply got out from the forest. Mahogany was first used in ship-building by Cortez about 1530, but it was not imported into England until 1724. (For account of its introduction see Lunan's 'Hortus Jamaicensis.') The tree is one of the most majestic and beautiful in the vegetable world, and requires at least 200 years to arrive at maturity. The season for cutting commences in August, its leaves at that time assuming a yellowish-red hue, easily discernible, from an eminence or the top of a tree, to the quick-sighted Carib hunter (as he is called) who leads the gang of wood-cutters, with unerring sagacity, to the patch or clump which he has selected. Mahogany works as freely, and bends as readily, as English oak. It is stiffer even than teak, and in the present day would prove the best wooden backing to our iron ships, for the following reasons:—1. Shot does not splinter it like teak, but, on the contrary, the projectile buries itself in the fibre; moreover the durability and firmness of the wood is well known, offering a better resisting medium. 2. Metals do not corrode so rapidly when in contact with it as with other woods; such as teak, for instance; a chemical analysis having proved that "a decoction of its chips or shavings had hardly any chemical reaction, and scarcely affected *iron* and copper." 3. Economy: the sale of mahogany planks when a ship is

siderable size, and is therefore proportionably valuable; and moreover we have a broad and deep river, the Rama, by means of which rafts could be at once floated to the sea within eight miles of the shipping port. Here, then, is an enterprise certain and safe, which might be opened up, and which, while it would enrich those engaged in it, would at the same time clear the land in the vicinity of the railway, ready for the settlement of emigrants.

On and about the next section, skirting the border of the Lake, I should consider the best locality for settlement. Here there are hundreds of thousands of acres of the finest pasture-land, on which vast herds of cattle might increase and multiply in sufficient numbers to stock the market with hides, and supply the fleets of the world with salt and preserved meat; while, at various degrees of elevation, there is ample room for farms, hamlets, villages, and towns to spring into existence. The savana land is bounded at the northern extremity of the Lake by Alto Grande, a huge mountain 3000 feet high, clothed to its very summit with grass, and upon which alone, choosing any degree of temperature, thousands of people now struggling for a bare subsistence in their own country might find happiness and plenty for themselves and children. Again, to the eastward, the broken range of the Cordilleras approaches within twenty miles of the line marked out for the railway, and con-

broken up from old age, or from the necessity of a *reconstruction* of the navy, realizes a profit on the original outlay, the wood having become harder and more suitable for the cabinet-maker, from its age; beautiful furniture has been made from H.M.S. Gibraltar, built of mahogany at Havana, more than a hundred years ago.

tains within itself the accumulated treasures of untold ages. The best authorities on this matter declare that the Chontales Mountains are second to none in the world for the richness of the mineral deposits buried in their strata; and this is proved by the quantity of gold annually brought to the towns by the rude untutored Indian, in spite of his curiously primitive method of extracting the precious metal. Nothing is wanting to enable men to realize large fortunes from the above source, but the opening of roads, by which machinery could be conveyed to the gold-bearing districts; for at present there are merely the rudest paths, along which, in some places, it would be rash to proceed without a guide, and over which it would be impossible to convey the appliances necessary for crushing the ore.

These two sections, comprising about 160 miles in length, may be said to be comparatively unoccupied; one moiety, viz. the land between the Atlantic and the Lake, is so entirely, with the exception of some settlement of Rama Indians, who are prepared to welcome English settlers, and who would be found most valuable auxiliaries; the other moiety, viz. the country bordering on the Lake, is inhabited by a few herdsmen, whose ranchos number about twelve, and are scattered at wide intervals along the shore; the *only* village is that of San Miguelito, described in my journal. So that there would be no impediment whatever,—on the contrary, every inducement,—to the rapid settlement of the country by Anglo-Saxons. The land is at present valueless in a money point of view; but the mere fact of laying down the iron road would convert it into property which would command a high price in the market.

The remaining sections of the proposed railway would run through land more or less occupied by the natives of the country. Their interests would be so manifestly advanced by the undertaking that it would command the cordial approbation of all classes; and ground would be granted free of cost to the Company, so as to ensure the line passing through the respective properties of the various land-owners. Seldom, indeed, has any project been undertaken which could at the outset offer so many guarantees for its successful accomplishment. Every sort of material which can be required in the construction of the work is at hand in abundance,—labour, provisions, timber, stone, etc.; and all that is necessary will be to introduce the manufactured iron for the tramway, and the ready-made iron or wooden houses to form the stations and settlements. Labour is abundant and cheap, and of the very best quality: I allude to the Carib inhabitants of Honduras, the Bay Islands, and Mosquito. These men will bear comparison with any labouring population in the world for endurance, capability for work, faithfulness, and orderly behaviour. I have had some experience of their good qualities; and I have never heard but one opinion as regards their excellent character, both from residents and visitors to the coast. They would be of the greatest value on the section between the Lake and the Atlantic, as they are acknowledged to be amongst the best woodmen in the world. At the present moment, owing to the abandonment of the Bay Islands and Mosquito, it would be easy to settle some thousands of these men, with their wives and families, in the vicinity and along the line of the railway. Their chief occupation has been mahogany-cutting; but, from the cause just mentioned, the trade is declining, and numbers are consequently out of employment. They speak English and Spanish, a great addition to the value of their services. Their numbers are variously estimated, it being almost impossible to arrive at the exact amount, owing to their migratory habits, entire families removing to that part of the country which affords the most work; but the Carib mahogany-cutters alone cannot be less than 6000 men. These people would without hesitation form settlements along the present Mosquito country if proper inducement was offered to them; and then, while the men were engaged on the works of the railway, women and children could attend to the cultivation of cotton in the vicinity of their various villages. I have made careful inquiries into this matter, and can answer for its practicability. The pay of these men is on an average 2*s.* per day, with rations consisting of pork (salt) and biscuit. The native Indian would not cost much more than half that sum; but then he would not labour half so well as a Carib, to say nothing of his not being accustomed to the peculiar work (road-making), in which the latter is especially skilled. For instance, the roads, which it is necessary to construct for the conveyance of the mahogany to the water, are often some miles in length; they must be levelled as much as possible, carefully grubbed, and bridges built across the small rivulets. The blocks of timber are conveyed on trucks drawn by oxen, and any inequality in the road would be fatal to progress; but this rarely happens, for the Carib appears to have an instinct for the selection of easy roads; he is, in point of fact, a black Macadam, brought up from his boyhood to the work, and unrivalled in it; in short, the man of all others most useful in the construction of a tropical railroad. The mahogany-cuttings are generally carried on by gangs of men who work by contract. The average amount of work performed by one man per day is a cutting thirty feet wide by about a hundred and fifty feet in length; that is to say, that a gang of ten men could cut, clear, and grub nearly two miles in a week; or, in other words, a hundred men would form a good substantial mule-road from Gorgon Bay to the Lake of Nicaragua in one month. The Caribs construct their huts with incredible quickness, thatch them with palm-leaves, hang up their hammock, light a fire, fry their pork, and make themselves quite at home in no time. A strip of calico round the loins is their working-day suit, but on holidays they come out in gorgeous apparel.

I have gone carefully into the matter of estimates both for railroad and colony, and append statements of cost, not, as will be seen, depending upon my own experience in these affairs, but seeking and obtaining the best information in my power. In addition to the value of the practical and business-like part of Mr. Griffin's letter, so much interest must be attached to his preliminary remarks by the general public, that I consider any excuse for the insertion of the entire correspondence quite unnecessary. I take this opportunity of stating that my intention in writing this book is not simply to lay *my* proposals before those only whose especial business it is, to deal with such matters, but to endeavour to place the subject in as clear and practical a manner as I possibly can before the great body of my countrymen, so as to leave it with *them* to judge whether the undertaking and carrying out of such a transit project as I propose, in the interest of England, would tend to advance the commercial and political position of the country; in other words, whether it would *pay them* to embark in it, and therefore, by the force of public opinion, *compel* those who now govern this land, and who appear to find a difficulty in initiating any independent action of their own (either for the benefit of the nation at home, or to advance its true interests abroad), to open their eyes to the true aspect of affairs in Central America.

The words of Mr. Cobden at Rochdale, reported in the 'Times' of October 25th, 1862, are pointedly applicable to the present occasion, and may here be repeated and re-urged. Mr. Cobden said, "What was wanted was that the discussion of this question should be *forced* upon the Government (*Liberal*) from our own standpoint, our own point of view; that we should insist that gentlemen should not tell us what was said in the time of Grotius, but look at and deal with the [question] as it exists. A great many of our public men and leading writers came from college into public life deeply read and well learned in the history of Athens, *but knowing sadly too little of what was actually occurring around us.*"

CHAPTER XVII.

MR. GRIFFIN'S RAILWAY WITHOUT WOODEN SLEEPERS.—PRESENT "CONSUMPTIVE" SYSTEM.—ECONOMIC PROPOSAL.—ESTIMATE OF NICARAGUAN RAILROAD.—COLONIZATION.—PROBABLE RECEIPTS OF THE NEW TRANSIT.—MONTHLY MAIL TO AUSTRALIA.—NEW ZEALAND.—GREAT BARRIER ISLAND.—GENERAL SUMMARY.

I SHALL now lay before my readers an estimate of the cost of constructing a single line of rails from Realejo to Gorgon Bay; and, in the first place, I shall introduce Mr. Griffin's letter, to which I particularly wish to draw attention. I ought however to state that the plan proposed by Mr. Griffin is not new in its principle; the iron sleepers and hollow supports having been used by Mr. Robert Stephenson in the construction of the railway from Alexandria to Cairo with signal success, as described in my paper on Suez, already alluded to.* Mr. Griffin's plan however is so great an improvement, not only upon the old one adopted in Egypt, but upon the present railway system generally, that it may almost be said to be a new invention.

* Proceedings of the Royal Geographical Society, vol. iii. p. 174.

"New Adelphi Chambers, John Street, W.C.,
"January 12th, 1863.

"Sir,—No one who has for a moment studied your proposal for a new and independent route which would connect the Atlantic and Pacific, can fail to be struck with the immense importance of the subject. It would indeed be a matter reflecting little honour on a maritime and commercial nation such as we are, to continue dependent upon our present rivals in trade, and possibly our future enemies on the ocean, for the only means of transit to our colonies and possessions. We ought unquestionably to have a direct highway in our own hands, beyond the control of any other Power whatever. I trust that the important work you have undertaken will be carried out to completion, and that it will redound not only to the advantage and glory of our country and its commercial interests, but also to the high honour and substantial benefit of yourself, as the originator of, and labourer in, so important a work.

In reply to the questions contained in your last favour, relative to the cost of the 'permanent ways' now in use, and my railway in particular, I would just, *en passant*, remark that it was scarcely possible to invent a more complete misnomer than that of 'permanent way' as applicable to the very defective system which has hitherto been adopted in the construction of most of the railways in this country. The many fatal accidents that have happened to the public from this cause are sufficiently well known,—not to mention the loss of rolling-stock, the claimed compensation, the law expenses, and other charges which the railway companies have had to bear from these defects; but these losses, considerable though they have been, and causing a serious deduction from the dividends of the subscribers, form, after all, but a small part of the very expensive outlay which the companies have had to bear, not only in the first cost of the line, but in the rapid deterioration of material, and the continued and costly expenditure of labour in keeping the said 'permanent way' in repair. Truly it should have been called the '*consumptive way*.'

I need not remark to one of your profession that iron is stronger than wood, and that it is more durable under certain conditions. I believe that the time is not distant when every railway in the kingdom will be laid upon iron sleepers, instead of wood; at least, it will be so if the directors study their own interests, and the interests of those whose property is committed to their care and management. Were I required to enumerate all the defects of the prevailing system of wooden sleepers, chairs, fishplates, wood keys, iron spikes, bolts and nuts, screws, trenails, etc., the task would be difficult, for their name is 'legion;' but I may mention a few of the most prominent.

"In the first place, where the traffic is considerable, fresh sleepers have to be laid every two years (average for renewing the whole line, about seven); the wedges, 7000 to 8000 in every two miles, are drawn out by the contraction and expansion of the rails from temperature and the vibration of passing trains, the enlargement of the holes of spikes and bolts, and the loosening of nuts and screws; besides which, the chairs oscillate to and fro, and destroy the *aplomb* of the rails; the fishplates become loose, and jump up and down with the attached ends of the rails at every passage of a wheel. These, and many more than these, are defects which it is easy to remedy by a proper system. Then consider again the labour and cost of men daily employed (six to every two miles of road) in inspecting, screwing-up, driving-up, and tightening every wedge, twice a day; upon the integrity or failure of any one of which, the lives of hundreds may depend; resetting displaced and sunken sleepers; the trouble and time employed in shifting the rails; and from the great number of separate parts—from 26,000 to 30,000 in a single mile; the consequent loss of material—in itself a very serious item; add to this the original expense of the 'permanent way,' the time required to place it in position, and some idea may be formed of the immense outlay which must be occasioned. Having for many years been interested in railway matters, a knowledge of these facts led me to study the subject deeply; and, after gleaning the opinions of many of our most eminent practical engineers with whom I have been thrown in contact, upon the advantages and disadvantages of the various systems that had been tried, it led me to invent what I style the 'Economic System,'* and which, where it has been tried, has given the most unqualified satisfaction, and has been found to combine advantages as to economy, stability, and permanency, which no other plan hitherto adopted is known to possess. I give you an extract from a letter addressed to me by an eminent engineer of one of our large metropolitan lines, bearing testimony to the efficiency of my plan; and I challenge the whole profession to produce so secure, durable, and economical a line. He says, 'In answer to your inquiry I have much pleasure in saying that up to the present date your permanent way has fully borne out the good opinion I at first formed of it. The traffic is so heavy at this spot that our rails are ordinarily renewed every seven or eight months, whereas those fixed on your sleepers have already been down that time, and appear as perfect as ever.' As a proof of the rapidity with which my sleepers can be laid down, and the rails fixed, an inspector of another metropolitan line declared, in the presence of several eminent engineers, that he could lay down five or six miles of my railway while he was laying down one under the ordinary system, and that when down it required no further attention. In reply to your first question, as to 'the weight per mile of my railway complete,' I have given you the weights, number of pieces, and present price of a mile of road, using a rail of sixty pounds per yard, on my own system; and also, for the purpose of comparison, the weight, number of pieces, and price of a mile, upon the system now in use; by which you will see that in the article of material alone, there would be a saving (including all royalties) of £563. 9*s*. in money, upwards of 20,000 loose parts, and 106 tons of weight, in every mile of single way.

* The accompanying plate will give some notion of the simplicity of construction of Mr. Griffin's railway; and from it also an idea may be formed, by the uninitiated reader, how rapidly a line so made may be jointed and laid down over any gradient.

Vincent Brooks, Lith

"NUMBER OF PARTS, WEIGHT, AND COST, OF ONE MILE OF PERMANENT WAY.

"*Ordinary System.*

			£	s.	d.
95	tons:	440 rails, 60 lbs. per yard, at £5. 10*s.* per ton	£522	10	0
70	"	3,520 chairs, at £4. 2*s.* 6*d.* per ton	288	15	0
7	"	1,004 fish-plates, at £11 per ton	77	0	0
110	"	1,760 cross-tie sleepers, 10 × 5 × 9, at £5. 10*s.* per load	605	0	0
3	"	3,520 wood keys, at £5 per thousand	17	12	0
3½	"	7,040 iron spikes, at £14 per ton	49	0	0
2	"	2,008 bolts, 2,008 nuts, 2,008 washers, } at £20 per ton	40	0	0
2	"	3,520 trenails, at £5 per thousand	17	12	0
292½	"	26,828 loose parts.	£1617	9	0

"*Economic System.*

			£	s.	d.
95	tons:	440 rails, 60 lbs. per yard, at £5. 10*s.* per ton	£522	10	0
80	"	2,008 sleepers, at £4. 5*s.* per ton	340	0	0
6½	"	753 tiebars, at £7 per ton	45	10	0
5	"	3,514 iron keys, etc.	46	0	0
186½	"	6,715 loose parts.	£954	0	0
		Royalties, shipping charges, etc.	100	0	0
			£1054	0	0

"Having already alluded to the durability, saving of labour, and security, specially appertaining to my railway, I need not again refer to it. I would therefore, in reply to your second question, as to the 'price for a rail over which the locomotive would not be required to travel more than twenty miles an hour, and principally for passengers,' observe, that, as the permanent way varies not only according to the requirements of the traffic, or weight and size of material employed, but with the market-price of such material, and which is constantly changing, I could only give you an approximation as compared with the prices above stated, by saying that a lighter rail,—such, for instance, as one of fifty pounds,—would cost so much less in proportion to its weight than the heavier one; but that it would not be desirable very materially to diminish the weight and consequent strength of the sleepers and tie-bars, upon which must depend the security of the whole, the weight of the rolling stock being nearly the same, although the speed be diminished, and thereby the wear and tear lessened.

"Being aware of the serious depredations on railway materials in India and other foreign countries, the result of the multiplicity of small detached parts, and more especially in a system of iron permanent way which has been very extensively used, and the patent for which has now expired, I have for a very considerable period devoted my attention to the manner of forming sleepers so as to dispense with chairs altogether; and have consequently effected a saving, as before stated, of upwards of 20,000 separate pieces in every mile of road, and at the same time combined extreme simplicity with the arrangement. The fastenings are so securely locked that no one who is not provided with the key required for the purpose can remove any portion; but with the key, the parts can be separated in a moment, as only *four distinct pieces* are used in the construction.

The least intelligent person can put the line together, and it can be laid on cleared ground with gradients as steep as those of any railway in this country; moreover, when so laid, it is immediately ready for use, and possesses any amount of elasticity which may be required, besides making less noise and vibration, and affording an easier motion in travelling than on any ordinary transverse-sleeper road. Requiring no skilled labour, I cannot but think it peculiarly adapted for such communication as you propose, twenty men being sufficient to lay down your whole line as fast as the land could be cleared. The cost of such road, complete in every respect, delivered free on board ship, would not exceed £1100 per mile of single way. I shall be happy to supply for this sum such a line as I feel sure would answer every requirement of your engineer; but if it should be deemed more desirable to give out contracts for public competition, there would be my royalties in addition. The total weight of your line, complete, would be about 187 tons per mile of dead weight. You may have a cheaper line, but not of such weight as I should recommend for a really permanent way.

"The following information on the subject of bridges, from one of the largest and most eminent engineering houses in that particular line of business, will answer your last question; and any further information that you may require and it is in my power to give, I shall be most happy to afford.

"And remain, Sir, yours faithfully,

"GEORGE FEATHERSTONE GRIFFIN, C.E.

"Captain Bedford Pim, R.N.,
"Junior United Service Club."

Copy of a Letter from Messrs. Head, Ashby, and Co.

"Teesdale Iron Works, Stockton-on-Tees,
"November 5th, 1862.

"Sir,—I had your letter of the 4th this morning. I find, from carefully going into the matter, that we can make wrought-iron plate girder bridges for a single line of road, *including* cross girders, at £4. 15*s.* (say four pounds fifteen shillings) per foot run, for bridges up to 50 feet span, and £5. 5*s.* per foot run for similar ones up to 70 feet span. You must add a margin to this to cover contingencies, and a liberal one for freight, as they are rather awkward for shipping. It is almost impossible to quote per foot run for cast-iron bridges, as the weight will vary so materially for every foot of increased span. As a guide, however, we can make them, including face girders, parapets, and hand-railings, for £5. 15*s.* per ton all round; this of course only applies to straight girders, and not to such ones as Southwark and Westminster. Trusting that this may be of service to you,

"I am, yours faithfully,

(Signed) "J. ASHBY.

"To G. F. Griffin, Esq., C.E."

Taking Mr. Griffin's statement for a basis, we have the following estimate:—

Railway complete	per mile	£1,100
Bridges*	"	800
Stations	"	50
Carriages, trucks, locomotives, rolling stock	"	1,500
Surveying, engineering, clearing, etc.	"	350
Freightage, insurance	"	500
Electric telegraph	"	30
Contingencies	"	170
Total cost per mile	"	£4,000

That is, a sum of £900,000 for the entire line. Add to this, five per cent. on the proposed capital, viz. £1,000,000, for preliminary expenses, leaving the same sum for the temporary line, and it will be seen that this magnificent undertaking may be accomplished at a cheaper rate than would be at first supposed; and why should it not? The great cost of our English lines has resulted from exorbitant law-charges and fabulous prices paid for the land, both of which would be avoided in the case of the Nicaraguan Railway. Then, again, why should we not profit by the great experience which many years' acquaintance with the working of railways in various parts of the world has brought home to us, and by this means avoid the errors and improve the improvements of our predecessors? In short, it is time that the "iron road," the most powerful wedge for opening up new countries, and thus spreading civilization, the world has ever seen, should no longer be trammelled with the artificial chains by which it is bound, in the shape of lawyers, grasping landowners, greedy contractors, *et hoc*

* This calculation is based on the number required for the Panama railroad; but it must be remembered that for seventy miles, from Realejo to Tipitapa, there will probably be neither cuttings, bridges, nor any work whatever, beyond laying the rails on the road.

genus omne. If it was *fairly* put on its mettle, people would be astonished at the profitable nature of railway undertakings; and the future progress of civilization would surprise every one by the wonderful ratio of its increase. Refer back to the account of the Panama Railway as a proof how cheaply the line might be managed.

Perhaps £1,000,000 sterling may, in the eyes of some individuals, appear an awful sum; but I would especially draw attention to the fact that this money will not be invested on a mere conjectural undertaking, but in one having some basis to start from; I allude to the concession of land which will be granted by the Nicaraguan and Mosquitian Governments to a company formed for the purpose of making the transit. The amount of waste lands to be conceded ought to be at least 400,000 acres for the purpose of colonization alone.* Then after laying down the line, the accumulation of surplus land will in itself be considerable, and doubtless fetch a high price for town lots, while the possession of the entire Atlantic harbour is alone a mine of wealth. In short, I think there cannot be a doubt that if judiciously managed, the land would become a source of profit of no inconsiderable magnitude, equal in value to at least one-half the proposed capital. While on this subject, I will just allude to the question of colonization. It will be unnecessary to enlarge upon the numerous advantages which present themselves for the

* By the colonization decree of Nicaragua, dated the 23rd of November, 1855, each immigrant could obtain a holding of 250 acres, and after six months' residence secure the title. A family was allowed to have a hundred additional acres, and all implements, live-stock, etc. etc., admitted into the country free of duty.

consideration of the immigrant. I have gone into that matter in a previous chapter, where the inducement the country, its climate, and its producing powers offers to all classes of colonists, from the capitalist to the working man, has been described; but I think the proposal of the Emperor of the French, with certain modifications, might be adopted with the most satisfactory result; as he truly says, it is not alone sufficient to offer a fine climate and prolific soil to the intending immigrant; other inducements, in the shape of a free, or at all events a cheap, passage for himself and family, a weather-tight habitation, and a sufficiency of food until he is able to gather in his own crop, must be held out to him, and easy terms made for the gradual purchase of the land, and the repayment of the cost of housing and of maintenance. It is astonishing how cheaply this might be done. For instance, a man and his family could be settled in Central America as under:—

Passage money	£10	0	0
Land, 40 acres, at 5*s*.	10	0	0
*House (wooden) containing two rooms, 22 feet by 10 feet, thoroughly weather-tight	30	0	0
Freight for ditto	5	0	0
Provisions for six months for 3 persons	21	0	0
Contingencies	4	0	0
Total outlay for establishing and supporting immigrant family for six months	£80	0	0

* These houses are made with double boards having inodorous felt or waterproof canvas between them, and are therefore perfectly weather-tight; the roofs are shingled and felted, the windows are glazed, and the doors well hung and latched. Wooden churches complete, cost about 23*s*. per sitting. An ordinary labourer can put up these buildings, exact directions and a model being forwarded with each. The fullest information can be obtained from the builder, Mr. Richardson, 99, Euston Road, London, N.W.

Thousands of poor families, upon the assurance of so fair a start, and the guarantee of support for the first six months, would gladly try their fortune in Nicaragua, and their presence would be of incalculable value to the country, as well as to the company. The £80 might be looked upon as a loan, to be paid off in ten years by yearly instalments of £8, plus five per cent. on the whole sum, until the entire debt was liquidated; that is to say, £12 per annum; this obligation might be cancelled by a certain amount of labour in the service of the company; by which means pressure on the immigrant would be avoided, while the company would reap a handsome money-profit, to say nothing of gain in other respects. This plan is of course a crude one, and no doubt susceptible of many improvements and some reduction in the expenditure; nevertheless it contains the germ of a project by means of which a healthy infusion of new blood might be poured into the veins of Nicaragua, which is a country that only requires such a spur to stand out in bold prominence before the world.

Let us now consider the sources of revenue and profit which will fall into the hands of those possessing such a transit as I have proposed. In the first place, I would impress upon the reader the fact that a route through Nicaragua is not a new project, subject to all the risks and blunders incidental to first efforts in any undertaking, but that it has been practically ascertained—even with all the disadvantages resulting from repeated changes from river-boat to lake-steamer, and thence to land-carriage, with the attendant discomforts and risk upon each transhipment—to be popular with the travelling public; in proof of which I append the following statement, taken from the New York custom-house returns for the year ending March 16th, 1856,—a year, be it remembered, in which the uncertainty of political affairs in Nicaragua must have influenced many to take the Panama route, as the safer of the two:—

California passengers, *viâ* Panama	. . . .	27,283
„ „ *viâ* Nicaragua	. . .	24,568

This is simply the number of passengers from the port of New York alone, and has no reference to the thousands of travellers from other parts of the United States, and from the various European nations. Indeed, this preference cannot fail to be always the case; for passengers, mail, treasure, and light freight, will be irresistibly attracted to the shortest and quickest means of transport; and even by the rough passage, so to speak, improvised, from ocean to ocean, through Nicaragua there is a gain of one day and a half* over that by the Panama railway; therefore, when it is considered that the railroad I propose will run across from ocean to ocean without a break; that the facilities for embarkation and disembarkation will be unrivalled; that in reaching the northern ports a saving of many hundreds of miles over Panama will be effected; that the actual sea-voyage will be shortened at least four days; that the climate is healthy, scenery magnificent, and all sorts of provisions abundant and cheap,—the very opposite of which rules at Panama,—when all this is thought

* The time occupied in the voyage from New York to San Francisco, as shown by official tables in 1855, is the following:—Average passages, *viâ* Panama, 24 days, 9 hours; *viâ* Nicaragua, 22 days, 22 hours.

of, I do not think it is too much to say that three-fourths of the present traffic across Panama will be diverted to Nicaragua. Of course all the trade of the southern ports, such as Valparaiso, Callao, Payta, Guayaquil, and Buenaventura, will seek the speediest route for their traffic; and that must be *viâ* Panama, which has at least three days' advantage over Nicaragua in all communication with the southward. At present, an American company is straining every nerve to occupy the River San Juan route. Their privileges expired on the 19th of October, 1862, unless they succeeded in passing over 500 passengers. It is just a question whether they have not forfeited their charter, because they cannot keep open a *regular* river communication; although, no doubt, passengers have been forwarded from ocean to ocean, on the very day, or at all events within a few hours of the time stipulated: but, with true American sagacity, this was done simply to keep a hold on the transit, and the period of highest water on river and harbour was seized upon to pass the passengers across. Every exertion is now being made to gain time, so as to decide what is best to be done; money without stint is wanted to ensure keeping the river navigation open, and the question is—can it be obtained? I mention this fact to show the value our American cousins place upon the Nicaraguan route; but even supposing their transit could be made a reliable one, it would in no way affect the one I propose, the superior comfort and speed of which is beyond question.

By the financial statement of the Panama Railway Company, for the year ending 31st December, 1860, it appears that—

The gross e rnings from 31st Deccember, 1859, to 31st December, 1860, amounted to	$1,550,875
Deduct interest on bonds and liabilities, running expenses, including materials, repairs, subsistence, labour and office expenses	617,104
Clear profit . . .	$933,771

Now three-fourths of this sum may fairly be laid down as the amount which would be *immediately* earned by the proposed railway, that is to say, a sum of $700,329, or £145,902 sterling, which would be at the rate of nearly 15 per cent. upon the calculated outlay of £1,000,000; but in addition to this a large increase may fairly be expected:—

1st. From British Columbia and Vancouver Island,* to which rising colonies such a means of communication is of the last importance, as at present the obstructive policy of America retards its advance, and indeed checks our commercial growth altogether in the Pacific; its present position, therefore, is no criterion of what it will become directly; a rapid means of access is opened by the mother-country.†

* The two colonies of British Columbia and Vancouver Island may be said to be still in their infancy. The total white inhabitants hardly exceed 15,000, while the exports and imports are but little more than half a million, but with the ample resources at the command of the settlers, civilization must advance with rapid strides. Gold, silver, copper, and coal, lie in untold quantities in the territory.

† In Mayne's 'British Columbia,' pp. 357–8, it is stated that the great drawback to the Panama route "is often experienced in the fact that there is no certainty of finding a Pacific steamer ready to sail, and that very often the traveller has to stop at Panama a week or ten days."

By the way of New York, Captain Mayne states that "the traveller may have to stay a few days (at New York), but this is better than waiting at Panama, the great advantage of this line being that it is connected with the Pacific Mail Company's steamers to San Francisco, and therefore there is no chance of being kept eight or ten days on the Isthmus,"—in other

2nd. It is by this route that the commerce of the teeming millions of Japan would be fostered and brought in a steady stream to our warehouses; and moreover to the North of China the Nicaraguan transit would also be a boon of great value, as it is by far the best means of communication with that country.

3rd. From local traffic, for it must be remembered that the line passes through the heart of the country, and Central America contains nearly 3,000,000 inhabitants, and vast resources, only waiting the introduction of enterprise and energy to be developed in a remarkable degree.

4th. The gain in time over any other route between England and New South Wales or Queensland, is very considerable; for instance, the shortest passage to Sydney is at present fifty-five days, *viâ* Gibraltar and the Isthmus of Suez, but by my route it could be done with ease in forty-four days, and no navigation in the world can compare with that of the Pacific for fine climate and beautiful weather; in fact, it is the sea of all others for rapid passages, so that comfort, safety, and speed may be relied on,—a combination not attainable elsewhere.

All the advantages of the existing steam-line *viâ* the Isthmus of Suez are enjoyed by Melbourne; Sydney and Brisbane being necessarily behind in the commercial race, so that no doubt that section of Australia would gladly avail itself of the proposed route. It will hardly

words, we may go through if we avail ourselves of the *entire* American line of transit, but that England *does not possess any* CERTAIN means of reaching our colonies in a given time.

be believed, that at this moment there is only *one* mail a month to our most important colony, and a short time ago, during the period of uncertainty occasioned by Captain Wilkes's invasion of the 'Trent,' even that lengthy interval was increased by the breaking down of one of the postal steamers between Ceylon and Australia, by which all communication was cut off with the mother-country about two months, during the crisis with America; and the Australians left in the most alarming state of uncertainty, whether war might not be raging between Great Britain and Federal America, and whether the first intimation of such an event might not be a bombardment similar to that meted out to Greytown. Again, the loss of the 'Colombo' has brought home to us still more recently the weakness of the link between the mother-country and her principal colony; and one is at a loss to conceive how the Australians can be so blind to their own interests as to continue with us, when they would gain so much by setting up for themselves. I heard the other day, at the Royal Geographical Society, a discussion on this matter, in which it was expressly stated that a severance from our colonies would be very unwise; and the speakers, mostly governors or officials, said they had never heard the idea seriously proposed in the country, one gentleman going so far as to say that such a notion would be scouted in Australian society, although it is notorious that Dr. Lang, the Member for Sydney, introduced a motion with the object of effecting a separation from England. The meeting to which I allude was a crowded one, and as the other side of the question did not transpire, we cannot be said to know the real Australian views on the subject; the fact is, that governors, officials, and others connected with the Government, like all the rest of the world, no doubt, firmly believe "there is nothing like leather." The Australian society, in which the excellencies and the magnates of the land shine, it may be presumed, is far too polite to tell *them* that their room would be preferred to their company; but to suppose for one moment that the main body of the people are not aware that they could do their business better and cheaper without brokers, and that the supineness of the mother-country is neither more nor less than a heavy clog upon their progress, is absurd. No doubt we should have cause to regret the severance of our colonies,—*we* should be the real losers by it;* but the most prejudiced observer must admit that we are doing our best to cut the connection, and the wonder is, that Australia has not left us long ago. As I stated in the first chapter of this book, the surest way to knit our dependencies to us, and *retain* their commerce when they become powerful, is to keep open the most rapid interchange of ideas and commodities; and this I hold to be strictly the duty of a

* The imports and exports of the Australian Colonies for the year 1861, exclusive of gold, amounted to—

Exports	£23,163,080
Imports	26,742,686
Total . .	£49,905,766

As regards gold, it was discovered in Australia in 1851, when £907,113 was produced; in 1855 this sum swelled into £11,513,230; and since then there has been a steady increase.

The passenger traffic is very considerable: for many years it has not fallen below 50,000 per annum, but the average for the last ten years is nearer double that amount.

Government caring one jot for the interests of the community. *Is a monthly communication with Australia the way to do this?* The Peninsular and Oriental Company have offered to convey the mails once a fortnight, but the official mind, with infantile simplicity, still remains in its swaddling-clothes of red tape; and any post may bring us the news that the Australian Parliament has determined to stand the humbug no longer.

The loss of the 'Colombo' brings home to our minds certain facts in connection with the route by which at present our communications with Australia are kept up, *viâ* the Isthmus of Suez. It is uncertain; it is trying to the constitution; it necessitates repeated changes before reaching the journey's end. A great deal of boisterous weather, with its attendant risks, may be expected. The terrific heat of the Red Sea and many variations of temperature, trying enough to healthy persons, but often fatal to the delicate, must be encountered; while not less than six changes *viâ* Marseilles and four *viâ* Gibraltar, between England and Australia, increase the wear and tear to both body and mind in no slight degree. Nevertheless this line is eminently useful, and will probably continue the chief means of communication with the West and South of Australia; but to New South Wales, Queensland, and other districts on the eastern side* of this *fifth quarter of the globe*, the quickest postal ser-

* The growth of our new colonies in this part of the world is wonderful, and it ought to be the earnest aim and effort of every true statesman to knit them to us "with hooks of steel." In 1851, the colonies of Victoria, Queensland, and Tasmania had no existence; of the former there was only one rude hut at Ballarat, and within a radius of forty miles of that place the population did not exceed 500 persons; in 1861, Ballarat contained

vice must be *viâ* the Central American Isthmus; and no doubt the jealousies and asperities between the Melbourne and Sydney sections might be put an end to by this opening of the proposed western route, and which, by an arrangement with its eastern contemporary, ought at least to ensure to Australia a semi-monthly, if not a weekly mail, by simply running alternately. For instance, news dated at the beginning of the month would reach Melbourne first by the eastern route; then a mail dated at the middle of the month would come to hand earlier at Sydney, which would thus take its turn. Conflicting interests might in this manner be reconciled, the *entente cordiale* of the entire community re-established, and our Australian relatives brought nearer home,—a consummation surely not unworthy the earnest consideration of any statesman truly loving his country.

Of the excellence of the ports on the eastern side of Australia, it will not be necessary to say one word; their capacity, safety, and the facility of ingress and egress, are well known,—indeed, the advantages of Sydney Harbour are proverbial; but of another colony it will be proper to give some description, for of all places it will benefit most largely by opening a western route,—I allude to New Zealand.* These islands have been called

22,111 inhabitants, whilst the population of the area mentioned above nearly reached 106,000 persons. There are now 600 miles of railway and 500 more in progress, about 900 places of worship, the same number of public and private schools, a university, public library, museum of arts, 10 savings-banks, several hospitals and asylums,—but not a single workhouse, —in a territory bigger than the British Isles. A full share of this prosperity is sure to reach the mother-country, if she will only open such a route as will enable it to travel safely and speedily to us.

* Nothing can prove more forcibly the rapid progress making in

the Britain of the South, and a more appropriate title could not have been conferred upon them; they are indeed Old England at the antipodes, having, curiously enough, exactly the same superficial area, and it does not require much foresight to predict their future glory and greatness. New Zealand is one of the youngest children of the mother-country, and has been hitherto the most neglected, but will notwithstanding become the flower of the flock; insular position, fine climate, magnificent harbours, unbounded mineral and vegetable wealth, sufficiently indicate its prosperous future: all that is wanted is a steady supply of the Anglo-Saxon

the importance and wealth of New Zealand than the following statement:—

In 1840, the total European population of the colony was 2050, in 1850 it was 22,108, in 1860 it was 83,919; and at the close of the year 1861 the Registrar-General states it to exceed 101,000.

In 1853 the value of the imports was £597,827, and in 1860 they had increased to £1,547,783. In 1853, the exports amounted to £303,282, and in 1860 they were £588,953. By the latest accounts received in this country, the value of the imports in the quarter ending June, 1862, was £976,518, against only £484,762 in the corresponding quarter of 1861; while the exports for the same periods were £662,177 and £229,299 respectively: making a difference of £432,878 in favour of the quarter in 1862.

In 1853, the ordinary revenue of the colony was £80,103, in 1860 it had increased to £231,298; that for the Province of Auckland alone having been respectively in the two years £36,395 and £72,364.

In 1853, the number of ships that cleared inwards was 238, of a total tonnage of 65,504, and in 1860 the number was 397, of 140,222 tons. In the former year, 229 vessels, of a total of 62,891 tons, cleared outwards; in 1860, the number being 398, of 140,393 tons.

In 1860, 237 vessels, of a total of 8473 tons, were registered, against 186 vessels, of 6662 tons, in 1857.

From 1853 to 1860, the quantity of wool exported increased from 1,071,340 lbs. to 6,665,880 lbs.

Recent accounts from the colony state that the quantity of gold shipped from New Zealand since its discovery there, a period of sixteen months, was 516,483 ounces, of the value of £2,065,932.

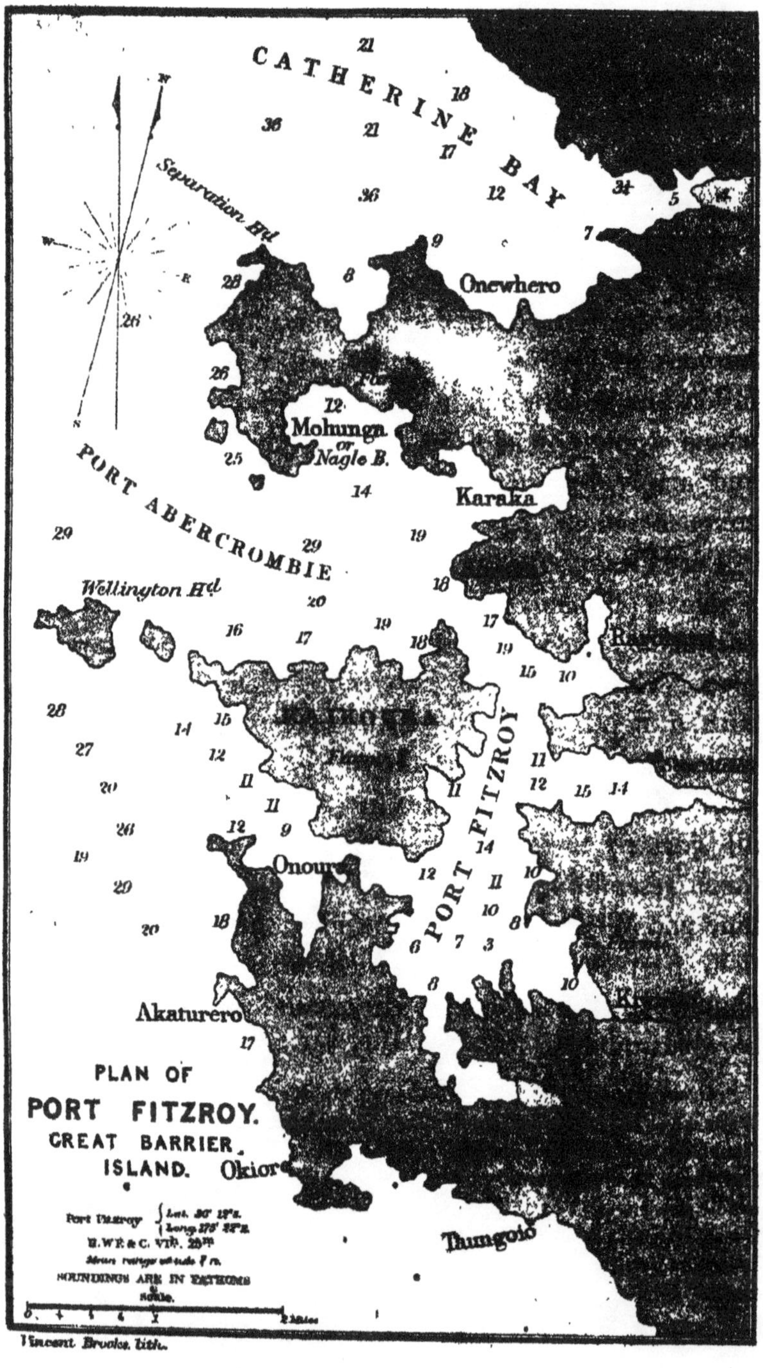

Vincent Brooks, lith.

element, and in no way can this be effected with such ease and certainty as by shortening the road over which such a supply has to travel.

The line of great circle sailing between Realejo and Sydney, passes close to the Northern Island; by deviating a few miles from this course, steering round the southern end of Great Barrier Island,* and making the harbour of Fitzroy the port of call, a stream of population and wealth might be poured into New Zealand which would spread from one extremity to the other, and amply reward the mother-country by increase of commerce alone.

Port Fitzroy, the inner harbour of Port Abercrombie, is unexceptionable; the largest ships can enter and depart at any time, as will be seen by the accompanying plan. The entrance is two cables' lengths in width, with a depth of more than twenty fathoms. One writer states that "Port Fitzroy is a magnificent harbour, well sheltered from all winds, and surrounded on all sides by the most beautiful and romantic scenery, much resembling that of some of the lakes of Cumberland and Westmoreland. The great depth of the harbour near its centre is a disadvantage, but there is abundance of good anchorage ground in the numerous bays surrounding it." Another informs us that "Port

* Great Barrier Island is 23 miles long, contains about 70,000 acres, and is situate at the mouth of the Gulf of Hauraki, at the head of which is Auckland, a distance of 55 miles. From a recent report by Mr. Heaphy, the Provincial Land Surveyor, we learn that the most valuable portion of the island lies round Ports Fitzroy and Abercrombie, and is owned by the Great Barrier Company, who have established several farms, which are succeeding well. The island is valuable on account of its forests of kauri timber, its metallic lodes, and its secure harbours.

Fitzroy is one of the finest harbours in the world, perfectly easy of access, and sheltered from all winds." Its situation at the mouth of the Gulf, in the direct track of the capital, Auckland, is such as to make it a very desirable port of call for the mail steamers employed in the proposed route,—indeed, the terminus in New Zealand, which lies within the shortest line of passage, is undoubtedly the Great Barrier Island, where there is every facility for coaling and obtaining supplies, if necessary, and the detention of the mail steamers might be made of the most trifling nature.

I must now proceed to sum up. Not another word need be said as to the necessity and value of rapid and frequent communication with our colonies and commercial marts, for the present state of affairs in the Western world is absolutely barbarous, and suicidal to our best interests. The advantages to be derived from opening a new route across the Pacific are thoroughly understood in Australia and New Zealand,* where the colonists would be only too glad to avail themselves of the facilities offered. The same applies to British Columbia; and our merchants in London can quite well judge of the result of a closer intercourse with Japan and its millions of inhabitants. I therefore estimate the following

* Since writing the above it has transpired that the Postmaster-General of New Zealand has arrived in England, charged with power, in conjunction with the Agent for New South Wales, to conclude a contract for carrying out a project for a steam line *viâ* the Central American Isthmus, a Committee of the House of Representatives of New Zealand having "recommended the appropriation of a sum not exceeding £30,000 per annum, from 1st January, 1864, for five years, as a contribution towards the colonial portion of a subsidy for such a service." New South Wales has agreed to vote £50,000 per annum.

ing scale of returns from the different countries enumerated above, which would immediately follow the opening of the Nicaraguan railroad; how this will swell year by year we have ample precedent to prove.

	Per annum.
Three-fourths of the existing traffic of the Panama Railway	£145,000
Trade with Japan and the north of China, and Sandwich Islands	25,000
Trade with Australia, New Zealand, and Polynesia	55,000
Total	£225,000

In other words, one quarter of the proposed outlay, or 25 per cent., is the very least that may be reckoned upon as a return to the shareholders. I have been most careful to allow a wide margin for outlay, and to place the returns at a low figure; therefore I have no hesitation in putting forward the statement that 25 per cent. may confidently be anticipated as the profits which would accrue to the Nicaraguan Railway Company.

It will be observed that in the above estimate I have confined myself exclusively to the consideration of what would be derived from the railway traffic alone,—I have not even included the postal subsidies; but there is another source which, while it would consolidate the undertaking, would, at the same time, bring in no trifling sum to the exchequer,—I mean the disposal and settlement of the waste lands in the vicinity of the line of rails. And judging by the precedent afforded by emigration projects properly conducted, this alone would not be less than 15 per cent.; take the Canada Company for instance,—its shares, with £32 paid on them, are selling at £102.

In short, a calm and dispassionate consideration of the subject, based on the most moderate calculations, will, I feel sure, convince the people of this country,

1. That the Nicaraguan transit will knit our colonies to us, and *secure* the advantages resulting from their daily-increasing commerce.

2. That the opening of the route will be a death-blow to the undisguised determination of the Americans to drive us out of the Pacific, and to monopolize that trade themselves; and

3. That, as far as anything human can be certain, here is an undertaking which will prove one of the most remunerative of the day, returning an enormous percentage to the shareholders; in short, it will *pay well.*

CHAPTER XVIII.

THE IMPORTANCE OF MOSQUITO TO ENGLAND.—OUR FOREIGN POLICY.—A BRILLIANT CONCEPTION.—PROTECTORATE OF MOSQUITO.—THE SPIRIT OF MINISTERS.—HER MAJESTY'S PROMISE.—INDEPENDENCE OF MOSQUITO.—BADINAGE OF THE 'NEW YORK HERALD.'—CHRISTIAN PRINCIPLES!—MARKED DISPLEASURE OF THEIR LORDSHIPS.—APATHY OF GOVERNMENT.—THE DUKE OF NEWCASTLE.—THE YOUNG GIANT.—EUROPEAN INTERNATIONAL HIGHWAY.—CONCLUSION.

"*Some careful observers affirm that a quiet possession of the Mosquito country would one day be more valuable to Great Britain than all the islands which that nation possesses in the West Indies.*" Thus wrote the Abbé Reynal in the last century, in his 'Philosophical and Political History of the East and West Indies;' and his words at this day assume the significance of prophecy.

Indeed, it is impossible to exaggerate the importance of Mosquito to our country; it ought at this moment to be the cynosure of all English eyes, and the people of England should strain every nerve, during the present favourable opportunity, to repair the damages, and rectify the mistakes, made by the Ministry now in power. Most unfortunately for the nation, its foreign policy has been wielded by those who, however capable in other respects, cannot by any perversion be said to have represented English feeling, or in even the remotest degree to have improved our relations with foreign countries. In proof of this, I need only remind my readers of a few Liberal acts, such as diplomacy at Vienna; the "*extraordinary*" Schleswig-Holstein dispatches, addressed to a *small* friendly and kindred power, and forwarded at a time, from a place, and in a manner, neither over-courteous, very graceful, nor particularly judicious; the proposed cession of the Ionian Islands to Greece,—in other words, the dismemberment of the empire, without the consent of Parliament. The value of that protectorate *may* be *nil;* its retention may be a very disagreeable duty; nevertheless it *is* a duty; and as well might the trustees of a school make a present of the funds in their keeping to a hospital, as our Government offer to cede these islands to the Greeks. The property is not ours to give; and this fact makes the conduct of Ministers the more provoking; for if the offer was made under a full sense of the responsibilities incurred by the trusteeship, was it not very like dotage? And if the duty was forgotten or not understood, was it not very like a species of ignorance which we cannot hope to amend, and which is found to be dangerous in even the smallest matters?* Thus far as regards the morality; but it is equally clear that placing a position of so much importance as Corfu in the hands of a weak state like Greece was not a *brilliant* conception; indeed, it would seem to offer, as it were, a premium to the legion of malcontents in that quarter, who only want such a hotbed as Corfu would

* No one but a *Liberal* minister would ever have thought of labouring for years to drive the Papacy out of Italy, and then offer to establish it at Malta, under the protection of the English flag.

prove, to give rise to the gravest complications of the Eastern question, such as would speedily involve this country in another vast expenditure, another display of ignorance and mismanagement, and another mourning in sackcloth and ashes, characteristic of our Crimean campaign,—a page of history it were well had never been written, and which has nothing to illuminate it but individual bravery and devotion.

If our policy with near neighbours, and concerning localities at our very doors, fails to come up to the requirements of the nation, is it to be expected that in more distant parts of the world, removed in a great measure from public observation, ministerial action should be regulated in a more enlightened manner? Accordingly we find that the very act in progress of consummation as regards Corfu, has been perpetrated in the case of Mosquito, our envoy having made a treaty in reference to that country such as might have been expected from the antecedents of his employers.*

* Her Gracious Majesty cannot be aware that she is pledged to "use her good offices with the Chief of the Mosquito Indians, so that he shall accept the stipulations" which are contained in a treaty recognizing "as belonging to and *under the sovereignty of* the Republic of Nicaragua, the country hitherto occupied or claimed by the Mosquito Indians." That is to say, our good Queen, who has gained the affection of her subjects by her uniform love of justice, has engaged to use her good offices for the furtherance of a policy utterly repugnant to those principles which have elevated our beloved country to its proud position. Her present Ministers, not content with merely abandoning a *weak* country, have actually given it away without the smallest reference to those most deeply interested; and this act is made more distressing by the fact that just as the philanthropists of our country had succeeded in introducing the Christian religion (which, under Providence, has been the means of making us the great and glorious nation we are), Mosquito is suddenly handed over to Nicaragua, which is Roman Catholic, without the slightest warning, or any care for

In the sketch which I have given of the Mosquito country, it will be remembered that the Spaniards never succeeded in subjecting the indomitable natives of this part of America to their sway; but, on the contrary, they found it to their interest to pay tribute to the King of Mosquito for permission to use the River San Juan, so as quietly to carry on their commerce with Nicaragua and Costarica. Moreover, not a single Spanish settlement was ever permitted to exist along the entire Mosquito coast; the natives being as invincibly hostile as the Bayano Indians on the Isthmus of Panama; therefore, that the Mosquito Indians were free and independent there cannot be a question, and that they *maintained* their position and freedom during the occupation of the surrounding country by the Spaniards there cannot be a shadow of doubt.

In 1822, when the Spanish American colonies revolted, the Spanish tribute for permission to ascend the river San Juan unmolested ceased; but the sudden opening of the long hermetically sealed ports drew general attention to the great political and commercial value so justly their due. Amongst other places the port of Greytown was not overlooked, some English settlers, under a grant from the King of Mosquito, taking up their residence there. They were the first to occupy the land, and for years carried on a trade with the interior of the country, without being molested in any way by Nicaragua, until that Republic was urged to do so by the United States.

the future spiritual welfare of the natives thus cruelly left to their fate. Can we, a Protestant nation, permit any minister to disgrace us in this way?

As soon as the Central American people were free from Spain, they claimed the right inherent in them of forming themselves into independent states; and, of course, even supposing Mosquito to have been subject to Spain, it could have done the same, but this was not necessary. Mosquito remained, after the revolution, in precisely the same condition as it had continued since the conquest; governed by its hereditary king and its own laws and customs, and with the full concurrence, aid, and support of an English protectorate.

Thus it will be seen that the Mosquito Indians have ever maintained their independence; that, even supposing such had not been the case, they possessed the right, in common with other communities at the time of the Revolution, of choosing their own form of government, and therefore the claim of Nicaragua was and is simply preposterous. Lastly, as regards the Port of Greytown, it unquestionably belonged to Mosquito, if only from the fact that it was first occupied by that Power. In short, there is no lack of proof in law and equity regarding the claims of Mosquito, and abundant evidence of the absurdity of the views put forward by Nicaragua, at the instigation of the United States. Indeed Nicaragua has no more right to Mosquito than Spain has to Portugal.

For nearly two hundred years there has been a close friendship between Mosquito and England, and many have been the benefits *we* have derived from the same, not only in commerce (pp. 71–2), but in actual warfare, first, in the aid afforded to the boldly conceived enterprise of Nelson directed against the Spanish power in

America, and subsequently in punishing the Republic of Nicaragua. The formal protectorate into which we entered with Mosquito was the result of an enlightened policy, and it ought to have been binding upon us at all risks. We quartered our flag with theirs; we formed settlements along their coast; we crowned and educated their kings; and at the especial request of one, the predecessor of his present Majesty, Protestant missionaries were induced to settle in the country, and devote themselves to Christianizing and educating the natives. The king's letter, dated the 12th of February, 1840, seeking Her Britannic Majesty's aid, contains the following expression of his wishes, and shows his progress in civilization:—"That salutary laws may be established in my kingdom, like those which Her Majesty's subjects have the happiness to enjoy, and to introduce among us the blessings of the Christian religion, which alone can ensure us lasting peace."

These sentiments are enlightened, and the requests then made have been responded to; indeed, in every respect, even to naming the principal seaport after one of our statesmen, we fully committed ourselves to Mosquito: and truly we were wise to do so; for if ever a people were deeply interested in any matter, Englishmen were, in maintaining as close a tie as possible with Mosquito. Where will you find a country to equal it as a cotton-field? and where else will you *very shortly* find a gate to the Pacific but through that territory? The public, unfortunately, are only just beginning to open their eyes to the dangerous nature of our foreign policy. Surely the subserviency of our various Liberal

Governments to American intimidation is not in accordance with the real character of John Bull. Read the Report to Congress, in the Appendix of this work; why, the Americans have such a contempt for us that they *openly* point out the commercial course they intend to pursue. Read Mr. Adams's dispatches to his Government at Washington, recently published in the 'Times.' Why, an English gentleman of the mildest temper would have turned any one out of his house who presumed to speak to him as Mr. Adams says he addressed Lord Russell. A diplomatic education is not necessary, thank God, to teach a man independence and proper self-respect. I fear indeed its tendency may be quite the contrary when we find the *spirited* foreign policy of our administration to mean "an incessant alternation between insult and abject submission," leaving us without friends in Europe, and embittering the enmities of America; the *spirit* which permits the blockade of Nassau and Bermuda, the attack on the 'Herald' and other vessels within gun-shot of British shores, and the burning of the 'Blanche' in neutral waters.

I make these remarks in the earnest hope of arousing the attention of my countrymen to their danger. Do they not perceive that the same policy which characterized Lord Aberdeen's Government, and deluded the Czar of Russia as to the real temper of the English people, is precisely the same as that of the present Administration towards America, and that we are drifting *helplessly* into troubled waters? *

* "The grovelling and cold-blooded selfishness of the British Ministry towards the Confederate States is fast engendering towards that country a

In dealing with a nation of bullies, quiet decision, and a determined resentment of the slightest liberty, is the only course that can be pursued with safety. Has Government done this? Certainly not. Indeed, as regards the Americans, they have brow-beaten us more than ever. As I stated above, it was through their intimidation,—I write the word with shame,—that the series of disgraceful Central American treaties was negotiated. It was, no doubt, desirable to settle the Mosquito question; it was the *bête noire* of each successive Liberal government; but no one of that party seemed to understand the key to all the trouble. No less than *nine* treaties have been drawn up within the last fifteen years, with a view to arrange matters. That called the Clayton-Bulwer has attained the most notoriety. The 'New York Herald,' December 17th, 1858, says: "Whether Mr. Clayton took Sir H. L. Bulwer for a fool, history may determine;" but it was the general impression in the American Senate that Bulwer had overreached him. "Mr. Clayton was much affected by his failure; and it is believed to have hastened his death." Such appears to

bitterness of feeling in this that cannot fail to tell upon the future relations of the two governments, and still more materially upon the business intercourse of their people. If we credit appearances, nine-tenths of the British people are with us and for us, an equal or greater proportion of the press, and a large minority, if not a majority, of the ministry. Yet so passive is their sympathy, that they permit, almost without remonstrance . . . Russell and Palmerston, to place the British nation in an attitude towards us heartlessly and cruelly unjust. There can be no doubt that those who direct the policy of England secretly rejoice in the fact that the late United States are arrayed against each other in bitter strife, literally threatening the complete annihilation of each other, thus relieving her of a powerful rival of whom she lived in continual dread."—*Richmond Whig, December* 29, 1862.

have been the spirit in which this important matter has been dealt with. The waste of time and money, and the irritation, caused by this *diplomacy*, can be more readily imagined than described. At last, in 1857, Sir William Gore Ouseley was sent out to Central America to settle the various points in dispute; but, unfortunately for the country, just as the matter had been placed by him on a thoroughly English basis, the whole policy of Downing Street was changed by the incoming of the Whigs, and Mr., afterwards Sir Charles Lennox Wyke, was charged by the new Government to make an end of the subject, probably on any terms. The treaties concluded by Mr. Wyke with Nicaragua and Honduras are inserted in the Appendix.* They are as extraordinary specimens as can be found anywhere. The Mosquito Indians have been compressed within the smallest possible space. The Bay Islands have been abandoned; Greytown has been given up to Nicaragua; the protectorate of Mosquito relinquished, and our ancient allies declared to be *subject* to Nicaragua; indeed, if we had been compelled to ratify these treaties at the point of the bayonet, they could not have been more humiliating. This is indeed liberalism with a vengeance. Lord Russell was not content with saying to Mosquito—We cannot protect you any longer, because the States have insisted that we should give in our adhesion to the Monroe doctrine,

* This *diplomatist* has, it appears, been acting in a similar manner in Mexico:—"In this, as in every other case, Sir C. Wyke had not condescended to take the slightest notice of the existence of any Englishman but himself in Mexico, or to take the counsel or ask the opinion of those whose interests were so vitally at stake, but in this, as in everything, treated them with hauteur."—*Lempriere's* '*Notes in Mexico*,' 1861–2, p. 414.

excluding "all interference on the part of European governments in American affairs;" but he actually *hands over* a *weak* but independent people, without the slightest reference to their wishes, though bound to us by the closest ties, to the tender mercies of an adjacent country, differing from them in customs, language, and religion. Is not such diplomacy atrocious? Can any one read the accounts lately received from our missionaries (pp. 81–85) without burning with indignation at this abandonment of England's Christian principles? Why have these good men been inveigled into a false position, and induced to toil so many years in Mosquito for the advancement of a religion which has made England the great nation she is, and which her people are bound by every law, human and divine, to extend to others, only to be summarily handed over to a power professing a religion which we hold to be corrupt?

It is impossible to exaggerate the folly of our policy in Central America. If people will just for one moment imagine the result to England should the route across Suez, by any chance, be closed, they may form some idea of what will be danger if we allow ourselves to be hoodwinked by the Americans, while they strain every nerve to shut us out from any avenue of approach to the Pacific. Think of the vast interests we have in that direction; only imagine the shock it would be to our prosperity if the cherished aim of the Americans, of diverting all the western trade from London to the warehouses of New York, is carried out by them. We must not forget that our rival is much *nearer* British Columbia, Japan, New Zealand, and Eastern Australia than we are; and now, by the monopoly of the Panama Railway transit, virtually holds the key of the Gate of the Pacific. Over and over again we have been warned to "beware how we trust ourselves in the power of a rival, and perhaps a foe;" we have totally disregarded that advice hitherto, and already are paying for our blindness. What I fear in the present case is, that the public may not take alarm until it is too late, for certainly they will receive no intimation of the danger from their own Government; indeed, my efforts have met with nothing but rebuff from that quarter, and to prevent the possibility of any charge against the gentlemen in Downing Street of complicity with my proceedings, I think it just to them to insert the correspondence which has passed between us.

I first received a letter from the late Commander-in-chief on the North American and West Indian station, referring to some of the paragraphs which from time to time appeared in the 'New York Herald,'* and desiring explanation. This was the prelude to a lengthy correspondence, in which the utility of my project, I must say, was never questioned; but, as the small black cloud on the horizon of the United States had not at that time been observed—although our nervous Ministers

* 'New York Herald' of the 13th and 14th of February, and 31st of March, 1860:—

"INTERESTING FROM CENTRAL AMERICA.

"I have just this moment been informed that Captain Bedford Pim, R.N., commanding H.B.M. steamer Gorgon, now here, who returned yesterday from a visit to Managua, has a new project for a route *vià* this isthmus, which he has submitted to the Nicaraguan Government. Captain Pim proposes to make Monkey Point (some forty miles up the coast) a starting-point, run a railroad thence to San Miguelito, on Lake appear to have been ceaselessly looking out for squalls from that quarter—it was thought necessary that the Government should be prepared with the usual "*disavowal and disapproval*," in the shape of the following letter:—

"'Nile,' at Halifax, 21st June, 1860.

"Sir,—With reference to the correspondence on the subject of your purchase of land at Monkey Point, I enclose, for your

Nicaragua, thence by steamer across the Lake to the river Sapoa, and from thence again by railroad to the Bay of Salinas, on the Pacific Ocean. There is a good harbour at each terminus, and the route is said to be feasible.

"It is believed that the visit of Captain Pim, of the 'Gorgon,' to Granada and Managua, had some connection with the proposed transit, especially as the Captain has purchased from the Mosquito king a large tract of land near Monkey Point.

"*Who is Captain Pim?*

"As Captain Pim has been introduced to the citizens of Greytown, it is but right that the readers of the 'Herald' should also be made acquainted with that gentleman.

"Captain Pim is a favourable specimen of Young England. He was one of the officers of the 'Resolute,' under Captain Kellett; and 'Pim's musical-box' was one of the articles found in the cabin, and restored *in statu quo*. Since that time Captain Pim has distinguished himself in China, where he was engaged in a hand-to-hand conflict with several long-tailed celestials.

"He is a man of about thirty-five, ruddy complexion, English leg-of-mutton whiskers, short thick-set frame, and eyes full of fun and mischief; he is somewhat addicted to slang, and, though not possessing the owl-like dignity considered by some necessary to the rank of a naval commander, is, nevertheless, to use his own phraseology, 'a stunnin' good fellow.'

"Captain Pim has been gazetted three times for gallant conduct. Would it not be expedient to introduce into our navy, also, the principle of promotion for bravery? At present, the man who lives the longest is sure to reach the highest rank, and naval officers progress as people do at the post-office window, all in a long line. This system is one which might be sometimes advantageously departed from.

"Let those officers whose whole naval history is contained in the 'Naval Register' be content to advance in the rule of seniority; but let gallant information, a copy of a letter I have received from the Admiralty, dated the 29th ult., relative thereto.

"I am, Sir,

"Your obedient servant,

"ALEXANDER MILNE,

"*Rear-Admiral and Commander-in-Chief.*

"Commander Pim,

"H.M.S. Gorgon, Portsmouth."

achievements be followed by immediate actual promotion, apart from party politics and party influence."

"*New Transit route across the Isthmus.—Preliminary arrangements for its completion.*

"Captain Pim is vigorously prosecuting his new Transit project, *viâ* Monkey Point. He has just completed a comprehensive chart of the harbour (Gorgon Bay), got up in beautiful style, showing the depth of the water from his own soundings, as well as the islands here and there dotting the Bay, and also giving a truthful idea of the mainland to the northward. He has concluded arrangements with a gentleman, who is nearly ready to start with a competent party, to cut a road in a direct line from Monkey Point to San Miguelito, on Lake Nicaragua. Several gentlemen have already made investments in Captain Pim's lands, and a large party will start in a few days for Gorgon Bay, to begin a settlement there. The Captain is a regular go-ahead, driving man, and success to him!"

"ASPINWALL, March 20, 1860.

"*Total obscuration of the star of Monsieur Belly.—A French war-vessel at Cartagena, with a corps of engineers to survey the Atrato route.*

"The English steamer arrived yesterday morning from San Juan. She reports all the citizens of that famous place in a state of effervescence, and ready to abandon 'Greytown' for Monkey Point,—a new embryo city, destined as the Atlantic terminus of the newly-discovered transit route of Captain Pim, of her Britannic Majesty's steamer Gorgon. He is now the hero of Greytown, for the star and fame of Monsieur Belly are clean gone out for ever. Captain Pim's scheme, however, is much more reasonable and practicable than the Frenchman's, and something may come of it.

"By the arrival of a small coaster from Carthagena yesterday, I learn that a French man-of-war was in that port, with a full and thoroughly equipped corps of engineers on board, destined for a survey of the Atrato route. *So the French and English are still looking for some other transit to the Pacific than the Panama Railroad.*"

(COPY.)

"Admiralty, 29th May, 1860.

"Sir,—With reference to your letter of the 20th April last, No. 42, transmitting the explanation of Commander Bedford Pim, of the 'Gorgon,' respecting the purchase of land at Monkey Point, Mosquito, I am commanded by my Lords Commissioners of the Admiralty to acquaint you that they have received a communication from her Majesty's Secretary of State for Foreign Affairs upon this subject, and stating that, in his opinion, the proceedings of Commander Pim should be disavowed and disapproved.

"My Lords are unable to account for an officer in Commander Pim's position having failed to perceive that his proceedings and conduct on the occasion were liable to be misrepresented, as the acts of an officer in her Majesty's service, authorized by her Majesty's Government. His extreme imprudence in taking such steps, under the peculiar circumstances in which he was placed, is deserving of the strongest censure; he is therefore to be informed that he has incurred the marked displeasure of their Lordships, and has proved himself to be unfit for the duties with which he has been entrusted.*

"I am, Sir,

"Your obedient servant,

(Signed) "W. G. ROMAINE.

"Rear-Admiral Sir Alexander Milne, K.C.B.,
"Halifax, N.S."

* Observe the date. In June I arrived at Portsmouth from the West Indies; H.M.S. Gorgon (one of the *failure paddle-wheel* frigates), then under my command, being in a very dilapidated condition, and requiring breaking up or *reconstruction;* the latter was of course determined upon, and we remained in Portsmouth harbour more than *four months*, going through that process. I then received orders to proceed on special duty to the Cape of Good Hope, the 'Gorgon' to remain there as part of the squadron. She is still there. After taking the ship to her destination and performing the duty required of me, I found that private affairs required my presence in England; I therefore exchanged into H.M.S.

Previous to the receipt of the above document, I felt more or less desponding as to my power of bringing prominently under the notice of my countrymen, so as to enforce attention, the momentous question at issue, but this *official* letter cheered me; I knew there was now a propect of success, and that the Government had unwittingly paid me the greatest compliment. They were simply true to their instincts and traditions; and when I remembered that at the time Waghorn proposed the Overland route, the official mind desired "no steam to India at all," that, George Stephenson's proposals were laughed at, and that, a similar influence was even then opposing the Thames embankment, I was convinced that every great effort for the welfare of the nation must abide a like test of its value.

I have thought it a duty to introduce the above correspondence, because I am desirous that Ministers should by no possibility be "*misrepresented;*" and I think it is *due to them*, to prevent any one from supposing for one moment that my act was "the act of an officer in her Majesty's service, *authorized* by her Majesty's Government." Moreover, it would not be honest to my countrymen to shirk from the whole truth.

In bringing my book to a conclusion, I shall sum up briefly the details which I have urged at length in the preceding pages. Any one can easily convince himself that we have commercial interests in the Pacific,

Fury, then on her way home, and paid that ship off at Portsmouth, in June, 1861: having had, as the reader will perceive, the privilege of contributing the usual £200 per annum (the sum it costs a naval officer nowadays, over and above his pay, to command with credit one of H.M. ships) for the space of a year *after* I was pronounced unfit.

comprising a vast portion of the trade of the nation; that the introduction of steam-power has revolutionized the old-fashioned method of doing business, necessitating the most rapid interchange of correspondence and ideas, even an hour's gain in time being often of the first importance to the merchant; and that, to keep pace with other countries nearly concerns our very vitality, for to stand still is to retrograde, and once behind, it is very, very difficult to make up the lost ground. Our interests in the West nearly balance those of the East. Look at Australia, New Zealand, Polynesia, Japan,* Northern China, and British Columbia; it is upon the development of these countries, and the *securing* to ourselves their commerce, that the continuance of England's greatness hinges; but we are quietly allowing all these advantages to slip through our fingers. The question has been treated by the Government of this country with marvellous apathy or ignorance; it is time, however, that the eyes of the public should be opened, and then it will be their own fault, and they will only have themselves to blame, if the best interests of the nation are allowed to be sacrificed without let or hindrance.

It seems hardly credible that there is only one monthly mail to Australia; that sixty days is the time occupied in the carriage of a letter to New Zealand; that we have not even yet drawn on the resources of

* "A letter from Lyons states that a first cargo of silk has arrived there from Japan. It reached Europe, not by the Chinese seas and India, but by the Pacific and the Isthmus of Panama."—*Paris 'Times' Correspondent, January 28th*, 1863.

The French, at all events, are fully alive to their commercial interests.

Japan, while to this hour British Columbia is struggling into maturity in *spite* of the indifference of those who should grapple that colony " to their hearts with hooks of steel." Contrast the career of California under American auspices, and that of British Columbia under English; in the case of the former, the Government of the United States devoted their earnest attention to its welfare. Read the report to Congress in the Appendix, and it will be seen that every nerve was strained in behalf of the young state, and vast has been the reward. It has not only added immensely to the exports and imports, and therefore the wealth of the mother-country; but in swelling the proportions of the Union it has increased its political status in a wonderful degree, and, in a strategical point of view, gained for that nation a commanding position on the shores of the Pacific. In the case of the latter, what are the facts? No one can doubt that, politically and commercially, the prosperity of Vancouver Island and British Columbia* is of much greater value to England, than that of California is to the United States, and that the former under proper management and encouragement could, and would, overshadow the American state in a very few years; but can we dare to hope for this consummation, when we are told by authority that the mere "*apprehension*" of hostilities with the United States was sufficient to intercept *govern-*

* Read the first leading article in the 'Times' of January 28th, 1863, on British Columbia, especially the account of its coal-fields: "It has an unlimited quantity of a fair bituminous coal, lighter by ten per cent. than Welsh coal, and answering well for steaming purposes." From this source a cheap and abundant supply of fuel might be supplied for the great lines of steamers which I propose in the Pacific.

mental communications for the space of "six weeks"? Is it not enough to make an Englishman blush for his nationality when such a fact is coolly promulgated to the world? I for one felt it keenly, and addressed the following letter to our Colonial Secretary; but, I am sorry to say, not even the usual *official* reply has been vouchsafed. I regret this, not from any personal pique at the absence of that courtesy which every gentleman has a right to expect from another, but because of the evidence thus afforded of that melancholy apathy, as regards the welfare of the nation, which seems to rule in the present Government.

"Junior United Service Club, S.W., July 10, 1862.

"My Lord Duke,—The great importance of an independent route to British Columbia is sufficiently indicated by your Grace's speech in the House of Lords on the 4th inst.

"I do myself the honour to solicit your Grace's attention to a new route through Central America, described in the enclosed abstract of a paper, read by me at the Royal Geographical Society, four months ago.

"Its advantages are:—

"1st. The postal service would be secure.

"2nd. English interests generally would be independent of the Panama Railway.

"3rd. There would be a great highway in British interests, offering the shortest, healthiest, safest, and cheapest route to New Zealand, Australia, Polynesia, and Japan.

"4th. British Columbia could be reached four days earlier than by any existing route.

"5th. Without the responsibility of a national possession, the adjacent lands (which before the emancipation of the negroes exported the finest Sea Island cotton, and which are nearer home and more easily reached than even New Orleans) would again be opened up.

"Some influential gentlemen, with whom I have been for several weeks in communication, propose to establish the new route by means of a company. It is not intended to ask for a guarantee, but it would greatly promote our enterprise, which I believe to be of national importance, if it should meet with your Grace's approbation.

"I should feel it an honour to communicate all the details of my plan, and the facts, which I collected on the spot, should your Grace desire further information on the subject.

"I have the honour to be,

"Your Grace's most obedient servant,

"BEDFORD PIM,

"*Commander Royal Navy, late Senior Officer in Central America.*

"To His Grace the Duke of Newcastle,
Secretary of State for the Colonies."

If the reader will reflect for one moment, he cannot fail to be astounded at the policy which our Government has adopted in Central American affairs, and especially the Mosquito question.* Look at Nicaragua! her geographical position fits her for the commerce of the universe; she is in reality the centre of the New World. Mosquito, to say nothing of its intrinsic worth, offers an Atlantic port; an easy means of reaching this vast wealth, besides being on the highway to all our interests to the westward; but what has the Government done? why, gone out of their way to perform a gratuitous act of gross injustice to old friends and allies, and deprived their country of a vantage-ground of vital importance

* By what right does England fix empirical boundaries to claims of possessions which have no lawful existence, and acknowledge authority where no Spanish or Nicaraguan red tape has ever yet dared to show itself?

to her commercial welfare. Such conduct, however inexcusable, is happily not irretrievable; at the proper period, resources are brought to light under the dispensations of an all-wise Providence, which have been long provided, but remain out of sight until circumstances arise which make their application self-evident. This, I am sanguine enough to believe, is the case with the discovery of the new route through Nicaragua, and which only requires the requisite English energy to be shortly an accomplished fact.

It is now certain, that in the new order of things, the giant arms of steam must shortly embrace the whole world: whether this will be accomplished through the Americans, or by us, remains to be seen. We have stretched across the Isthmus of Suez, and with astonishing results pushed steam to the eastward; we must now do the same by way of the Nicaraguan Transit to the westward; or it is certain our transatlantic kinsmen will do so, and then good-bye to Australia, New Zealand, British Columbia, and all connection with that side of the New World.

I wish now to draw attention to the physical strength of the rivalry with which we have to cope on the other side of the Atlantic, and in doing so I must go a little into figures, to show the relative proportions of the two countries.

The United Kingdom of Great Britain and Ireland numbered in 1861, 29,313,000; the United States in 1860 numbered 27,477,090; the Slaves, 3,952,801; total, 31,429,891.

In the year 1871, the estimated population of Great

Britain and Ireland, assuming the rate of increase to be the same as between 1851 and 1861, viz. nearly six per cent.,—in England it was twelve per cent.,—will be 30,989,000, while in the United States the population by 1870 will have attained 42,323,341; and at the same ratio, that is to say, at the rate of 34·6, the average decennial increase per cent. of our kinsmen on the other side of the Atlantic, their population will in 1890 have reached the enormous amount of 76,677,872—in other words, be just double the number which the census returns of this country will then show. It behoves our statesmen to ponder well over these figures.

So much for the increase of the two countries, which is largely in favour of America,* and will go far to give her the victory, unless we infuse more energy into our movements; for it cannot be too often urged that, in addition to numerical superiority, there is the strongest national feeling against us; "to humble England" is at present the day-dream of all "patriotic Americans;" and when to this be added their self-evident commercial interest in so doing, I do not think the danger is trifling, or that we can afford to relax for one second the most strenuous exertions to frustrate their machinations. Our neighbour, the Emperor of the French, is thoroughly alive to the aggressive policy of the United States, and to check this before it destroys European interests in the New World, has been no

* "The increase of the American people has been most remarkable since the development of the means of communication has produced a corresponding development of trade, and the improvements in navigation enormously increased the power of exchanging the products of industry."—*Malthus's 'Exposition of the Principles of Population.'*

doubt the motive-power of his policy in Mexico, as clearly pointed out in the following extract from his letter to General Forey.

"We have an interest in the Republic of the United States being powerful and prosperous, but not that she should take possession of the whole Gulf of Mexico, thence command the Antilles as well as South America, and be the only dispenser of the products of the New World." Again: "To restore to the Latin race on the other side of the Atlantic all its strength and *prestige*, to give security to our West India colonies and those of Spain, and to establish a friendly influence in the centre of America," is the mission of France.

We will now look a little at the relative commercial positions of London and New York as regards the western trade of which I have been speaking; and one glance at the map will be sufficient to point out that New York holds the most commanding position of the two,—not alone because it is nearer in actual distance, but because its citizens hold the key of the Pacific,—I allude to the Panama railroad; and had not the present struggle in America upset all commercial undertakings, in that country, a line of American steamers would have been running between Australia, New Zealand, and New York, by means of which the commerce of those colonies would have been carried off under our very noses; and I also know for a fact, that a new line of steamers was to have been placed on the Atlantic to compete with the Royal Mail Steam Packet Company; and who can doubt with what result, for Englishmen do not nowadays prefer to pay £35 to travel in an English steamer when they can get the same accommodation for £25,—to say nothing of performing the voyage in less time.

If we are to maintain our position as a first-rate Power,—and to do this we must spare no pains to extend and increase our commerce in all directions,—then it is high time to be up and stirring. The United States for many years have been brandished as a rod in pickle for this country. We should not have tolerated the language used towards us if it had been addressed by any other Power; but somehow we have so quietly submitted to their kicks, and allowed them to pick up the halfpence, that Americans are perfectly convinced that we entertain a chronic fear of them; and they even use the argument afforded by our conduct in the 'Trent' business, when their hands were tied, as a proof of our cowardice; in short, there can be no question of the action which will be taken on the other side of the Atlantic directly a favourable opportunity occurs. If they succeed in shutting the Gate of the Pacific against us, and keeping it fastened, I cannot see how we are to retain Australia, New Zealand, and British Columbia. Our Administration may be quite prepared to let those colonies set up for themselves whenever they like, and to consider their loss as colonies in reality a gain; but the abstraction of their commerce into American channels is quite another affair; that is the true point at issue, and it will assuredly take place if we do not very shortly open a speedy means of communication with them, and keep that transit open at all hazards. What I should propose would be a *European International Highway* in the interests of the Old World. The selfish Monroe doctrine, "America for the Americans," should be treated with the contempt it merits. I should be heartily glad to see the two nations, in a friendly spirit, emulating each other in the cause of civilization; but I cannot shut my eyes to the fact that the Yankees have invariably rejoiced at our disasters and difficulties; spoken of the annexation of our property as already accomplished; and taken every opportunity of showing that the spirit of the nation against us is more consonant with the character of the red Indians of their continent, than that of an Anglo-Saxon people.

I have pointed out a means by which American designs against us may be foiled, and a desirable highway of nations be opened. I have placed my project before the Government, with what result the correspondence above will prove; it now remains with the public to decide whether they choose to permit this apathy of their interests, this meek surrender of important rights. The matter is now before them, and, I trust I have shown clearly that if the Americans are allowed to monopolize every avenue of approach to the Pacific, and to close the gate against us, the result must be, to use their own words,—"*to throw into the warehouses and shipping of the United States the entire commerce of the Pacific Ocean.*"

APPENDIX.

1. Treaty of Friendship, Commerce, and Navigation, between Her Majesty and the Republic of Nicaragua. *Signed at Managua, February 11th,* 1860.

2. Treaty between Her Majesty and the Republic of Nicaragua, relative to the Mosquito Indians, and to the Rights and Claims of British Subjects. *Signed at Managua, January 28th,* 1860.

3. Treaty between Her Majesty and the Republic of Honduras, respecting the Bay Islands, the Mosquito Indians, and the Rights and Claims of British Subjects. *Signed at Comayagua, November 28th,* 1860.

4. Extracts from an Official Report to the American Congress, on the Communications between the Atlantic and Pacific.

5. Extracts from Convention and Amended Charter of the American Atlantic and Pacific Ship Canal Company, 19th June, 1857, and Explanatory Articles respecting the same, 15th October, 1857.

APPENDIX.

I.

EXTRACTS FROM A TREATY OF FRIENDSHIP, COMMERCE, AND NAVIGATION, BETWEEN HER MAJESTY AND THE REPUBLIC OF NICARAGUA.

Signed at Managua, February 11, 1860.

Presented to both Houses of Parliament by Command of Her Majesty. 1860.

Article II.—The two high contracting parties being desirous of placing the commerce and navigation of their respective countries on the liberal basis of perfect equality and reciprocity, mutually agree that the citizens of each may frequent all the coasts and countries of the other, and reside therein, and shall have the power to purchase and hold all kinds of property which the laws of the country may permit any foreigners, of whatever nation, to hold, and to engage in all kinds of trade, manufactures, and mining, upon the same terms with subjects or citizens of other countries. They shall enjoy all the privileges and concessions in these matters which are or may be made to the subjects or citizens of any country; and shall enjoy all the rights, privileges, and exemptions, in navigation, commerce, and manufactures, which native subjects or citizens do or shall enjoy, submitting themselves to the laws there established, to which native subjects or citizens are subjected.

The high contracting parties further engage that neither will grant any favour to any other nation, in respect of commerce and navigation, which shall not immediately become common to the other contracting party.

ARTICLE XV.—The subjects of her Britannic Majesty residing in the Republic of Nicaragua, and the citizens of the Republic of Nicaragua residing in the dominions of her Britannic Majesty, shall be exempted from all compulsory military service whatsoever, whether by sea or land, and from all forced loans, or military exactions or requisitions; and they shall not be compelled, under any pretext whatsoever, to pay any ordinary or extraordinary charges, requisitions, or taxes, other or higher than those that are or may be paid by native subjects or citizens.

ARTICLE XVII.—British subjects residing in the territories of the Republic of Nicaragua shall enjoy the most perfect and entire liberty of conscience, without being annoyed, molested, or disturbed, on account of their religious belief. Neither shall they be annoyed, molested, or disturbed, in the proper exercise of their religion, in private houses, or in the chapels or places of worship appointed for that purpose, provided that in so doing they observe the decorum due to Divine worship, and the respect due to the laws of the country. Liberty shall also be granted to bury British subjects who may die in the territories of the Republic of Nicaragua, in convenient and adequate places, to be appointed and established by themselves for that purpose, with the knowledge of the local authorities, or in such other places of sepulture as may be chosen by the friends of the deceased; nor shall the funerals or sepulchres of the dead be disturbed in any wise, or upon any account.

ARTICLE XX.—The Republic of Nicaragua hereby grants to Great Britain, and to British subjects and property, the right of transit between the Atlantic and Pacific Oceans, through the territories of that Republic, on any route of communication, natural or artificial, whether by land or water, which *may now or hereafter exist or be constructed under the authority of Nica-*

ragua, to be used and enjoyed in the same manner and upon equal terms by both parties, and their respective subjects and citizens; the Republic of Nicaragua, however, reserving its full and complete right of sovereignty over the same; and, generally, the Republic of Nicaragua engages to grant to Great Britain, and to British subjects, the same rights and privileges, in all respects, in regard to the transit and the rates of transit, and also as regards all other rights, privileges, or advantages whatsoever, whether relating to the passage and employment of troops, or otherwise, which are now or may hereafter be granted to, or allowed to be enjoyed by, the most favoured nation.

Article XXI.—Her Majesty the Queen of the United Kingdom of Great Britain and Ireland hereby agrees to *extend her protection to all such routes of communication as aforesaid, and to guarantee the neutrality and innocent use of the same.* Her Britannic Majesty also agrees to employ her influence with other nations to induce them to guarantee such neutrality and protection.

And the Republic of Nicaragua, on its part, undertakes to establish two free ports, one at each of the extremities of the communication aforesaid, on the Atlantic and Pacific Oceans. At these ports, no tonnage or other duties shall be imposed or levied by the Government of Nicaragua on the vessels of Great Britain, or on any effects or merchandise belonging to subjects of Great Britain, or of any other country, intended *bonâ fide* for transit across the said route of communication, and not for consumption within the Republic of Nicaragua. Her Britannic Majesty shall also be at liberty, on giving notice to the Government or authorities of Nicaragua, to carry troops, provided they are destined for a British possession, or places beyond sea, and are not intended to be employed against Central American nations friendly to Nicaragua, and munitions of war; and also to convey criminals, prisoners, and convicts, with their escorts, in her own vessels or otherwise, to either of the said free ports, and shall be entitled to their conveyance between them, without obstruction by the authorities of Nicaragua, and without any charges or tolls whatever for their transportation, or any of the said routes of communication. And no higher or other charges or tolls shall be imposed on the conveyance or transit of the persons and property of subjects of Great Britain, or of the subjects and citizens of any other country, across the said routes of communication, than are or may be imposed on the persons or property of citizens of Nicaragua.

And the Republic of Nicaragua concedes the right of the Postmaster-General of Great Britain to enter into contracts with any individuals or companies to transport the mails of Great Britain along the said routes of communication, or along any other routes across the isthmus, in closed bags, the contents of which may not be intended for distribution within the said Republic free from the imposition of all taxes or duties by the Government of Nicaragua; but this liberty is not to be construed so as to permit such individuals or companies, by virtue of this right to transport the mails, to carry also passengers or freight, except any messenger deputed by the British Post-office, in charge of mails.

ARTICLE XXII.—The Republic of Nicaragua agrees that, should it become necessary at any time to employ military forces for the security and protection of persons and property passing over any of the routes aforesaid, it will employ the requisite force for that purpose; but upon failure to do this for any cause whatever, her Britannic Majesty may, with the consent, or at the request of the Government of Nicaragua, or of the Minister thereof, at London or Paris, or of the competent legally-appointed local authorities, civil or military, employ such force for this and for no other purpose; and when, in the opinion of the Nicaraguan Government, the necessity ceases, such force shall be immediately withdrawn.

In the exceptional case, however, of unforeseen or imminent danger to the lives or properties of British subjects, her Majesty's forces are authorized to act for their protection without such previous consent having been obtained.

ARTICLE XXIII.—It is understood, however, that her Britannic Majesty, in according protection to such routes of communication, and guaranteeing their neutrality and security, always intends that the protection and guarantee are granted conditionally, and may be withdrawn if her Britannic Majesty should deem that the persons or company undertaking or managing the same, adopt or establish such regulations concerning the traffic thereupon as are contrary to the spirit and intention of this Treaty, either by making unfair discriminations in favour of the commerce of any other nation or nations, or by imposing oppressive exactions or unreasonable tolls upon mails, passengers, vessels, goods, wares, merchandise, or other articles. The aforesaid protection and guarantee shall not, however, be withdrawn by her Britannic Majesty without first giving six months' notice to the Republic of Nicaragua.

ARTICLE XXIV.—And it is further understood and agreed that, in any grant or contract which may hereafter be made or entered into by the Government of Nicaragua, having reference to the interoceanic routes above referred to, or any of them, the rights and privileges granted by this convention to her Britannic Majesty, and to British subjects, shall be fully protected and reserved; and if any such grant or contract now exist of a valid character, it is further understood that the guarantee and protection of her Britannic Majesty stipulated in Article XXI. of this Treaty shall be held inoperative and void, until the holders of such grant or contract shall recognize the concessions made in this Treaty to her Britannic Majesty, and to British subjects, with respect to such interoceanic routes, or any of them, and shall agree to observe, and be governed by, those concessions as fully as if they had been embraced in their original grant or contract; after which recognition and agreement, the said guarantee and protection shall be in full force: provided that nothing herein contained shall be construed either to affirm or deny the validity of any of the said contracts.

ARTICLE XXV.—After ten years from the completion of a

canal, railroad, or any other route of communication, through the territory of Nicaragua, from the Atlantic to the Pacific Ocean, no company which may have constructed or be in possession of the same, shall ever divide, directly or indirectly, by the issue of new stock, the payment of dividends, or otherwise, more than 15 per cent. per annum, or at that rate, to its stockholders, from tolls collected thereupon; but whenever the tolls shall be found to yield a larger profit than this, they shall be reduced to the standard of 15 per cent. per annum.

ARTICLE XXVII.—The present Treaty shall remain in force for the term of twenty years from the day of the exchange of ratifications; and if neither party shall notify to the other its intention of terminating the same, twelve months before the expiration of the twenty years stipulated above, the said Treaty shall continue binding on both parties beyond the said twenty years, until twelve months from the time that one of the parties may notify to the other its intention of terminating it.

ARTICLE XXVIII.—The present Treaty of Friendship, Commerce, and Navigation, shall be ratified, and the ratifications shall be exchanged at London as soon as possible within six months from this date.

In witness whereof the respective Plenipotentiaries have signed the same, and have affixed thereto their respective seals.

Done at Managua, this eleventh day of February, in the year of our Lord one thousand eight hundred and sixty.

(L.S.) CHARLES LENNOX WYKE.
(L.S.) PEDRO ZELEDON.

II.

EXTRACTS FROM A TREATY BETWEEN HER MAJESTY AND THE REPUBLIC OF NICARAGUA, RELATIVE TO THE MOSQUITO INDIANS, AND TO THE RIGHTS AND CLAIMS OF BRITISH SUBJECTS.

Signed at Managua, January 28, 1860.

Presented to both Houses of Parliament by Command of Her Majesty.

Article I.—On exchanging the ratifications of the present Treaty, Her Britannic Majesty, subject to the conditions and engagements specified therein, and without prejudice to any question of boundary between the Republics of Nicaragua and Honduras, will recognize as *belonging to and under the sovereignty of the Republic of Nicaragua*, the country hitherto occupied or claimed by the Mosquito Indians within the frontier of that Republic, whatever that frontier may be.

The British Protectorate of that part of the Mosquito territory shall cease three months after the exchange of the ratifications of the present Treaty, in order to enable Her Majesty's Government to give the necessary instructions for carrying out the stipulations of said Treaty.

Article II.—A district within the territory of the Republic of Nicaragua shall be assigned to the Mosquito Indians, which district shall remain as above stipulated, under the sovereignty of the Republic of Nicaragua.

Such district shall be comprised in a line which shall begin at the mouth of the River Rama in the Caribbean Sea; thence it shall run up the midcourse of that river to its source, and from such source proceed in a line due west to the meridian of 84° 15′ longitude west from Greenwich; thence due north up the said meridian until it strikes the River Hueso, and down the midcourse of that river to its mouth in the sea, as laid down in Baily's map, at about latitude from 14° to 15° north, and longitude 83° west from the meridian of Greenwich; and thence southerly along the shore of the Caribbean Sea to the mouth of the River Rama, the point of commencement.

But the district thus assigned to the Mosquito Indians may

not be ceded by them to any foreign person or State, but shall be and remain *under the sovereignty* of the Republic of Nicaragua.

Article III.—The Mosquito Indians, within the district designated in the preceding Article, shall enjoy the right of governing, according to their own customs, and according to any regulations which may from time to time be adopted by them, not inconsistent with the sovereign rights of the Republic of Nicaragua, themselves, and all persons residing within such district. Subject to the above-mentioned reserve, the Republic of Nicaragua agrees to respect and not to interfere with such customs and regulations so established, or to be established, within the said district.

Article V.—The Republic of Nicaragua being desirous of promoting the social improvement of the Mosquito Indians, and of providing for the maintenance of the authorities to be constituted under the provisions of Article III. of this Treaty, in the district assigned to the said Indians, agrees to grant to the said authorities, for the space of ten years, with a view to such purposes, an annual sum of five thousand hard dollars. The said sum shall be paid at Greytown, by half-yearly payments, to such person as may be authorized by the Chief of the Mosquito Indians to receive the same, and the first payment shall be made six months after the exchange of the ratifications of the present Treaty.

Article VI.—Her Britannic Majesty engages to use her good offices with the Chief of the Mosquito Indians, so that he shall accept the stipulations which are contained in this convention.

Article VIII.—All *bonâ fide* grants of land for due consideration made in the name and by the authority of the Mosquito Indians, since the 1st of January, 1848, and lying beyond the limits of the territory reserved for the said Indians, shall be confirmed; provided the same shall not exceed in any case the extent of one hundred yards square, if within the limits of San Juan or Greytown, or one league square if without the same; and provided that such grant shall not interfere with other legal grants made previously to that date by Spain, the Republic of Central America, or Nicaragua; and provided further, that no such grant shall include territory desired by the Government of the latter State, for forts, arsenals, or other public buildings. This stipulation only embraces those grants of land made since the 1st of January, 1848.

It is understood that the grants of land treated of in this Article shall not extend to the westward of the territory reserved for the Mosquito Indians in Article II. further than 84° 30′ of longitude, in a line parallel and equal with that of the said territory on the same side; and if it should appear that any grants have been made further in the interior of the Republic, the lands acquired *bonâ fide* shall be replaced with those that are within the limit defined under the regulations agreed upon. In case, however, any of the grants referred to in the preceding paragraph of this Article shall be found to exceed the stipulated extent, the Commissioners hereinafter mentioned shall, if satisfied of the *bona fides* of any such grants, confirm to the grantee or grantees, or to his or their representatives or assigns, an area only equal to the stipulated extent. And in case any *bonâ fide* grant, or any part thereof, should be desired by the Government for forts, arsenals, or other public buildings, an equivalent extent of land shall be allotted to the grantees elsewhere.

It is understood that the grants of land treated of in this Article shall not extend to the westward of the territory reserved for the Mosquito Indians in Article II. further than 84° 30′ of longitude, in a line parallel and equal with that of the said territory on the same side; and if it should appear that any grants have been made further in the interior of the Republic, the lands acquired *bonâ fide* shall be replaced with those that are within the limit defined under the regulations agreed upon.

In witness whereof the respective Plenipotentiaries have signed the same, and have affixed thereto their respective seals.

Done at Managua, this 28th day of January, 1860.

(L.S.) CHARLES LENNOX WYKE.

(L.S.) PEDRO ZELEDON.

Declaration.

In proceeding to the exchange of the ratifications of the Treaty concluded and signed at Managua on the 28th of January, 1860, between Her Majesty the Queen of the United Kingdom of Great Britain and Ireland and the Republic of Nicaragua, relative to the Mosquito Indians and to the rights and claims of British subjects, the undersigned, her Britannic Majesty's Principal Secretary of State for Foreign Affairs and the Envoy Extraordinary and Minister Plenipotentiary of the Republic of Nicaragua, hereby declare that the limitation laid down in the paragraph added by the Congress of the Republic to Article VIII. of the said Treaty applies to grants of land to the west of the meridian of 84° 30′ of longitude throughout the whole extent of the territory hitherto occupied or claimed by the Mosquito Indians within the frontier of the Republic, but not to grants in any part of the said territory to the east of that meridian line.

In witness whereof the undersigned have signed the present Declaration, and have affixed thereto their respective seals.

Done at London, the 2nd day of August, 1860.

(L.S.) J. Russell.
(L.S.) J. de Marcoleta.

III.

EXTRACTS FROM A TREATY BETWEEN HER MAJESTY AND THE REPUBLIC OF HONDURAS, RESPECTING THE BAY ISLANDS, THE MOSQUITO INDIANS, AND THE RIGHTS AND CLAIMS OF BRITISH SUBJECTS.

Signed at Comayagua, November 28, 1859.

Presented to both Houses of Parliament by Command of Her Majesty.

1860.

Article I.—Taking into consideration the peculiar geographical position of Honduras, and in order to secure the neutrality of the Islands adjacent thereto, with reference to any railway or other line of interoceanic communication which may be constructed across the territory of Honduras on the mainland, her Britannic Majesty agrees to recognize the Islands of Ruatan, Guanaca, Elena, Utile, Barbarete, and Morat, known as the Bay Islands, and situated in the Bay of Honduras, as a part of the Republic of Honduras.

The inhabitants of the said Islands shall not be disturbed in the enjoyment of any property which they may have acquired therein, and shall retain perfect freedom of religious belief and worship, public and private, but remaining in all other respects subject to the laws of the Republic. If any of them should wish to withdraw from the Islands, they shall be at full liberty to do so, to dispose of their fixed or other property as they may think fit, and to take with them the proceeds thereof.

The Republic of Honduras engages not to cede the said islands, or any of them, or the right of sovereignty over such islands, or any of them, or any part of such sovereignty, to any nation or state whatsoever.

Article II.—Her Britannic Majesty engages, subject to the conditions and engagements specified in the present Treaty, and without prejudice to any question of boundary between the Republics of Honduras and Nicaragua, to recognize as belonging to and under the sovereignty of the Republic of Honduras, the country hitherto occupied or possessed by the Mosquito Indians within the frontier of that Republic, whatever that frontier may be.

The British protectorate of that part of the Mosquito territory shall cease three months after the exchange of the ratifications of the present Treaty, in order to enable her Majesty's Government to give the necessary instructions for carrying out the stipulations of said Treaty.

Article III.—The Mosquito Indians in the district recognized by Article II. of this Treaty as belonging to and under the sovereignty of the Republic of Honduras, shall be at liberty to remove, with their property, from the territory of the Republic, and to proceed whithersoever they may desire; and such of the Mosquito Indians who remain within the said district shall not be disturbed in the possession of any lands or other property which they may hold or occupy, and shall enjoy, as natives of the Republic of Honduras, all rights and privileges enjoyed generally by the natives of the Republic.

The Republic of Honduras being desirous of educating the Mosquito Indians, and improving their social condition in the district so occupied by them, will grant an annual sum of $5000 in gold or silver, for the next ten years, for that purpose, to be paid to their headman in the said district; the payment of such annual sum being guaranteed to them by a mortgage on all woods and other natural productions (whatever they may be) of the state lands in the Bay Islands and the Mosquito territory.

These payments shall be made in half-yearly instalments, of $2500 each, the first of which payments shall be made six months after the exchange of the ratifications of the present Treaty.

ARTICLE IV.—Whereas British subjects have by grant, lease, or otherwise, heretofore obtained from the Mosquito Indians interests in various lands situated within the district mentioned in the preceding Article, the Republic of Honduras engages to respect and maintain such interests; and it is further agreed that her Britannic Majesty and the Republic shall, within twelve months after the exchange of the ratifications of the present Treaty, appoint two Commissioners, one to be named by each party, in order to investigate the claims of British subjects arising out of such grants or leases, or otherwise; and all British subjects whose claims shall, by the Commissioners, be pronounced well founded and valid, shall be quieted in the possession of their respective interests in the said lands.

In witness whereof the respective Plenipotentiaries have signed the same, and have affixed thereto their respective seals.

Done at Comayagua, the twenty-eighth day of November, in the year of our Lord one thousand eight hundred and fifty nine.

(L.S.) C. Lennox Wyke.
(L.S.) Francisco Cruz.

IV.

EXTRACTS FROM AN OFFICIAL REPORT TO THE AMERICAN CONGRESS, ON THE COMMUNICATIONS BETWEEN THE ATLANTIC AND PACIFIC.

January 16, 1849.

Mr. T. Butler King, from the Committee on Naval Affairs, made the following Report:—

The Committee on Naval Affairs, to whom was referred the "Memorial of Wm. H. Aspinwall, John L. Stephens, and Henry Chauncey, praying aid from the Government of the United States to construct a Railroad across the Isthmus of Panama," have examined the subject with much care, and submit the following Report:—

The intention of the memorialists is, if suitably aided by Government, to construct a railroad across the Isthmus of Panama, from the Atlantic to the Pacific Ocean. For this purpose they have procured a charter from the Government of New Granada, a copy of which is annexed to this Report, marked B (originally granted to a French company), which secures to them very extensive privileges on the Isthmus, provided the work shall be commenced within eighteen months from the date of the transfer of the charter to them, and completed within eight years. The original privilege granted to the French company was for ninety-nine years. This term has been reduced, in the contract with the memorialists, to forty-nine years, and a right has been reserved to the Government of New Granada to purchase the railroad at the expiration of twenty years.

The cost of the railroad, and the expense of its management in a tropical climate, will necessarily be so much greater than would be required in any work of similar extent in our own country, and the profits that may accrue on the investment are so uncertain, that, without efficient aid from Government, the memorialists will probably be compelled, as all others who have moved in this matter hitherto have been, to abandon the undertaking. It therefore becomes the duty of Congress to consider whether the tendency and interests of our commerce, agriculture, and manufactures, the convenience of governing and defending our widely extended territories on the shores of the Pacific, and of emigration to them, are objects of sufficient importance, when taken in connection with the proposed transport across the Isthmus of troops, munitions of war, and the mails, to justify the Government in giving such aid as may secure the completion of this great work within the time proposed—three years—*and place its future management in the hands of our own citizens*. Our commerce with all the countries bordering on the Pacific Ocean is rapidly on the increase, and especially with the South American republics and Mexico; and it is believed that a more frequent and speedy communication with China, and other countries of the East, will produce a rich harvest.

Great Britain is principally indebted to her skill in commerce and manufactures for her commercial ascendency, but she is also indebted in no small degree to her *position*. She not only has the ports of the continent of Europe as her neighbours, but she is *fifteen hundred miles*, or two weeks, nearer than we are *to all the other ports of the world, except the Atlantic ports of the American continent north of the Equator and the West Indies.* The cause of this is, that all vessels bound from our ports to places south of the Line, or beyond either of the Capes, cross the Atlantic to the Azores or Western Islands, for the purpose of finding favourable winds, while vessels from British ports run down to the same latitude and longitude without the necessity of crossing the ocean to avail themselves of the same advantages. This difference in favour of British commerce, running through our entire existence as a nation, has been a most serious obstacle for our merchants and navigators to contend with, and has of itself been a vast item in favour of the profits on British capital. Lieutenant M. F. Maury, Superintendent of the Observatory, has, within two or three years past, proposed a more direct route for vessels bound from our ports to ports on the Atlantic side of the American continent, south of the Equator and beyond Cape Horn, which will save about one thousand miles of the distance to those places, but all vessels bound round the Cape of Good Hope will be compelled to pursue the old route.

The construction of the proposed railroad across the Isthmus will not only do away this advantage over us, now possessed by European commerce and navigation, but will turn the tide in our favour.

The average distance from Liverpool, London, and Havre to Panama, is 4700 miles; from New York, the distance is 2000 miles; from Charleston, 1400; from Savannah, 1300; from New Orleans and Mobile, 1600—making an average distance from our principal exporting Atlantic and Gulf ports of about 1600 miles to Panama. If, therefore, we admit, for the sake of the argument, that European commerce with the Pacific Ocean, the East India and China Seas, will take the new route across the Isthmus—there will be a difference of 3100 miles in our favour. Add to this the 1500 miles now against us, and we find that we shall gain by this channel of communication, in our relative position to those parts of the world, a distance of 4600 miles, or of 42 days. *In the voyage out and home* we shall have the advantage of our European competitors of 9200 miles, and 84 days, as compared with the present route.

This is *admitting* that *European ships* will come freighted to the terminus of the railroad on this side of the Isthmus, with cargoes intended for the markets of the Pacific and China. That, however, will not be the case. The large number of vessels bound to the ports of the United States for cotton, rice, tobacco, lumber, flour, provisions, etc. etc., will bring the freights for those markets as ballast or cargoes, whence they will be conveyed to the railroad in our own fast-sailing coasting vessels and steamers. which will also bring to us the commerce of the Pacific. This is very obvious, because, if European ships were to sail with full cargoes direct to the railroad, they would run the risk of being compelled to return without freight, or come to the United States for it. We are so much nearer to the Isthmus than the ports of Europe, and our means of communication and information will be so frequent and certain, our lines of steamers and coasting vessels so constantly on the alert, and will move with such celerity, that heavy European-freighting ships will find it quite impossible to compete with them. If this view of the subject be correct, and we believe it is, *the construction of this railroad will throw into our warehouses and shipping the entire commerce of the Pacific Ocean.* Our ports are on the very wayside from Europe to the Isthmus of Panama, and our lines of steamers and packet ships across the Atlantic will come laden with the freights for that channel of trade. The commerce, therefore, from Europe to the East Indies, China, and the west coast of this continent, will be forced to pursue the old route, *or fall into our hands.*

It is thus shown that the new route across the Isthmus will bring us more than an average of 10,000 miles nearer to the East Indies, China, and the ports of South America on the Pacific, and will actually, for all the purposes of navigation and commercial intercourse, bring the ports of the west coast of Mexico, California, and Oregon, 14,000 miles nearer to us than they now are! With steamers on each side of the Isthmus that will go fifteen miles an hour—a speed ascertained to be quite practicable—passengers, the mails, and small packages of light and valuable goods may be conveyed from New York to San Francisco in fourteen days, and from our southern ports in less time: thus bringing these remote points, for all practical purposes, nearer than New York and New Orleans were twenty years ago.

The employment of steam-vessels would render the contrast in our favour still more striking. But the difficulty and expense of transporting heavy merchandise across the Isthmus *in its present state,* and the distance round the Capes, render the employment of steam in *the carrying trade* to the East Indies, China, and the west coast of America, quite impracticable. The most that can be done is to employ steam-packets in the conveyance of the mails and passengers. Let this railroad be completed, however, and *no part of the world will present as great advantages for the successful use of steam in ocean navigation as the Pacific.* Coal is found on all its borders, both American and Asiatic, in the greatest quantity and perfection. Its quiet waters seem to indicate steam as the proper agent to be employed in their navigation. The spirit and genius of the American people, and the extent of our territory on the west side of the continent, proclaim clearly enough that we are to become the legitimate heirs of a vast commerce that shall spread fleets of steam-ships over the bosom of this peaceful ocean.

Steamers, with a speed of twelve miles an hour, would go from New York, *viâ* the Isthmus (throwing out the fractions)—

To Calcutta	in 47 days.
To Canton	36 „
To Shanghae	35 „
To Valparaiso	17 „
To Callao	12 „
To Guayaquil	9½ „
To Panama	7 „
To San Blas	12 „
To Mazatlan	14 „
To San Diego	16 „
To San Francisco	18 „

When we consider the remarkable results presented in the foregoing table, and compare our present condition with what it will be when the proposed railroad shall be completed, and the advantages we shall then possess over all competitors for the commerce of the Pacific and the east, we need not be surprised that European capitalists have refused to lend their aid to the accomplishment of an undertaking which will not only deprive them of the decided superiority which they now possess over us in their intercourse with nine-tenths of the world—exclusive of ourselves—but will place us so far ahead in the race for commercial supremacy, *that they can never overtake us.*

Whether any considerations of this nature have been the secret cause of the failure of all the efforts hitherto made in Europe to open a communication across the Isthmus of Panama, we pretend not to say; but we think it by no means improbable that men who now hold in their hands the purse-strings of the world, would decline taking any steps which would so evidently deprive them of their commanding position, and transfer the seat of the money power to our shores.

If a wise sagacity has deterred them from aiding to advance us at their expense, we may justly be regarded as blind to our true interests if we hesitate to adopt such measures as will secure the prize which is offered to us. In all great public movements, it is as natural, as it is evidently proper, that every nation should consider well what course of policy will best promote its own prosperity and contribute to its security. With regard, therefore, to a channel of communication across the Isthmus of Panama, it was to be expected that, while European governments and capitalists would acknowledge its vast importance to the commerce of the *world*, they would not fail to perceive that its completion would transfer the seat of commercial empire to the western hemisphere. Hence the scheme of a ship canal has found no favour with them except in empty words, whilst a railroad is openly objected to as worse for them than no communication at all. . . . .

If any change is to be given to the course of European commerce with the west coast of America and the East Indies, by a communication across the Isthmus of Panama, it is quite clear that a *ship-canal* would be the only channel that could save it from falling into our hands, while it is equally certain that *our* interests point to a railroad as best suited, in all respects, to our progress.

California has now been added to our territory on the Pacific. Its beautiful and commodious harbours, its delightful climate, the fertility of its soil, and its mineral wealth, are attracting thousands, and, probably, tens of thousands of our fellow-citizens to it. *The most rapid means of communication should be established to facilitate their emigration, protect them in their new homes, supply their wants, and enable them still to participate in the blessings of our free institution.* They will be large consumers of manufactures of every description, and, for some years to come, at least, of our agricultural products also. . . . .

If, however, our commerce with that territory shall still be forced to find its way round Cape Horn, and pass twice through the tropics, our agriculture will be entirely deprived of this market, because it is well known that it is almost impossible to preserve flour, and many other articles equally perishable, so many months on shipboard in the warm latitudes through which they would have to pass. Therefore the Californian market would, of necessity, be supplied, at very high prices, from Chili, and other states bordering the Pacific. These views alone, if properly considered, possess sufficient force, it seems to us, to justify the favourable action of the Government on the application of the memorialists. . . . .

In a report which your committee had the honour to present to the House, at its last session, on "steam communication with China," the commerce of the United States with that country was so fully examined, that it is not deemed necessary on the present occasion to repeat the arguments then presented to show the vast importance of the proposed communication across the Isthmus, which was then, and is now regarded as the instrument *which is to change our commercial relations with the whole world,* and as being inseparably connected with our system of steam navigation. . . . .

We have already spoken of the commanding position which Great Britain occupies in the commercial world, and we deem it proper to remark still further on the advantages she has derived from it. At an early day she adopted the warehousing system. This enabled her own merchants and those of all other countries to place merchandise in bond, for consumption or exportation. It has been equally beneficial to her commerce and manufactures.

While it has exempted the merchants from paying duties on importations beyond actual consumption, it has enabled them to make up, with home manufactures and foreign commodities, assorted cargoes for all parts of the world. Foreigners have thus been induced to place immense amounts of merchandise in bond, that they might have the double advantage of consumption or re-exportation.

The manufacturer has thus been enabled to allow the raw materials, necessary to his pursuit, to remain in store until required for use, without being burdened with the payment of large sums in duties on importations not immediately wanted. *A vast supply has thus been constantly held, at the expense of the foreign producer.*

The total value of articles imported into the United States in 1848, was 154,977,876 dollars; the value of articles re-exported was 7,986,806 dollars. Thus it will be seen that *we* re-export but a little more than *one-twentieth* of our imports, and that the re-exportations from Great Britain are nearly five times larger in proportion to her imports than ours, and are actually *nine* times larger than ours. Now, if by the construction of the proposed work, we give such a direction to the course of trade as to bring us almost in a central position between Europe and Asia, it seems impossible to resist the conclusion that *our* warehouses must become the great depôts, and *our* cities the marts of modern commerce.

There are two important provisions in the charter, which it is proper to mention, as they limit very materially the privileges of the Company. The first is in Article 22, which stipulates "that the Company shall be obliged to convey, without delay, all the correspondence (mails) which may be delivered to it, and that the price of conveyance along the whole extent of the road shall not exceed eight reals—one cent a pound—per quintal." In the "schedule of duties and obligations" of the Company, Article 16 is as follows:—"The Company, on the receipt of the tolls and payments for transportation fixed by it, contracts the obligation to execute continually, with care, punctuality, and expedition, and *without any national preferences*, the transport of passengers, cattle, goods, merchandise, and materials of every description which may be entrusted to it, all which shall be transported without abatement of the rates of payment in favour of any one." These stipulations are proper, and present the intentions of the Granadian Government in a very favourable light; but it is well to remark that if this charter were in the hands of a foreign company, over whose movements *we* could not exercise control, and whose interests might be—*we may say, would be*—adverse to ours, it is by no means impossible that a future administration of that Government might consent to rescind these restrictions, and that heavy and ruinous exactions on our commerce might not be the consequence.

It may, therefore, be regarded as a fortunate circumstance that this charter has fallen into the hands of *our own citizens*, and that their application for aid may enable the Government, in granting it, *to place such restrictions on their future movements* as shall be a perfect guarantee against any action of the company adverse to our interests. This alone is a very weighty consideration with the committee in the recommendations which they are about to make.

The first section of the thirty-fifth article of the "Treaty of Peace, Navigation, and Commerce, with the Republic of New Granada," which was ratified in this city on the 12th day of June last, is as follows: —

"The United States of America and the Republic of New Granada, desiring to make as durable as possible the relations which are to be established between the two parties by virtue of this treaty, have declared solemnly, and do agree to the following points:—

"1st. For the better understanding of the preceding articles, it is, and has been stipulated between the high contracting parties, that the citizens, vessels, and merchandise of the United States, shall enjoy in the ports of New Granada, including those of the part of the Granadian territory generally denominated *Isthmus of Panama*, from its southernmost extremity, until the boundary of Costarica, all the exemptions, privileges, and immunities, concerning commerce and navigation, which are now or may hereafter be enjoyed by Granadian citizens, their vessels, and merchandise; and that this equality of favour shall be made to extend to the passengers, correspondence, and merchandise of the United States in their transit across the said territory from one sea to the other. The Government of New Granada guarantees to the Government of the United States that the right of way or transit across the *Isthmus of Panama* upon any modes of communication that now exist, or that may be hereafter constructed, shall be open and free to the Government and citizens of the United States, and for the transportation of any articles of produce, manufactures, and merchandise, of lawful commerce, belonging to the citizens of the United States; that no other tolls or charges shall be levied or collected upon the citizens of the United States or their merchandise thus passing over any road or canal that may be made by the Government of New Granada, or by the authority of the same, than is, under like circumstances, levied upon and collected from the Granadian citizens; that any lawful produce, manufactures, or merchandise belonging to citizens of the United States, thus passing from one sea to the other, in either direction, for the purpose of exportation to any other foreign country, shall not be liable to any import duties whatever, or, having paid such duties, they shall be entitled to drawback upon their exportation; nor shall the citizens of the United States be liable to any duties, tolls, or charges of any kind to which native citizens are not subjected for thus passing the said Isthmus. And, in order to secure to themselves the tranquil and constant enjoyment of these advantages, and, as an especial compensation for the said advantages, and for the favours they have acquired by the 4th, 5th, and 6th Articles of this treaty, the United States guarantee positively and efficaciously to New Granada, by the present stipulations, the perfect neutrality of the before-mentioned Isthmus, with the view that the free transit from the one to the other sea may not be interrupted or embarrassed in any future time while this treaty exists; and, in consequence, the United States also guarantee, in the same manner, the rights of sovereignty and property which New Granada has and possesses over the said territory."

The second section declares, that "the present treaty shall remain in full force and vigour for the term of twenty years from the day of the exchange of ratifications." And the third section stipulates that, "notwithstanding the foregoing, if neither party notices to the other its intention of reforming any of or all the articles of this treaty, twelve months before the expiration of the twenty years stipulated above, the said treaty shall remain binding on both parties, beyond the said twenty years, until twelve months from the time that one of the parties notifies its intention of proceeding to a reform."

This is, in fact, a *defensive league*, on our part, with New Granada, in which we virtually guarantee her sovereignty and independence for the term of twenty years, and as much longer as either party shall not notify the other of "its intention of proceeding to a reform" of the treaty. This is a very wide departure from our foreign policy hitherto, and its justification is only to be found in the exigency of the case—the overruling necessities of our position with reference to our territories on the Pacific. The pass across the Isthmus of Panama is the only route by which easy, regular, and *speedy* communication can be established with them, and by which, in fact, it has already been established; and there is no power on earth, except New Granada herself, which may say to us, "thou shalt not cross the Isthmus," without meeting the prompt resistance of the whole power of the Union. This treaty, therefore, is but a simple advertisement to all the world, that for the next twenty years, at least, we will, with the permission of New Granada, cross the Isthmus of Panama, and you must not interfere. This is what we should say if there were no treaty, and, therefore, there is no harm in saying it in the treaty. The stipulation which places the citizens of the United States on an equality, with respect to the transit of passengers and freight, with those of New Granada, was, doubtless, intended to protect American interests from unreasonable or improper exactions. But as the quantity of freight and number of passengers belonging to New Granada, which will pass over the railroad, will be small in comparison to the commerce and travel from the United States, it is doing that Government no injustice to imagine, that were this undertaking in the hands of a foreign company, it might consent to regulations which would not be felt by its own citizens, but which would be perfectly ruinous to ours; and besides, the treaty *does not provide that the commerce, citizens, or subjects of other countries* shall not be placed, by any company, on a more favourable footing than those of New Granada, and consequently than *ours.*

The guarantee of the Government of New Granada to the Government of the United States of "the right of way or transit across the Isthmus of Panama, upon any modes of communication that now exist or that may be hereafter constructed," simply means that the Government of New Granada will not forbid us from crossing the Isthmus on a railroad if we pay for it —or, that the citizens of the United States may be required to pay as much as the Government of New Granada may consent that the citizens of that republic shall pay—though the merchandise, subjects or citizens of other countries might be allowed to pass at half the price. To guard against impositions from any quarter, and secure the interests of the United States beyond contingency, the committee have deemed it proper, in the bill submitted herewith, to provide *that a large majority of the stock of the railroad shall be held by American citizens.*

Much has been said respecting a communication across the Isthmus of Tehuantepec, and representations have been made that the depth of water on the bar is sufficient to justify the construction of a ship-canal. This question has been effectually decided by the survey of Lieutenant William Leigh, United States Navy, who has recently made a very accurate survey of the bar at the mouth of the river Coatzacoalcos (the entrance to the harbour on the gulf side of the Isthmus), and found but twelve feet and a half of water at low tide, and but two feet rise of tide on the bar. A safe deduction for the swell of the sea would enable vessels drawing about twelve feet to cross the bar into the canal. The survey of Lieutenant Leigh has been published at the Observatory, and may be regarded as the highest authority for saying that, if a ship-canal were constructed across that Isthmus, it would not be possible to get ships into it. If, however, nature had imposed no obstructions at the entrance of the harbour, there are other considerations which, it is believed, are of sufficient weight to render the expenditure of money at that point inexpedient. There are few who have attentively observed the progress of opinion in this country during the last few years, who will deny that the people of the United States are now looking with much anxiety to the construction of a railroad from some point on the Mississippi river to the Bay of San Francisco; and it is not probable that twenty years will be allowed to pass before this great and necessary work will be accomplished. This road will form the great northern line of communication, while that across the Isthmus of Panama will be the southern. *There is no necessity for an intermediate line.* When the northern line shall be completed, it will become the great thoroughfare to California, Oregon, the islands in the North Pacific, Japan, China, Manilla, etc. etc.; while the southern line will be the channel of communication to the ports on the west coast of Mexico, South America, New Zealand, New Holland, and the islands of the South Pacific. It would probably cost one-half as much to construct a ship-canal across the Isthmus of Tehuantepec as it would to make a railroad from the Mississippi river to San Francisco. . . . .

The committee recommend, therefore, that a grant of two hundred and fifty thousand dollars per annum be made to the memorialists, for the purpose of enabling them to complete the work, on the conditions stated in their memorial, which is annexed to this Report, marked A. Their charter from the Government of New Granada allows them eight years in which to complete their railroad. They propose to finish it in three years. This will be a saving of five years. The above items show an annual saving of 4,250,000 dollars, which, for the five years, will amount to 21,250,000 dollars. It will, therefore, be perceived how very important it is that the road shall be completed as soon as possible. *One year's delay* will cause nearly as great a loss as the whole amount proposed to be granted to the Company, in yearly payments, for twenty years.

The proposed grant will be five per cent. on the investment, and will probably not greatly exceed the amount which the Government would pay annually for the services stipulated by the memorialists to be performed.

The committee recommend the passage of the bill herewith submitted.

V.

EXTRACTS FROM CONVENTION AND AMENDED CHARTER OF THE AMERICAN ATLANTIC AND PACIFIC SHIP CANAL COMPANY, 19TH JUNE, 1857, AND EXPLANATORY ARTICLES RESPECTING THE SAME, 15TH OCTOBER, 1857.

Whereas the supreme Government of Nicaragua did, on the 27th day of August, 1849, through their Commissioners, Hermangildo Zapida and Gregorio Juarez, enter into and sign a contract with the American Atlantic and Pacific Ship Canal Company, which said contract was ratified by the Congress of the Republic of Nicaragua on the 22nd day of September, 1849, and afterwards amended on the 9th day of March, 1850, which amendments were ratified and confirmed by the Congress of said Republic, and by decree of the supreme director, the 11th day of April, 1850;

And whereas, by Article 2 of said contract, the dimensions of the said ship-canal, to be constructed by the aforesaid Company, are defined and fixed;

And whereas it has been ascertained and determined by careful and thorough examination of engineers, that a Canal of the dimensions required in and by the aforesaid Article cannot be constructed, because of a want of water of sufficient depth in the Lake of Nicaragua;

And whereas by Article 30 of said contract, the Company are required to construct a railroad and water communication between the two oceans, should the construction of the said canal become impossible for reasons or causes therein named;

And whereas it is desirable that a railroad and water communication should be established as speedily as possible on terms advantageous to both the Republic and the Company:

The following amendments and addition to the aforesaid contract have been mutually agreed on, by and between the State and the Company.

Dated and signed in New York, 19th June, 1857, by A. J. de Irisarri, Minister Plenipotentiary, and H. G. Stebbins, President of the American Atlantic and Pacific Ship Canal Company.

Extracts from the "Amended Charter" of the American Atlantic and Pacific Ship Canal Company.

1. The obligation to construct the canal on the part of the Company is dispensed with, but in lieu of said canal the Company shall establish across the territory of the State between the two oceans a communication by water and railroad, within two years from the ratification of this contract by the proper authorities of Nicaragua.

2. Article 6 of the primary contract is stricken out, and in lieu thereof the following is inserted:—"The said State shall receive one dollar and fifty cents, of lawful money of the United States of America, for every passenger conveyed by said Company across the State;" defines how the money shall be paid, and number of passengers ascertained. [This article shall apply to all passengers conveyed by the Company by carriage, road, and water communication *during the two years allowed for the construction of the railroad.*]

3. Regulates the question of passports for persons intending to stay in Nicaragua.

4. In the event of the said State being invaded by any public or other enemy, the steamers of the Company may be employed by the Government of the said State for the transportation of their troops, ammunition, provision, etc., on the request of the proper officers. But whenever said steamers, or any one of them, shall be so used or employed, the Company shall charge

therefor the actual running expenses, and no more; which said charge shall be adjusted between the Company and the State, and the amount thereof deducted from the *per capita* tax herein agreed to be paid.

The provisions of this Article contained, as to any public or other enemy, shall not be applicable to the Government of the United States of America, or such other Government as may enter into treaty stipulations similar to those which may be entered into between said Government of the United States and the Republic of Nicaragua, for the protection of said Company.

The ratification of the amended Charter took place in Managua on the 27th day of July, 1857, and signed by Maximo Jerez and Tomas Martinez. And further, it was accepted, ratified by the constituent assembly of Nicaragua. By a clause in the ratification, it was left to the discretion of Mr. Irissari to deliver the same or not, as he might think fit.

The contract was handed to the Company by Mr. Irissari, and certain explanations appended thereto, which read as follows:—

Explanatory Articles.

Whereas I, Don Antonio José de Irisarri, representing the Government of Nicaragua, by virtue of the most ample authority conferred on me by the said Government, have required the American Atlantic and Pacific Ship Canal Company to make certain explanations of some Articles in the contract of the 27th August, 1849, and of 19th of June of the present year: and whereas the said Company have deemed it for their interest to make such explanations, we, the undersigned, on behalf of our respective principals, have agreed as follows:—

ART. 1. The said Company agrees to issue their certificates of capital stock thereof, and commence to make the transit across the Isthmus of Nicaragua within ninety days from this date. Stipulates for notice to Mr. Irisarri, when the stock-books shall be open.

2. The Company to deliver to Mr. Irissari 2000 shares of stock, according to primary contract of August, 1849.

3. Company not to issue over 30,000 shares of capital stock, and mode of inspection of books of Company pointed out.

4. Determines the proportion of profit on "Mail Matter" to be paid to Nicaragua to be fixed at one-sixteenth of the gross sum received; fixes also about the mails of the Government of Nicaragua, and official dispatches.

5 (*verbatim*).—In order to simplify and expedite the object proposed in Articles 33 and 34 of the contract of 27th August, 1849, whenever it may be necessary to appoint arbitrators to decide such disputes and controversies as may arise between the Government of Nicaragua and the Company, only one arbitrator shall be appointed by each party, and in case of their disagreement, if the arbitrators do not, within three days, select a third arbitrator, application shall be made within ten days to the three oldest ministers plenipotentiary, or ministers resident in default of ministers plenipotentiary, or *chargés d'affaires* in the absence of ministers resident, according to the dates of receptions at Washington, to select such third arbitrator; and the minister or diplomatic representative of Nicaragua shall in no case be one of the three authorized to select.

In case any one of the ministers or *chargés* shall excuse himself, or for any cause should not be able to act, his place shall be successively supplied by the next oldest minister or *chargé d'affaires*, according to the order of receptions in Washington, until the object is attained.

Persons interested in the Company, or the officers, agents, or *employés* thereof, cannot be appointed arbitrators, nor can the officers, agents, or *employés* of the Government of Nicaragua be so appointed. The arbitration shall take place in the City of New York.

6. Stipulations as to the colonists which the Company may locate on their land grants.

7. Relates to the mode of governing and defending them.

8. Stipulates that nothing in the convention of August 27th, 1849, or the contract of August 14th, 1851, nor in the foregoing convention of June 19th, 1857, shall be held or construed as a revival of the Accessory Transit Company, nor as an au-

thority to revive or continue the same, the said Accessory Transit Company being considered as extinct.

For any wilful breach or non-performance of any of these stipulations, or of the others contained in the contract of the 19th June of this present year, or of the aforesaid convention of the 27th August, 1849, the Government of Nicaragua may annul the said contracts, after having submitted the question to the decision of the arbitrators as aforesaid, and after they shall have decided the question against the Company. And each of the articles and stipulations aforesaid shall be considered and observed as an integral part of the contract.

Accepted, approved, ratified, and confirmed by the Government of Nicaragua, on the 27th July, 1857.

And in testimony whereof, etc.

Signed, 15th October, 1857.

A. J. de Irisarri,
H. G. Stebbins, *President.*

THE END.

CPSIA information can be obtained
at www.ICGtesting.com
Printed in the USA
LVHW100426110522
718424LV00003B/79

9 783375 003753